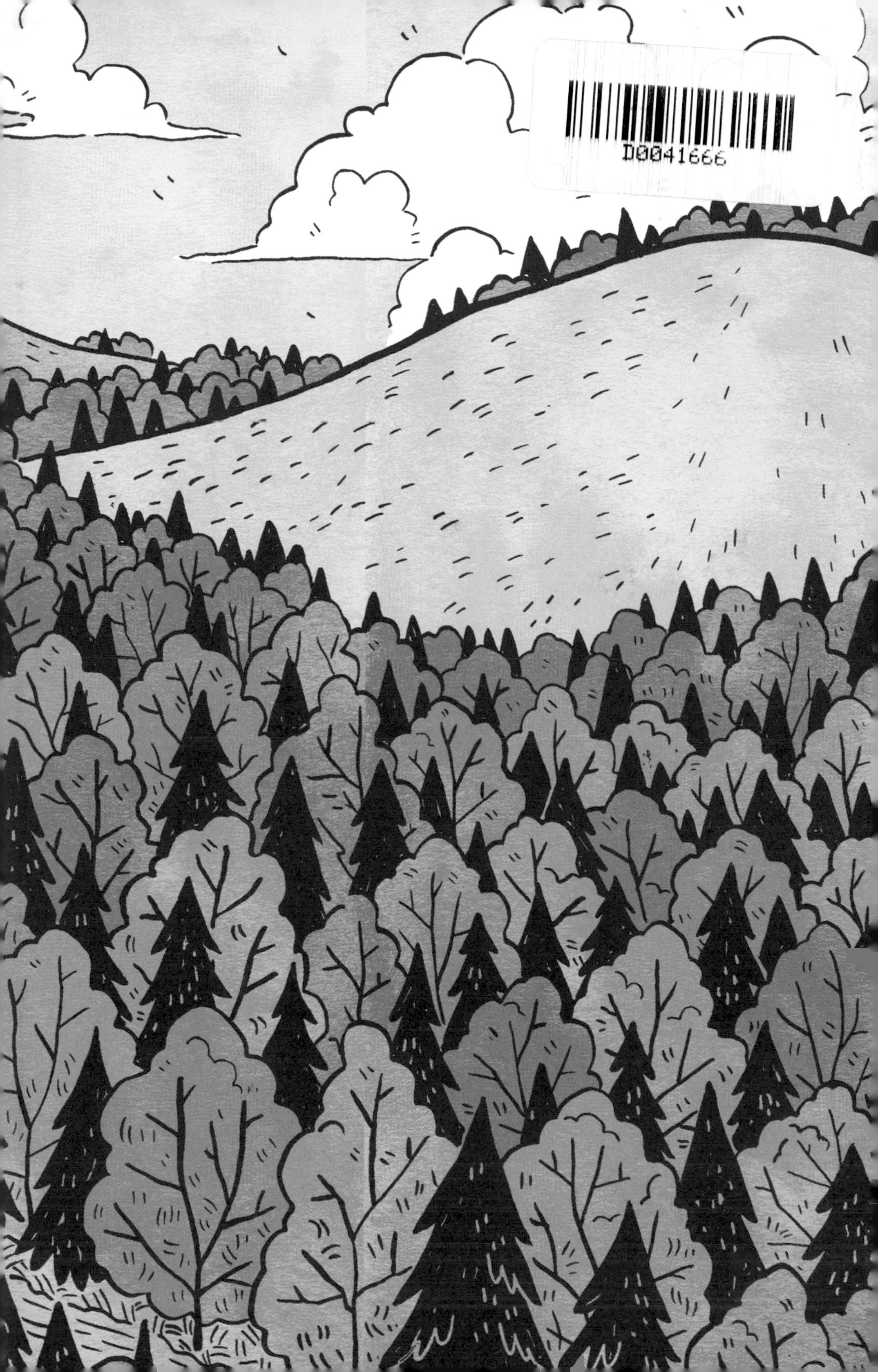

PILU
of the
WOODS

AN ONI PRESS PUBLICATION

PILU

of the

WOODS

WRITTEN, ILLUSTRATED,
COLORED, & LETTERED BY
MAI K. NGUYEN

EDITED BY
ROBIN HERRERA

DESIGNED BY
KATE Z. STONE

PUBLISHED BY ONI PRESS, INC.

JOE NOZEMACK, FOUNDER & CHIEF FINANCIAL OFFICER
JAMES LUCAS JONES, PUBLISHER
CHARLIE CHU, V.P. OF CREATIVE & BUSINESS DEVELOPMENT
BRAD ROOKS, DIRECTOR OF OPERATIONS
MELISSA MESZAROS, DIRECTOR OF PUBLICITY
MARGOT WOOD, DIRECTOR OF SALES
SANDY TANAKA, MARKETING DESIGN MANAGER
AMBER O'NEILL, SPECIAL PROJECTS MANAGER
TROY LOOK, DIRECTOR OF DESIGN & PRODUCTION
KATE Z. STONE, SENIOR GRAPHIC DESIGNER
SONJA SYNAK, GRAPHIC DESIGNER
ANGIE KNOWLES, DIGITAL PREPRESS LEAD
ARI YARWOOD, EXECUTIVE EDITOR
SARAH GAYDOS, EDITORIAL DIRECTOR OF LICENSED PUBLISHING
ROBIN HERRERA, SENIOR EDITOR
DESIREE WILSON, ASSOCIATE EDITOR
MICHELLE NGUYEN, EXECUTIVE ASSISTANT
JUNG LEE, LOGISTICS COORDINATOR
SCOTT SHARKEY, WAREHOUSE ASSISTANT

ONIPRESS.COM
FACEBOOK.COM/ONIPRESS • TWITTER.COM/ONIPRESS
ONIPRESS.TUMBLR.COM • INSTAGRAM.COM/ONIPRESS

@OHMAIPIE / OHMAIPIE.COM

FIRST EDITION: APRIL 2019

HARDCOVER ISBN: 978-1-62010-551-1
PAPERBACK ISBN: 978-1-62010-563-4
EISBN: 978-1-62010-564-1

PRINTED IN CHINA

LIBRARY OF CONGRESS CONTROL NUMBER: 2018940556

10 9 8 7 6 5 4 3 2

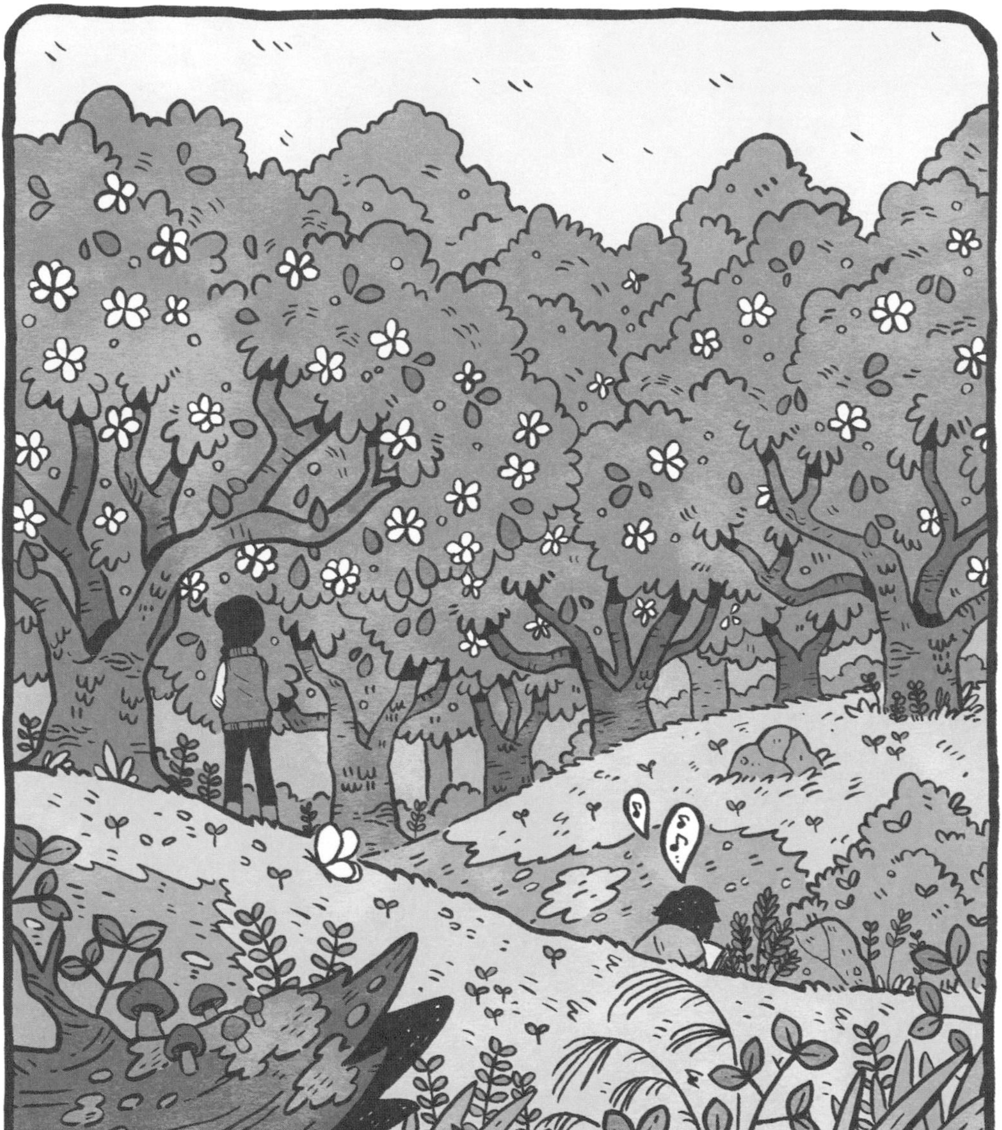

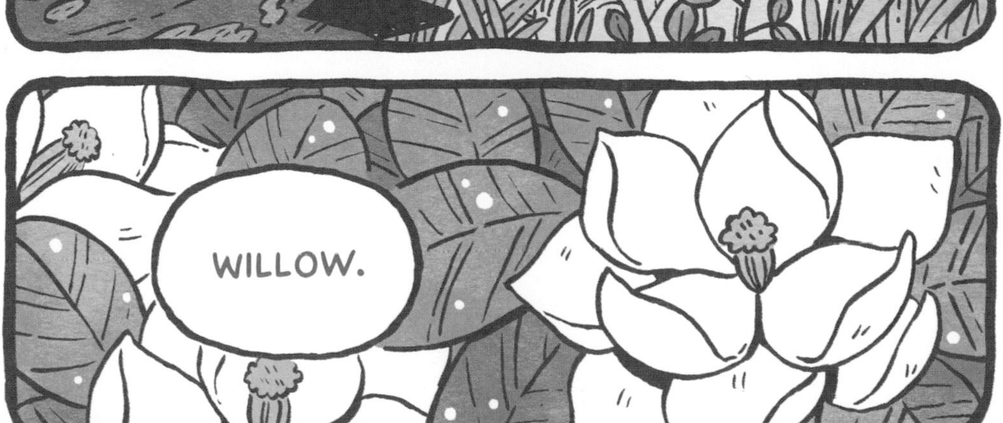
WILLOW.

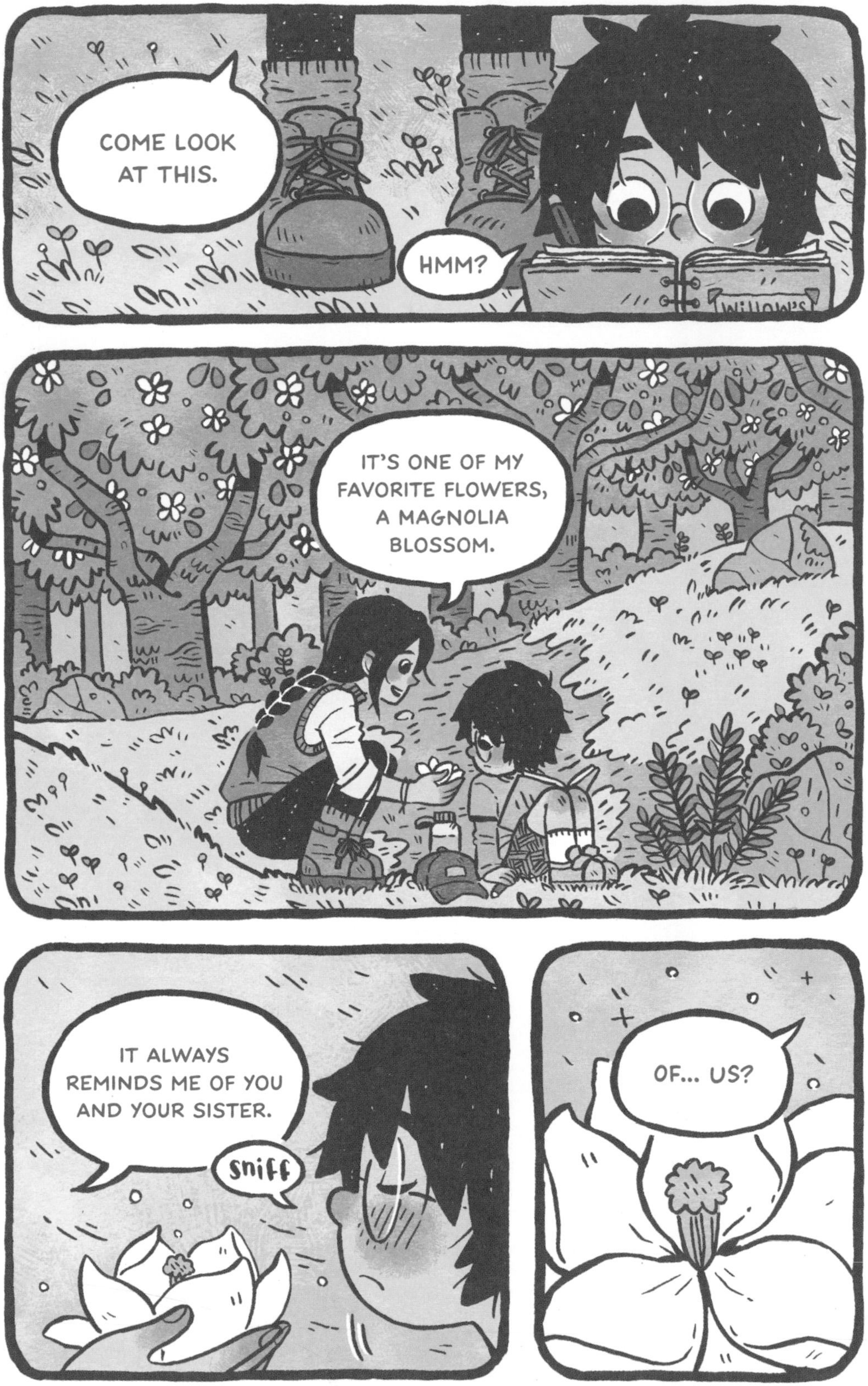
COME LOOK AT THIS.
HMM?
WILLOW'S
IT'S ONE OF MY FAVORITE FLOWERS, A MAGNOLIA BLOSSOM.
IT ALWAYS REMINDS ME OF YOU AND YOUR SISTER.
sniff
OF... US?

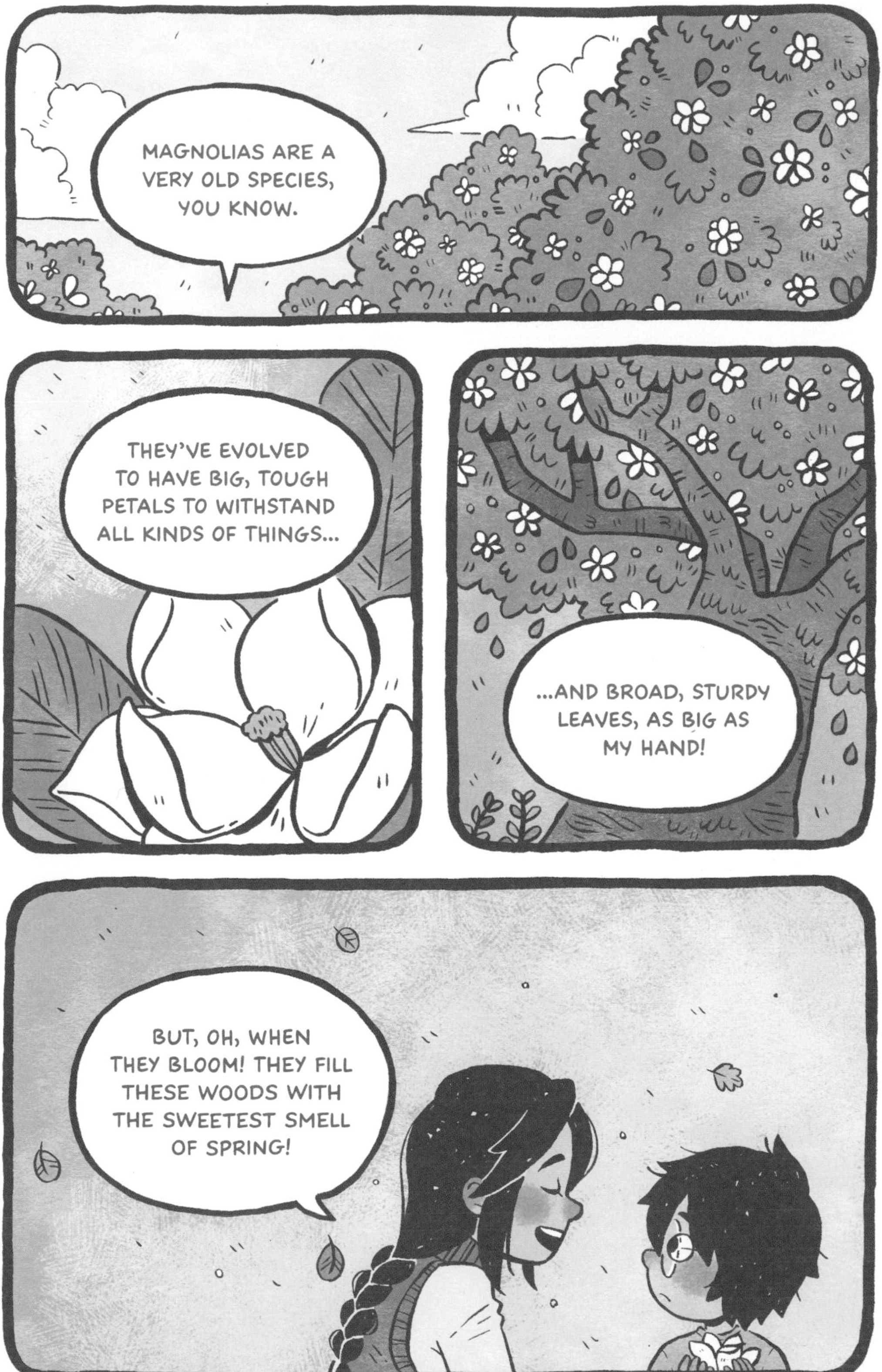
MAGNOLIAS ARE A VERY OLD SPECIES, YOU KNOW.
THEY'VE EVOLVED TO HAVE BIG, TOUGH PETALS TO WITHSTAND ALL KINDS OF THINGS...
...AND BROAD, STURDY LEAVES, AS BIG AS MY HAND!
BUT, OH, WHEN THEY BLOOM! THEY FILL THESE WOODS WITH THE SWEETEST SMELL OF SPRING!

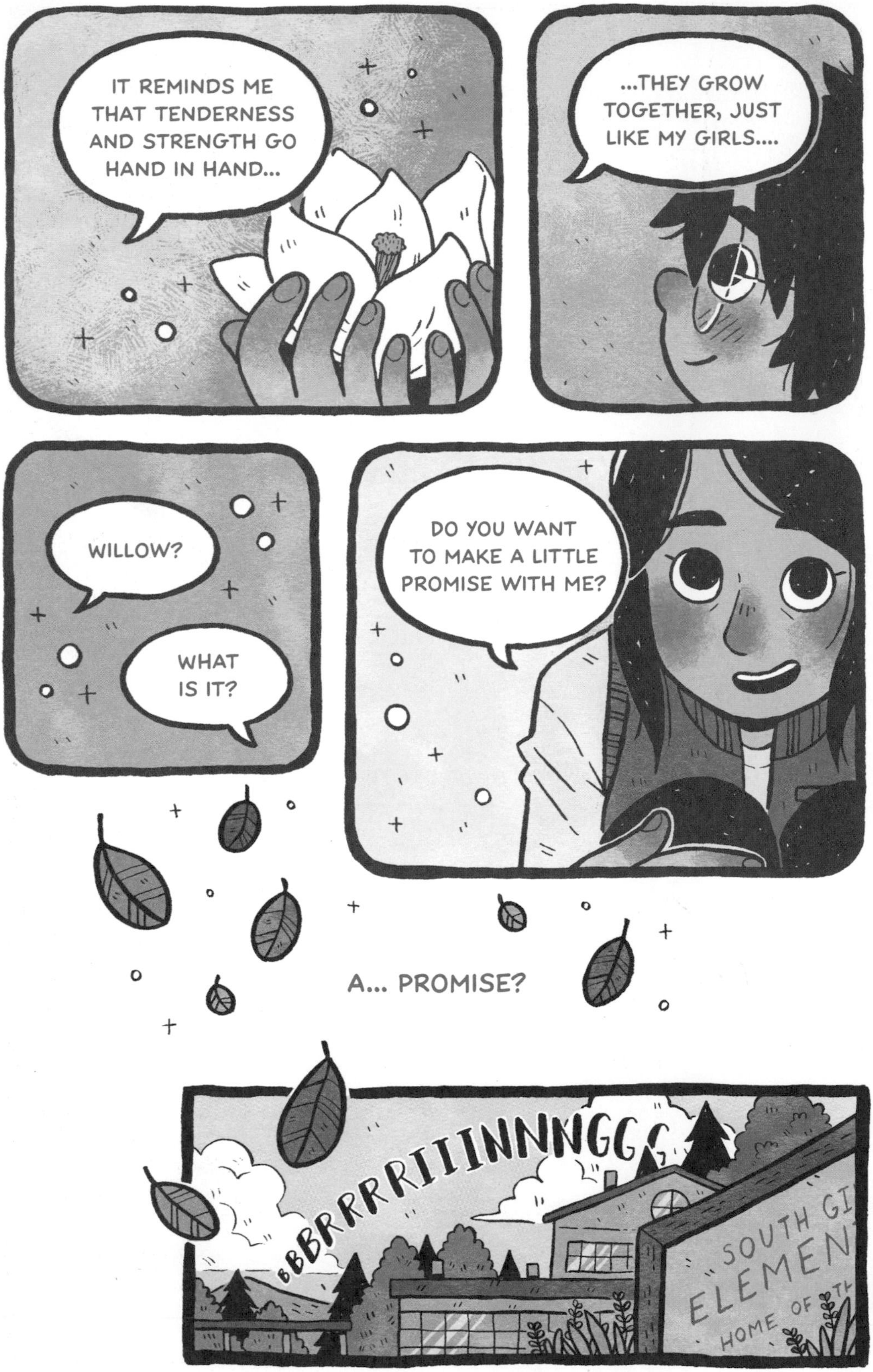

IT REMINDS ME THAT TENDERNESS AND STRENGTH GO HAND IN HAND...
...THEY GROW TOGETHER, JUST LIKE MY GIRLS....
WILLOW?
WHAT IS IT?
DO YOU WANT TO MAKE A LITTLE PROMISE WITH ME?
A... PROMISE?
BBBRRRRRIIINNNNGGG
SOUTH GI
ELEMEN
HOME OF TH

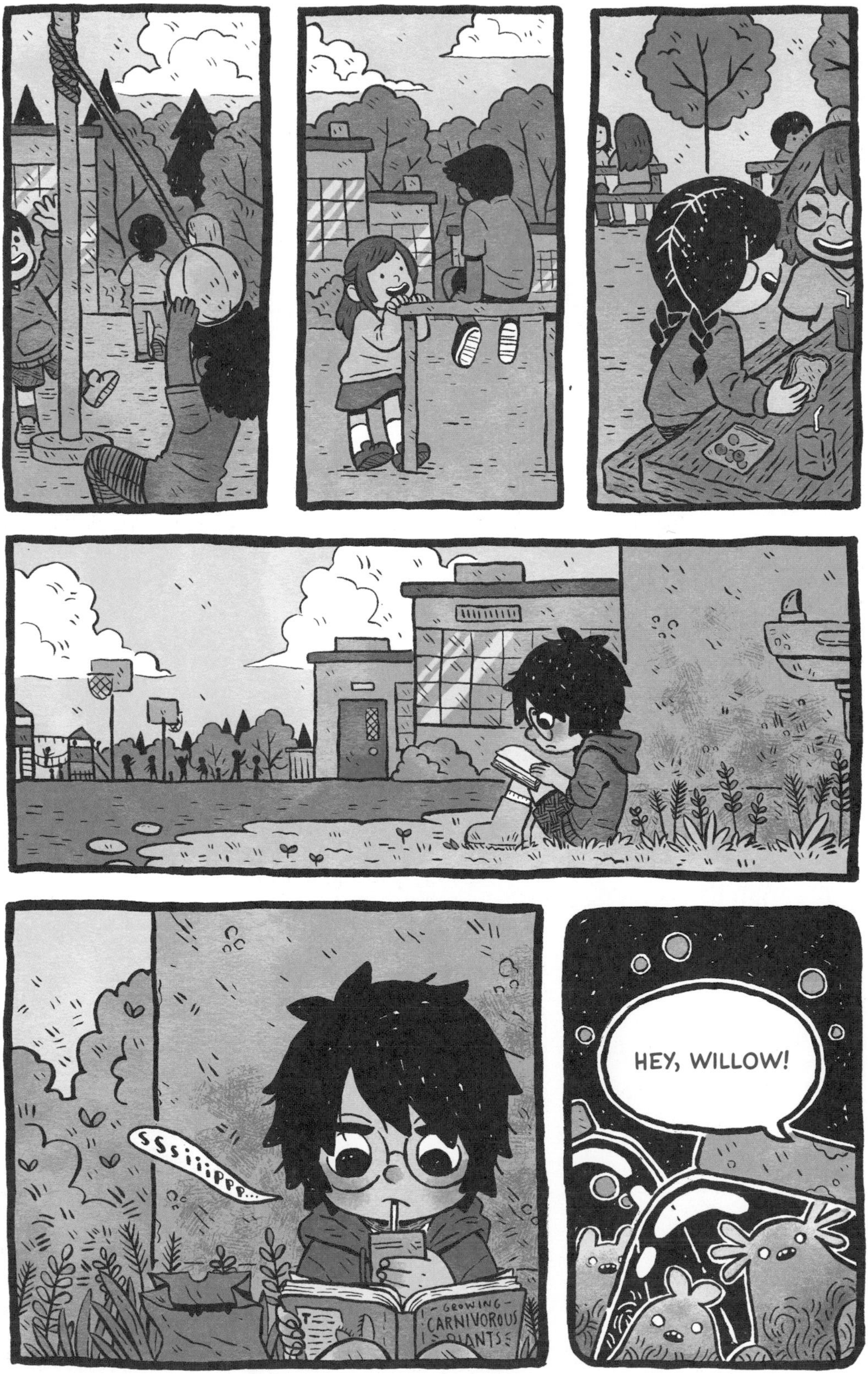
SSsiiiiPPP...
GROWING
CARNIVOROUS PLANTS
HEY, WILLOW!

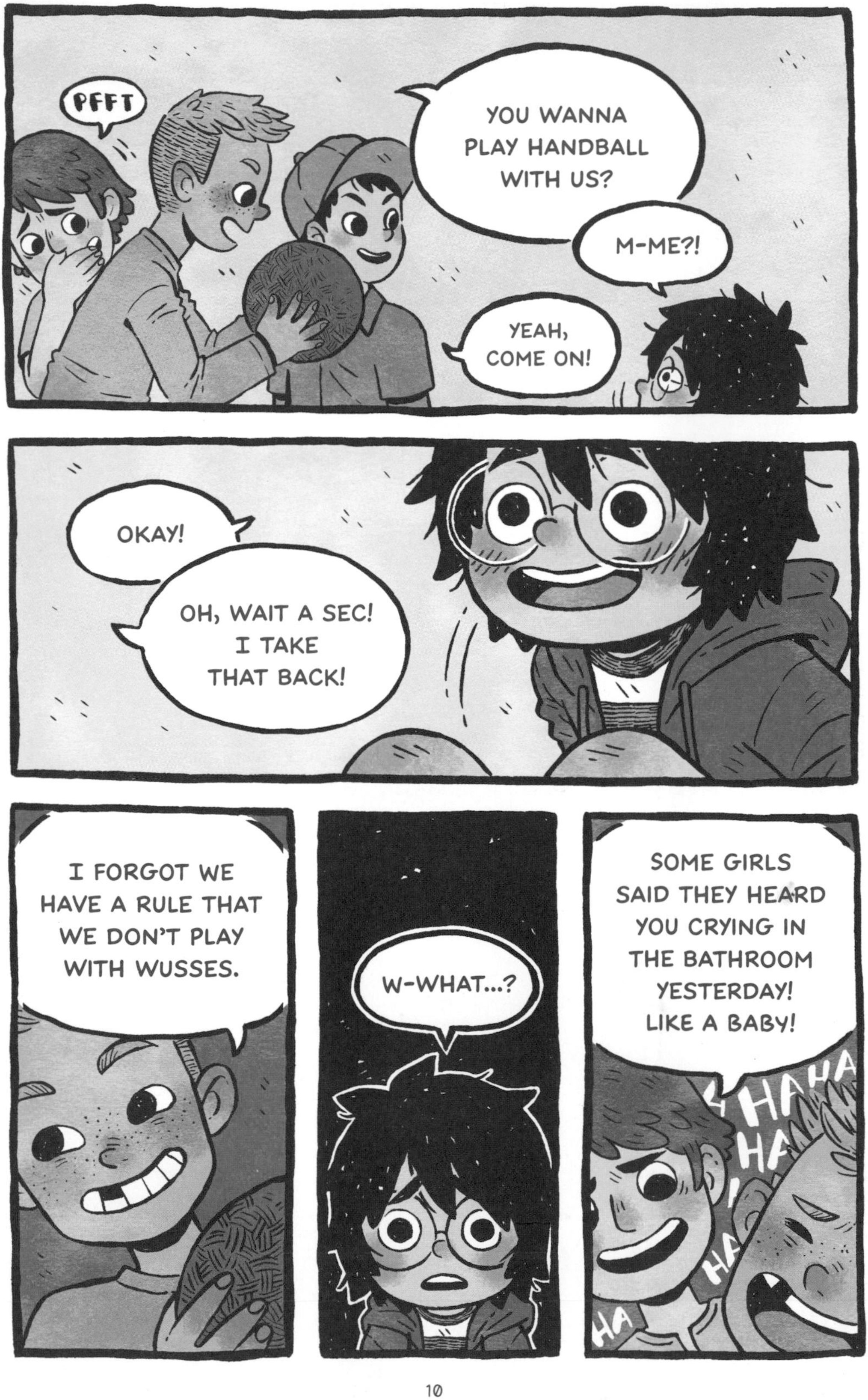
PFFT
YOU WANNA PLAY HANDBALL WITH US?
M-ME?!
YEAH, COME ON!
OKAY!
OH, WAIT A SEC! I TAKE THAT BACK!
I FORGOT WE HAVE A RULE THAT WE DON'T PLAY WITH WUSSES.
W-WHAT...?
SOME GIRLS SAID THEY HEARD YOU CRYING IN THE BATHROOM YESTERDAY! LIKE A BABY!
HAHA HAHA HA HA HA

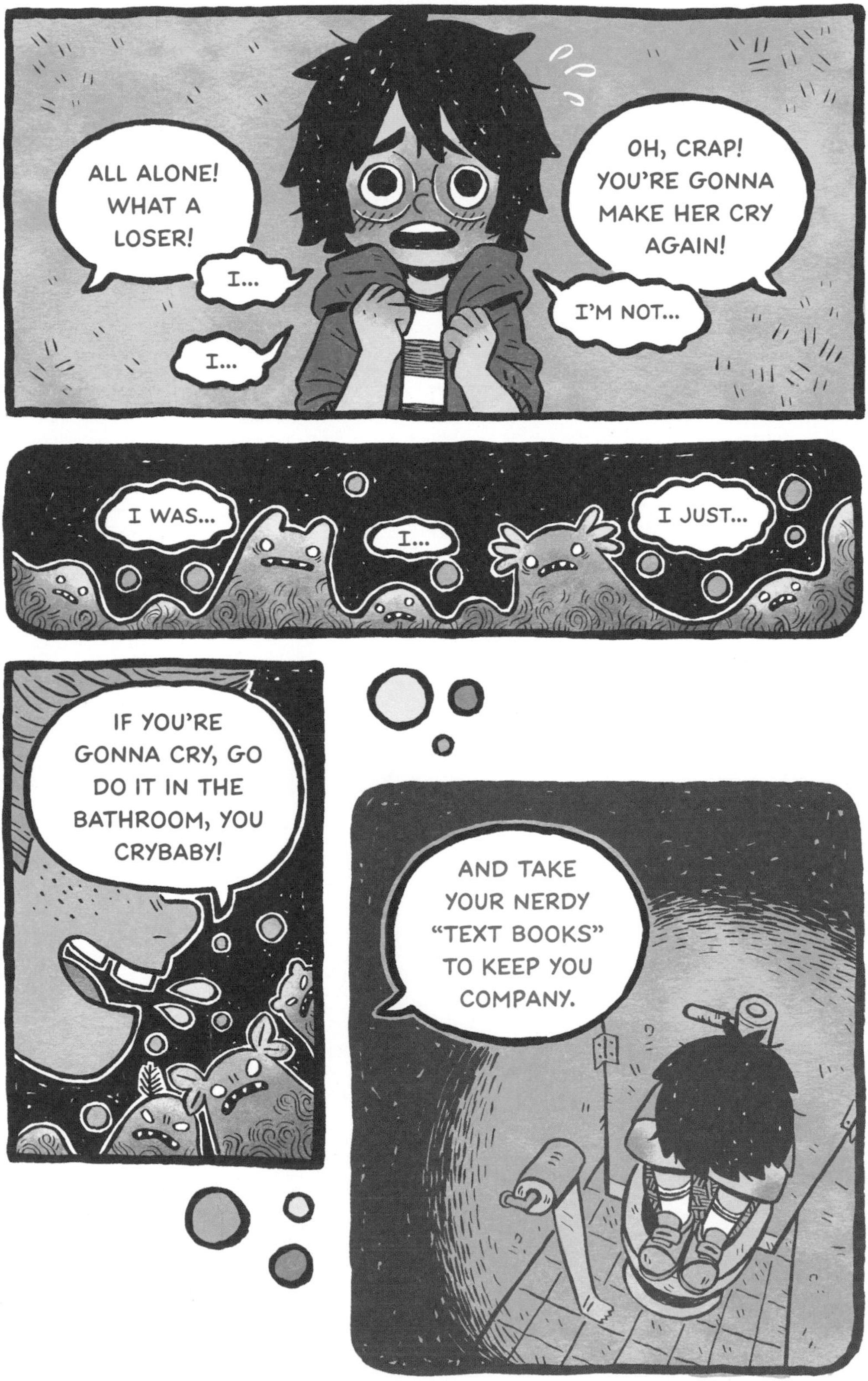
ALL ALONE! WHAT A LOSER!
I...
I...
OH, CRAP! YOU'RE GONNA MAKE HER CRY AGAIN!
I'M NOT...
I WAS...
I...
I JUST...
IF YOU'RE GONNA CRY, GO DO IT IN THE BATHROOM, YOU CRYBABY!
AND TAKE YOUR NERDY "TEXT BOOKS" TO KEEP YOU COMPANY.

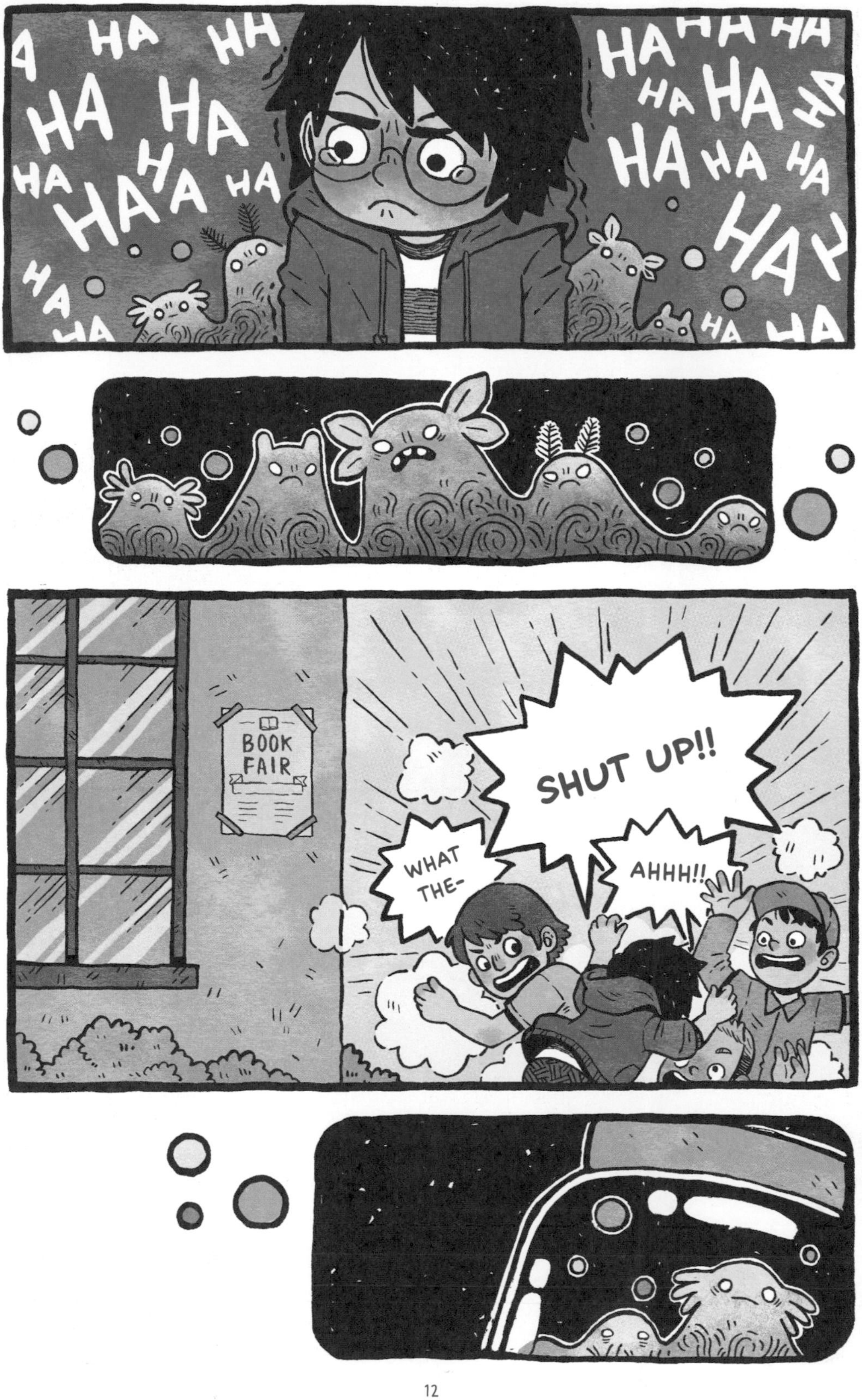
HA HA HA HA HA HA HA HA HA HA
HA HA HA HA HA HA HA HA HA HA HA HA
BOOK FAIR
SHUT UP!!
WHAT THE-
AHHH!!

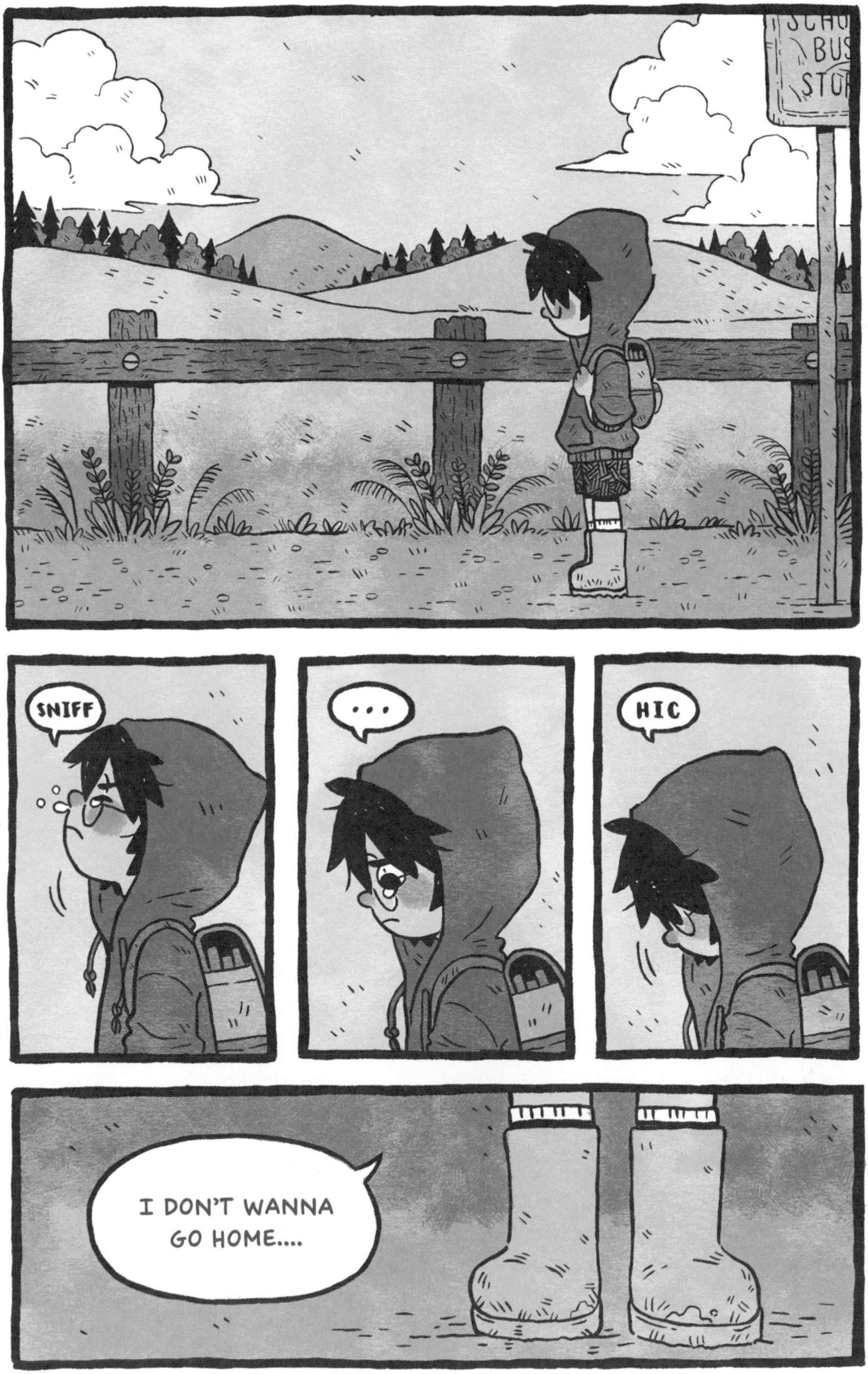
SNIFF
...
HIC
I DON'T WANNA GO HOME....

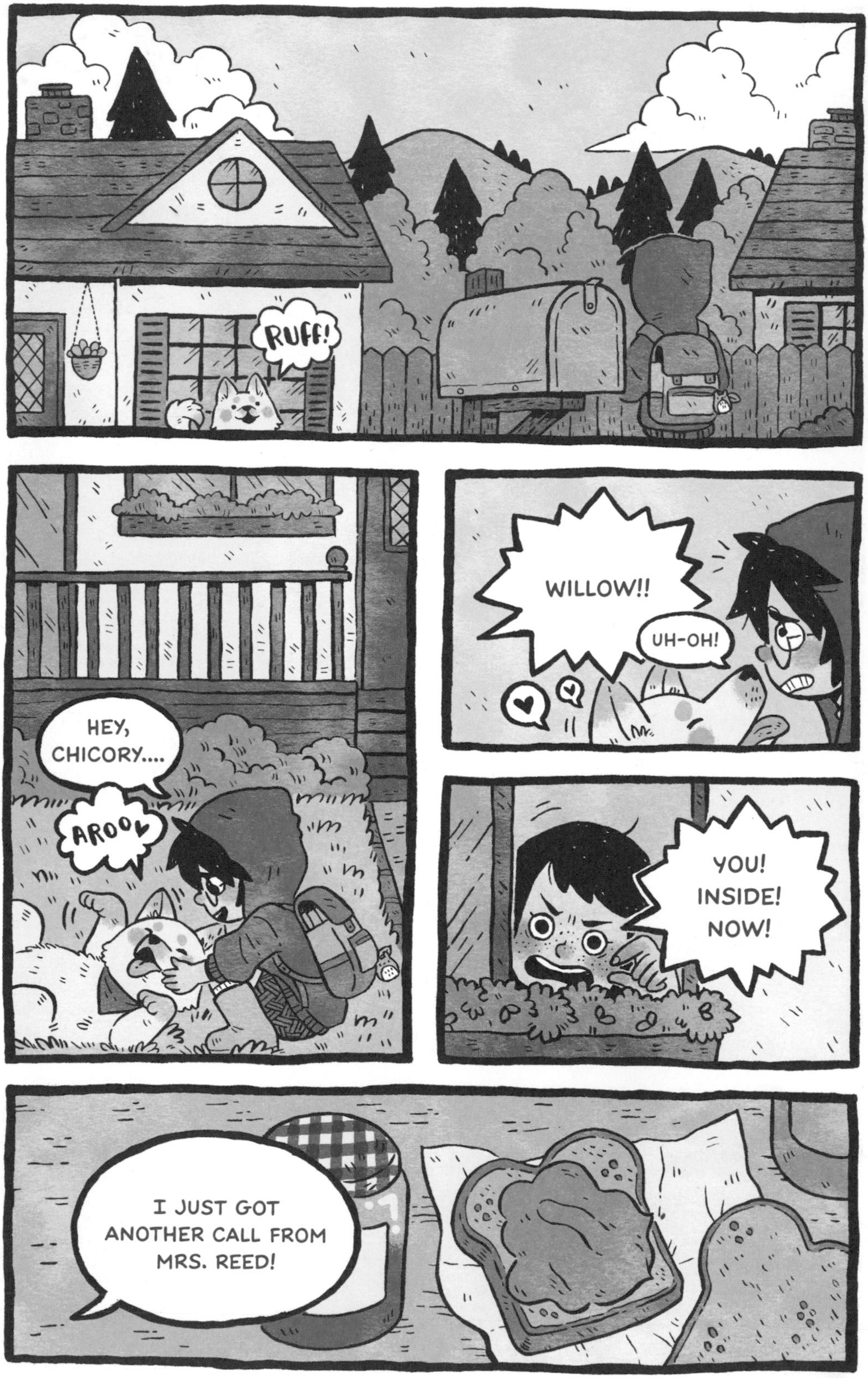
RUFF!
HEY, CHICORY....
AROO♥
WILLOW!!
UH-OH!
YOU! INSIDE! NOW!
I JUST GOT ANOTHER CALL FROM MRS. REED!

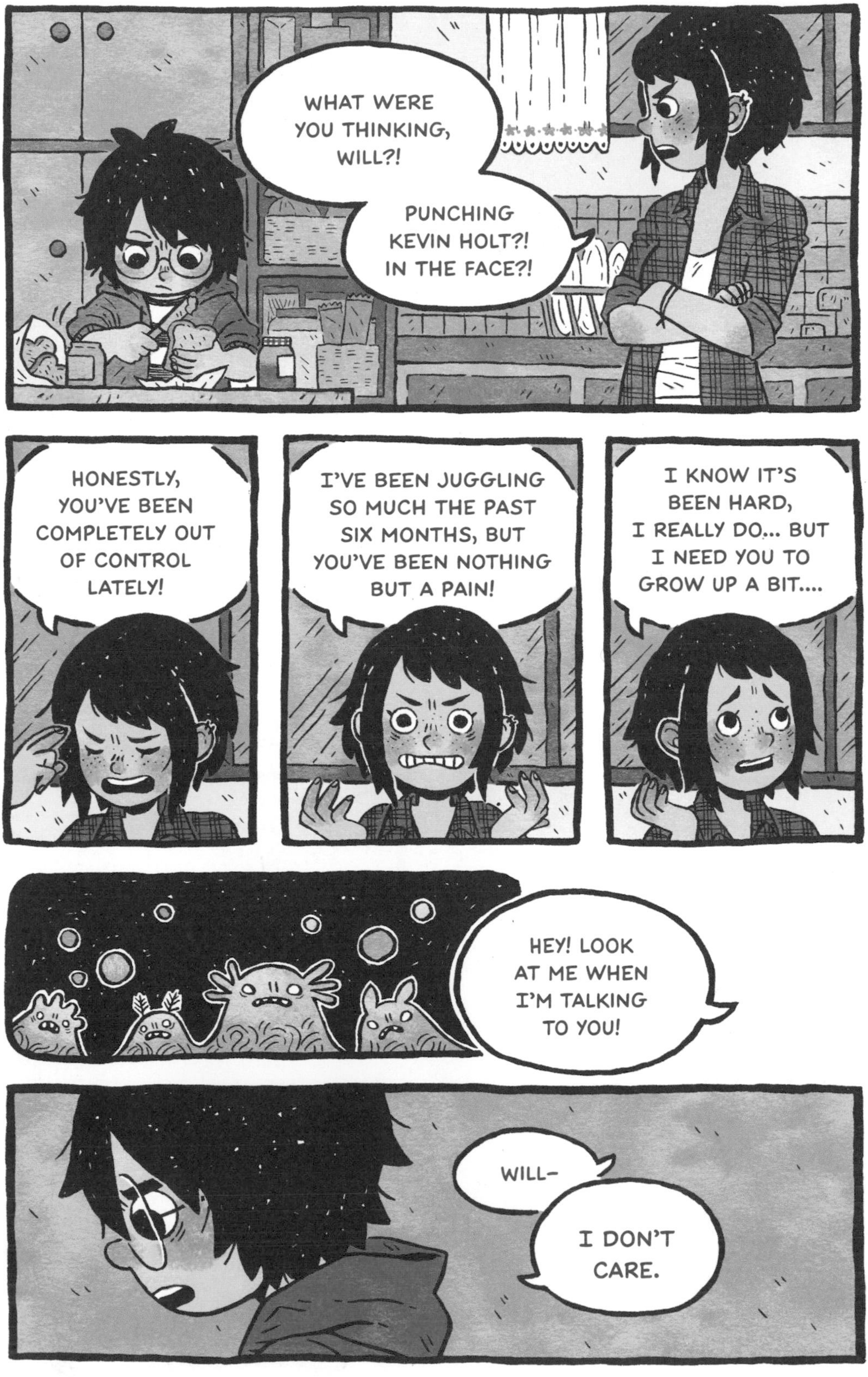
WHAT WERE YOU THINKING, WILL?!
PUNCHING KEVIN HOLT?! IN THE FACE?!
HONESTLY, YOU'VE BEEN COMPLETELY OUT OF CONTROL LATELY!
I'VE BEEN JUGGLING SO MUCH THE PAST SIX MONTHS, BUT YOU'VE BEEN NOTHING BUT A PAIN!
I KNOW IT'S BEEN HARD, I REALLY DO... BUT I NEED YOU TO GROW UP A BIT....
HEY! LOOK AT ME WHEN I'M TALKING TO YOU!
WILL–
I DON'T CARE.

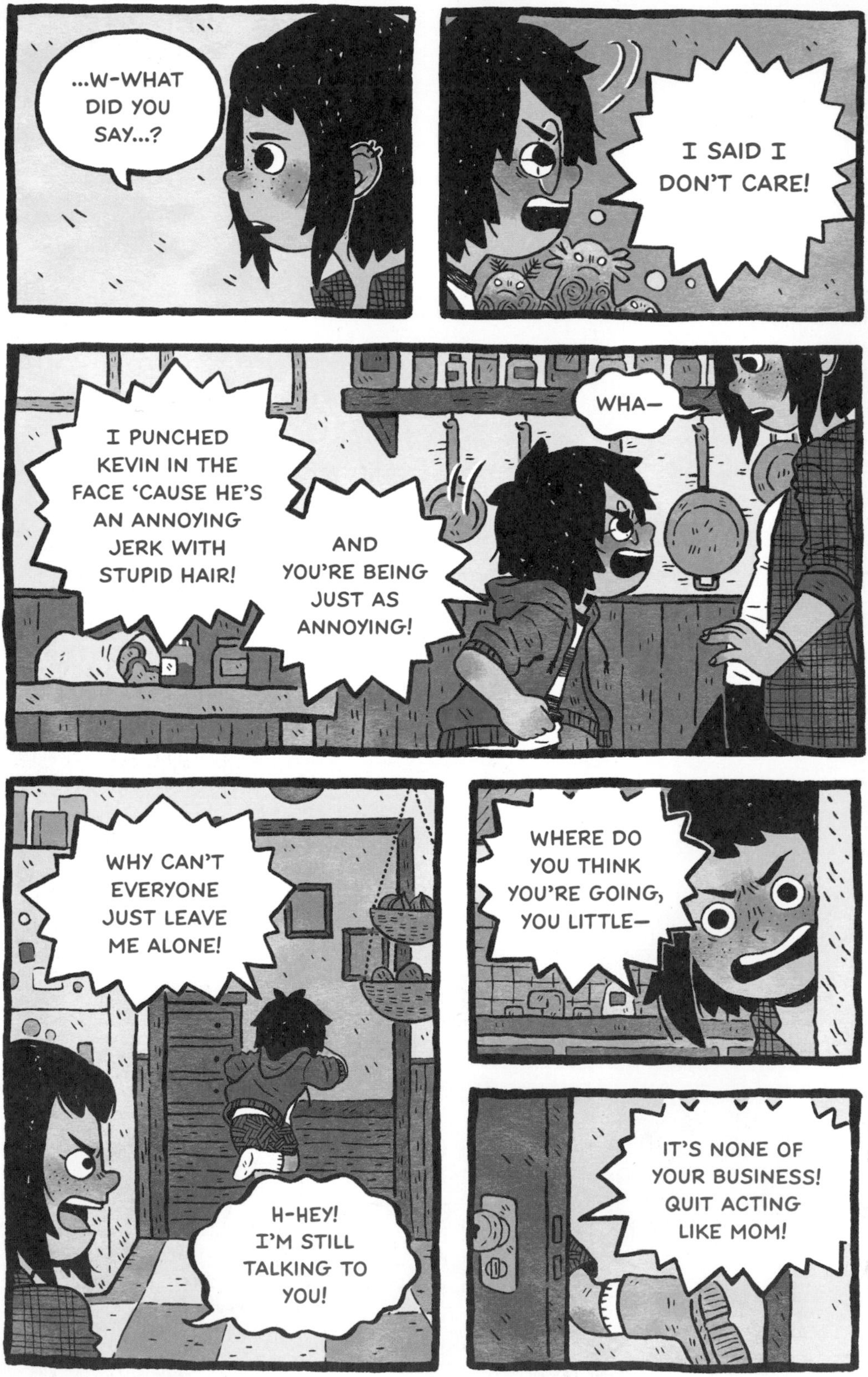
...W-WHAT DID YOU SAY...?
I SAID I DON'T CARE!
I PUNCHED KEVIN IN THE FACE 'CAUSE HE'S AN ANNOYING JERK WITH STUPID HAIR!
WHA—
AND YOU'RE BEING JUST AS ANNOYING!
WHY CAN'T EVERYONE JUST LEAVE ME ALONE!
H-HEY! I'M STILL TALKING TO YOU!
WHERE DO YOU THINK YOU'RE GOING, YOU LITTLE—
IT'S NONE OF YOUR BUSINESS! QUIT ACTING LIKE MOM!

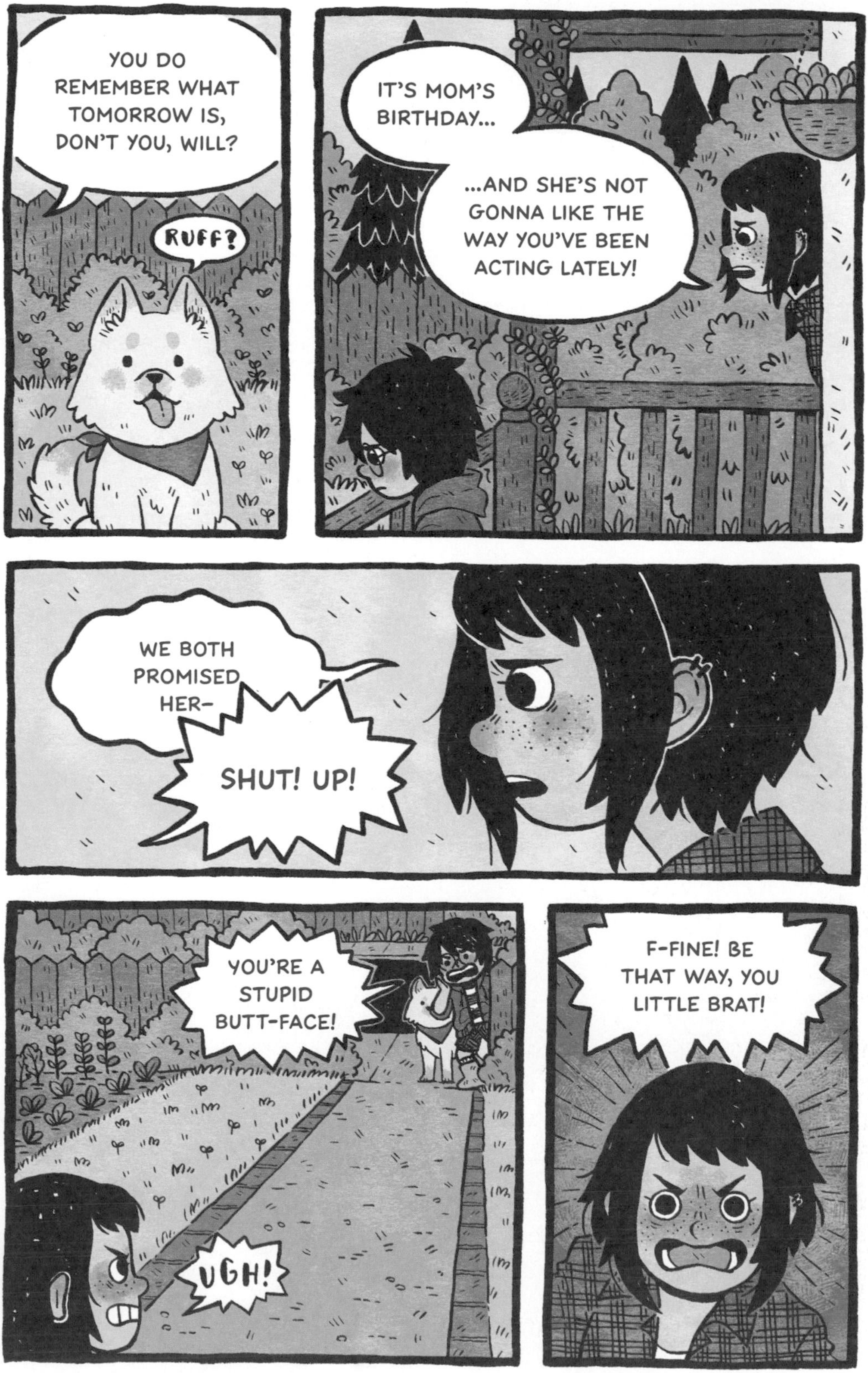
YOU DO REMEMBER WHAT TOMORROW IS, DON'T YOU, WILL?
RUFF?
IT'S MOM'S BIRTHDAY...
...AND SHE'S NOT GONNA LIKE THE WAY YOU'VE BEEN ACTING LATELY!
WE BOTH PROMISED HER-
SHUT! UP!
YOU'RE A STUPID BUTT-FACE!
UGH!
F-FINE! BE THAT WAY, YOU LITTLE BRAT!

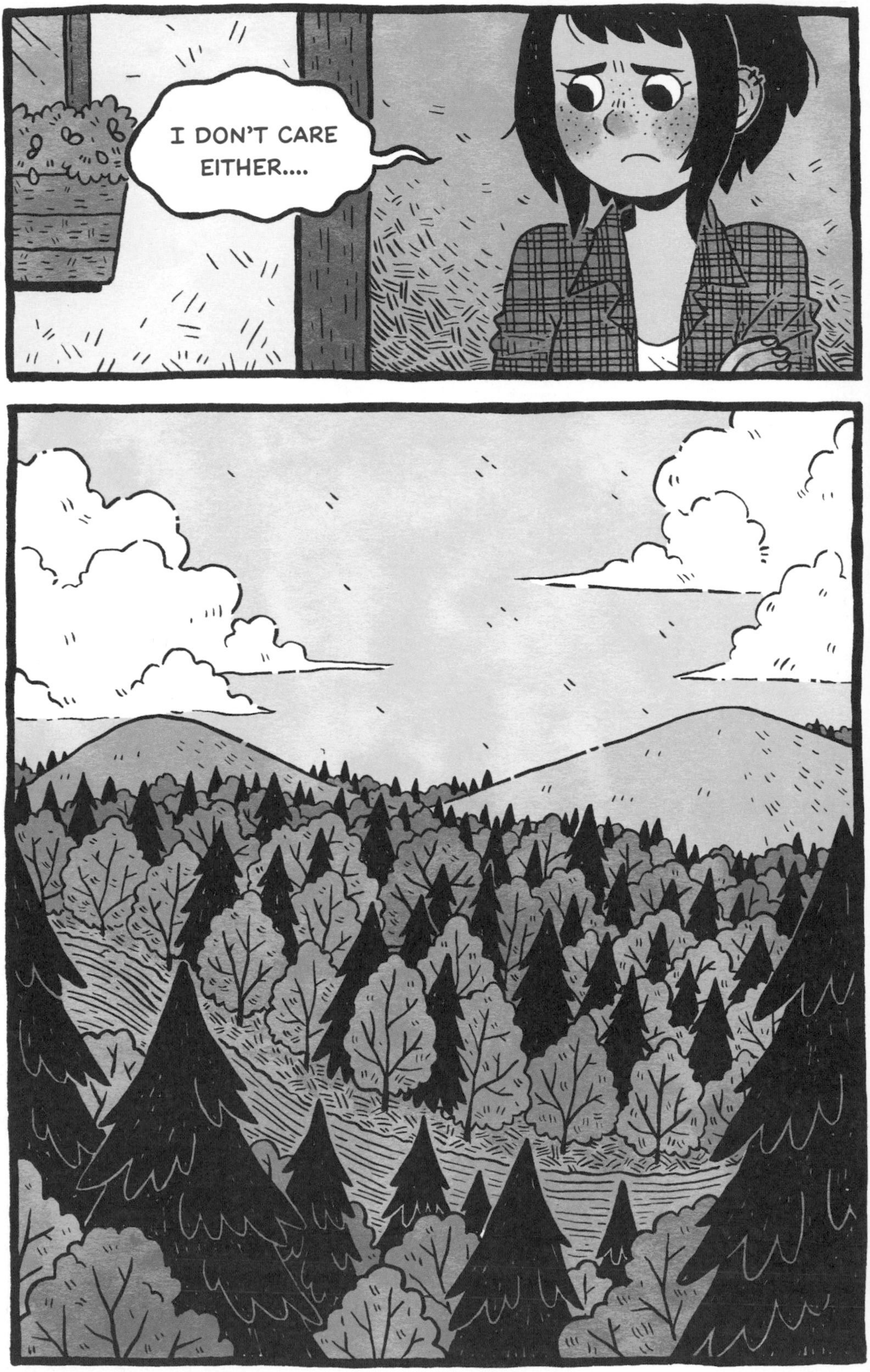
I DON'T CARE EITHER....

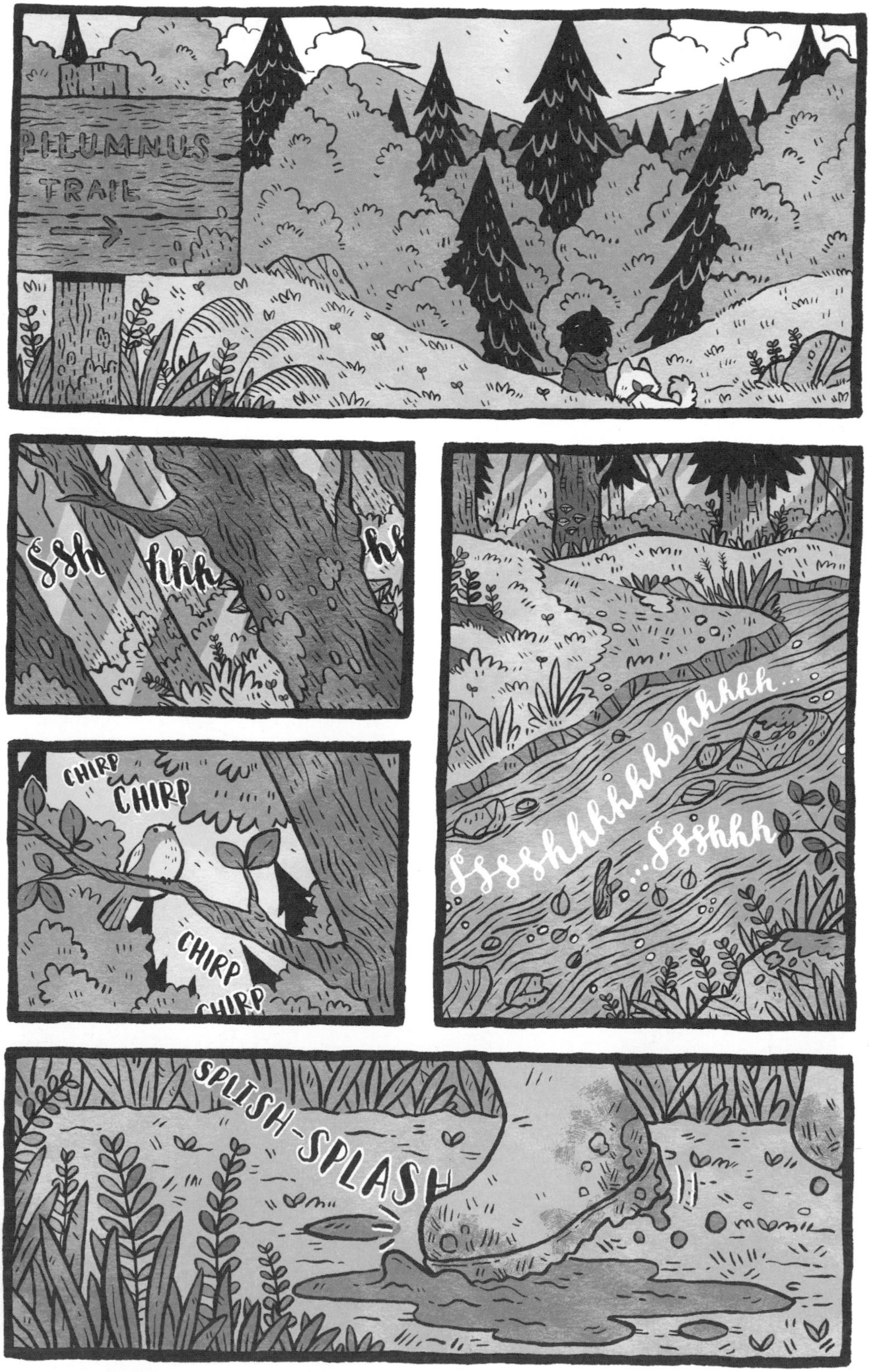
PILUMNUS
TRAIL
Sshhhh
CHIRP
CHIRP
CHIRP
CHIRP
Ssshhhhhhhhhhhhhh...
...Ssshhh
SPLISH-SPLASH

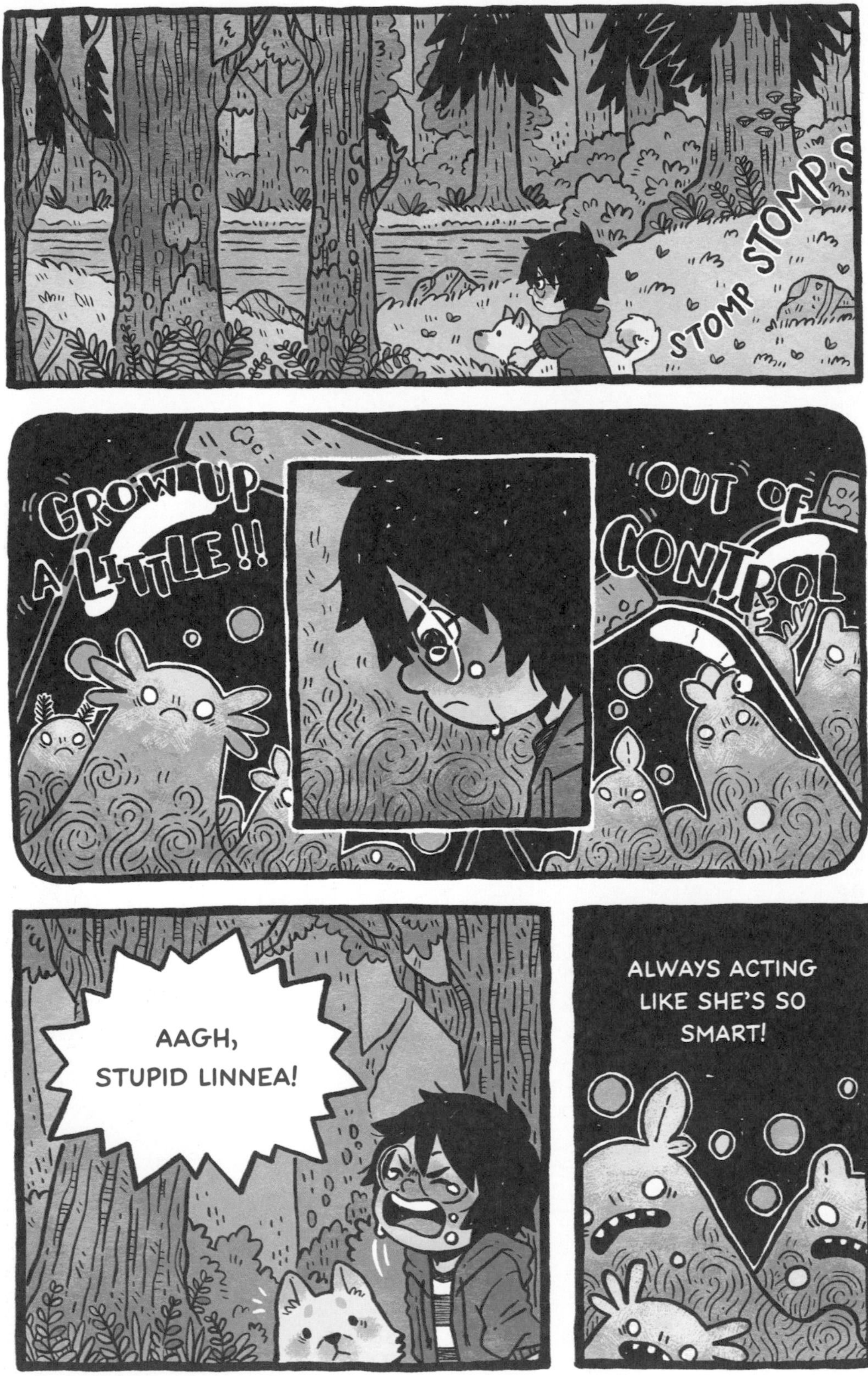
STOMP STOMP S
GROW UP A LITTLE!!
OUT OF CONTROL
AAGH, STUPID LINNEA!
ALWAYS ACTING LIKE SHE'S SO SMART!

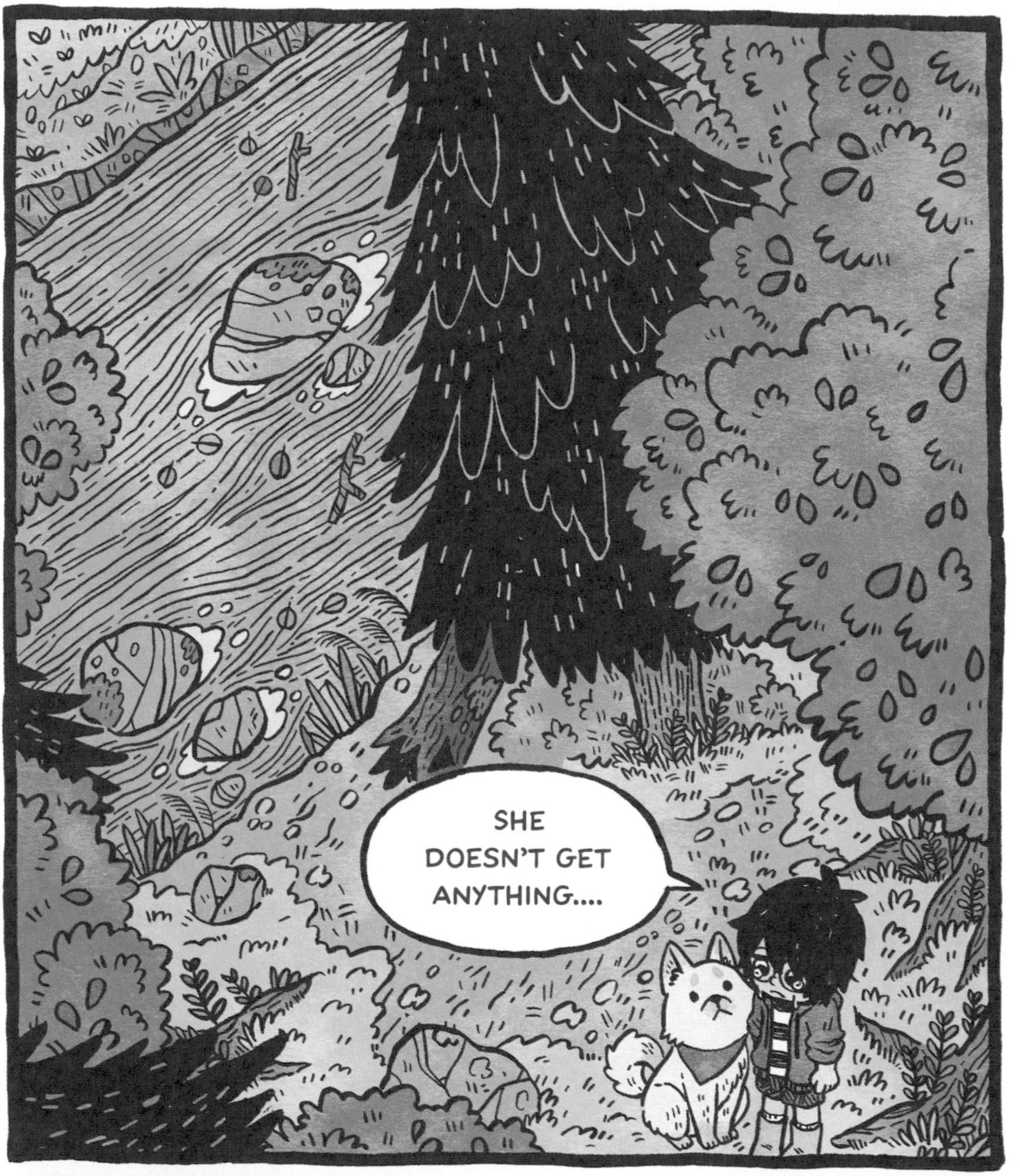
SHE DOESN'T GET ANYTHING....

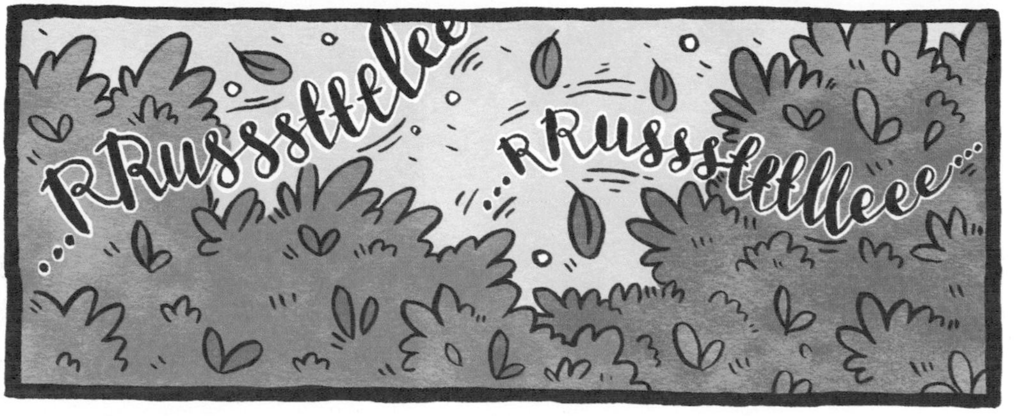
...RRUSSSTTLLEE
...RRUSSSTTTLLEEE...

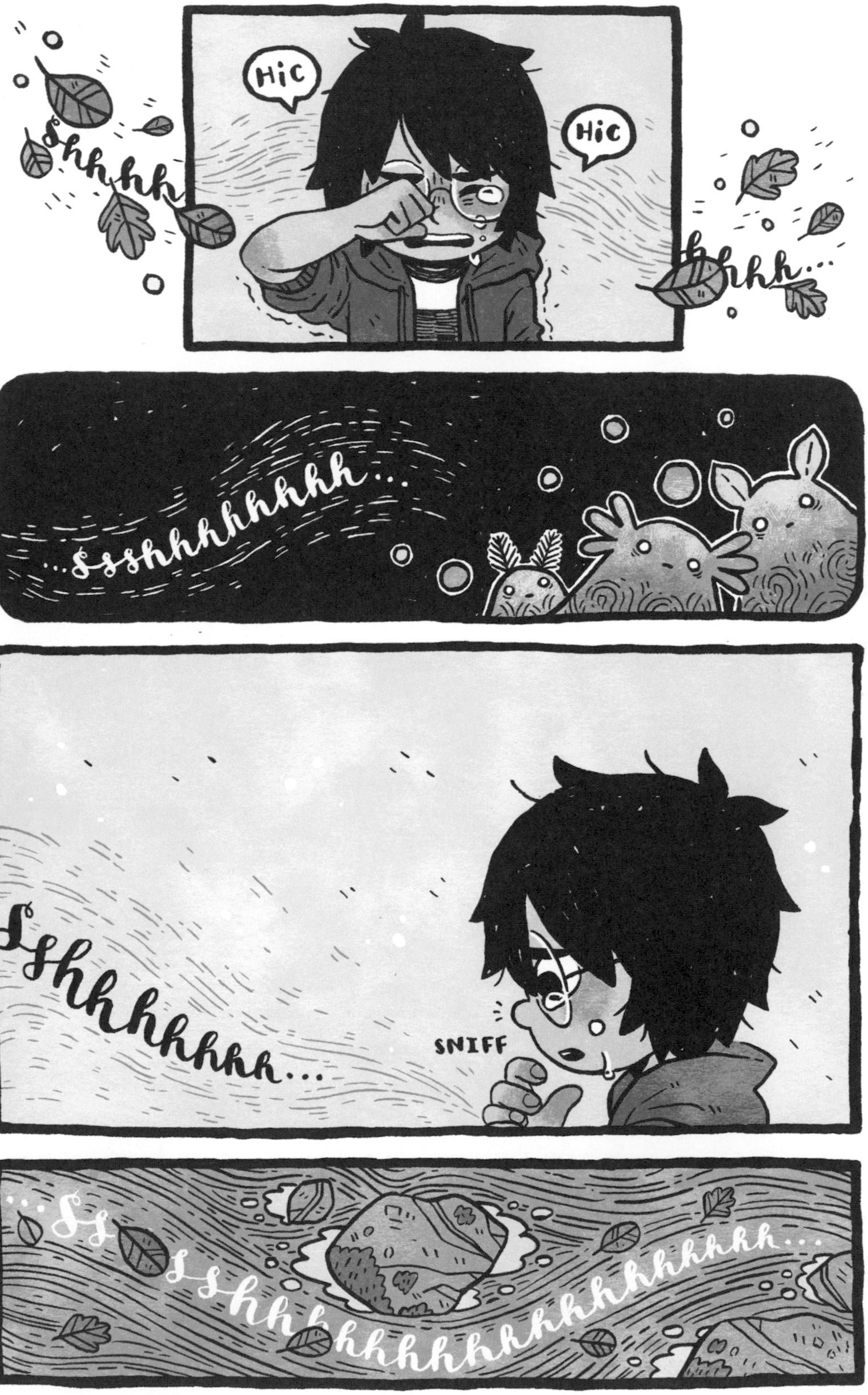
Hic
Hic
Shhhhh
hhhh...
...Ssshhhhhhhhhh...
SNIFF
Shhhhhhh...
...Ss shhhhhhhhhhhhhhhhhhhhh...

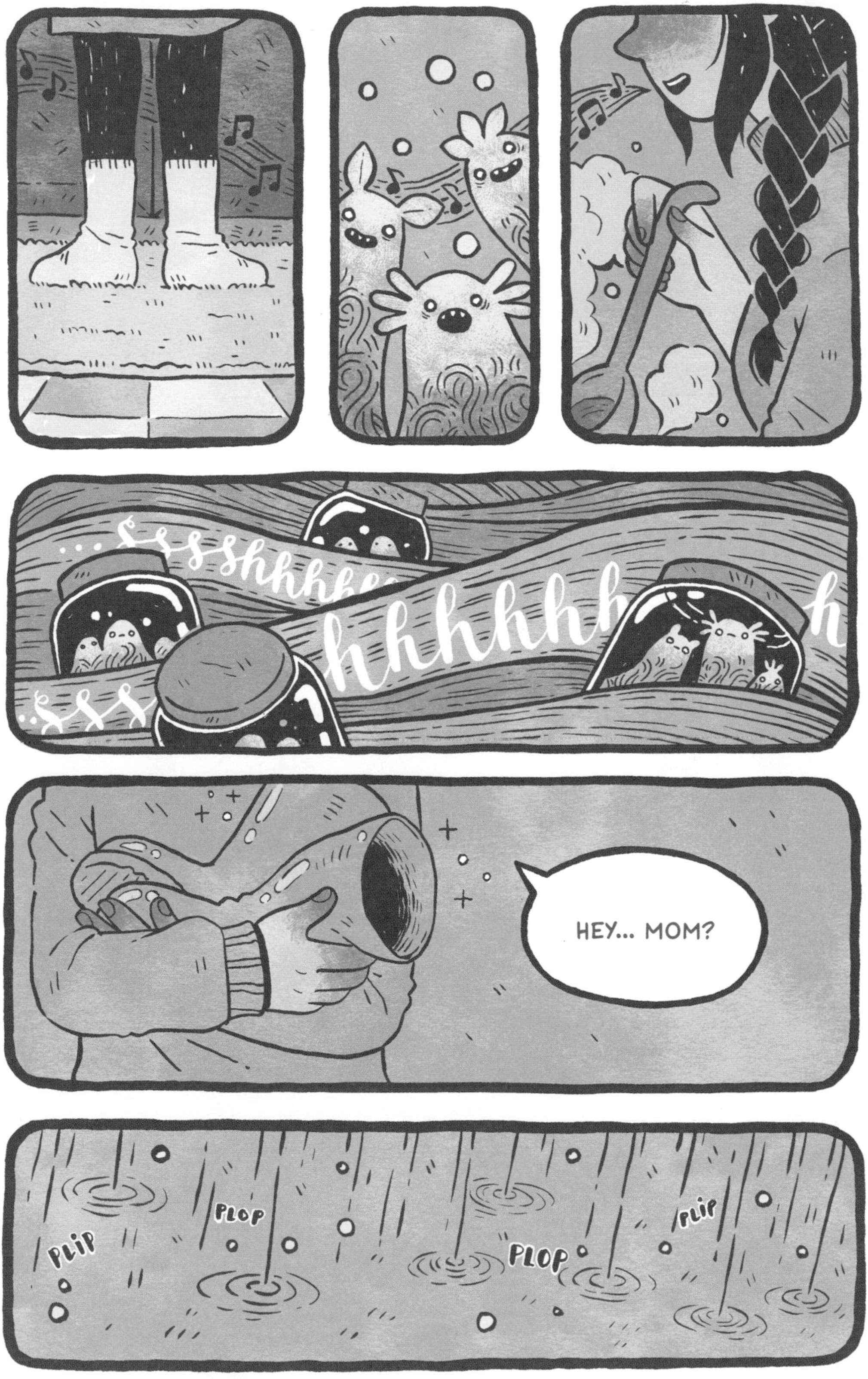
...Ssssshhhhhh
hhhhhhh
HEY... MOM?
PLIP
PLOP
PLOP
PLIP

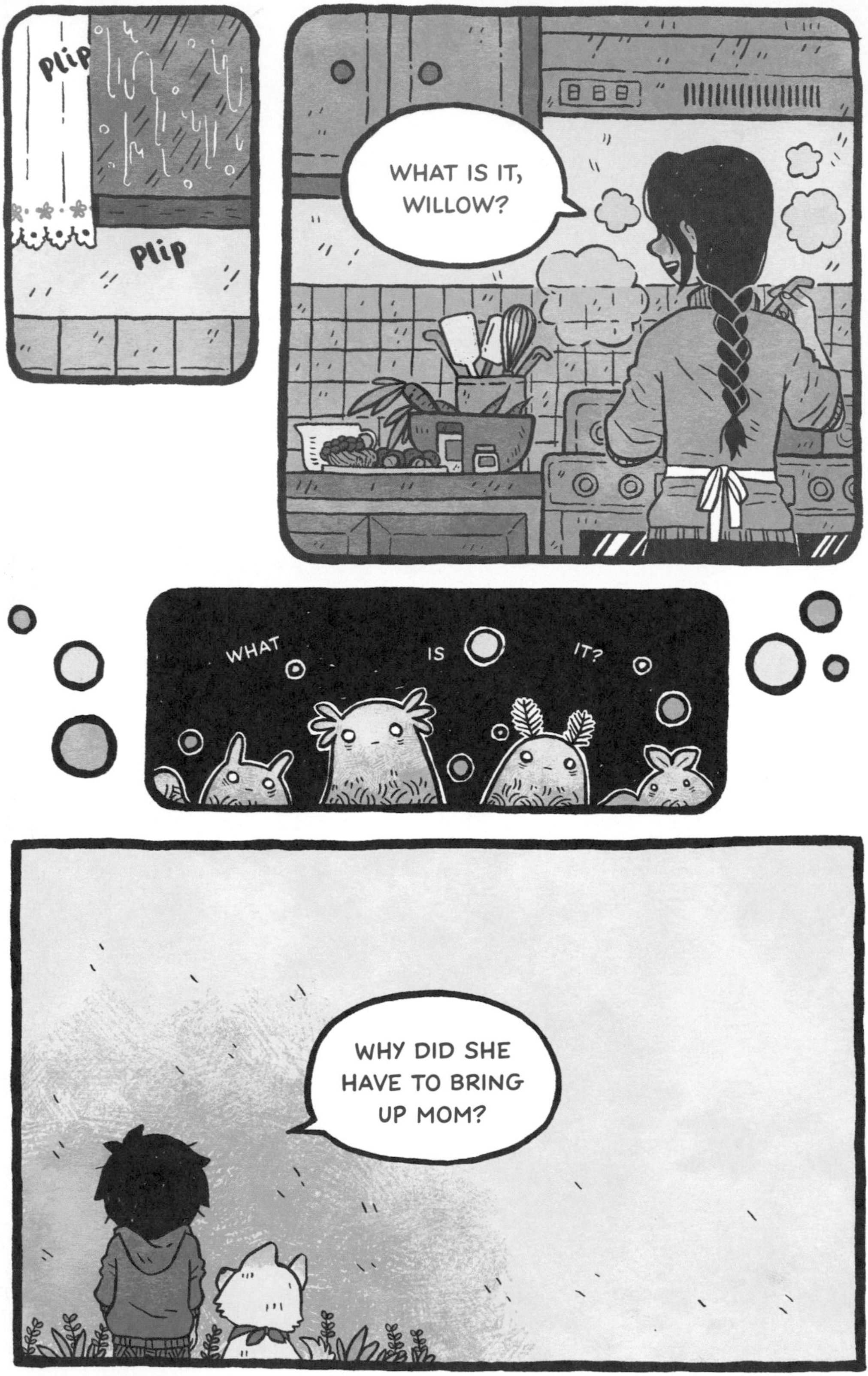
Plip
Plip
WHAT IS IT, WILLOW?
WHAT
IS
IT?
WHY DID SHE HAVE TO BRING UP MOM?

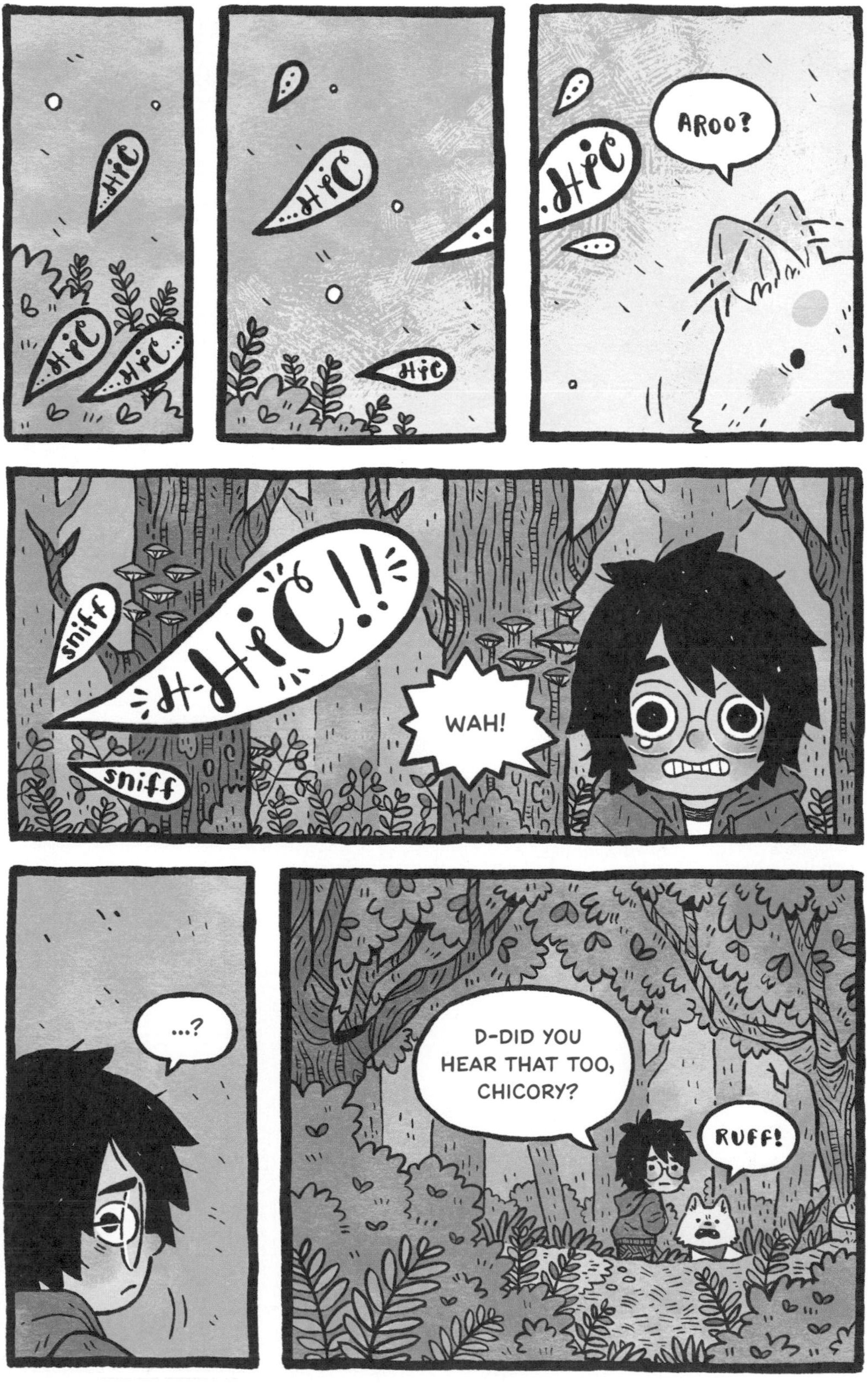
...Hic
Hic...
...Hic
...Hic
Hic
...Hic
AROO?
sniff
H-Hic!!
sniff
WAH!
...?
D-DID YOU HEAR THAT TOO, CHICORY?
RUFF!

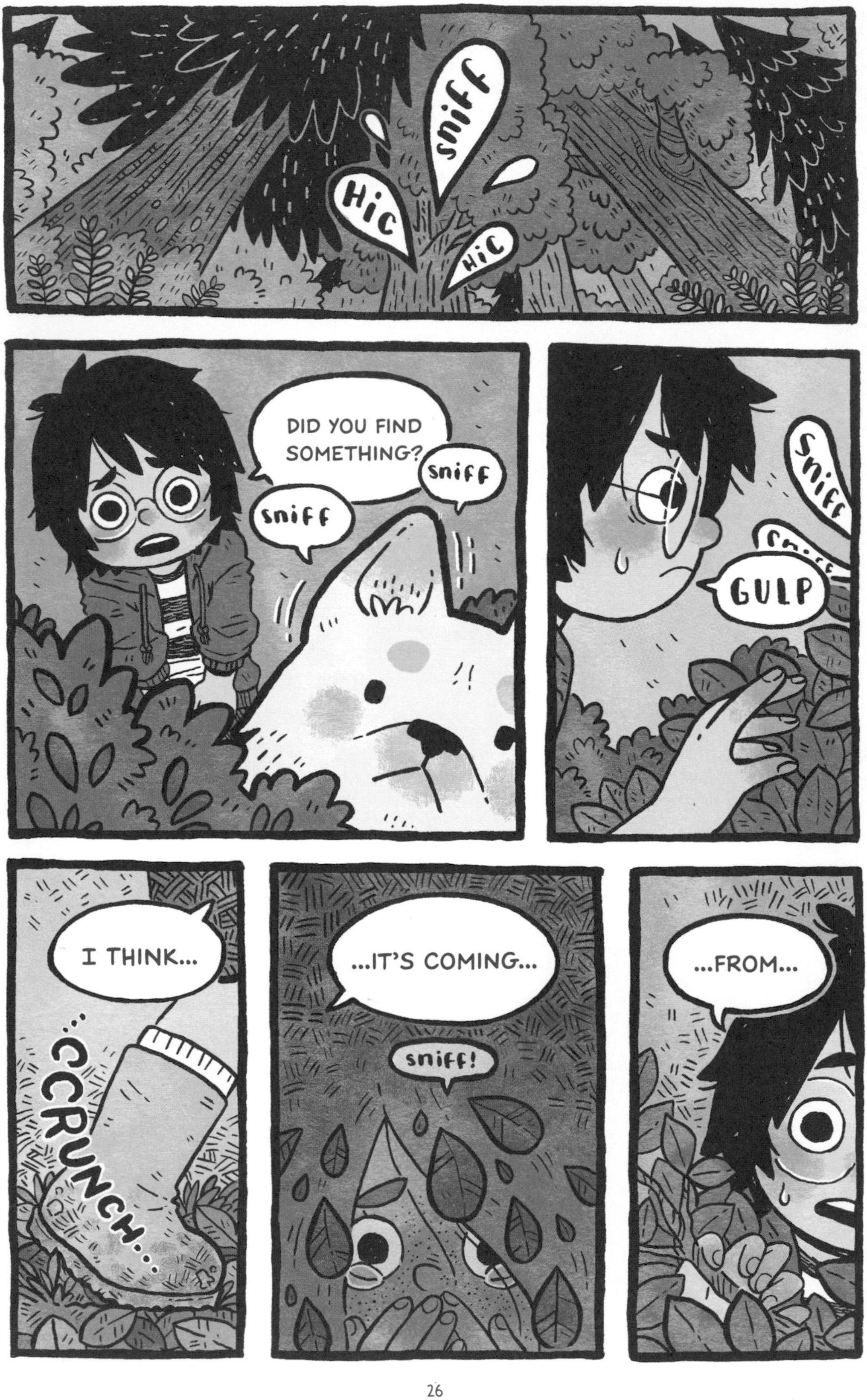
sniff
Hic
Hic
DID YOU FIND SOMETHING?
sniff
sniff
Sniff
GULP
I THINK...
...CCRUNCH...
...IT'S COMING...
sniff!
...FROM...

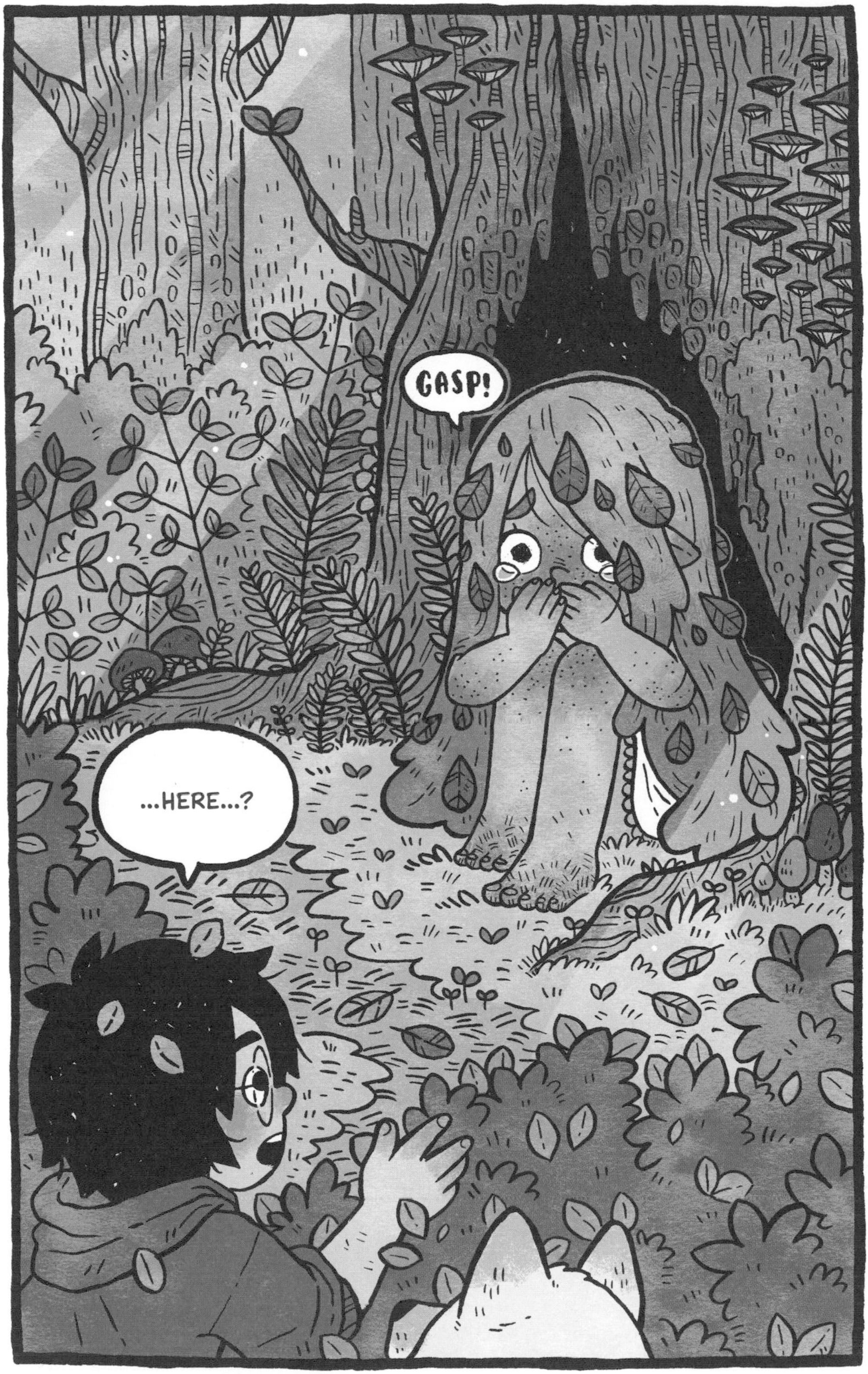
GASP!
...HERE...?

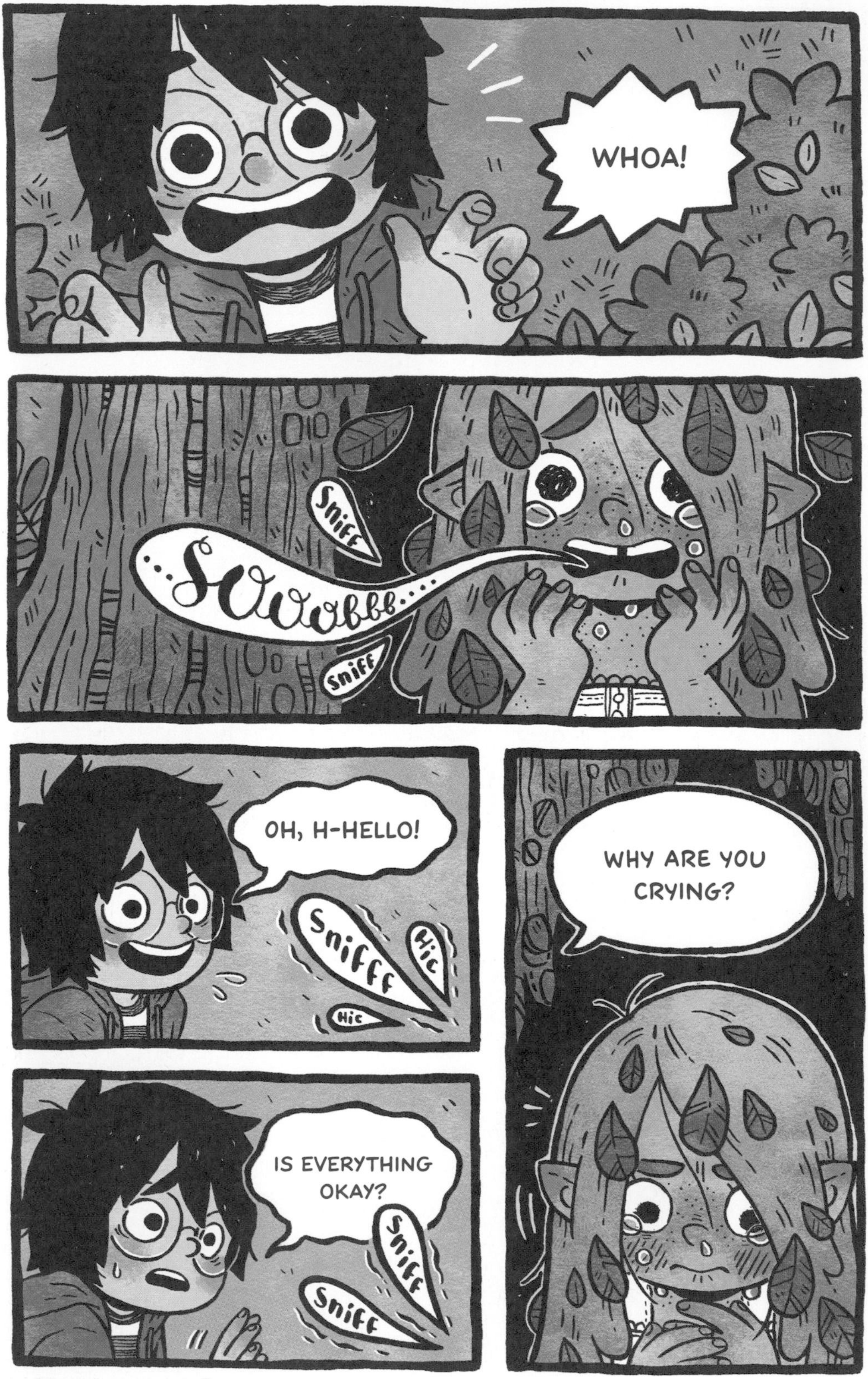
WHOA!
Sniff
...SOOObbb....
sniff
OH, H-HELLO!
Snifff
Hic
Hic
WHY ARE YOU CRYING?
IS EVERYTHING OKAY?
Sniff
Sniff

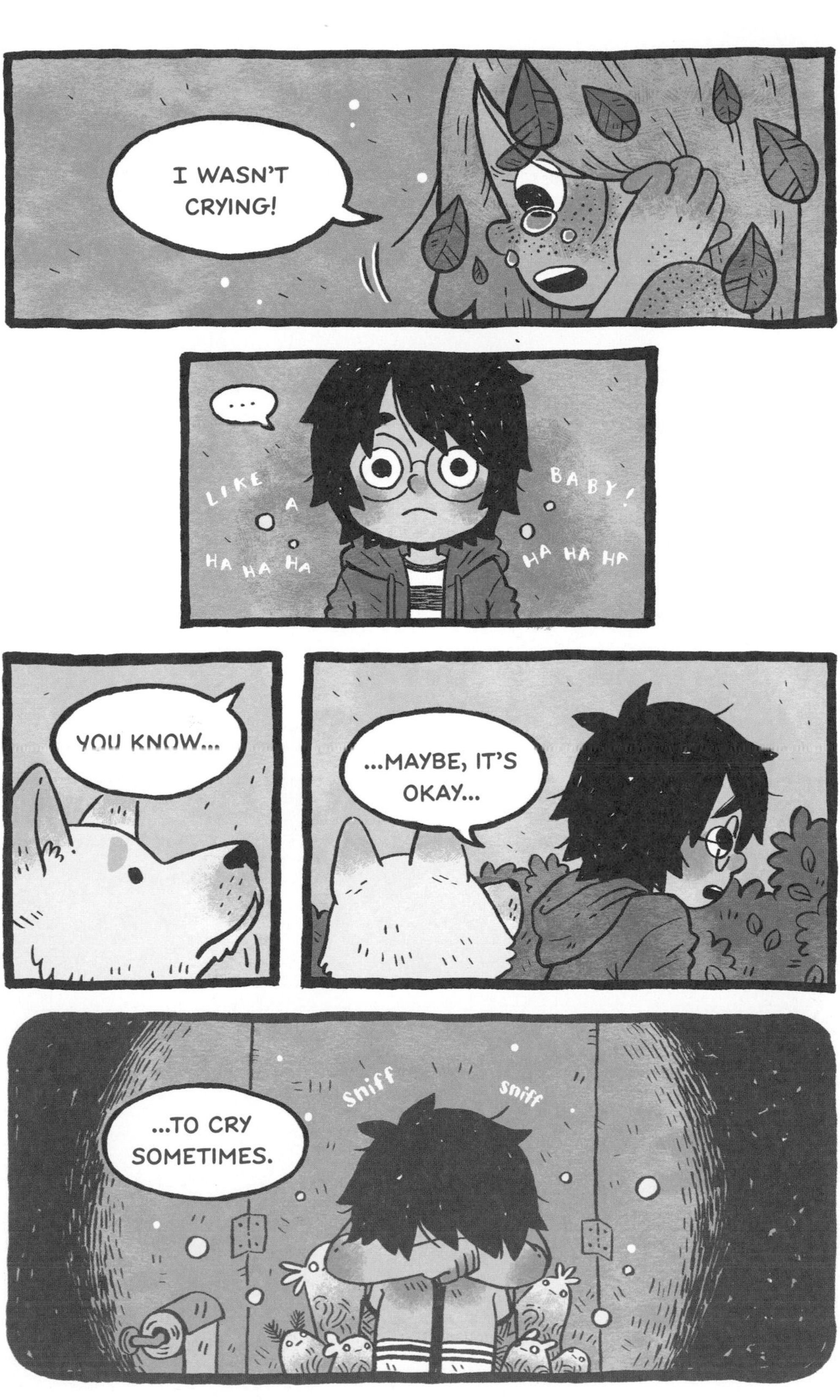
I WASN'T CRYING!
...
LIKE A BABY!
HA HA HA
HA HA HA
YOU KNOW...
...MAYBE, IT'S OKAY...
sniff
sniff
...TO CRY SOMETIMES.

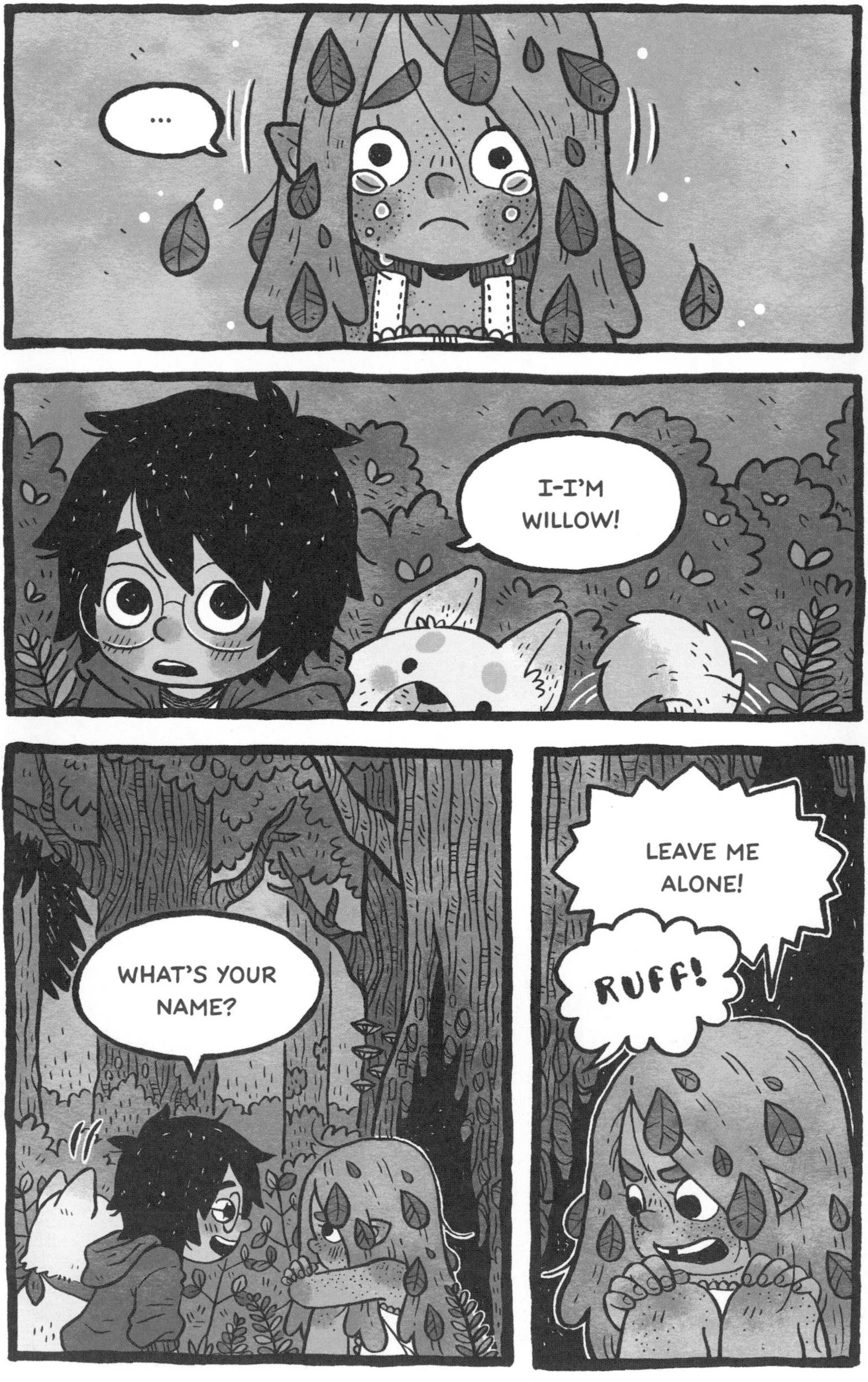
...
I-I'M WILLOW!
WHAT'S YOUR NAME?
LEAVE ME ALONE!
RUFF!

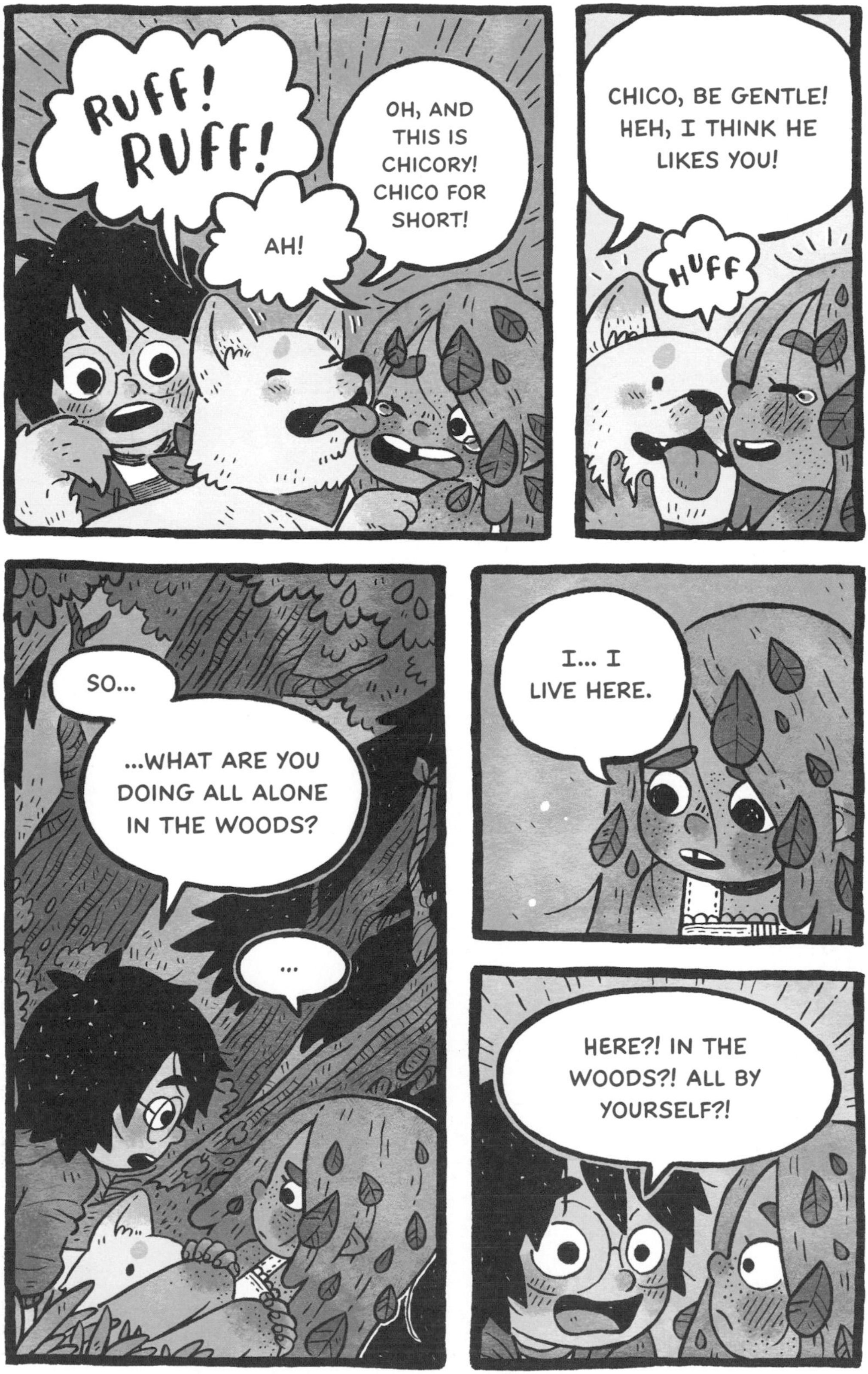
RUFF! RUFF!
AH!
OH, AND THIS IS CHICORY! CHICO FOR SHORT!
CHICO, BE GENTLE! HEH, I THINK HE LIKES YOU!
HUFF
SO...
...WHAT ARE YOU DOING ALL ALONE IN THE WOODS?
...
I... I LIVE HERE.
HERE?! IN THE WOODS?! ALL BY YOURSELF?!

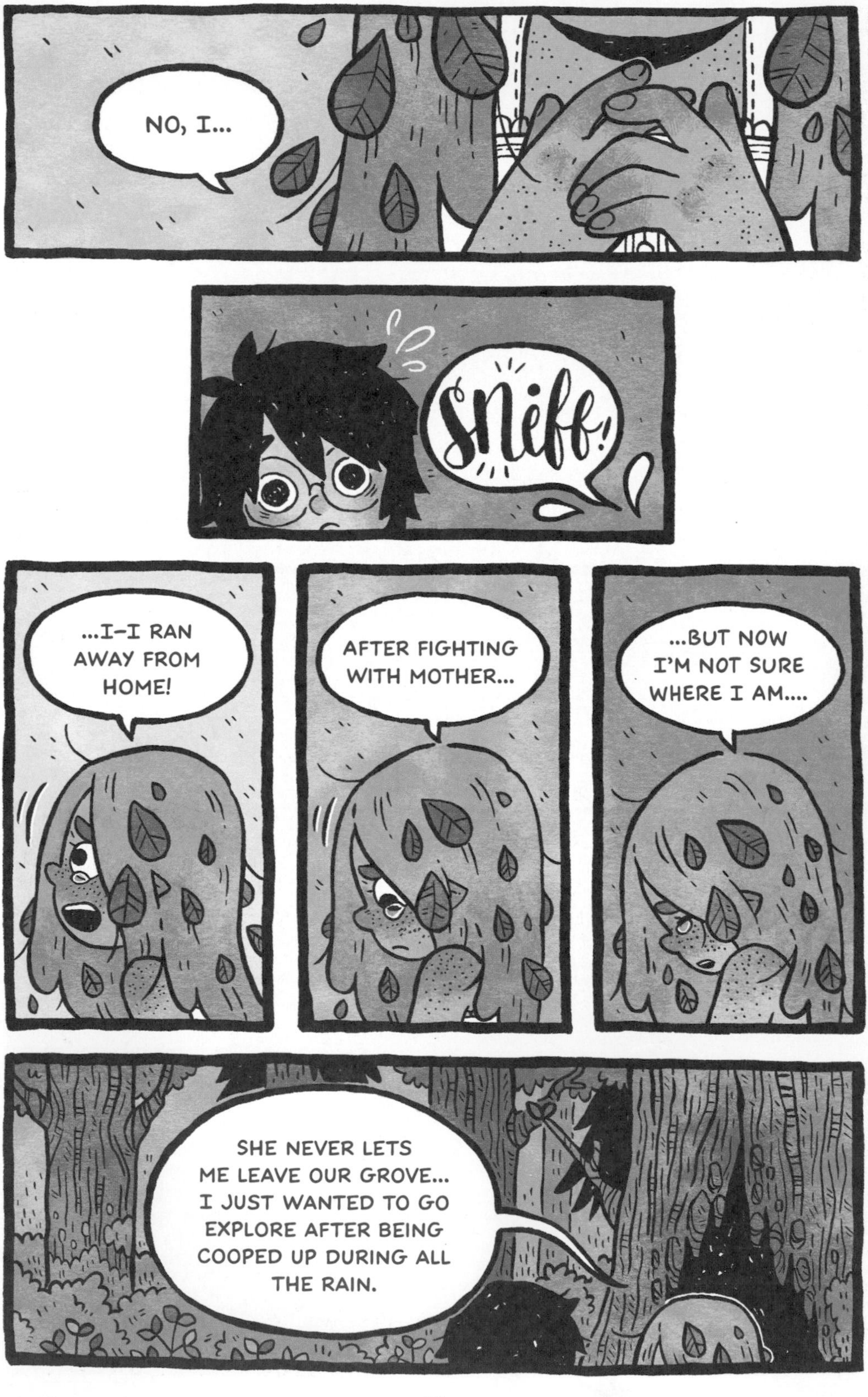
NO, I...
SNIFF!
...I-I RAN AWAY FROM HOME!
AFTER FIGHTING WITH MOTHER...
...BUT NOW I'M NOT SURE WHERE I AM....
SHE NEVER LETS ME LEAVE OUR GROVE... I JUST WANTED TO GO EXPLORE AFTER BEING COOPED UP DURING ALL THE RAIN.

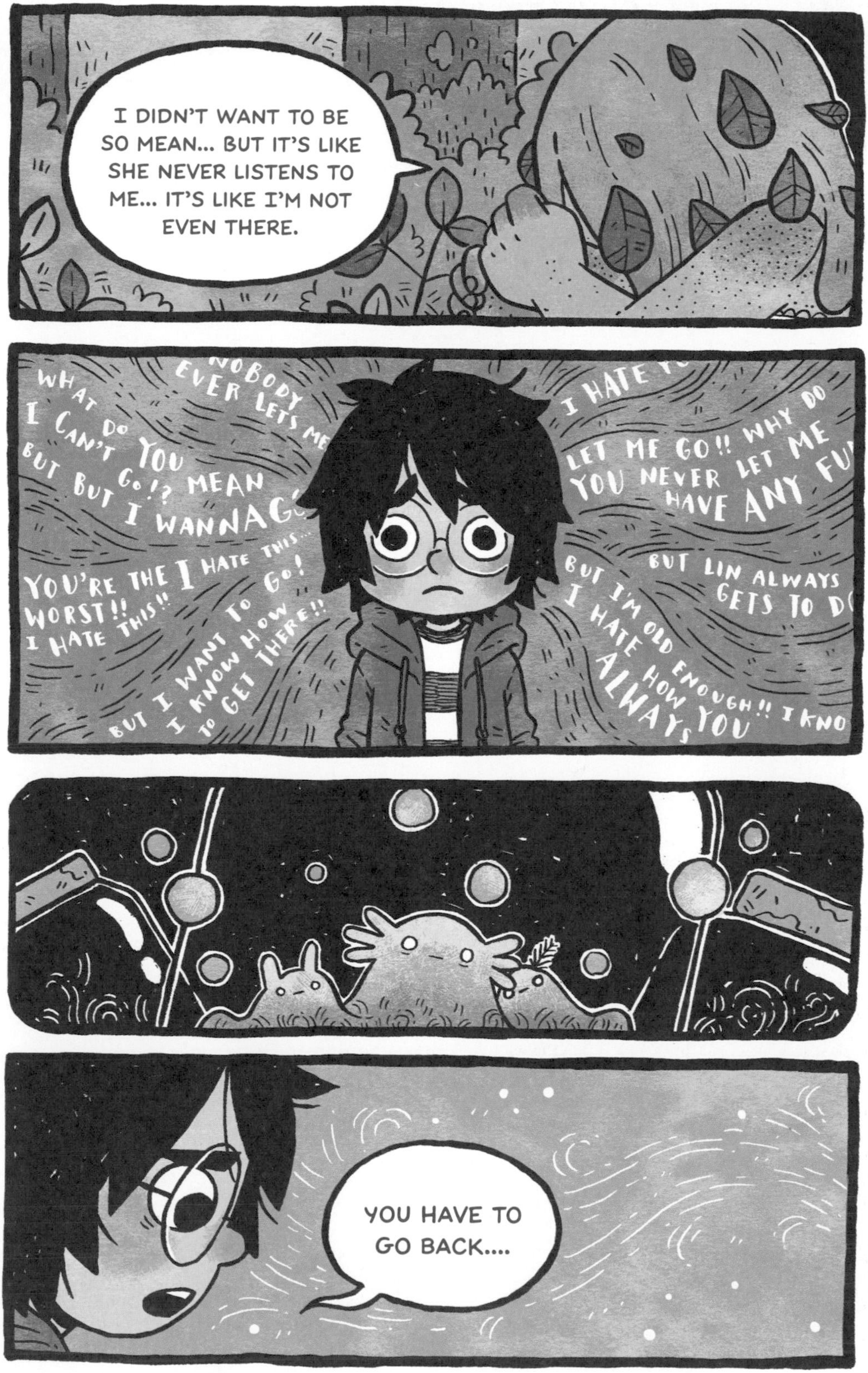
I DIDN'T WANT TO BE SO MEAN... BUT IT'S LIKE SHE NEVER LISTENS TO ME... IT'S LIKE I'M NOT EVEN THERE.
NOBODY EVER LETS ME
WHAT DO YOU MEAN
I CAN'T GO!?
BUT BUT I WANNA GO
YOU'RE THE WORST!!
I HATE THIS...
I HATE THIS!!
BUT I WANT TO GO!
I KNOW HOW TO GET THERE!!
LET ME GO!! WHY DO YOU NEVER LET ME HAVE ANY
BUT LIN ALWAYS
BUT I'M OLD ENOUGH!!
I HATE HOW YOU ALWAYS
YOU HAVE TO GO BACK....

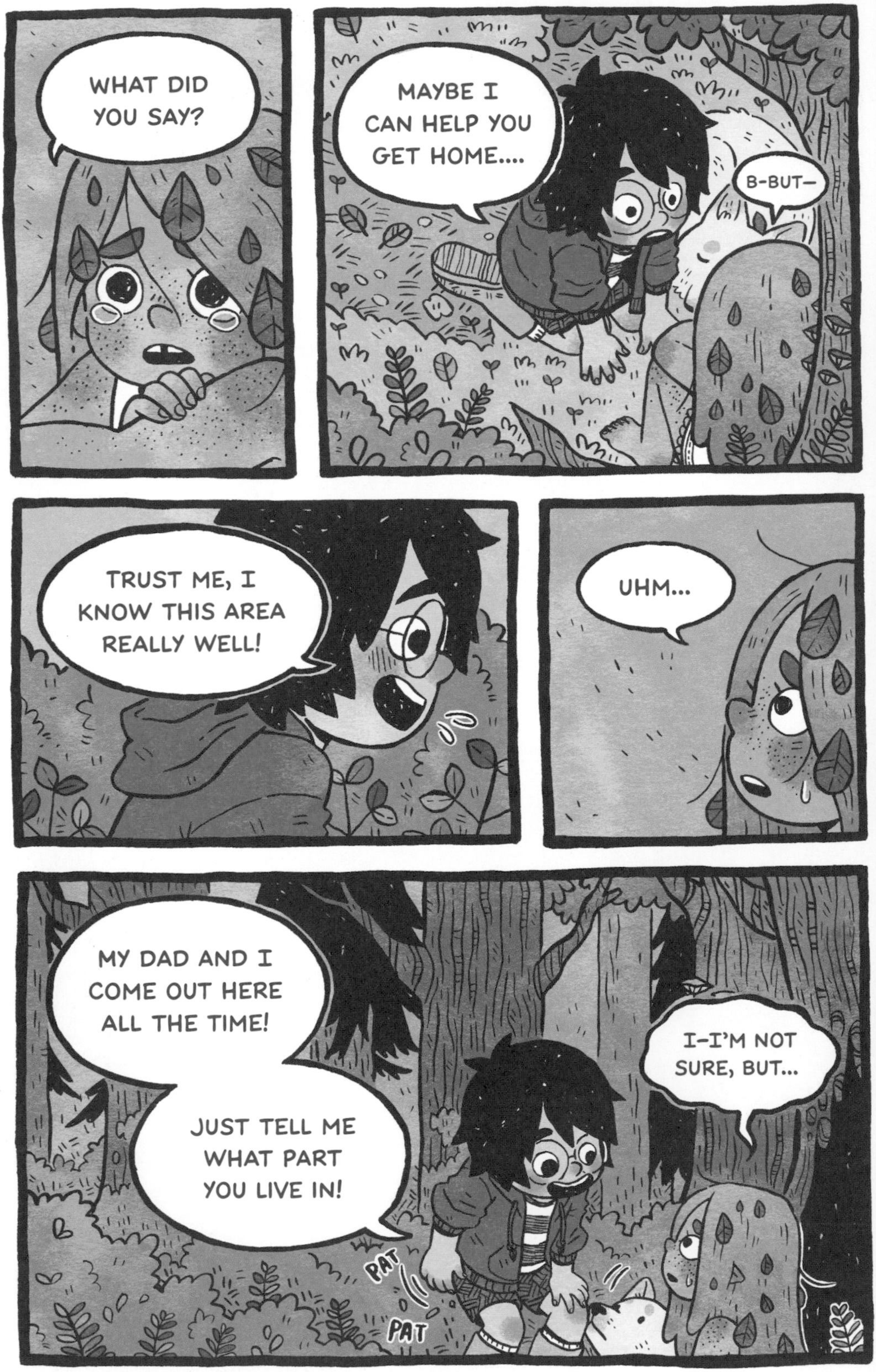
WHAT DID YOU SAY?
MAYBE I CAN HELP YOU GET HOME....
B-BUT—
TRUST ME, I KNOW THIS AREA REALLY WELL!
UHM...
MY DAD AND I COME OUT HERE ALL THE TIME!
JUST TELL ME WHAT PART YOU LIVE IN!
I-I'M NOT SURE, BUT...
PAT
PAT

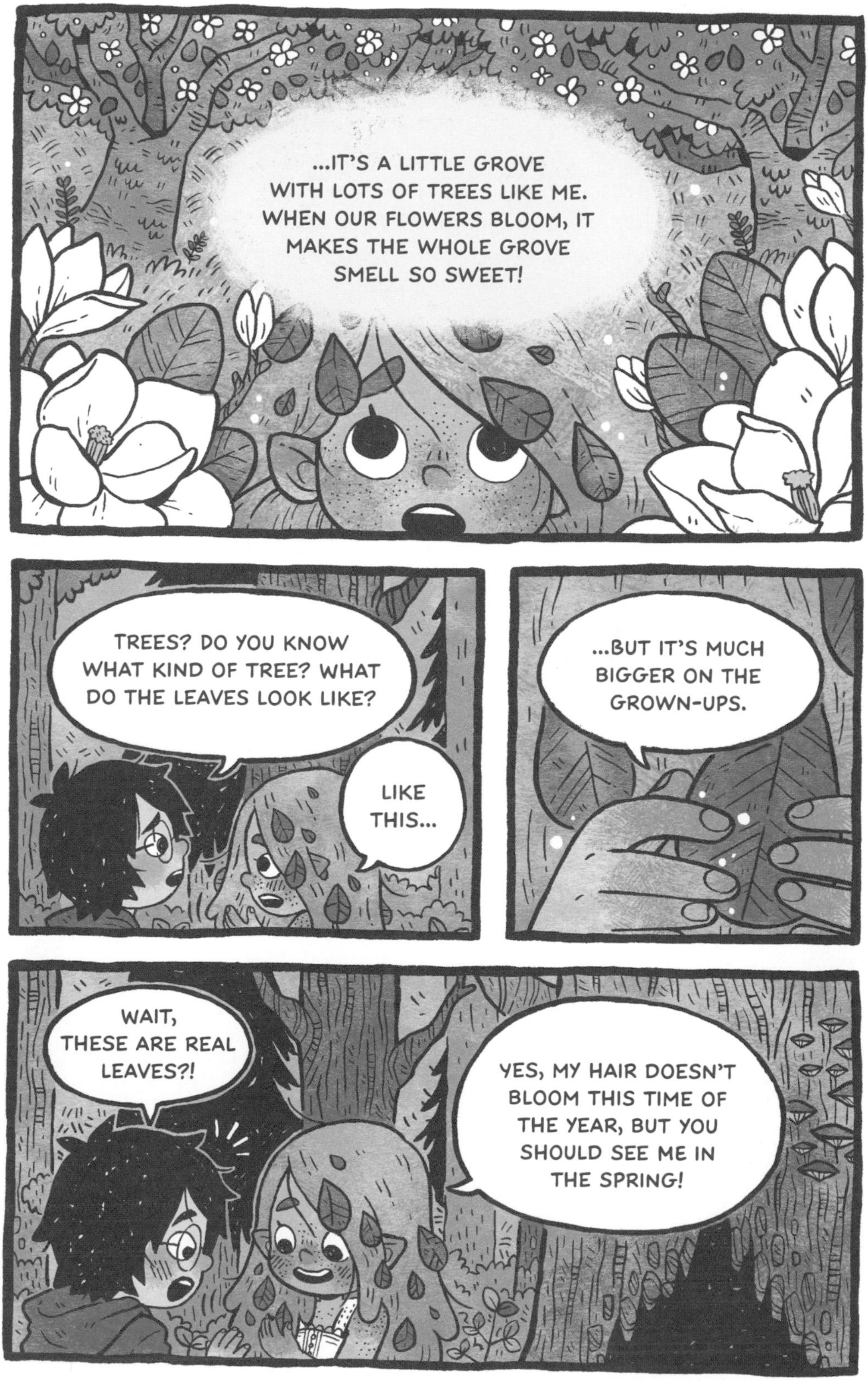
...IT'S A LITTLE GROVE WITH LOTS OF TREES LIKE ME. WHEN OUR FLOWERS BLOOM, IT MAKES THE WHOLE GROVE SMELL SO SWEET!
TREES? DO YOU KNOW WHAT KIND OF TREE? WHAT DO THE LEAVES LOOK LIKE?
LIKE THIS...
...BUT IT'S MUCH BIGGER ON THE GROWN-UPS.
WAIT, THESE ARE REAL LEAVES?!
YES, MY HAIR DOESN'T BLOOM THIS TIME OF THE YEAR, BUT YOU SHOULD SEE ME IN THE SPRING!

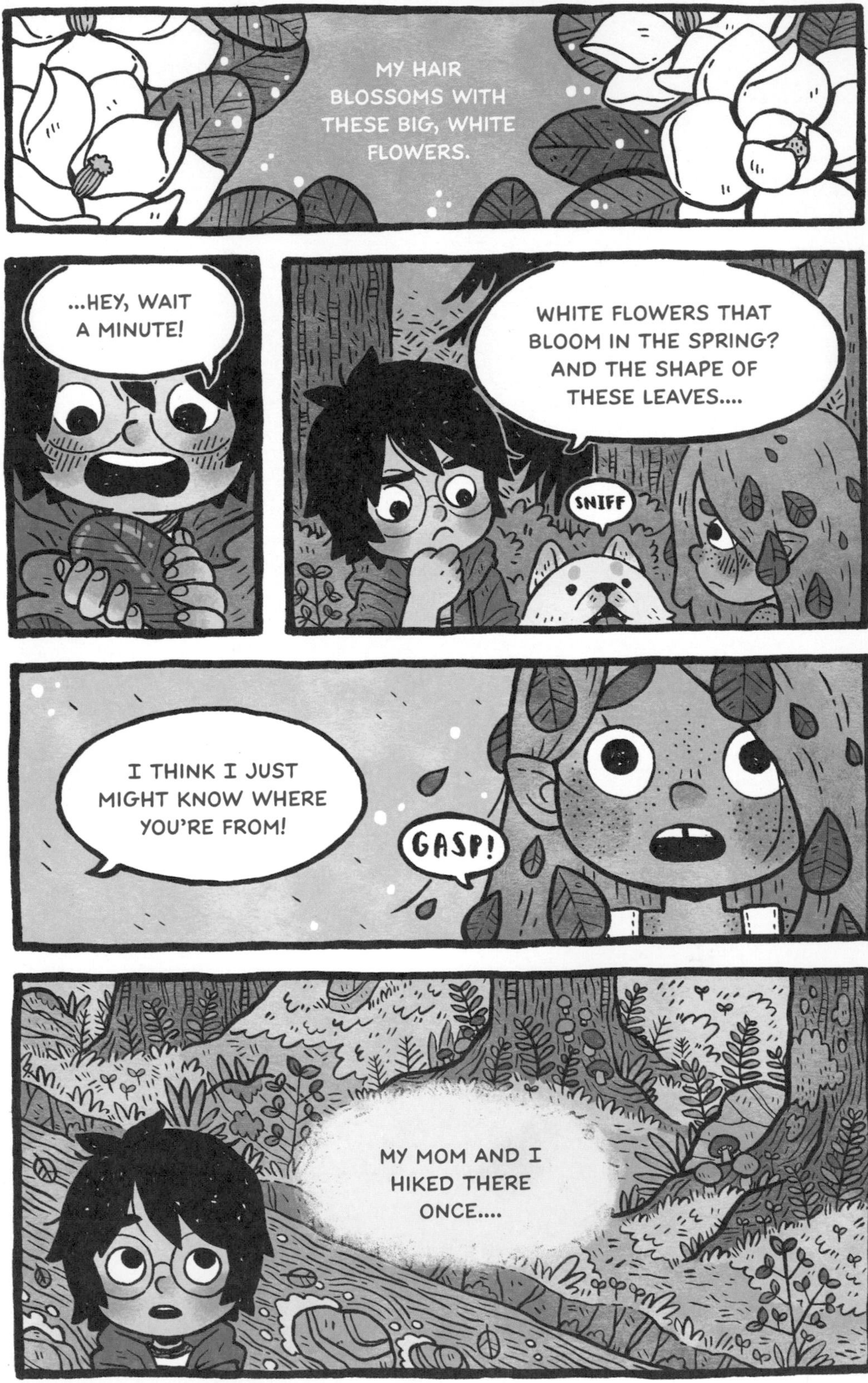
MY HAIR BLOSSOMS WITH THESE BIG, WHITE FLOWERS.
...HEY, WAIT A MINUTE!
WHITE FLOWERS THAT BLOOM IN THE SPRING? AND THE SHAPE OF THESE LEAVES....
SNIFF
I THINK I JUST MIGHT KNOW WHERE YOU'RE FROM!
GASP!
MY MOM AND I HIKED THERE ONCE....

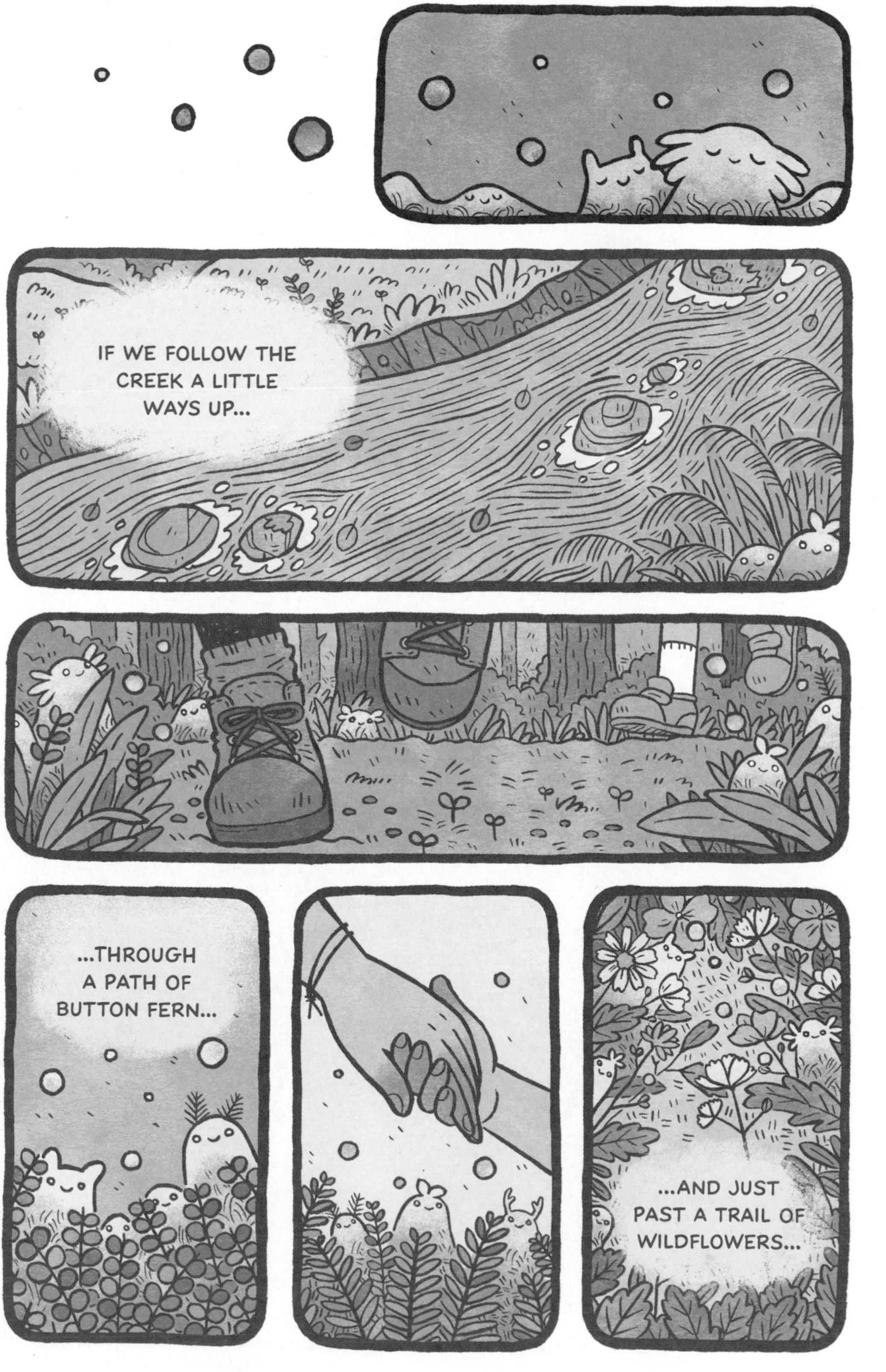
IF WE FOLLOW THE CREEK A LITTLE WAYS UP...
...THROUGH A PATH OF BUTTON FERN...
...AND JUST PAST A TRAIL OF WILDFLOWERS...

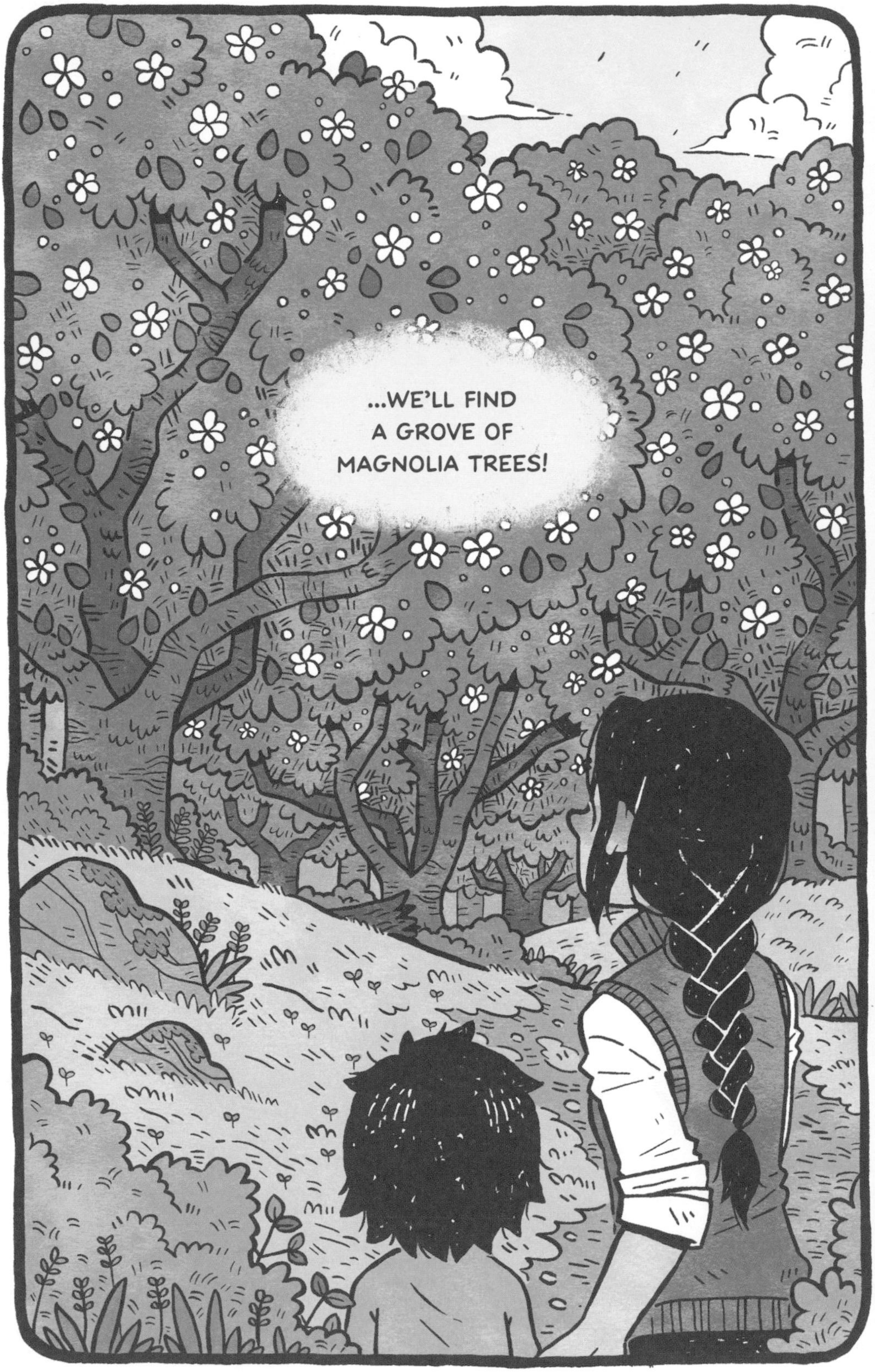
...WE'LL FIND
A GROVE OF
MAGNOLIA TREES!

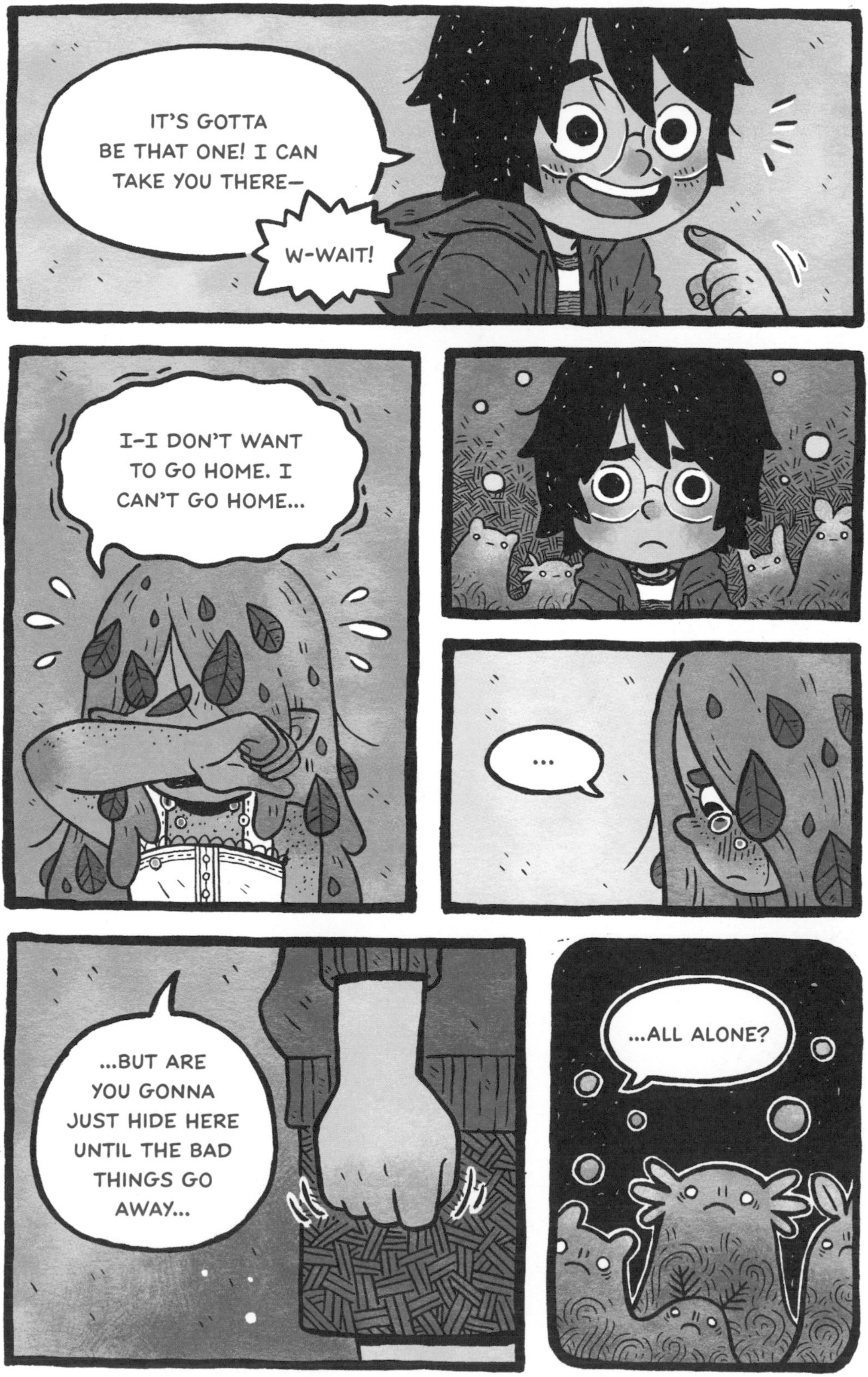
IT'S GOTTA BE THAT ONE! I CAN TAKE YOU THERE—
W-WAIT!
I-I DON'T WANT TO GO HOME. I CAN'T GO HOME...
...
...BUT ARE YOU GONNA JUST HIDE HERE UNTIL THE BAD THINGS GO AWAY...
...ALL ALONE?

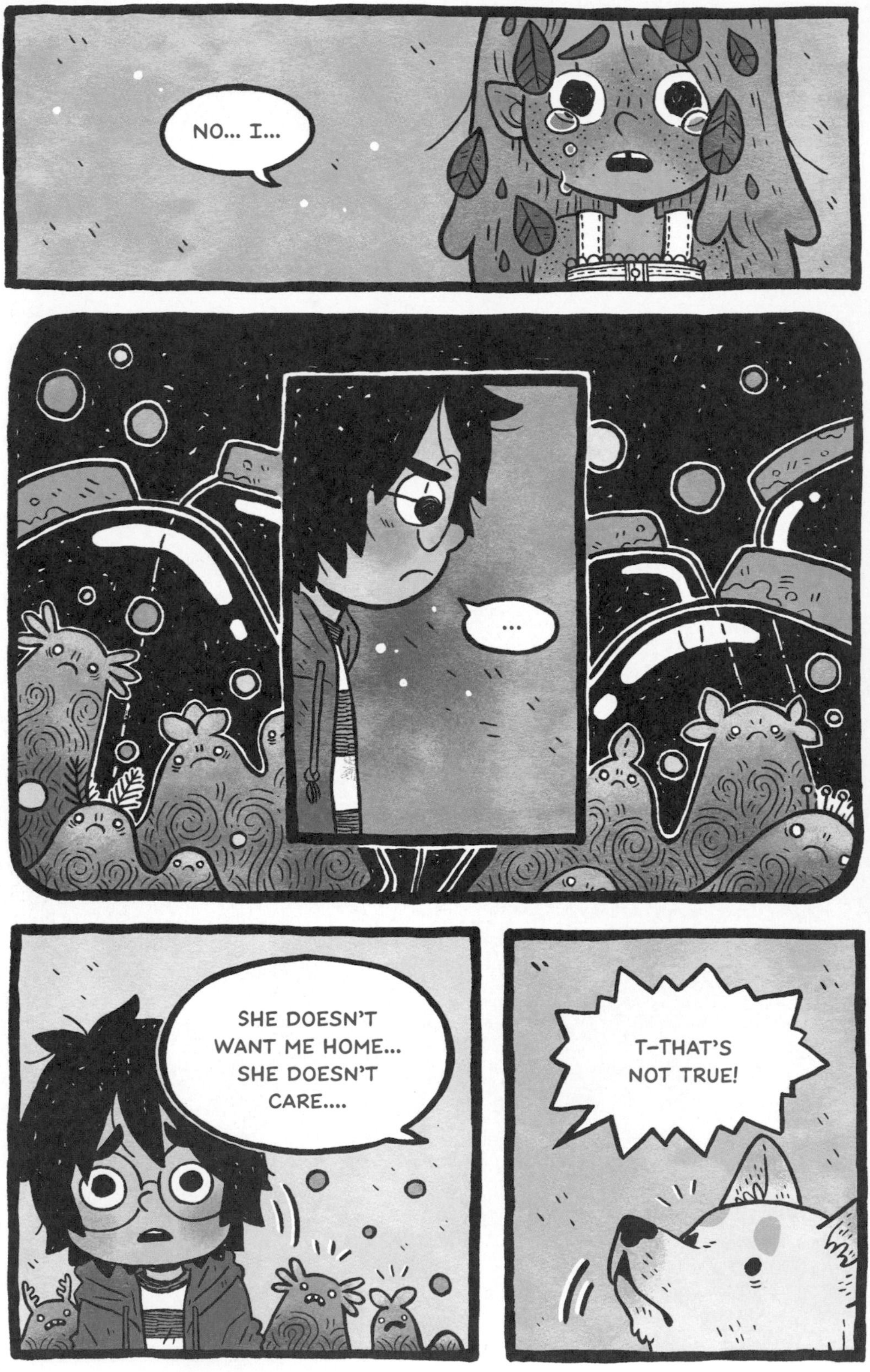
NO... I...
...
SHE DOESN'T WANT ME HOME... SHE DOESN'T CARE....
T-THAT'S NOT TRUE!

SHE PROBABLY DIDN'T WANT YOU TO LEAVE HOME BECAUSE SHE WAS WORRIED SOMETHING BAD MIGHT HAPPEN!

AT LEAST LET ME SHOW YOU HOW TO GET HOME.

B-BUT—

AND THEN YOU CAN DECIDE WHAT YOU WANT TO DO!

PLEASE!

...OKAY.

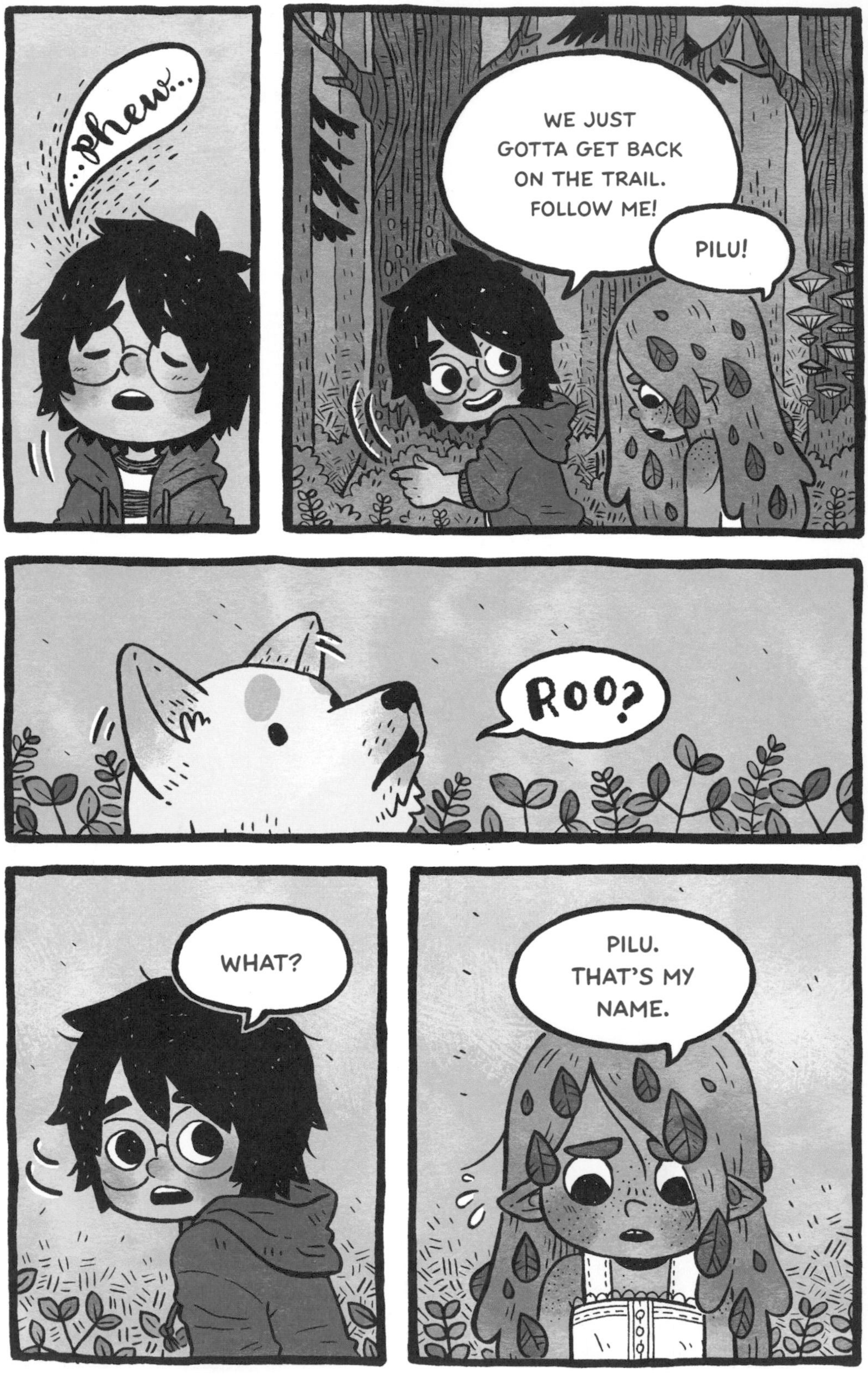
...phew...
WE JUST GOTTA GET BACK ON THE TRAIL. FOLLOW ME!
PILU!
ROO?
WHAT?
PILU. THAT'S MY NAME.

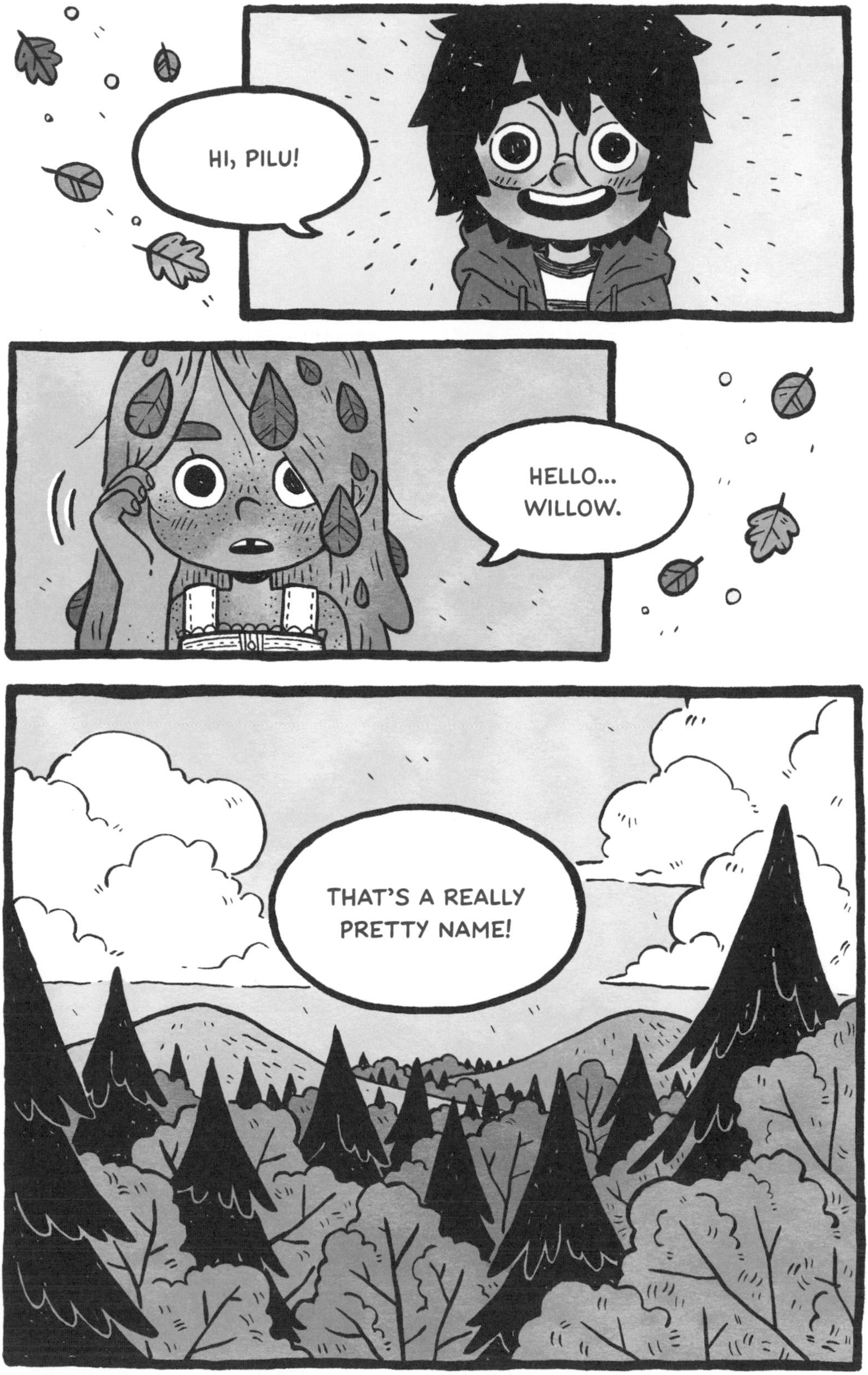
HI, PILU!
HELLO... WILLOW.
THAT'S A REALLY PRETTY NAME!

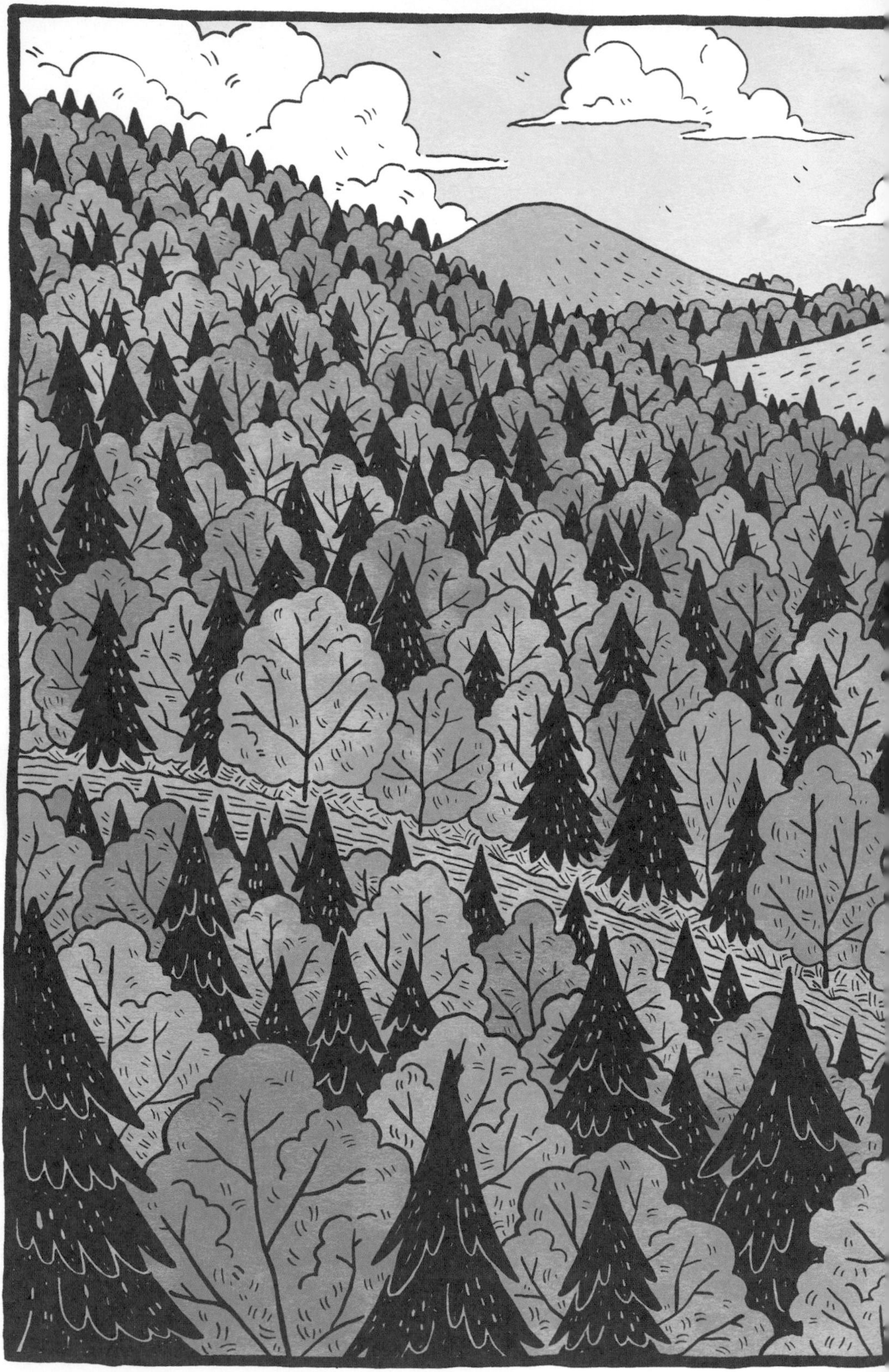

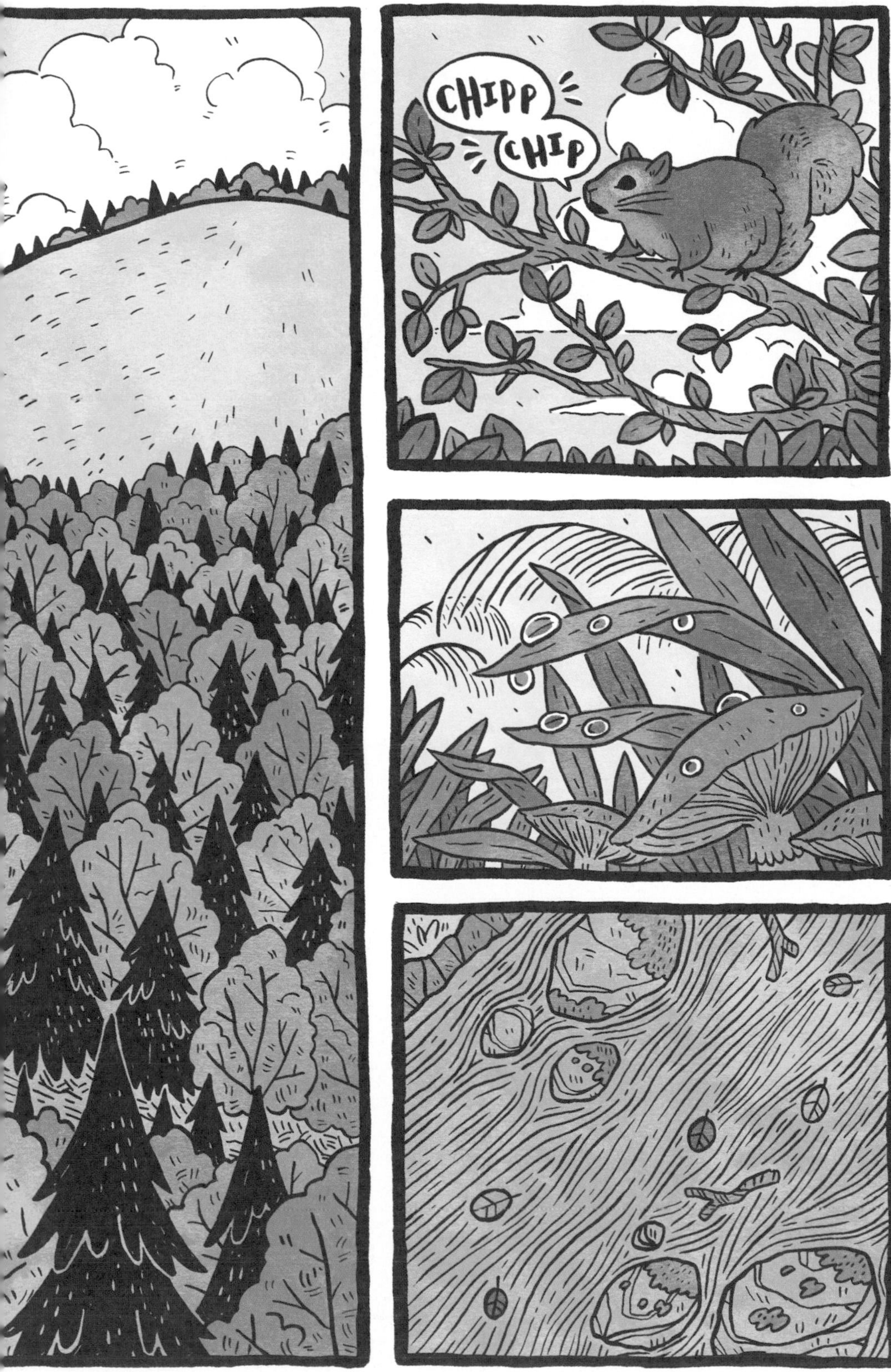
CHIPP
CHIP

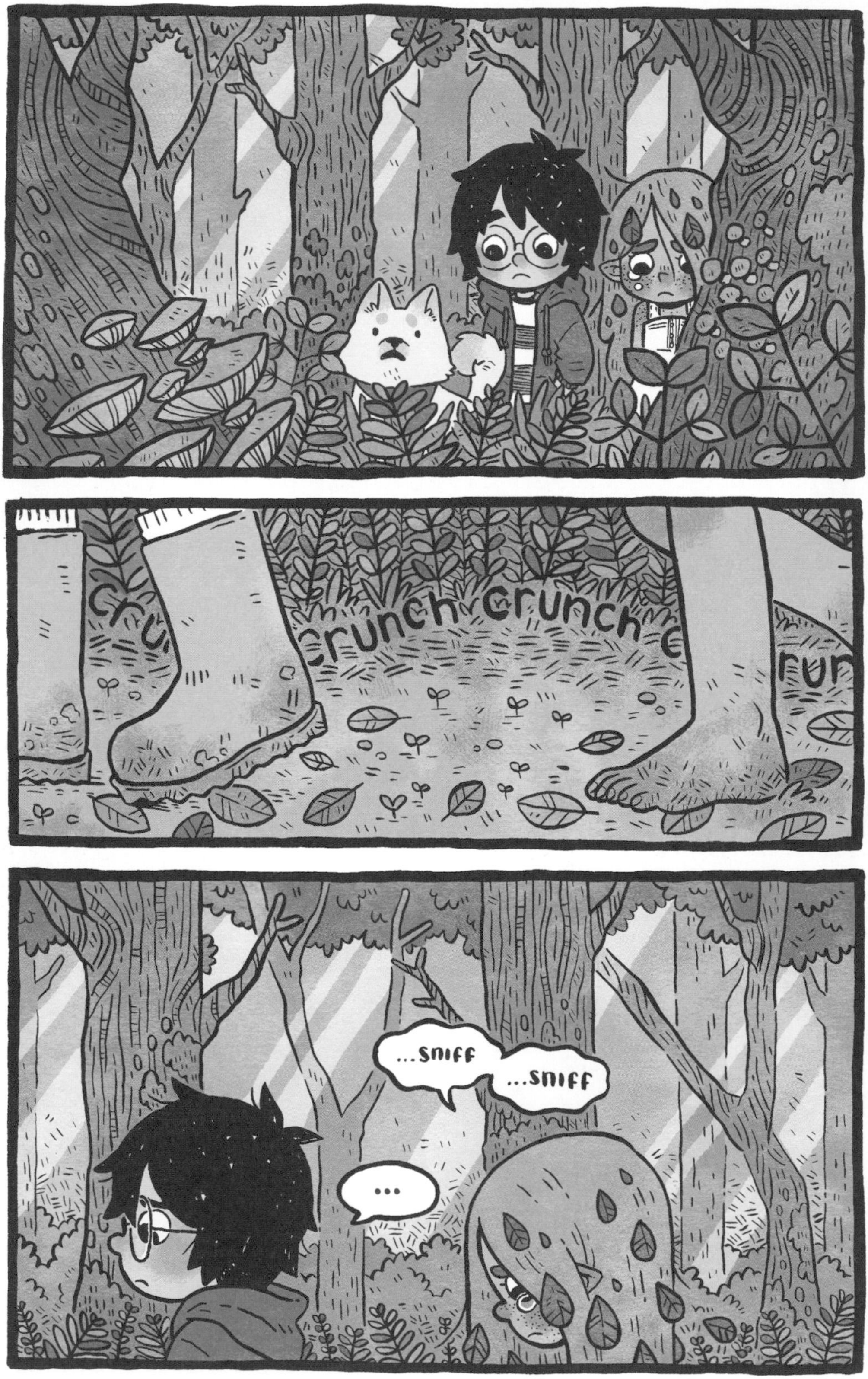
crunch crunch crunch crunch
...sniff
...sniff
...

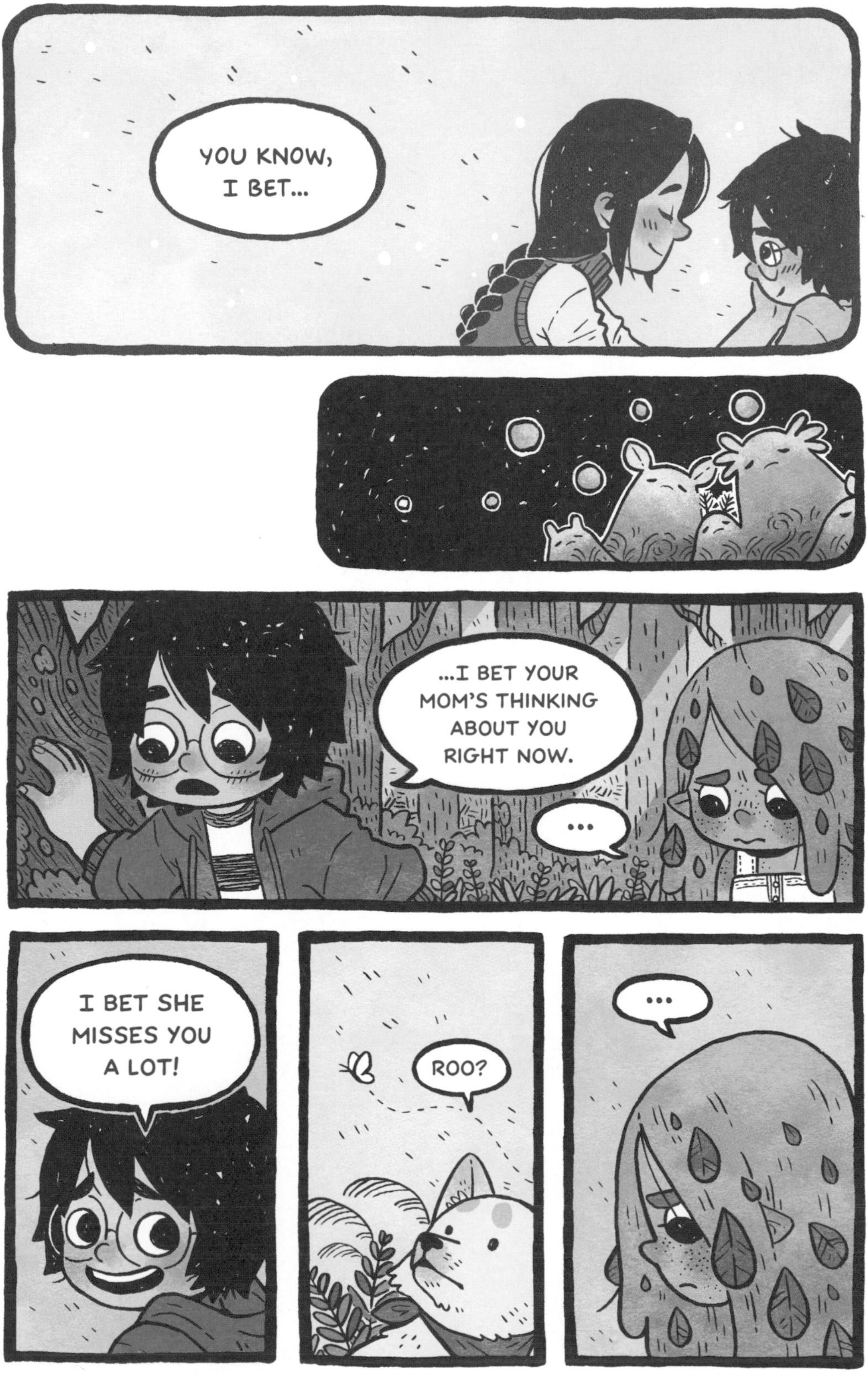
YOU KNOW, I BET...
...I BET YOUR MOM'S THINKING ABOUT YOU RIGHT NOW.
...
I BET SHE MISSES YOU A LOT!
ROO?
...

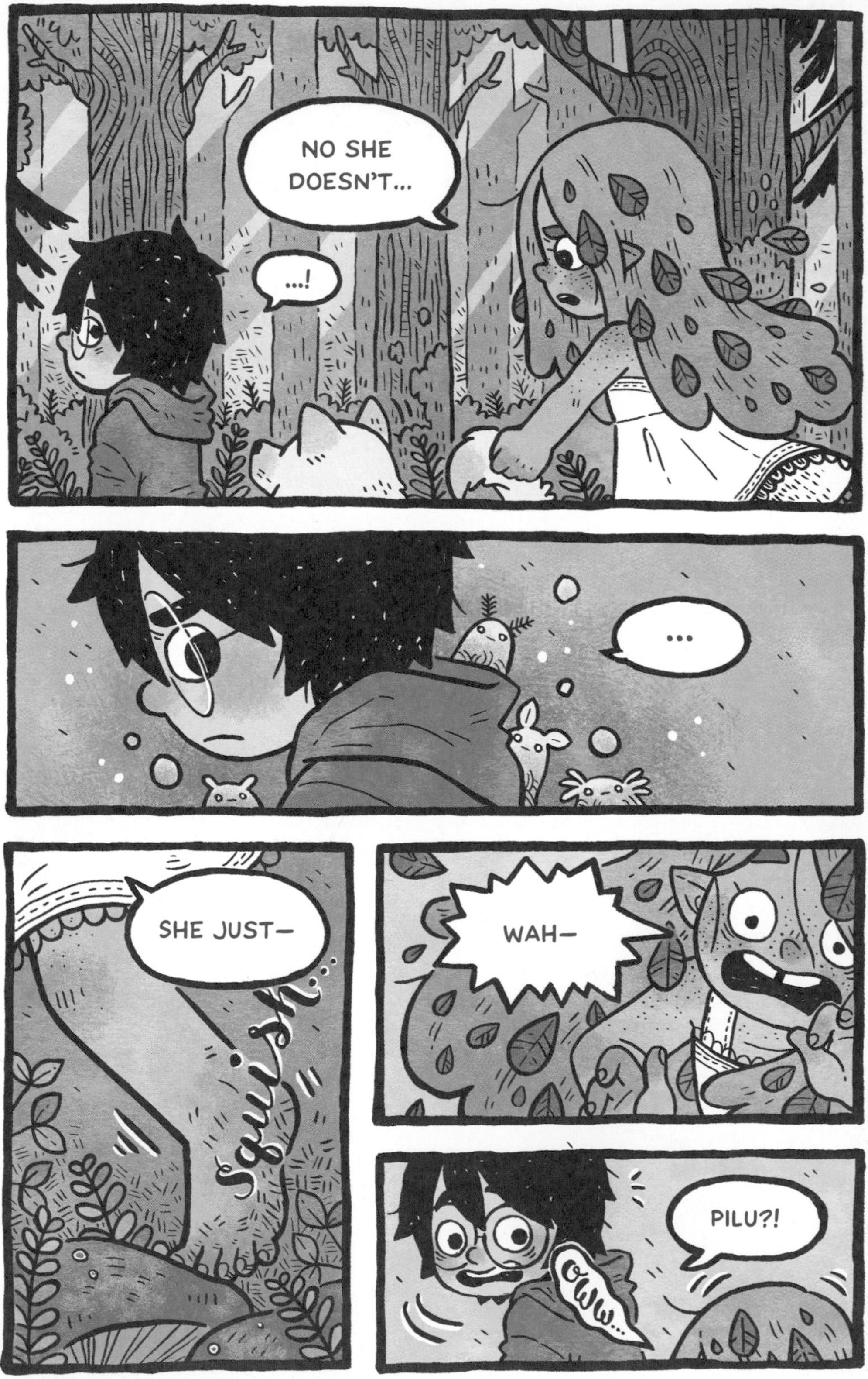
NO SHE DOESN'T...
...!
...
SHE JUST—
Squish
WAH—
PILU?!
OWW...

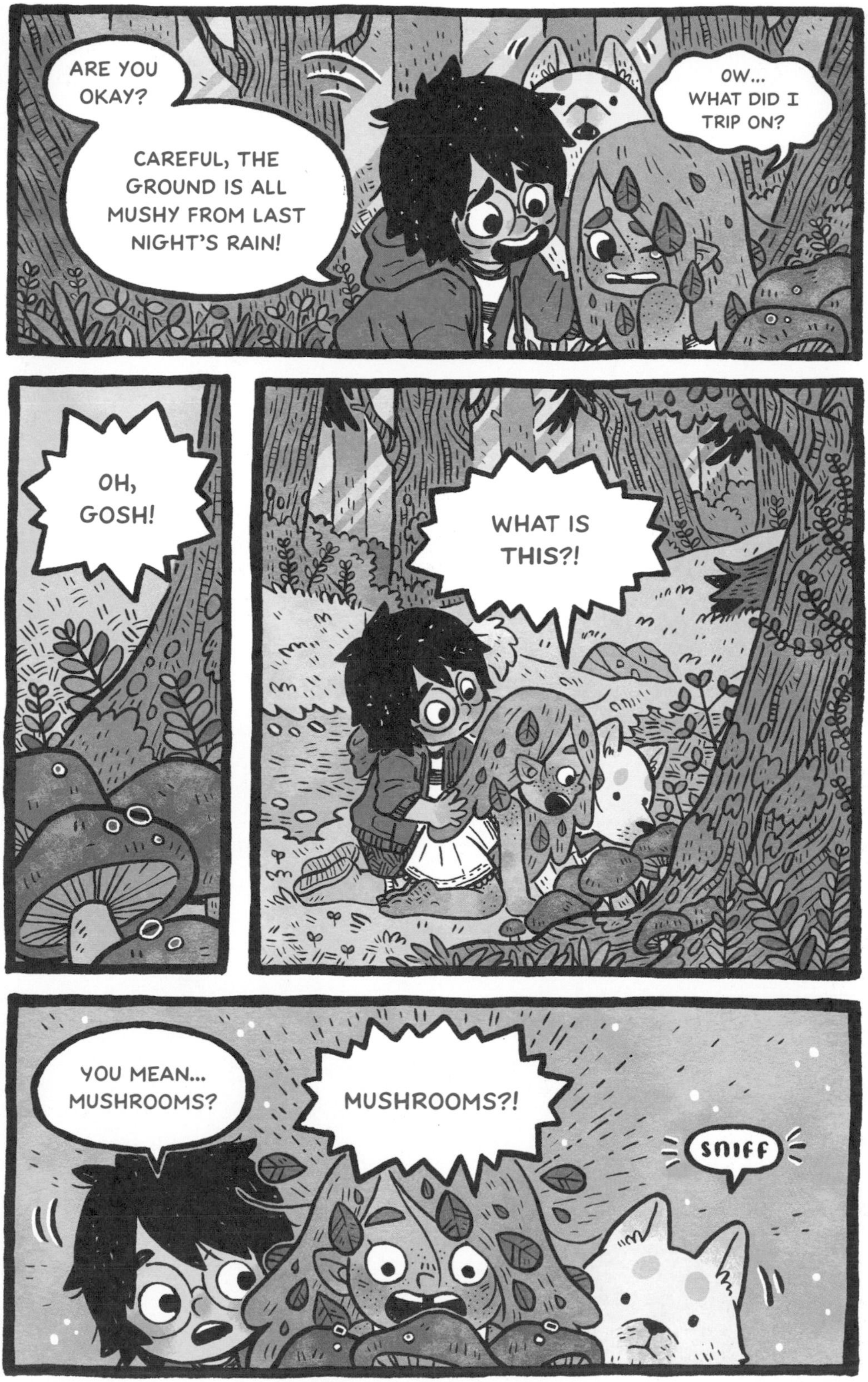
ARE YOU OKAY?
CAREFUL, THE GROUND IS ALL MUSHY FROM LAST NIGHT'S RAIN!
OW... WHAT DID I TRIP ON?
OH, GOSH!
WHAT IS THIS?!
YOU MEAN... MUSHROOMS?
MUSHROOMS?!
SNIFF

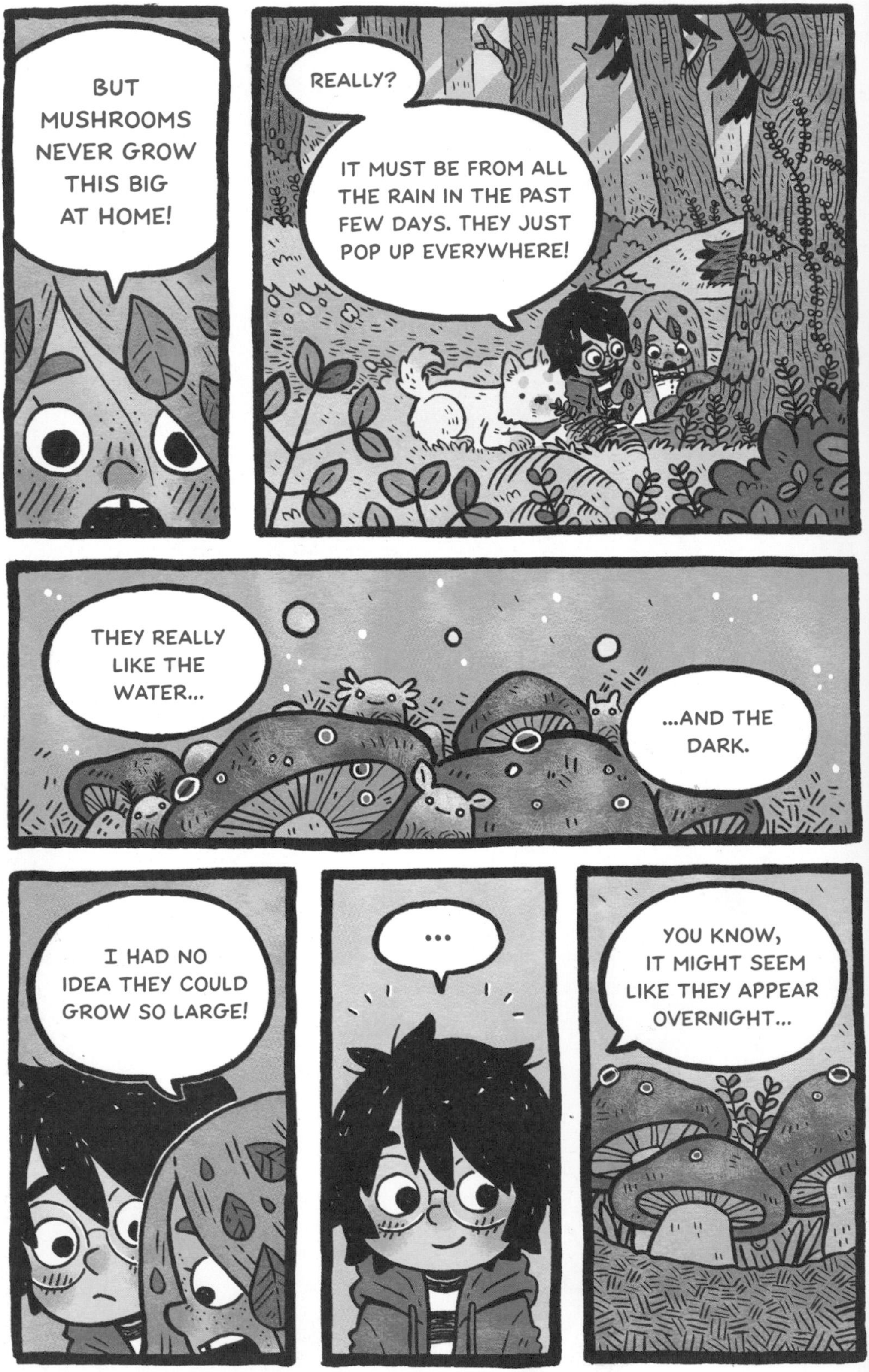
BUT MUSHROOMS NEVER GROW THIS BIG AT HOME!
REALLY?
IT MUST BE FROM ALL THE RAIN IN THE PAST FEW DAYS. THEY JUST POP UP EVERYWHERE!
THEY REALLY LIKE THE WATER...
...AND THE DARK.
I HAD NO IDEA THEY COULD GROW SO LARGE!
...
YOU KNOW, IT MIGHT SEEM LIKE THEY APPEAR OVERNIGHT...

...BUT MOST OF THE MUSHROOM IS GROWING UNDERGROUND...

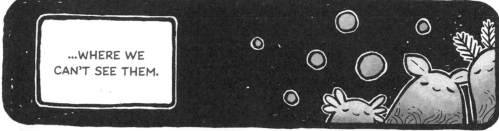

...WHERE WE CAN'T SEE THEM.

AND THEY'RE ALL GROWING TOGETHER FROM ONE BIG ROOT.

SO ONCE IT RAINS, THEY ALL JUST BURST OUT FROM THE GROUND!

AND SOMETIMES THEY DISAPPEAR JUST AS QUICKLY AS THEY APPEARED!

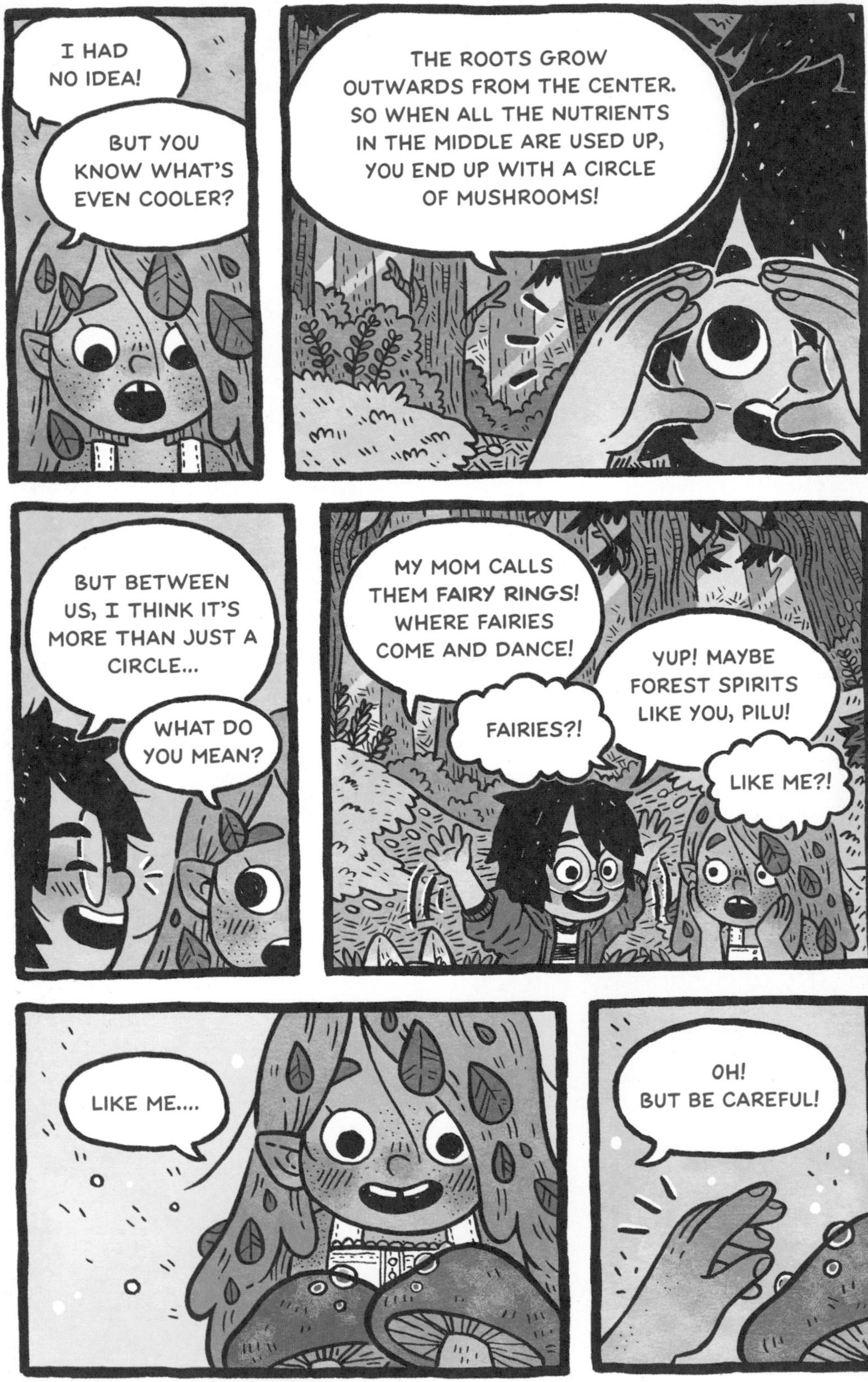
I HAD NO IDEA!
BUT YOU KNOW WHAT'S EVEN COOLER?
THE ROOTS GROW OUTWARDS FROM THE CENTER. SO WHEN ALL THE NUTRIENTS IN THE MIDDLE ARE USED UP, YOU END UP WITH A CIRCLE OF MUSHROOMS!
BUT BETWEEN US, I THINK IT'S MORE THAN JUST A CIRCLE...
WHAT DO YOU MEAN?
MY MOM CALLS THEM FAIRY RINGS! WHERE FAIRIES COME AND DANCE!
FAIRIES?!
YUP! MAYBE FOREST SPIRITS LIKE YOU, PILU!
LIKE ME?!
LIKE ME....
OH! BUT BE CAREFUL!

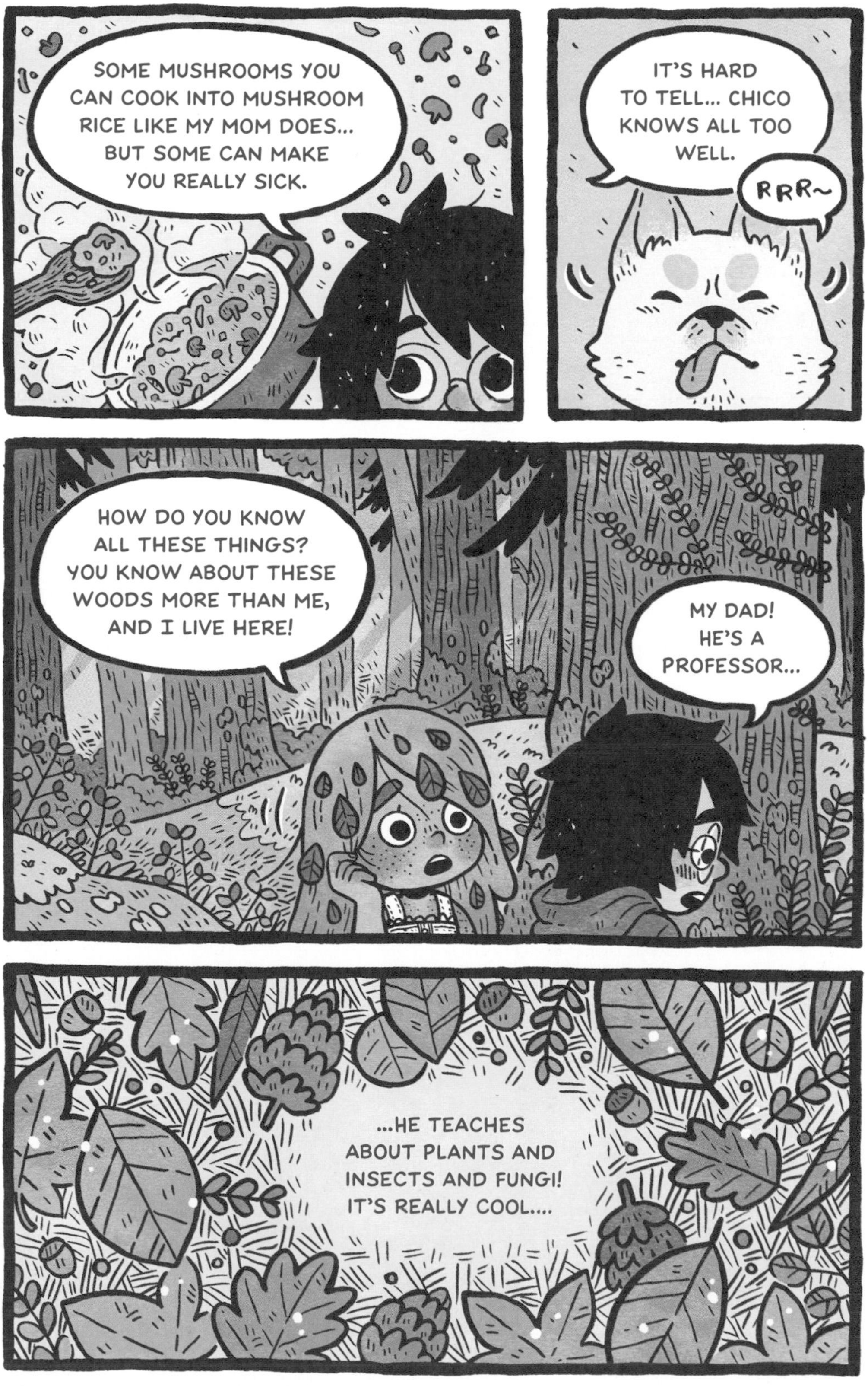
SOME MUSHROOMS YOU CAN COOK INTO MUSHROOM RICE LIKE MY MOM DOES... BUT SOME CAN MAKE YOU REALLY SICK.
IT'S HARD TO TELL... CHICO KNOWS ALL TOO WELL.
RRR~
HOW DO YOU KNOW ALL THESE THINGS? YOU KNOW ABOUT THESE WOODS MORE THAN ME, AND I LIVE HERE!
MY DAD! HE'S A PROFESSOR...
...HE TEACHES ABOUT PLANTS AND INSECTS AND FUNGI! IT'S REALLY COOL....

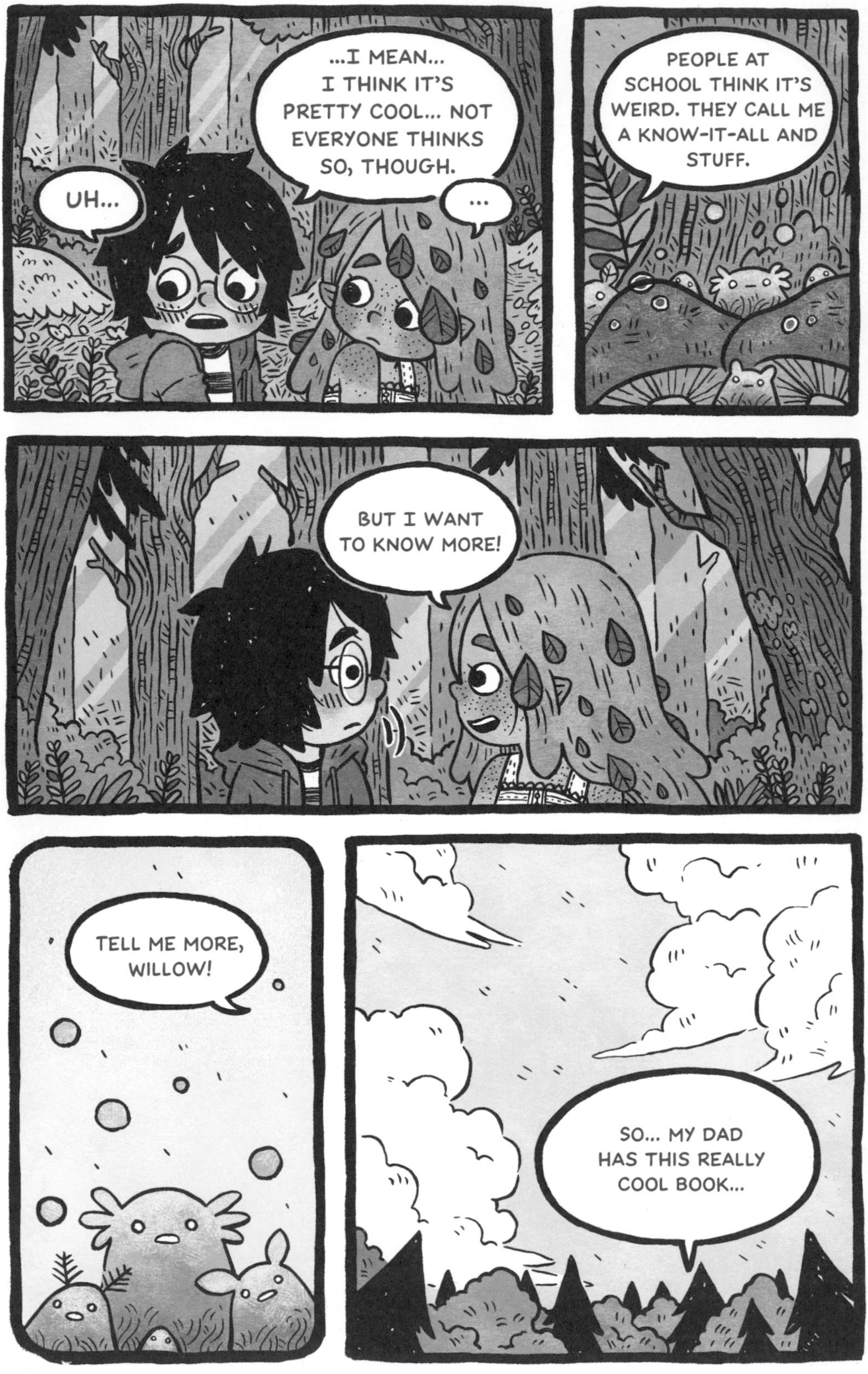
UH...
...I MEAN... I THINK IT'S PRETTY COOL... NOT EVERYONE THINKS SO, THOUGH.
...
PEOPLE AT SCHOOL THINK IT'S WEIRD. THEY CALL ME A KNOW-IT-ALL AND STUFF.
BUT I WANT TO KNOW MORE!
TELL ME MORE, WILLOW!
SO... MY DAD HAS THIS REALLY COOL BOOK...

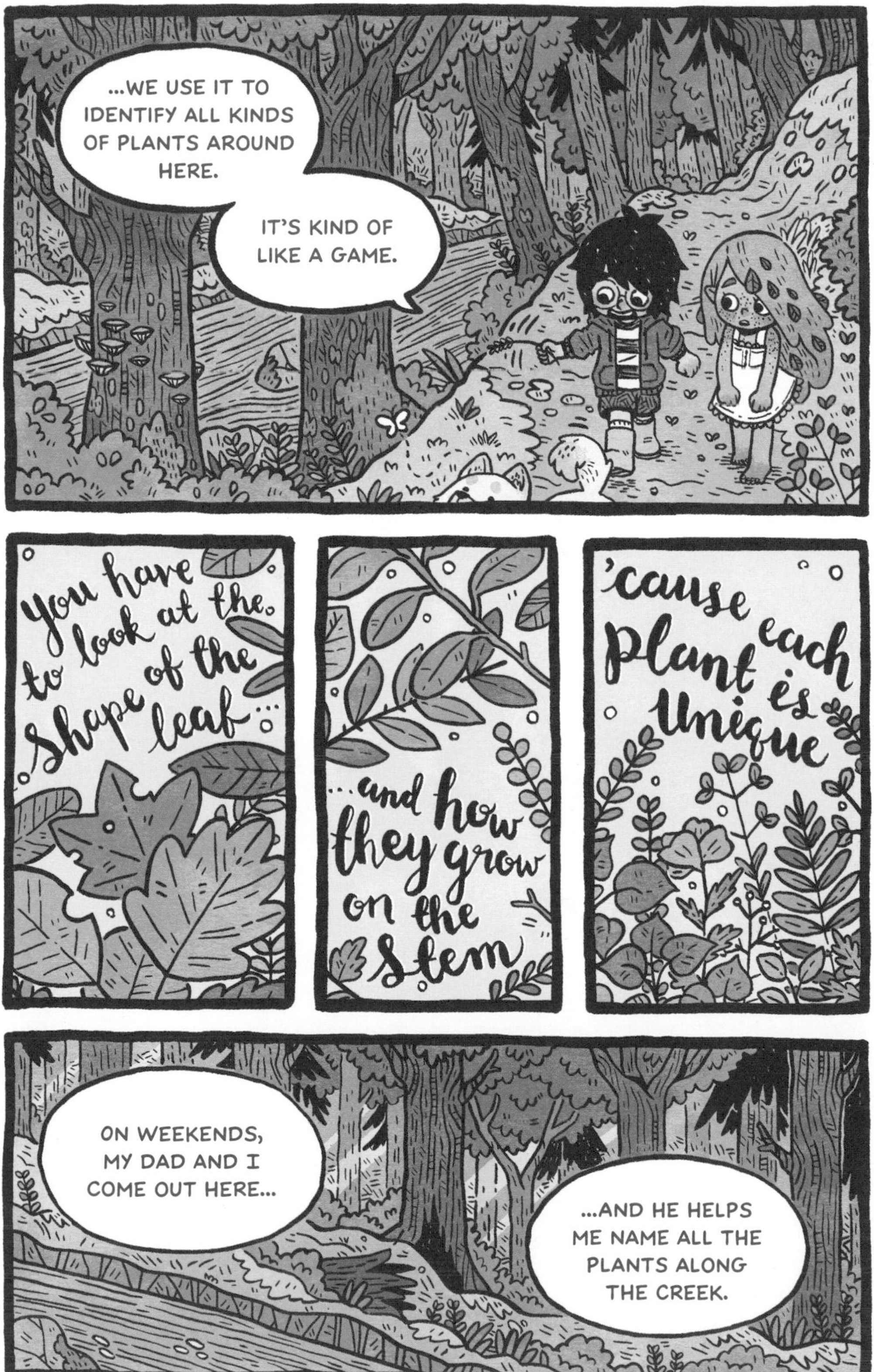
...WE USE IT TO IDENTIFY ALL KINDS OF PLANTS AROUND HERE.
IT'S KIND OF LIKE A GAME.
you have to look at the shape of the leaf...
...and how they grow on the stem
'cause each plant is unique
ON WEEKENDS, MY DAD AND I COME OUT HERE...
...AND HE HELPS ME NAME ALL THE PLANTS ALONG THE CREEK.

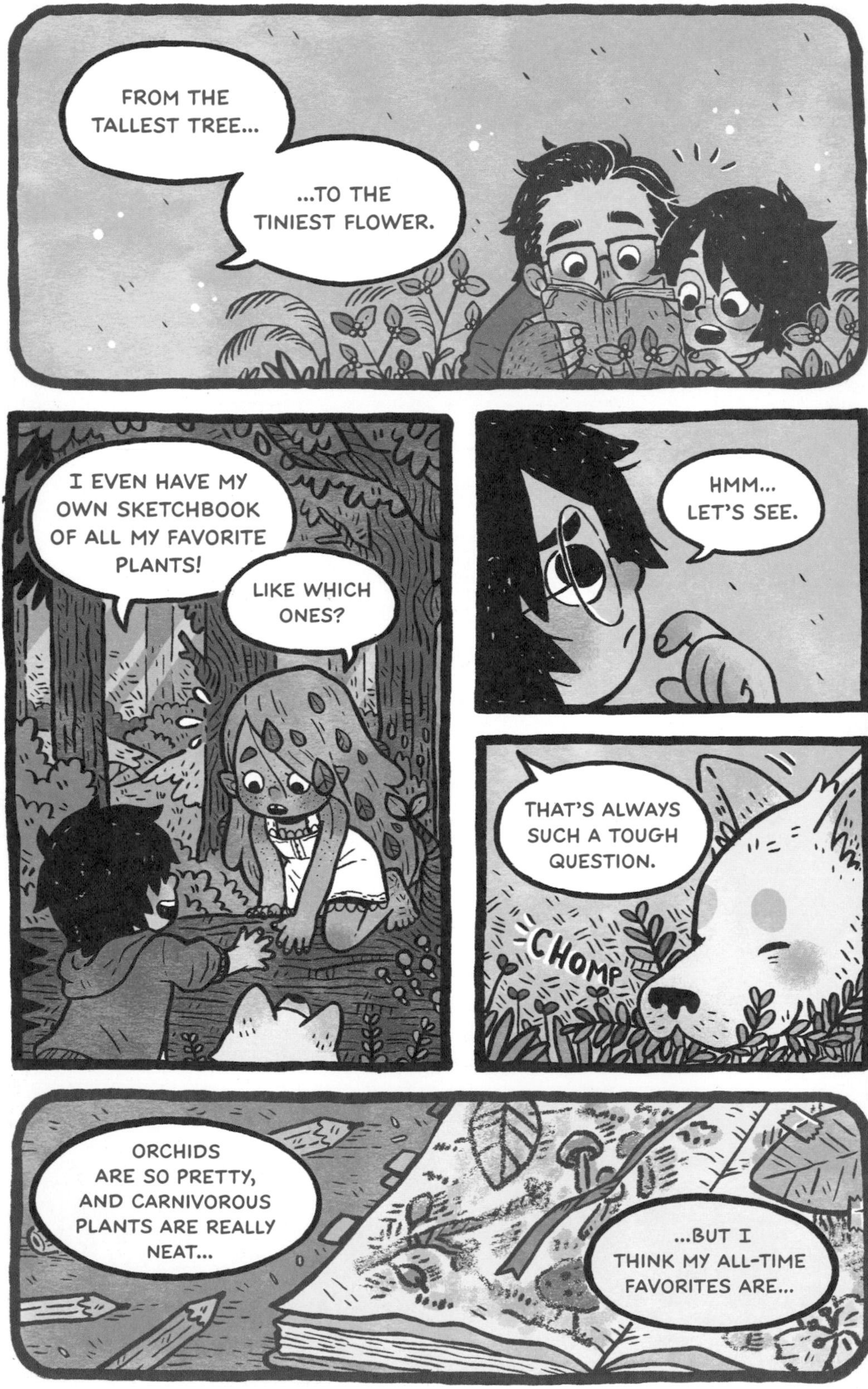
FROM THE TALLEST TREE...
...TO THE TINIEST FLOWER.
I EVEN HAVE MY OWN SKETCHBOOK OF ALL MY FAVORITE PLANTS!
LIKE WHICH ONES?
HMM... LET'S SEE.
THAT'S ALWAYS SUCH A TOUGH QUESTION.
CHOMP
ORCHIDS ARE SO PRETTY, AND CARNIVOROUS PLANTS ARE REALLY NEAT...
...BUT I THINK MY ALL-TIME FAVORITES ARE...

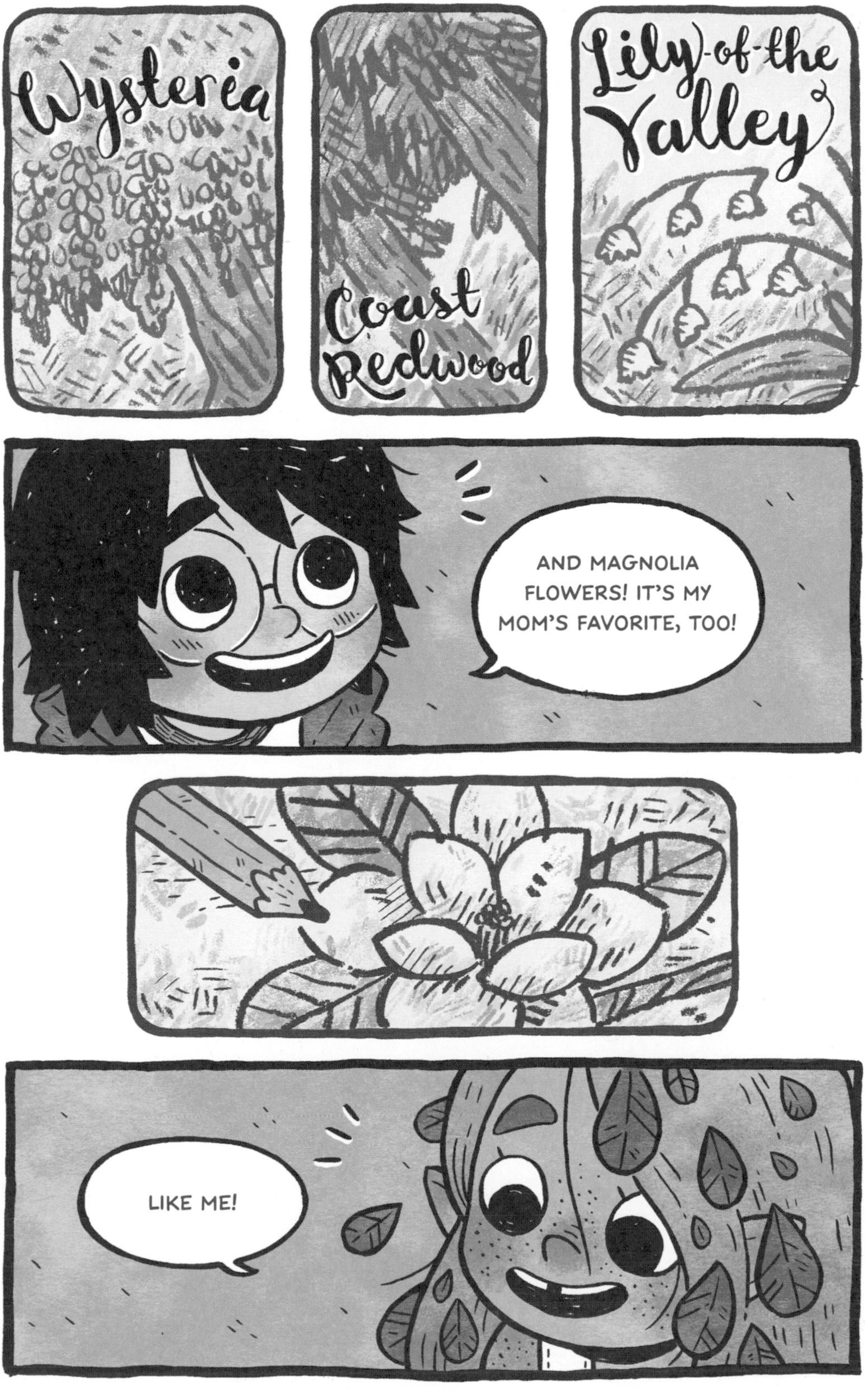
Wysteria
Coast Redwood
Lily-of-the Valley
AND MAGNOLIA FLOWERS! IT'S MY MOM'S FAVORITE, TOO!
LIKE ME!

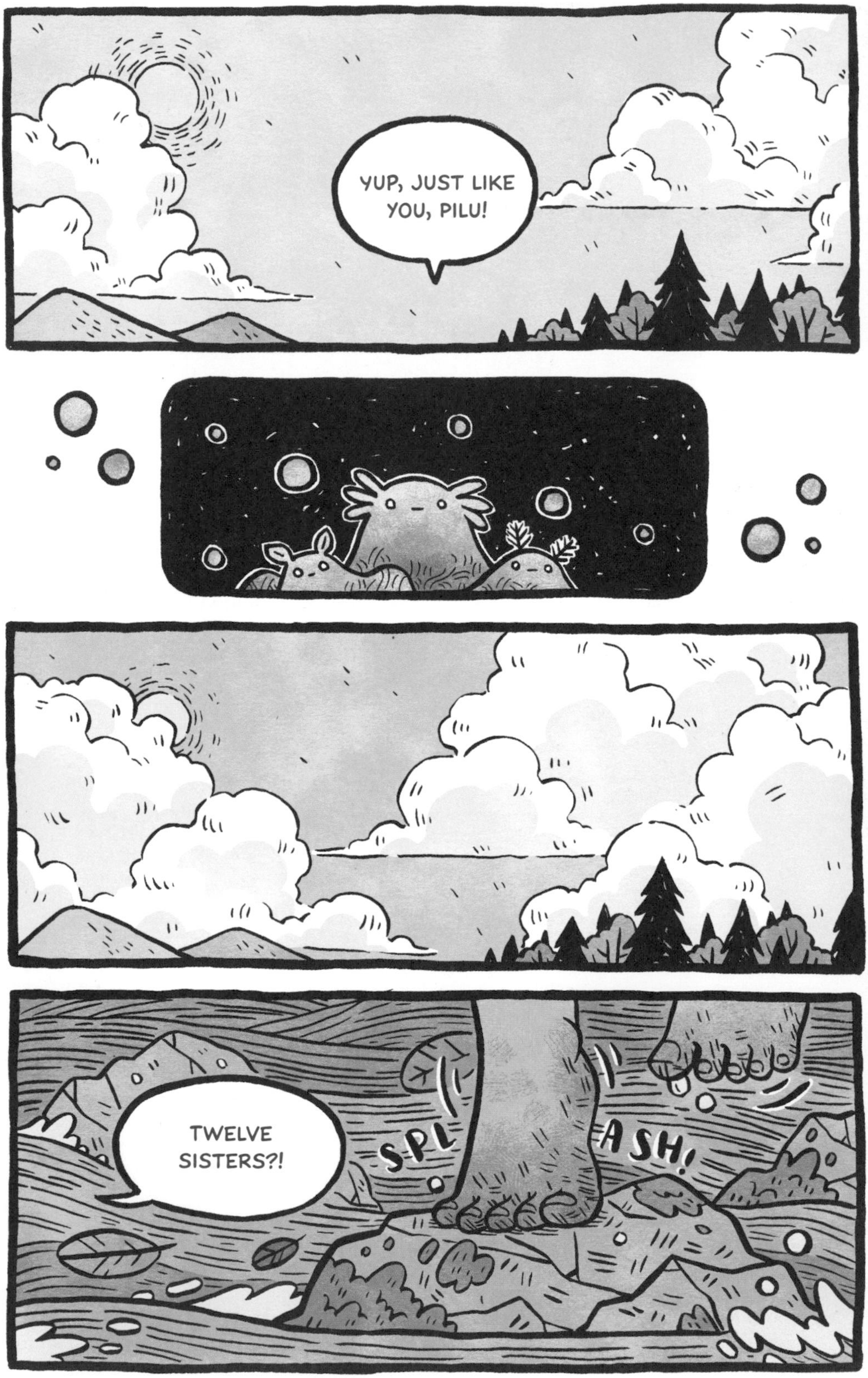
YUP, JUST LIKE YOU, PILU!
TWELVE SISTERS?!
SPLASH!

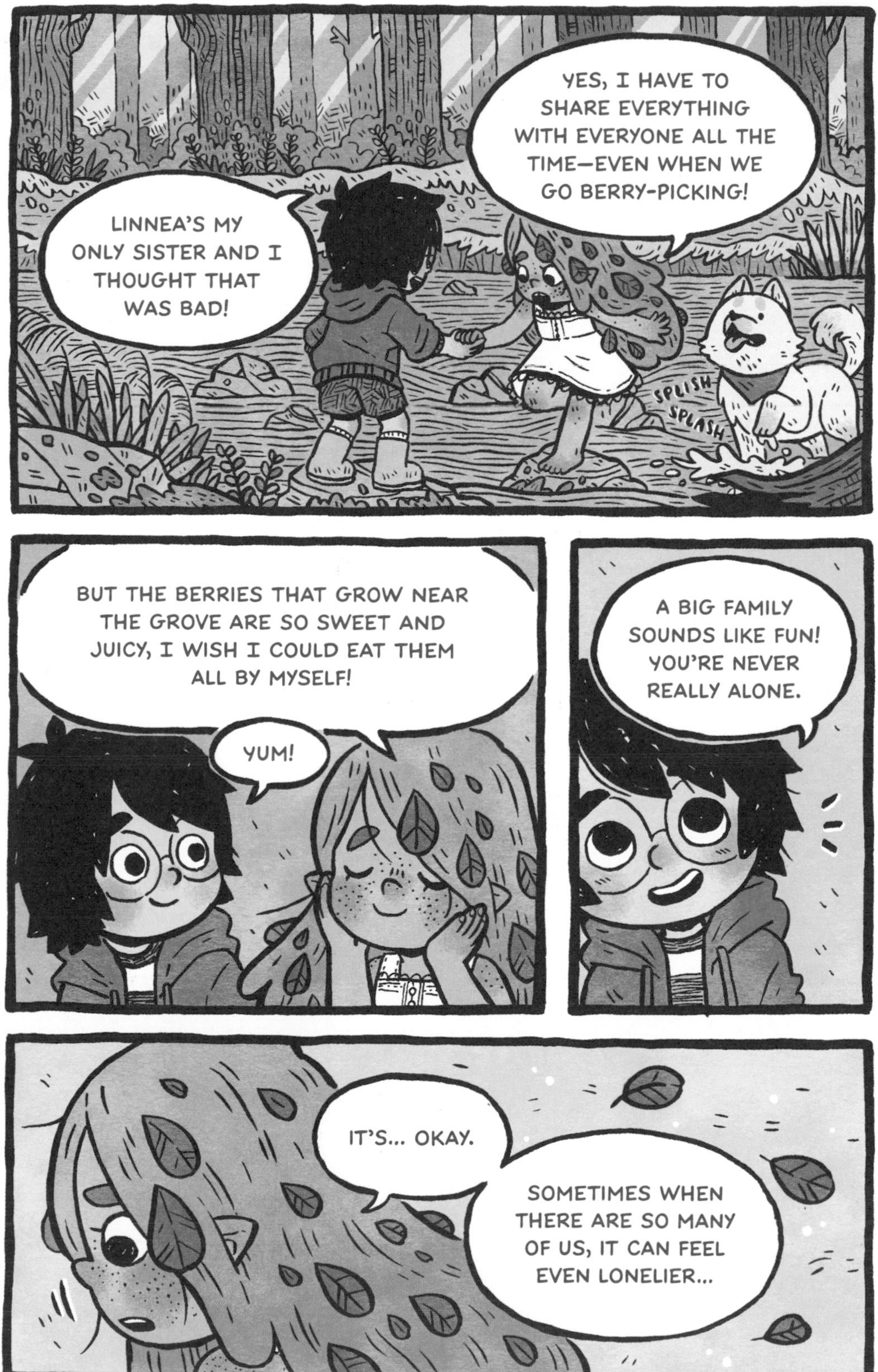
YES, I HAVE TO SHARE EVERYTHING WITH EVERYONE ALL THE TIME—EVEN WHEN WE GO BERRY-PICKING!
LINNEA'S MY ONLY SISTER AND I THOUGHT THAT WAS BAD!
SPLISH
SPLASH
BUT THE BERRIES THAT GROW NEAR THE GROVE ARE SO SWEET AND JUICY, I WISH I COULD EAT THEM ALL BY MYSELF!
YUM!
A BIG FAMILY SOUNDS LIKE FUN! YOU'RE NEVER REALLY ALONE.
IT'S... OKAY.
SOMETIMES WHEN THERE ARE SO MANY OF US, IT CAN FEEL EVEN LONELIER...

SOMETIMES I FEEL LIKE I COULD JUST DISAPPEAR AND NO ONE WOULD NOTICE....

...IS THAT WHY YOU RAN AWAY?

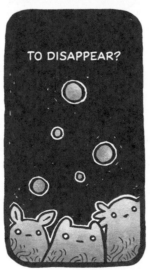

TO DISAPPEAR?

...

I DON'T REALLY THINK THINGS CAN JUST DISAPPEAR....

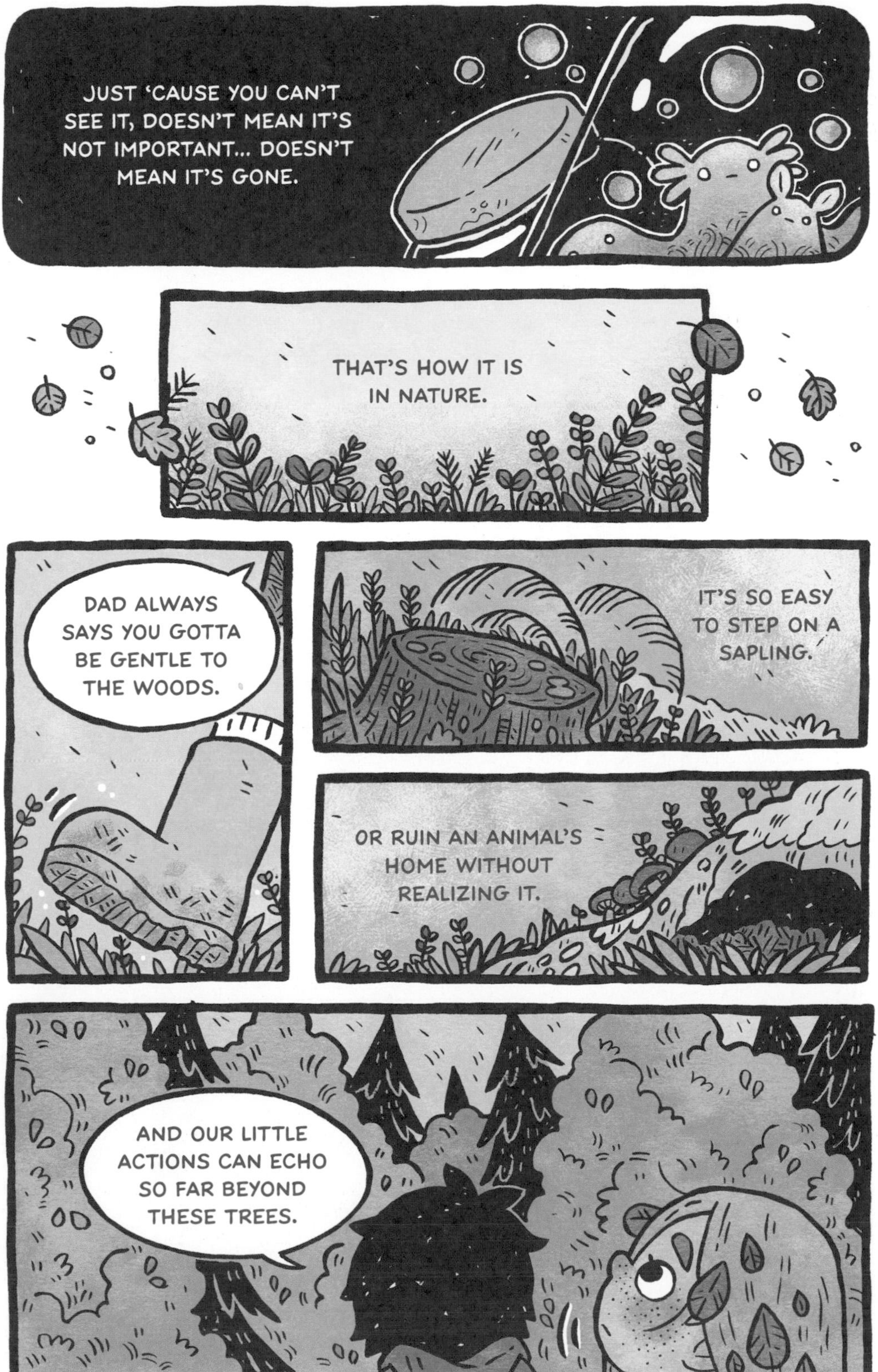
JUST 'CAUSE YOU CAN'T SEE IT, DOESN'T MEAN IT'S NOT IMPORTANT... DOESN'T MEAN IT'S GONE.
THAT'S HOW IT IS IN NATURE.
DAD ALWAYS SAYS YOU GOTTA BE GENTLE TO THE WOODS.
IT'S SO EASY TO STEP ON A SAPLING.
OR RUIN AN ANIMAL'S HOME WITHOUT REALIZING IT.
AND OUR LITTLE ACTIONS CAN ECHO SO FAR BEYOND THESE TREES.

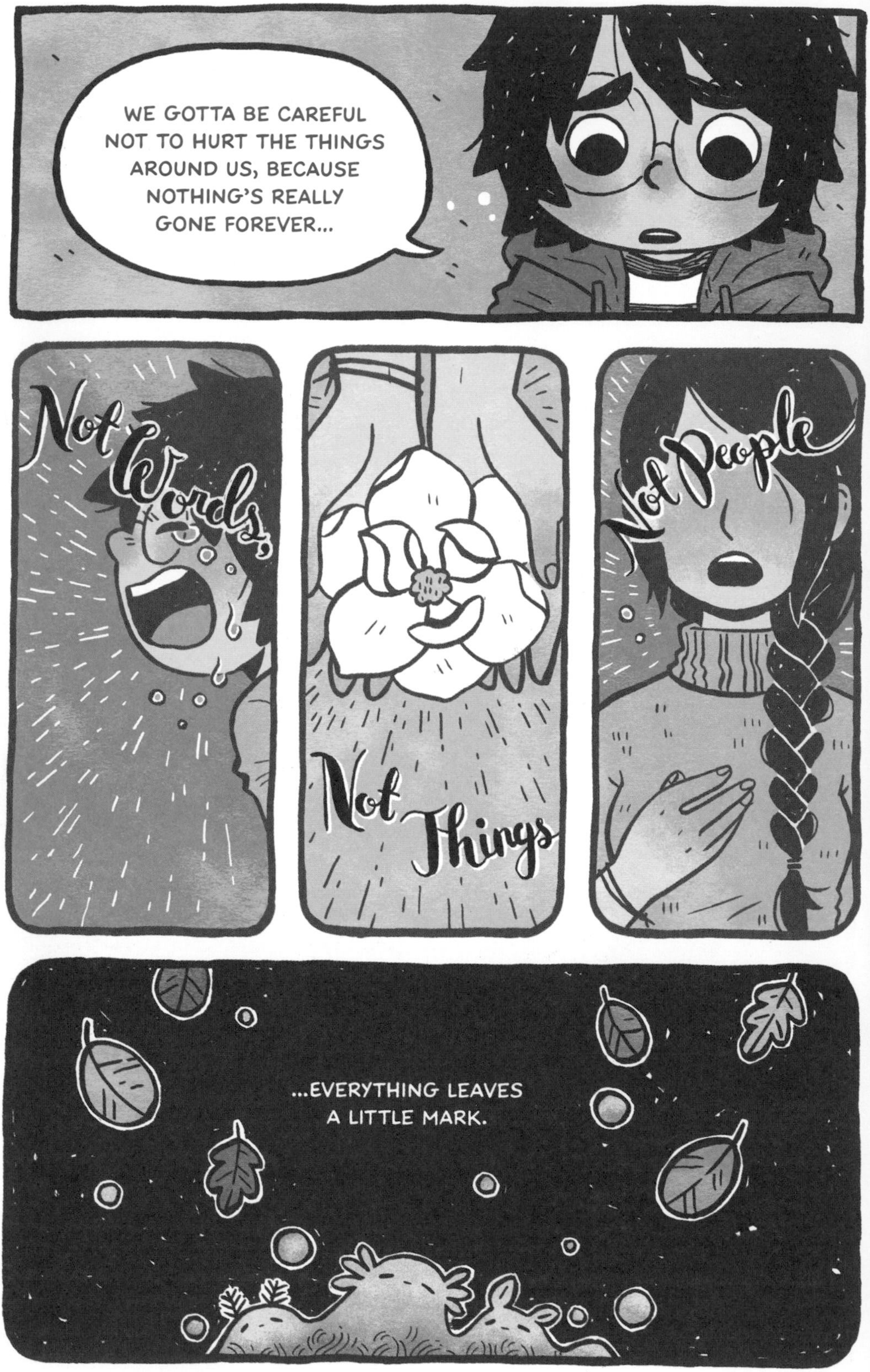
WE GOTTA BE CAREFUL NOT TO HURT THE THINGS AROUND US, BECAUSE NOTHING'S REALLY GONE FOREVER...
Not Words,
Not Things
Not People
...EVERYTHING LEAVES A LITTLE MARK.

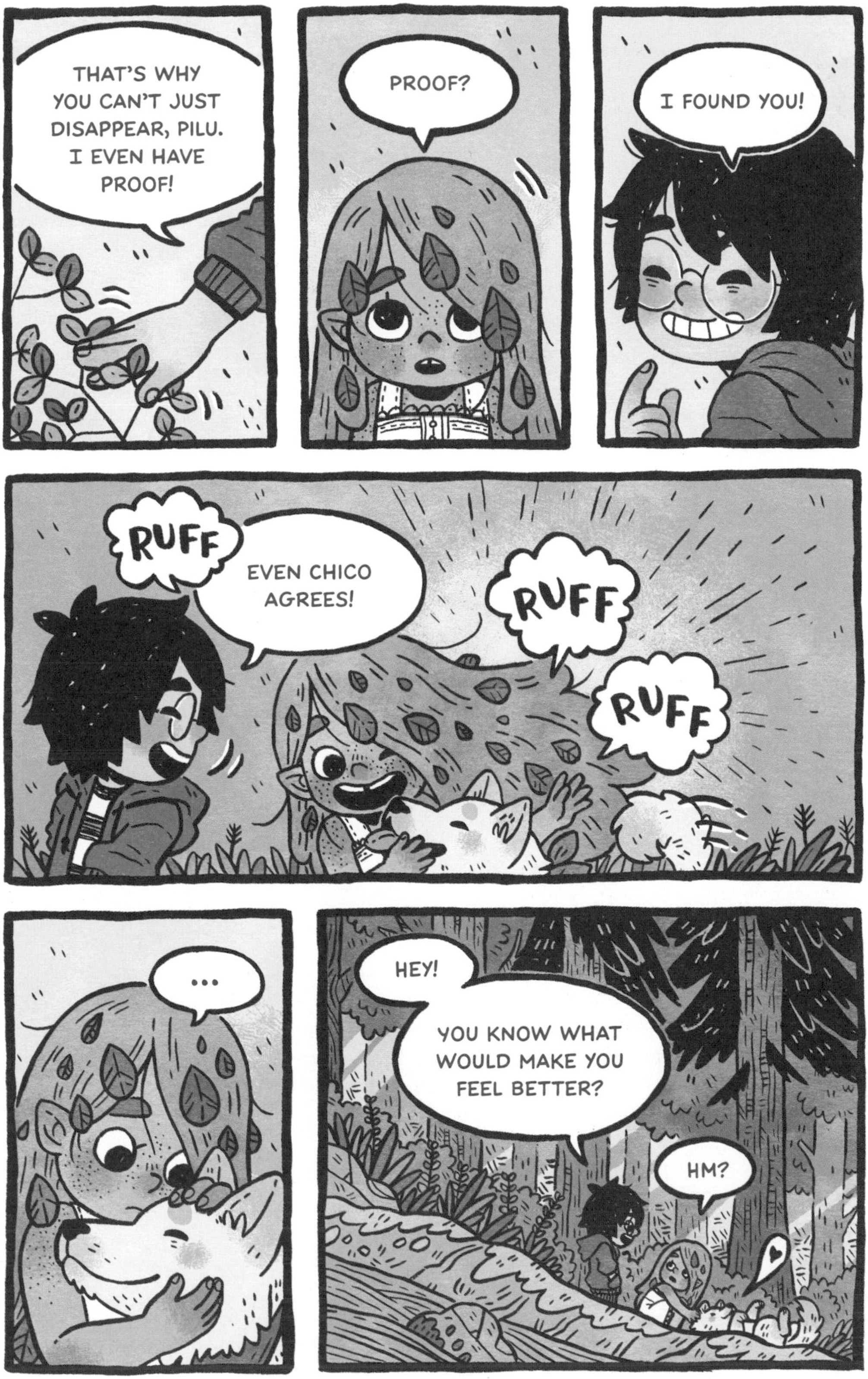
THAT'S WHY YOU CAN'T JUST DISAPPEAR, PILU. I EVEN HAVE PROOF!
PROOF?
I FOUND YOU!
RUFF
EVEN CHICO AGREES!
RUFF
RUFF
...
HEY!
YOU KNOW WHAT WOULD MAKE YOU FEEL BETTER?
HM?

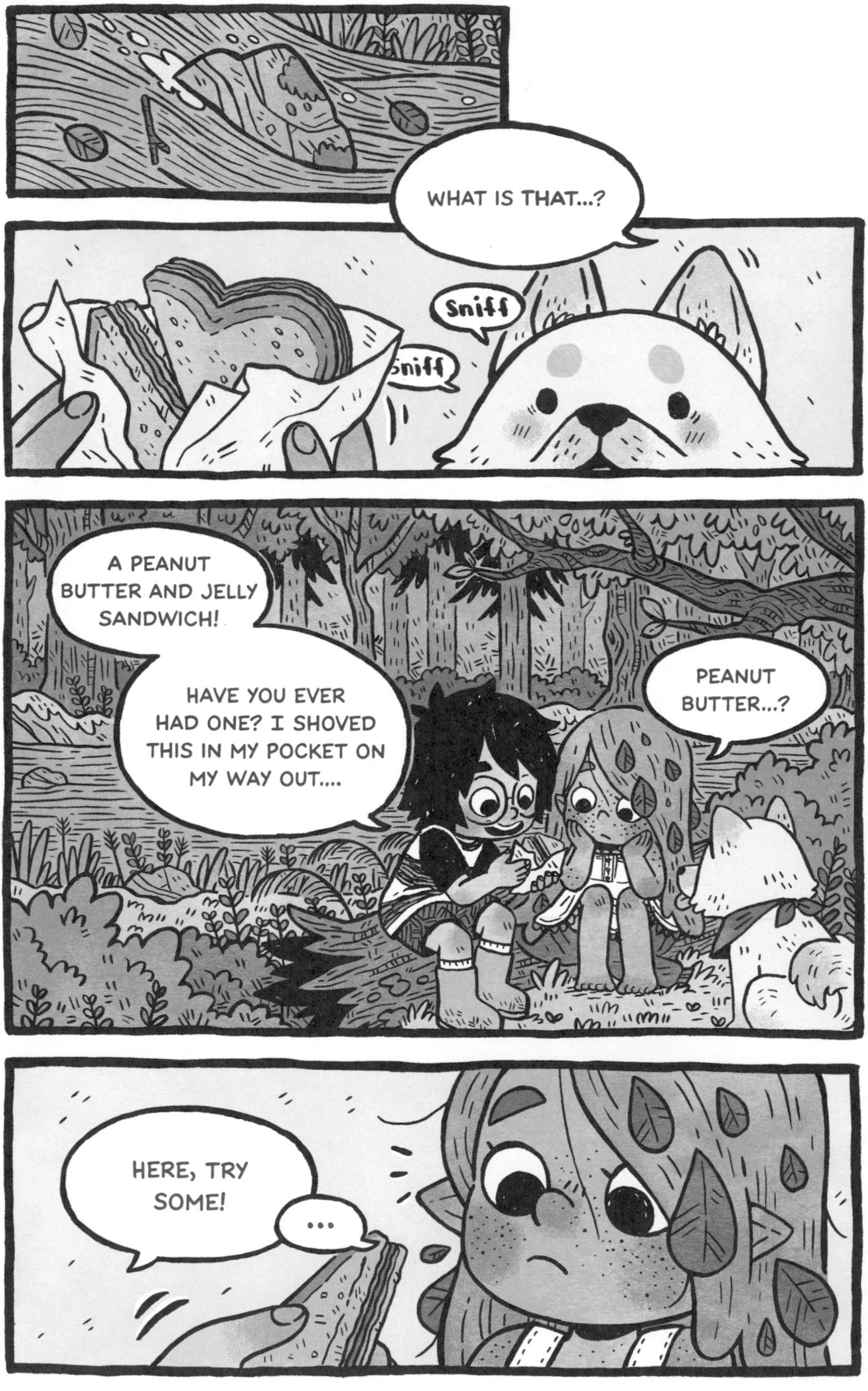
WHAT IS THAT...?
Sniff
Sniff
A PEANUT BUTTER AND JELLY SANDWICH!
HAVE YOU EVER HAD ONE? I SHOVED THIS IN MY POCKET ON MY WAY OUT....
PEANUT BUTTER...?
HERE, TRY SOME!
...

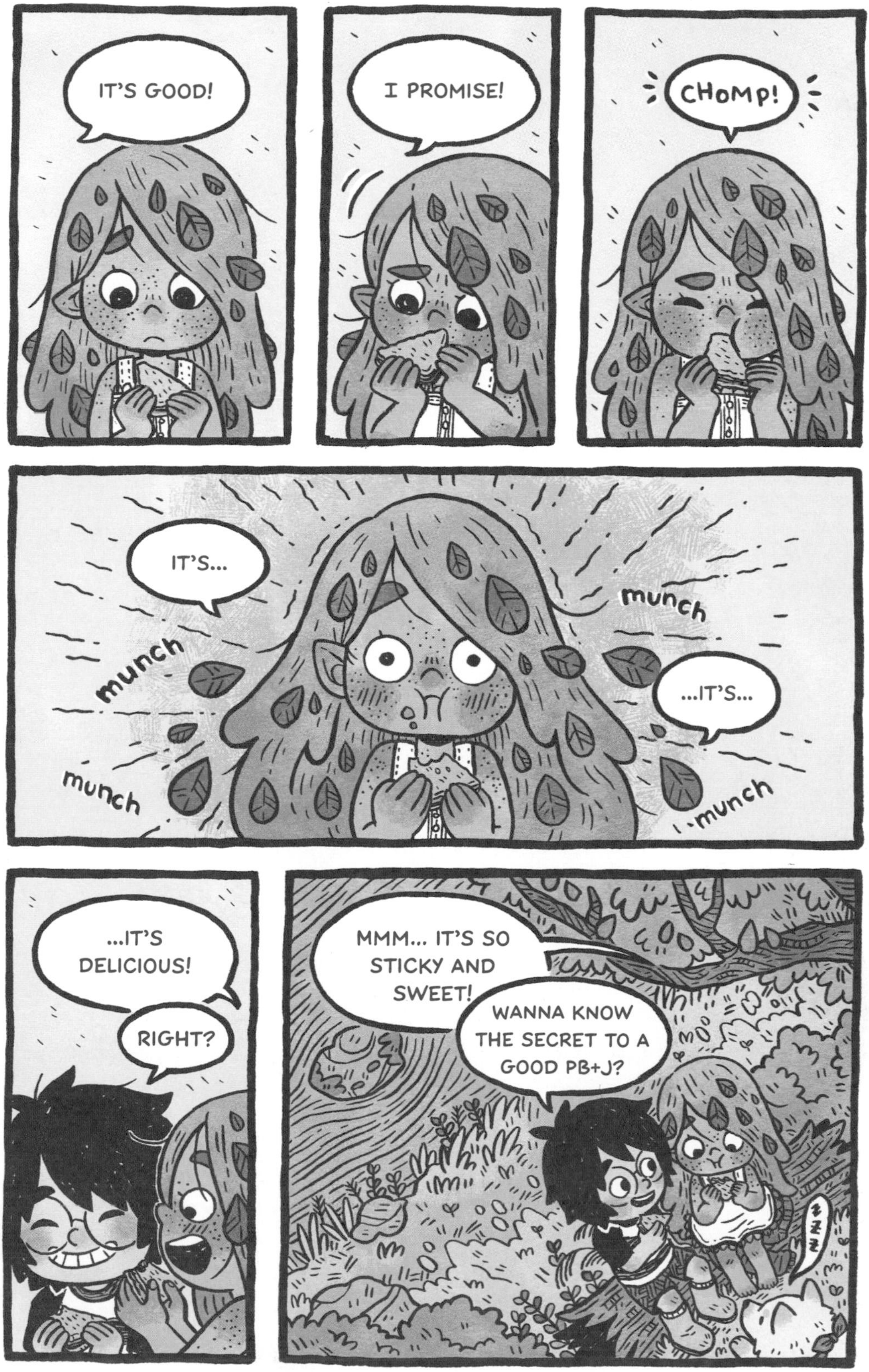
IT'S GOOD!
I PROMISE!
CHOMP!
IT'S...
munch
munch
munch
...IT'S...
munch
...IT'S DELICIOUS!
RIGHT?
MMM... IT'S SO STICKY AND SWEET!
WANNA KNOW THE SECRET TO A GOOD PB+J?

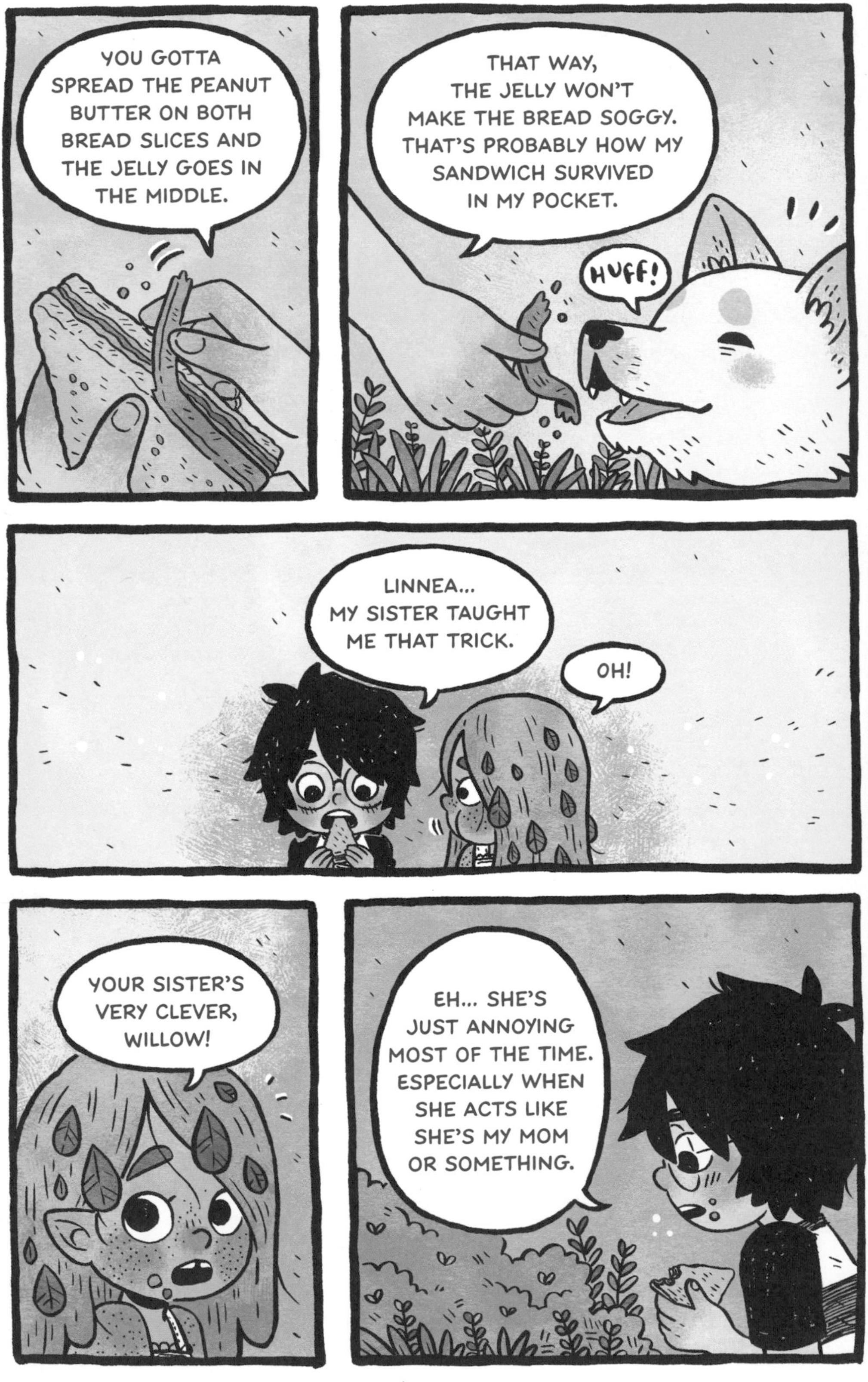
YOU GOTTA SPREAD THE PEANUT BUTTER ON BOTH BREAD SLICES AND THE JELLY GOES IN THE MIDDLE.
THAT WAY, THE JELLY WON'T MAKE THE BREAD SOGGY. THAT'S PROBABLY HOW MY SANDWICH SURVIVED IN MY POCKET.
HUFF!
LINNEA... MY SISTER TAUGHT ME THAT TRICK.
OH!
YOUR SISTER'S VERY CLEVER, WILLOW!
EH... SHE'S JUST ANNOYING MOST OF THE TIME. ESPECIALLY WHEN SHE ACTS LIKE SHE'S MY MOM OR SOMETHING.

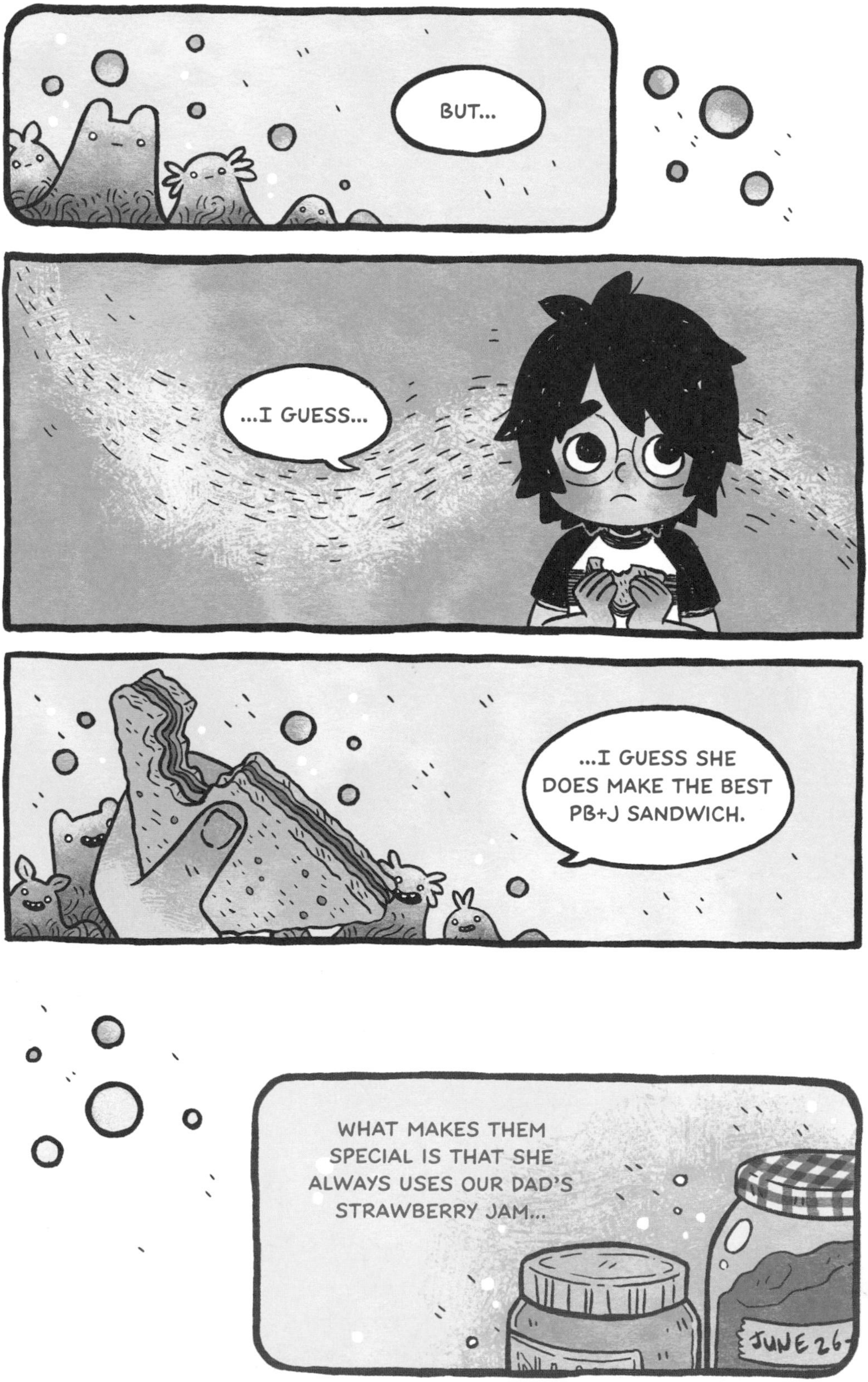

BUT...
...I GUESS...
...I GUESS SHE DOES MAKE THE BEST PB+J SANDWICH.
WHAT MAKES THEM SPECIAL IS THAT SHE ALWAYS USES OUR DAD'S STRAWBERRY JAM...
JUNE 26-

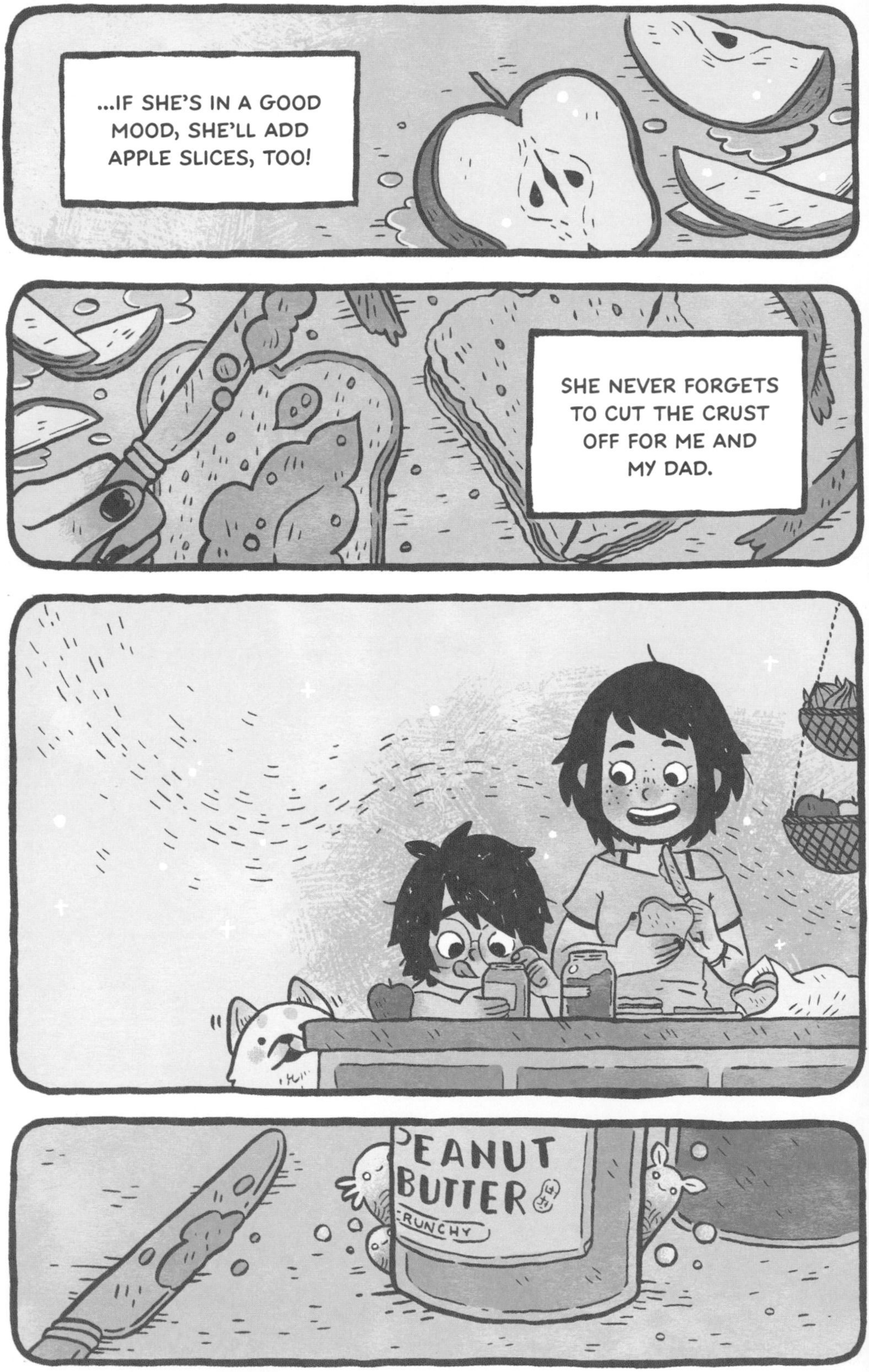
...IF SHE'S IN A GOOD MOOD, SHE'LL ADD APPLE SLICES, TOO!
SHE NEVER FORGETS TO CUT THE CRUST OFF FOR ME AND MY DAD.
EANUT BUTTER
RUNCHY

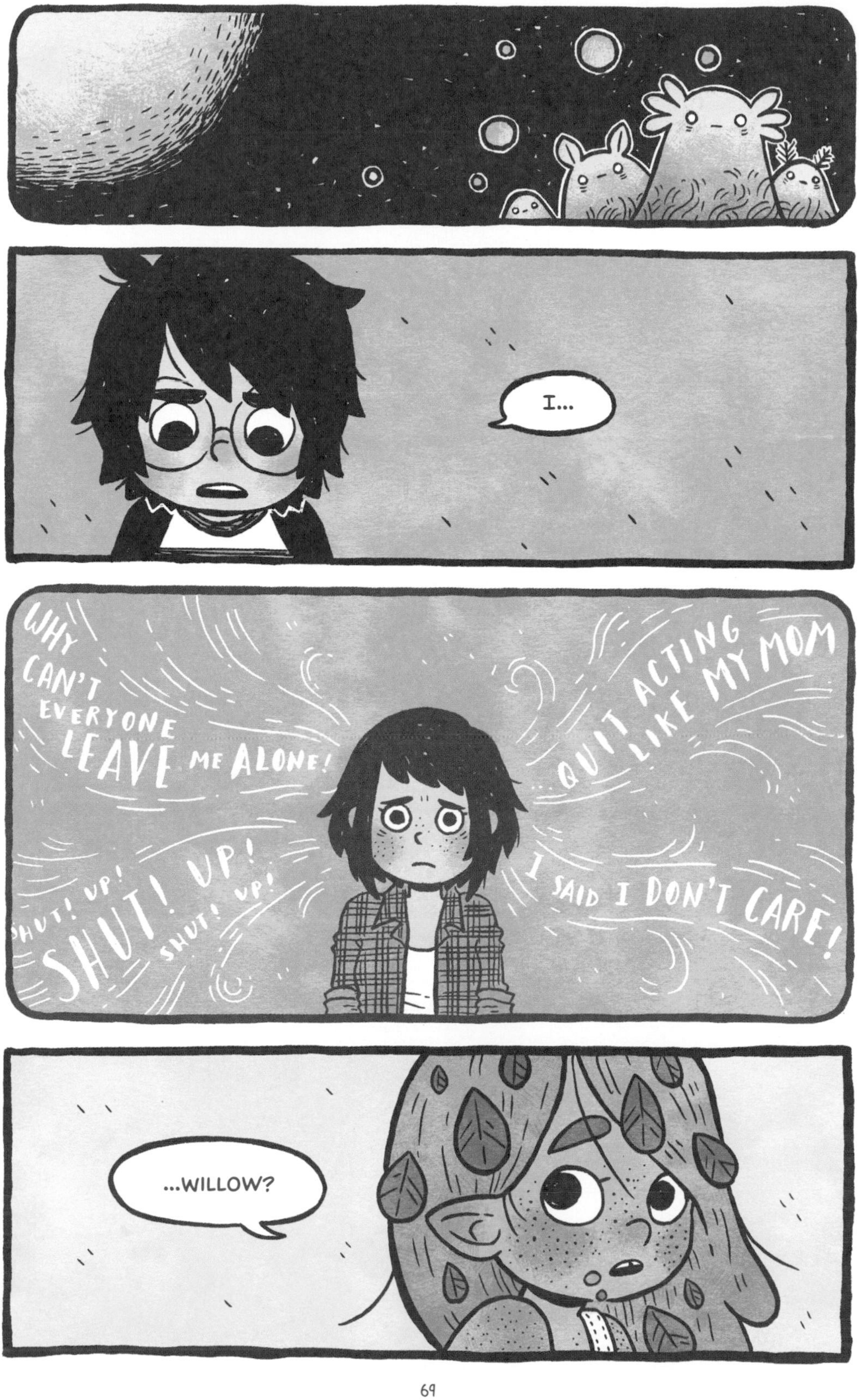
I...
WHY CAN'T EVERYONE LEAVE ME ALONE!
QUIT ACTING LIKE MY MOM
SHUT! UP! SHUT! UP! SHUT! UP!
I SAID I DON'T CARE!
...WILLOW?

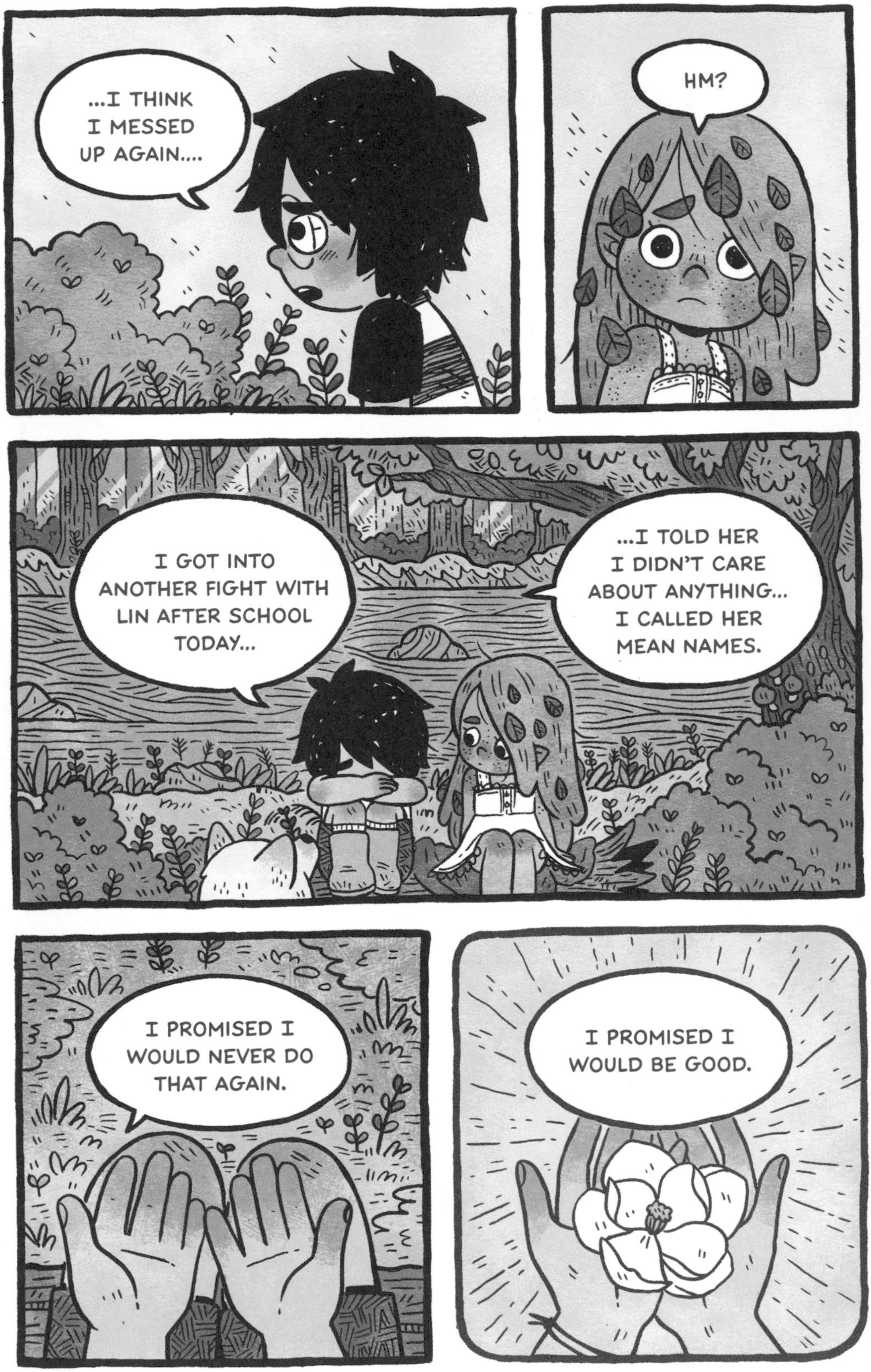
...I THINK I MESSED UP AGAIN....
HM?
I GOT INTO ANOTHER FIGHT WITH LIN AFTER SCHOOL TODAY...
...I TOLD HER I DIDN'T CARE ABOUT ANYTHING... I CALLED HER MEAN NAMES.
I PROMISED I WOULD NEVER DO THAT AGAIN.
I PROMISED I WOULD BE GOOD.

WHY DO I ALWAYS DO THIS?

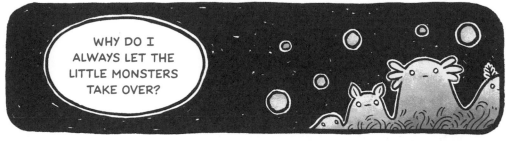

WHY DO I ALWAYS LET THE LITTLE MONSTERS TAKE OVER?

MONSTERS...?

ANGRY LITTLE MONSTERS...

...THAT'S WHAT I CALL THEM. THEY LIVE IN YOUR HEAD AND THEY'RE LOUDER THAN YOUR HEART...

THE SMALLEST THINGS SEEM TO SET THEM OFF... THEY ALWAYS START AS A WHISPER...

...THEN A NEVER-ENDING CHATTER.

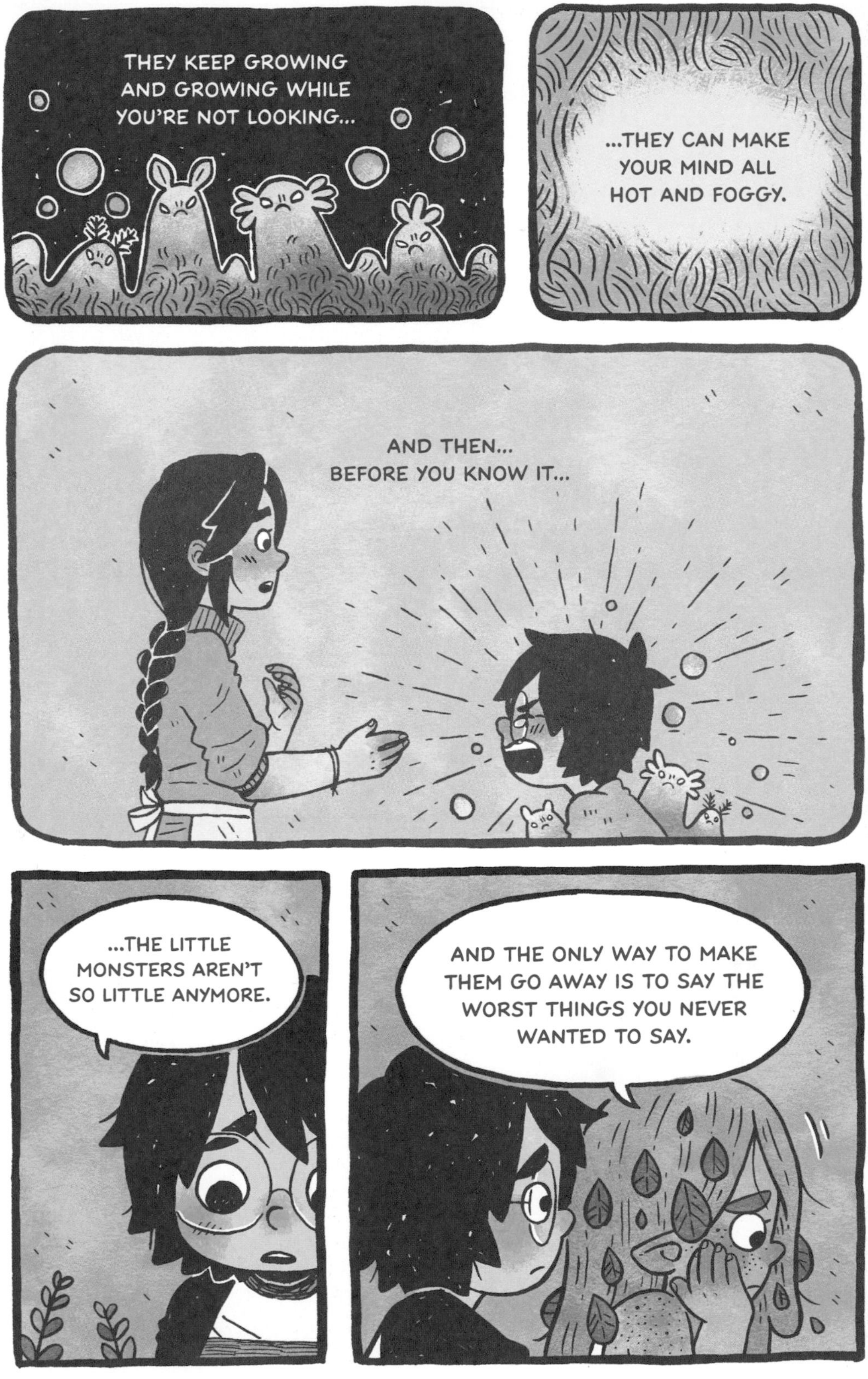
THEY KEEP GROWING AND GROWING WHILE YOU'RE NOT LOOKING...
...THEY CAN MAKE YOUR MIND ALL HOT AND FOGGY.
AND THEN... BEFORE YOU KNOW IT...
...THE LITTLE MONSTERS AREN'T SO LITTLE ANYMORE.
AND THE ONLY WAY TO MAKE THEM GO AWAY IS TO SAY THE WORST THINGS YOU NEVER WANTED TO SAY.

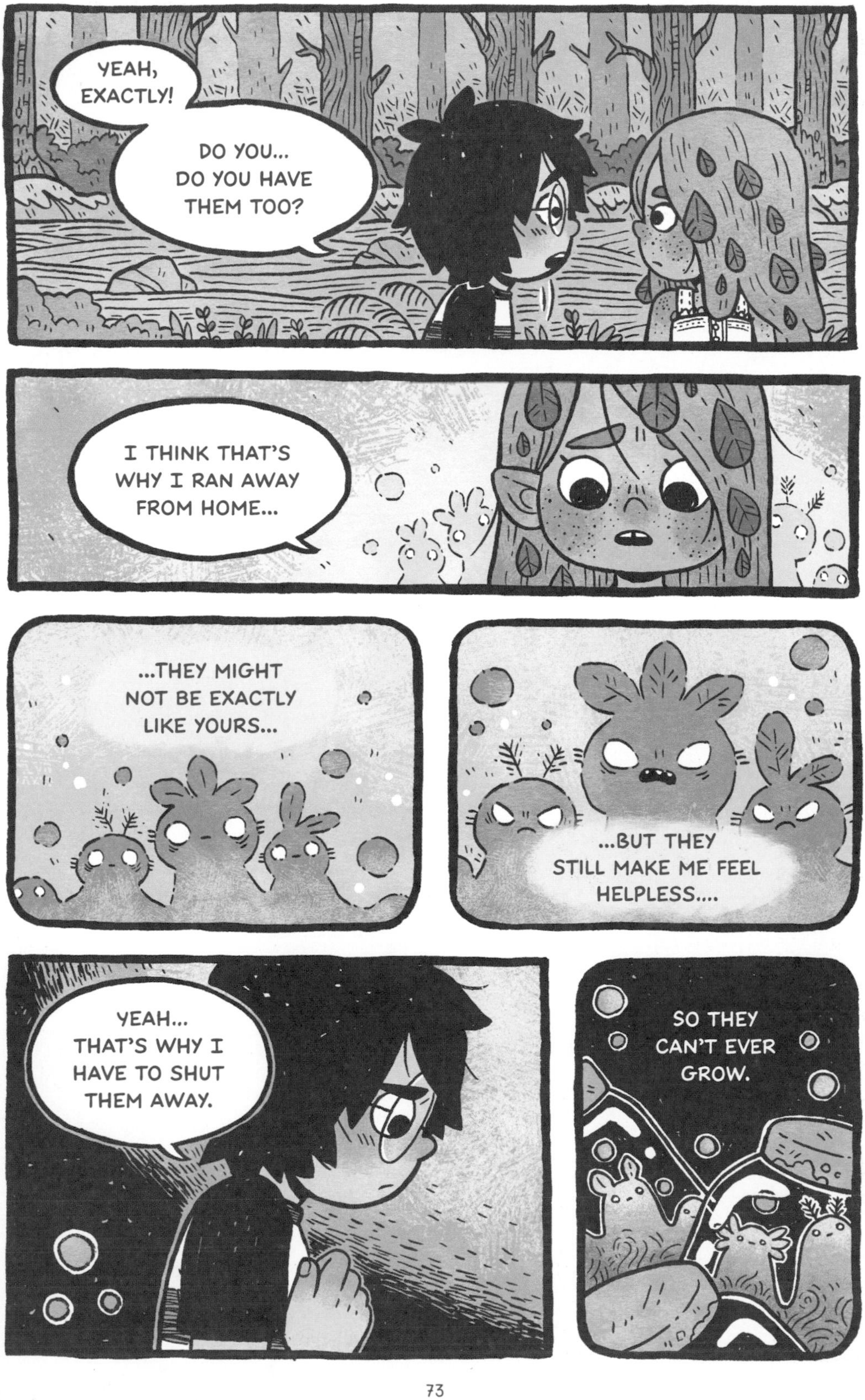
YEAH, EXACTLY!
DO YOU... DO YOU HAVE THEM TOO?
I THINK THAT'S WHY I RAN AWAY FROM HOME...
...THEY MIGHT NOT BE EXACTLY LIKE YOURS...
...BUT THEY STILL MAKE ME FEEL HELPLESS....
YEAH... THAT'S WHY I HAVE TO SHUT THEM AWAY.
SO THEY CAN'T EVER GROW.

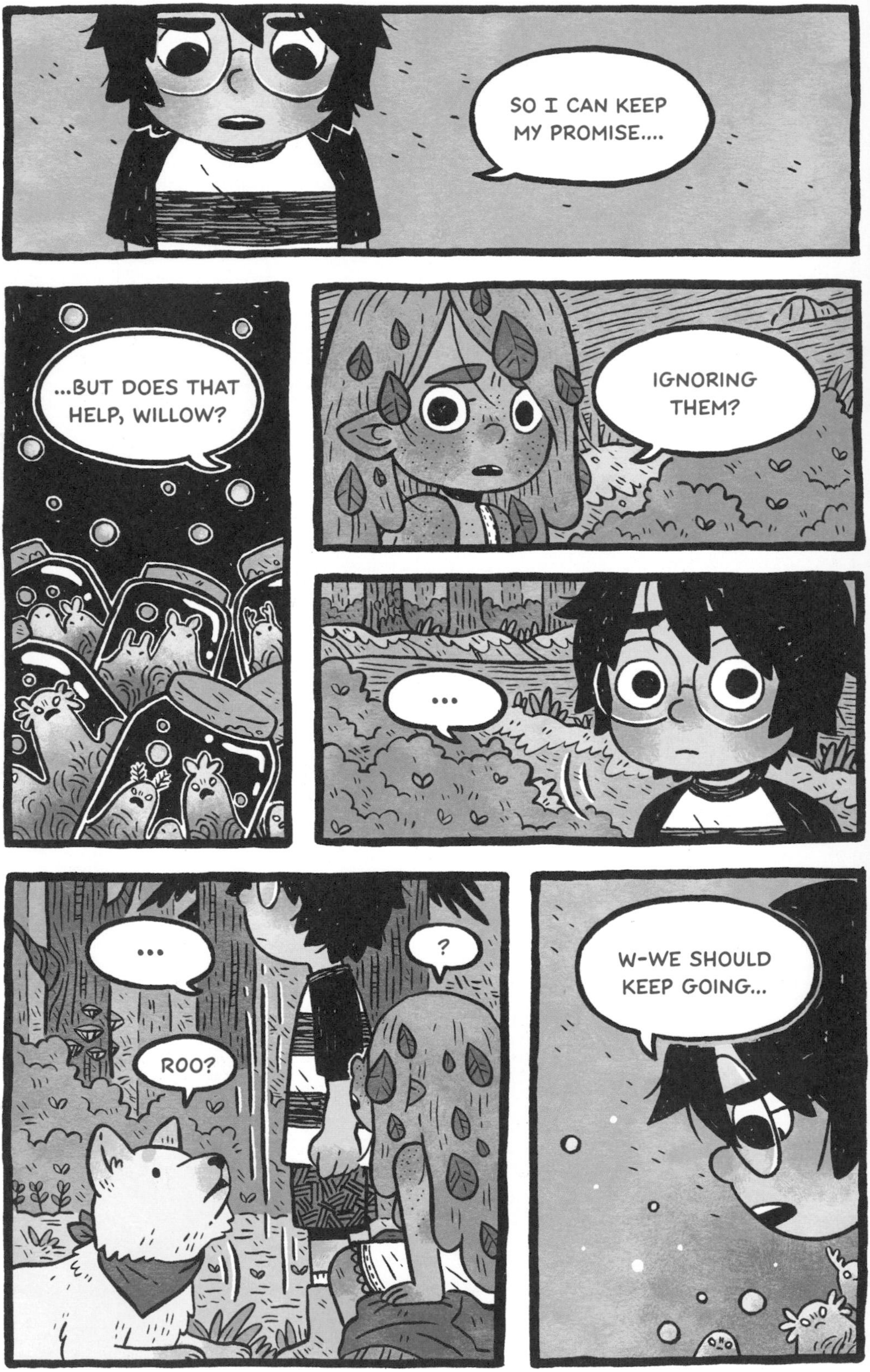
SO I CAN KEEP MY PROMISE....
...BUT DOES THAT HELP, WILLOW?
IGNORING THEM?
...
...
?
ROO?
W-WE SHOULD KEEP GOING...

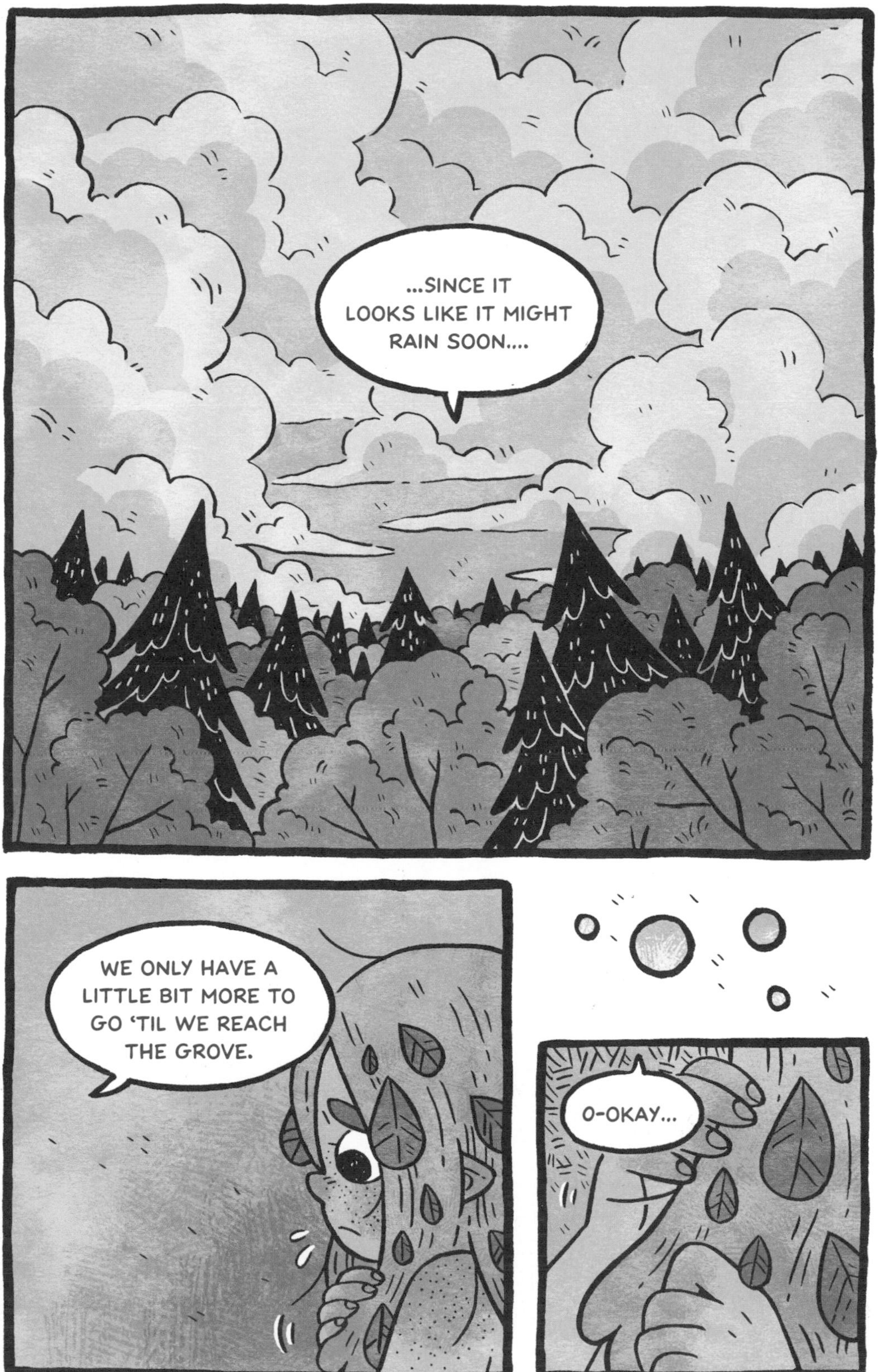
...SINCE IT LOOKS LIKE IT MIGHT RAIN SOON....
WE ONLY HAVE A LITTLE BIT MORE TO GO 'TIL WE REACH THE GROVE.
O-OKAY...

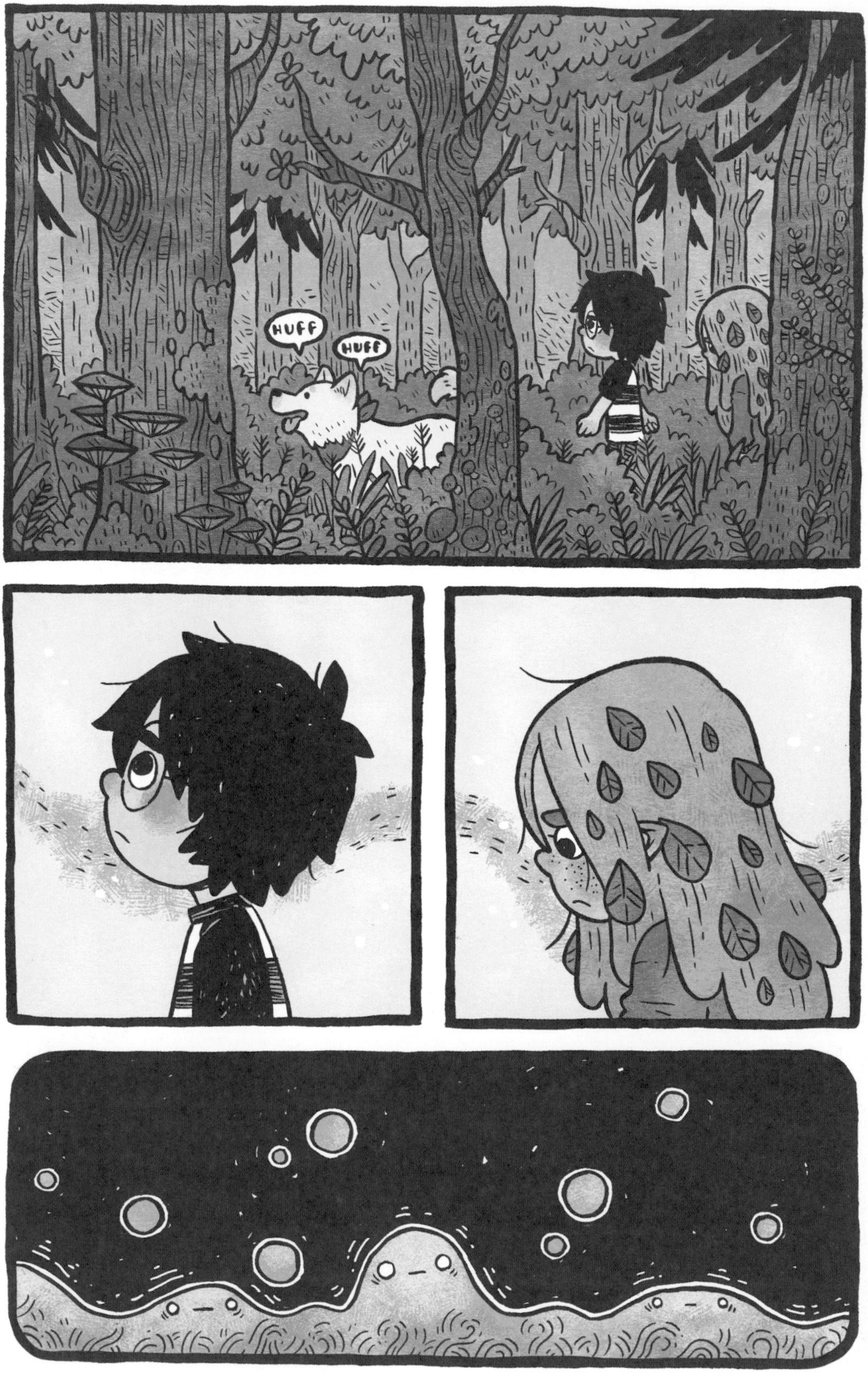
HUFF
HUFF

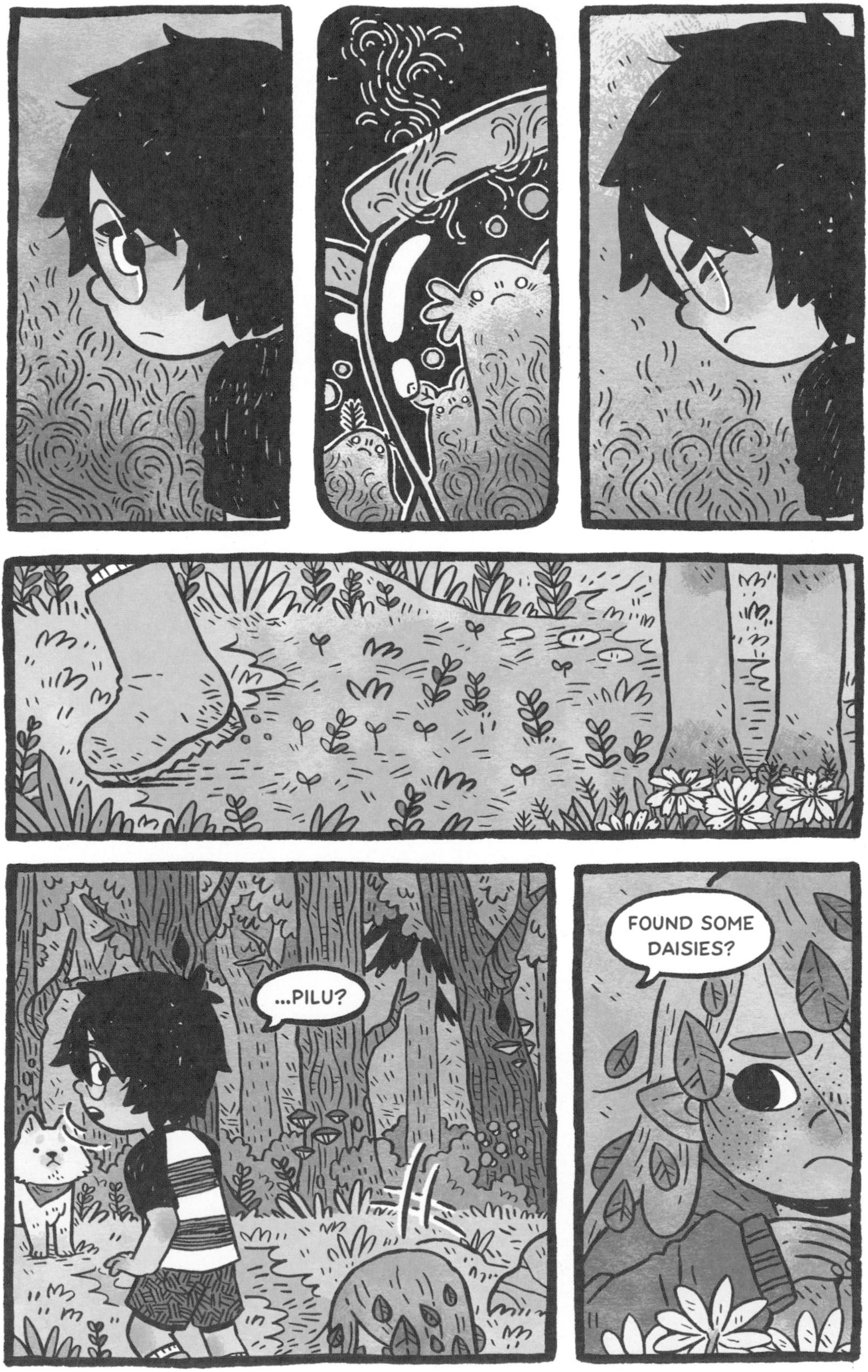
...PILU?
FOUND SOME DAISIES?

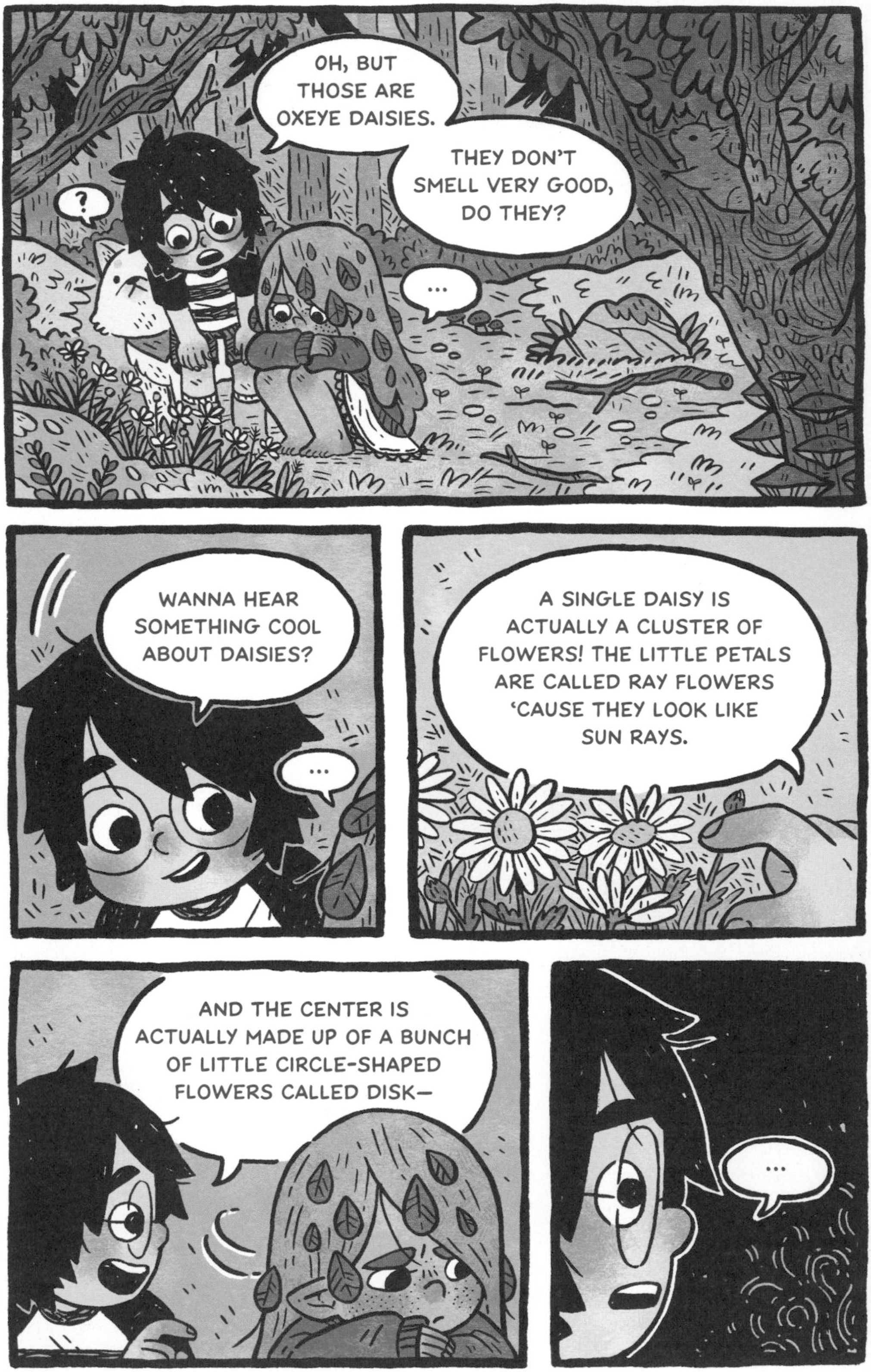

OH, BUT THOSE ARE OXEYE DAISIES.
THEY DON'T SMELL VERY GOOD, DO THEY?
?
...
WANNA HEAR SOMETHING COOL ABOUT DAISIES?
...
A SINGLE DAISY IS ACTUALLY A CLUSTER OF FLOWERS! THE LITTLE PETALS ARE CALLED RAY FLOWERS 'CAUSE THEY LOOK LIKE SUN RAYS.
AND THE CENTER IS ACTUALLY MADE UP OF A BUNCH OF LITTLE CIRCLE-SHAPED FLOWERS CALLED DISK—
...

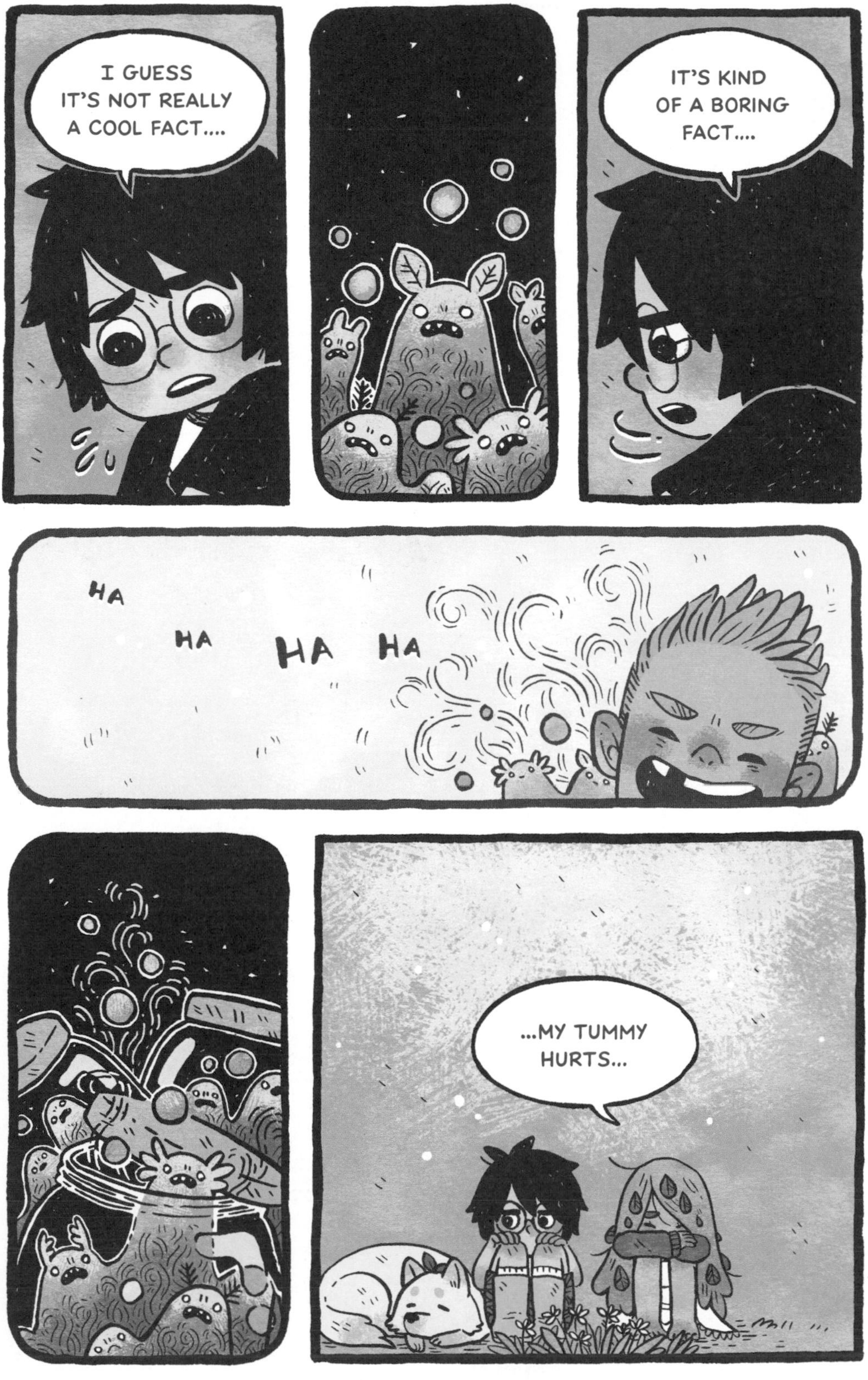
I GUESS IT'S NOT REALLY A COOL FACT....
IT'S KIND OF A BORING FACT....
HA
HA
HA
HA
...MY TUMMY HURTS...

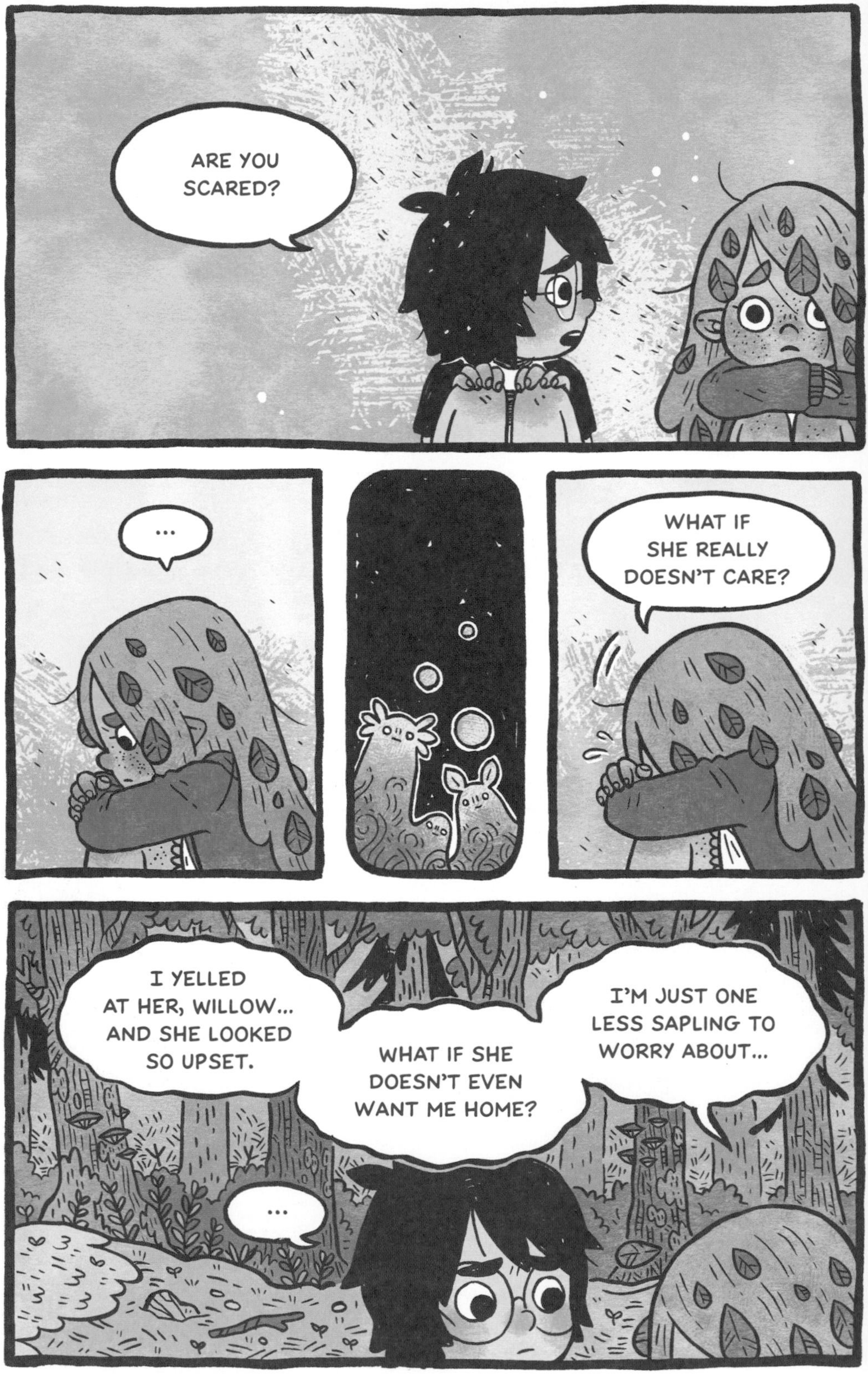
ARE YOU SCARED?
...
WHAT IF SHE REALLY DOESN'T CARE?
I YELLED AT HER, WILLOW... AND SHE LOOKED SO UPSET.
WHAT IF SHE DOESN'T EVEN WANT ME HOME?
I'M JUST ONE LESS SAPLING TO WORRY ABOUT...
...

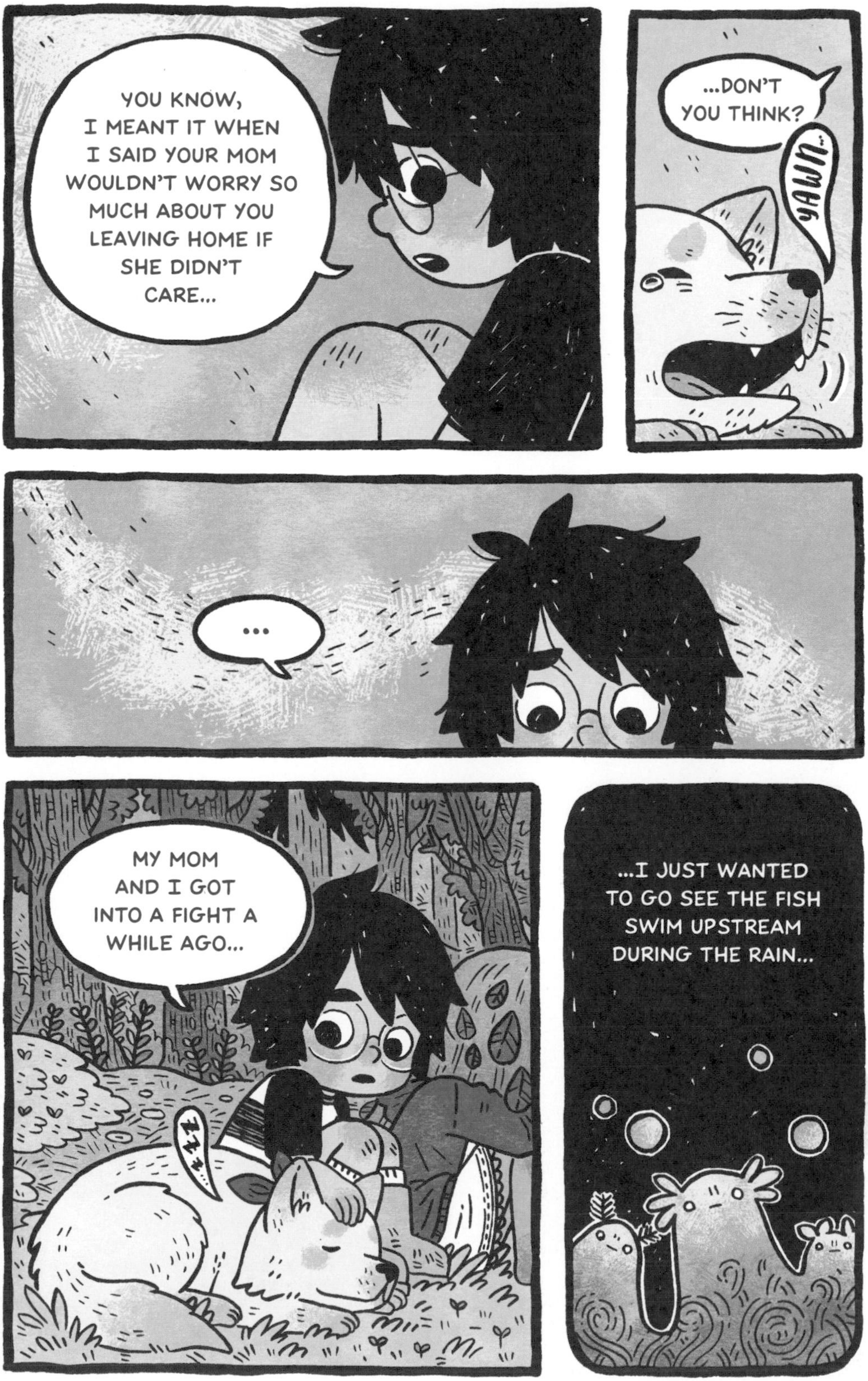
YOU KNOW, I MEANT IT WHEN I SAID YOUR MOM WOULDN'T WORRY SO MUCH ABOUT YOU LEAVING HOME IF SHE DIDN'T CARE...
...DON'T YOU THINK?
YAWN...
...
MY MOM AND I GOT INTO A FIGHT A WHILE AGO...
ZZZ
...I JUST WANTED TO GO SEE THE FISH SWIM UPSTREAM DURING THE RAIN...

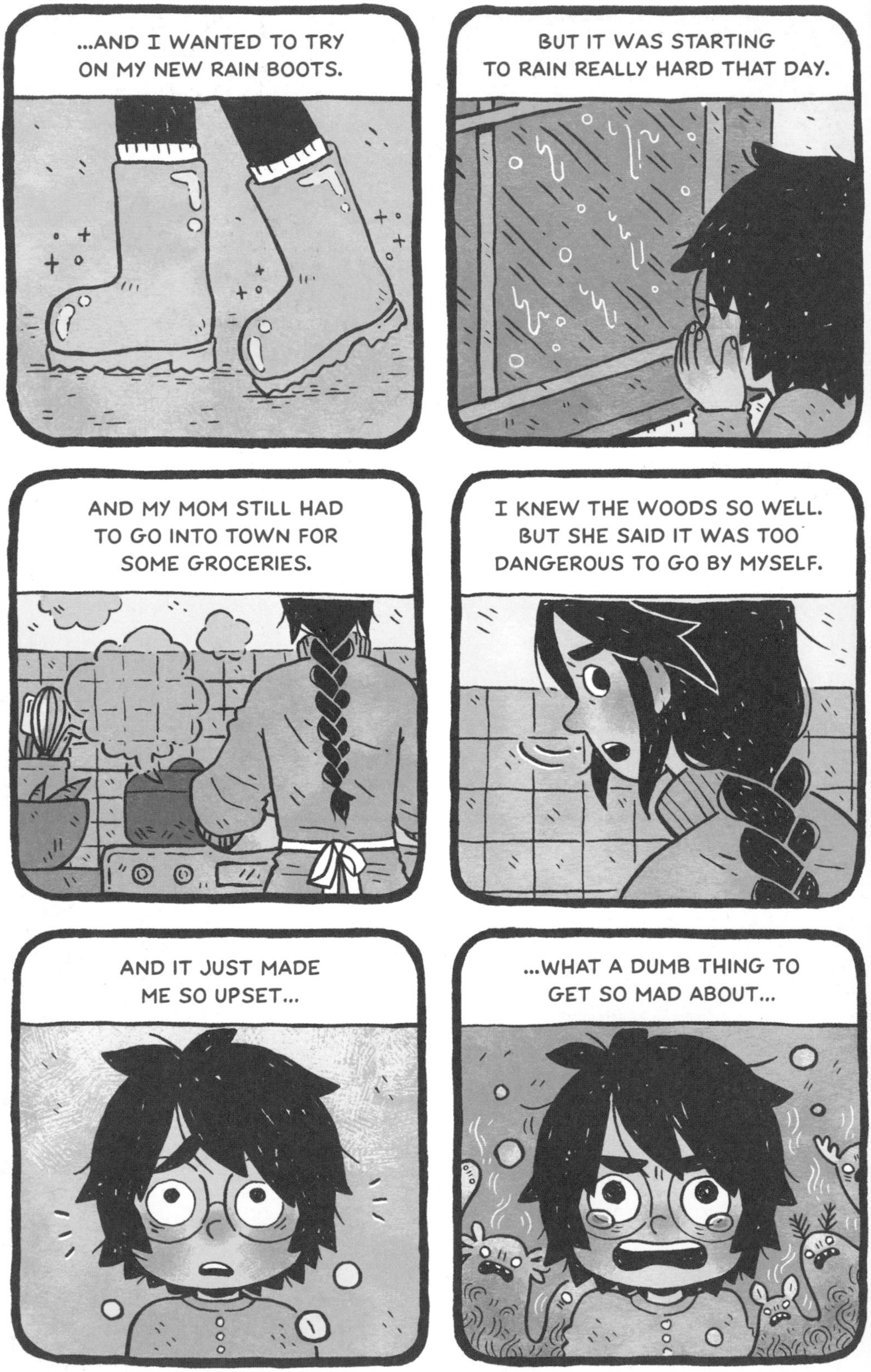
...AND I WANTED TO TRY ON MY NEW RAIN BOOTS.
BUT IT WAS STARTING TO RAIN REALLY HARD THAT DAY.
AND MY MOM STILL HAD TO GO INTO TOWN FOR SOME GROCERIES.
I KNEW THE WOODS SO WELL. BUT SHE SAID IT WAS TOO DANGEROUS TO GO BY MYSELF.
AND IT JUST MADE ME SO UPSET...
...WHAT A DUMB THING TO GET SO MAD ABOUT...

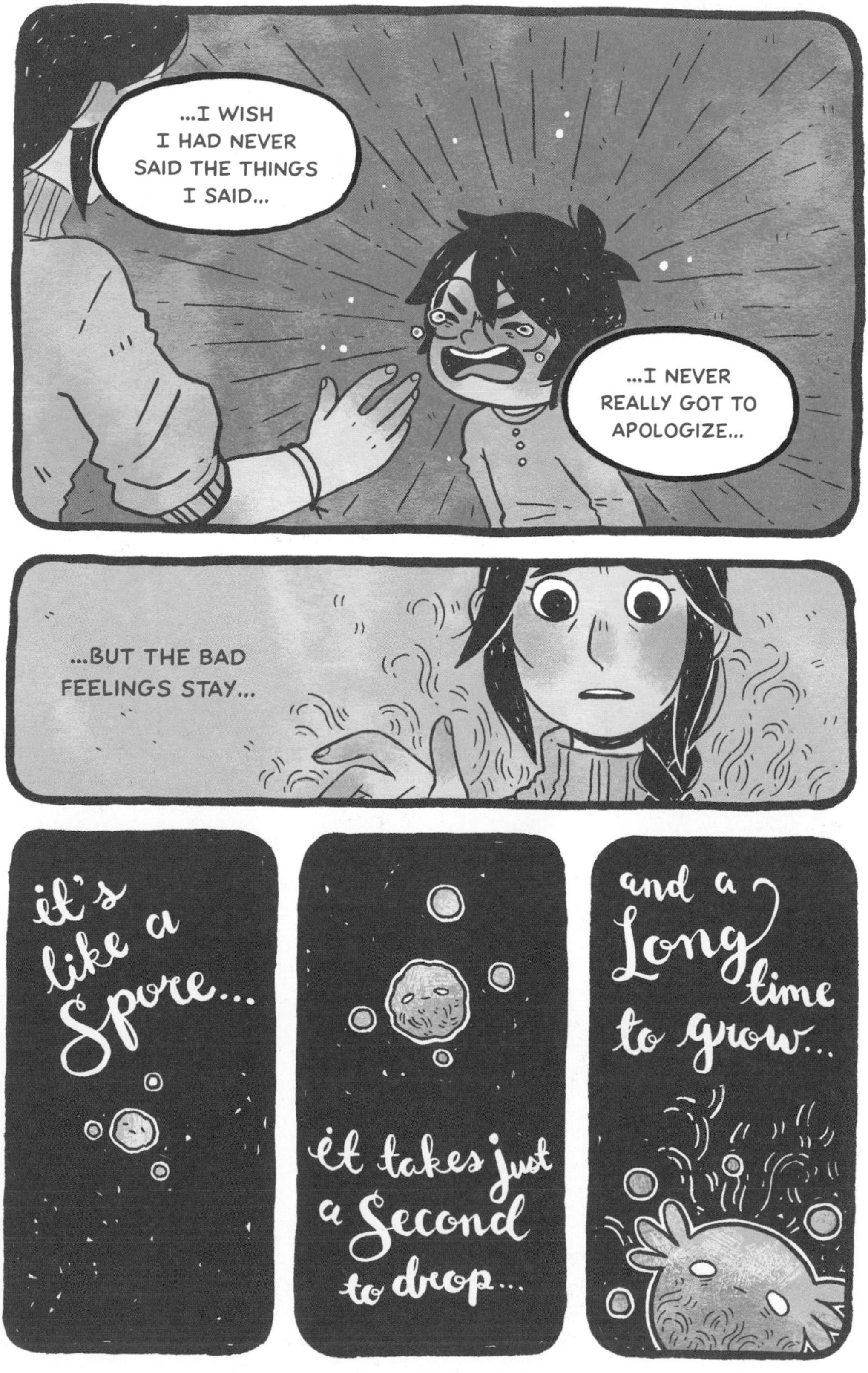
...I WISH I HAD NEVER SAID THE THINGS I SAID...
...I NEVER REALLY GOT TO APOLOGIZE...
...BUT THE BAD FEELINGS STAY...
it's like a Spore...
it takes just a Second to drop...
and a Long time to grow...

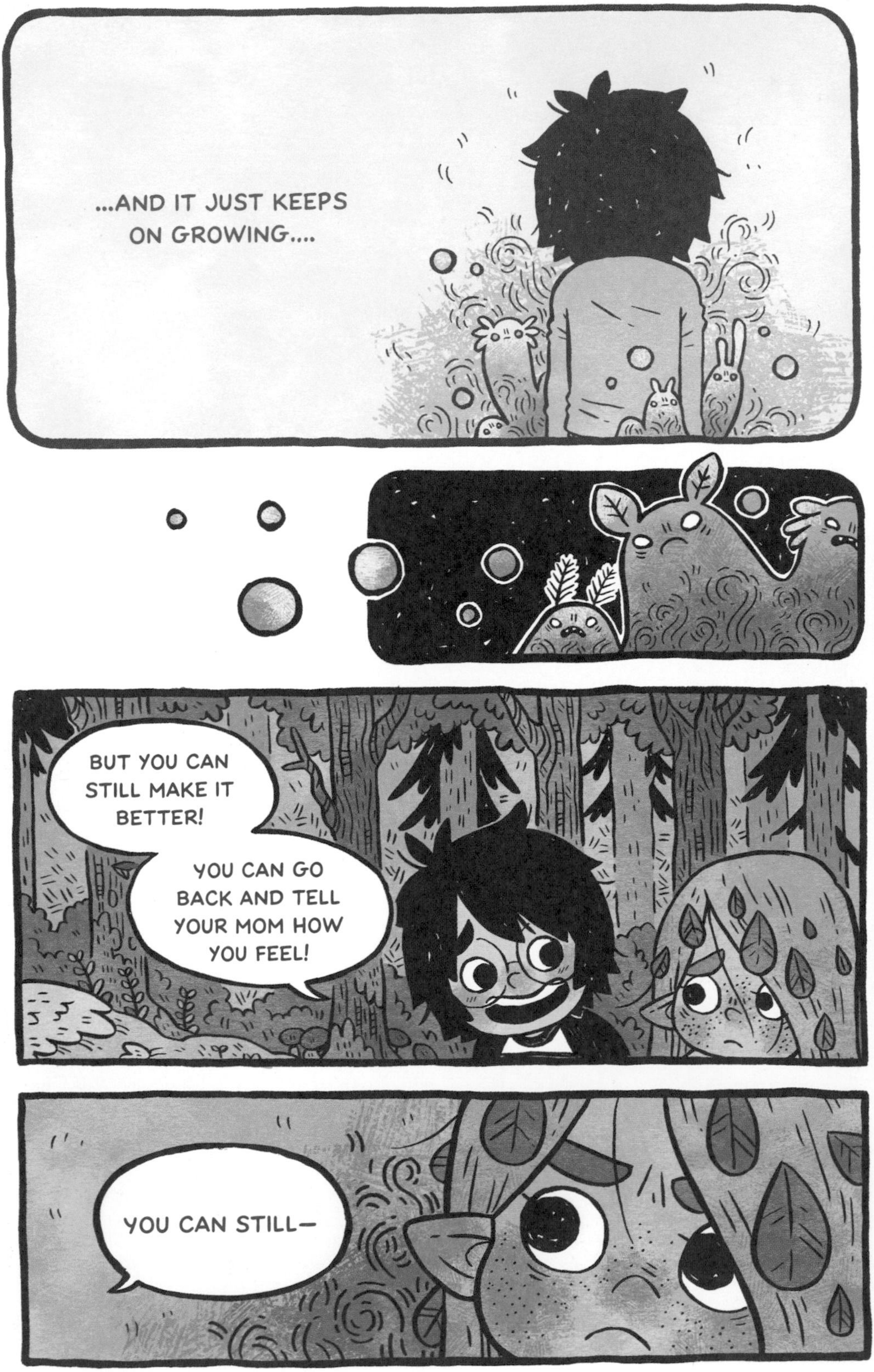
...AND IT JUST KEEPS ON GROWING....
BUT YOU CAN STILL MAKE IT BETTER!
YOU CAN GO BACK AND TELL YOUR MOM HOW YOU FEEL!
YOU CAN STILL—

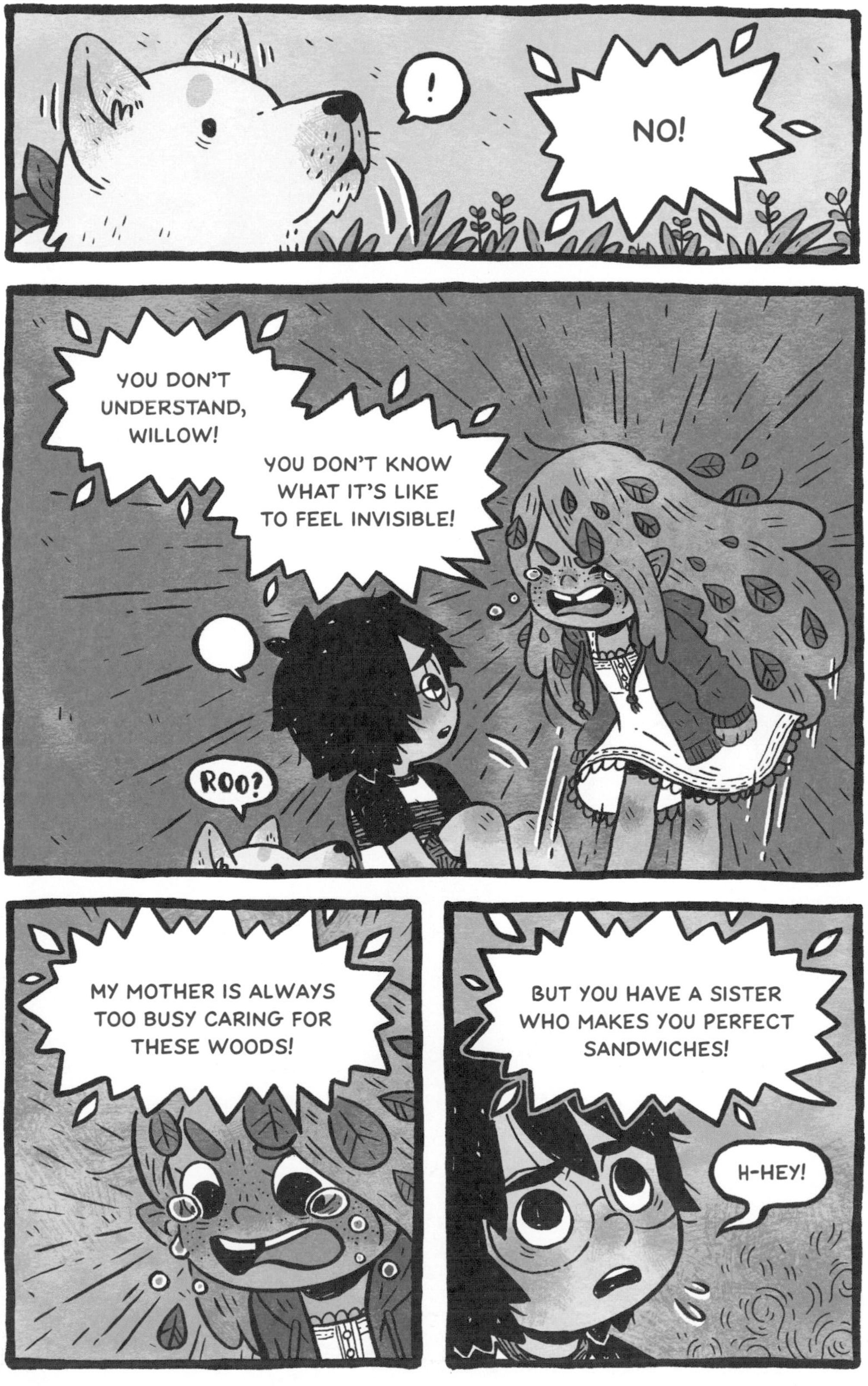
!
NO!
YOU DON'T UNDERSTAND, WILLOW!
YOU DON'T KNOW WHAT IT'S LIKE TO FEEL INVISIBLE!
ROO?
MY MOTHER IS ALWAYS TOO BUSY CARING FOR THESE WOODS!
BUT YOU HAVE A SISTER WHO MAKES YOU PERFECT SANDWICHES!
H-HEY!

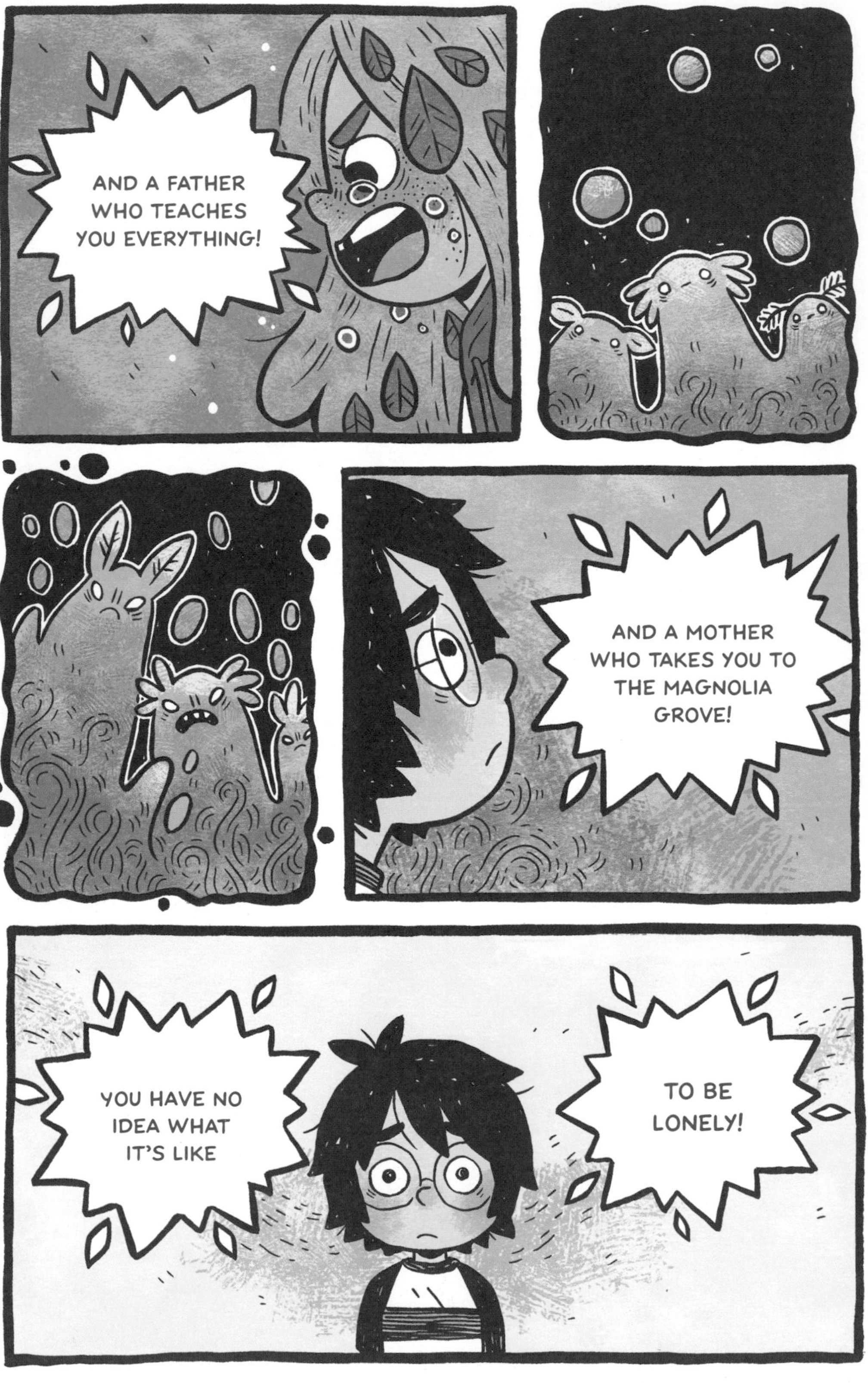
AND A FATHER WHO TEACHES YOU EVERYTHING!
AND A MOTHER WHO TAKES YOU TO THE MAGNOLIA GROVE!
YOU HAVE NO IDEA WHAT IT'S LIKE
TO BE LONELY!

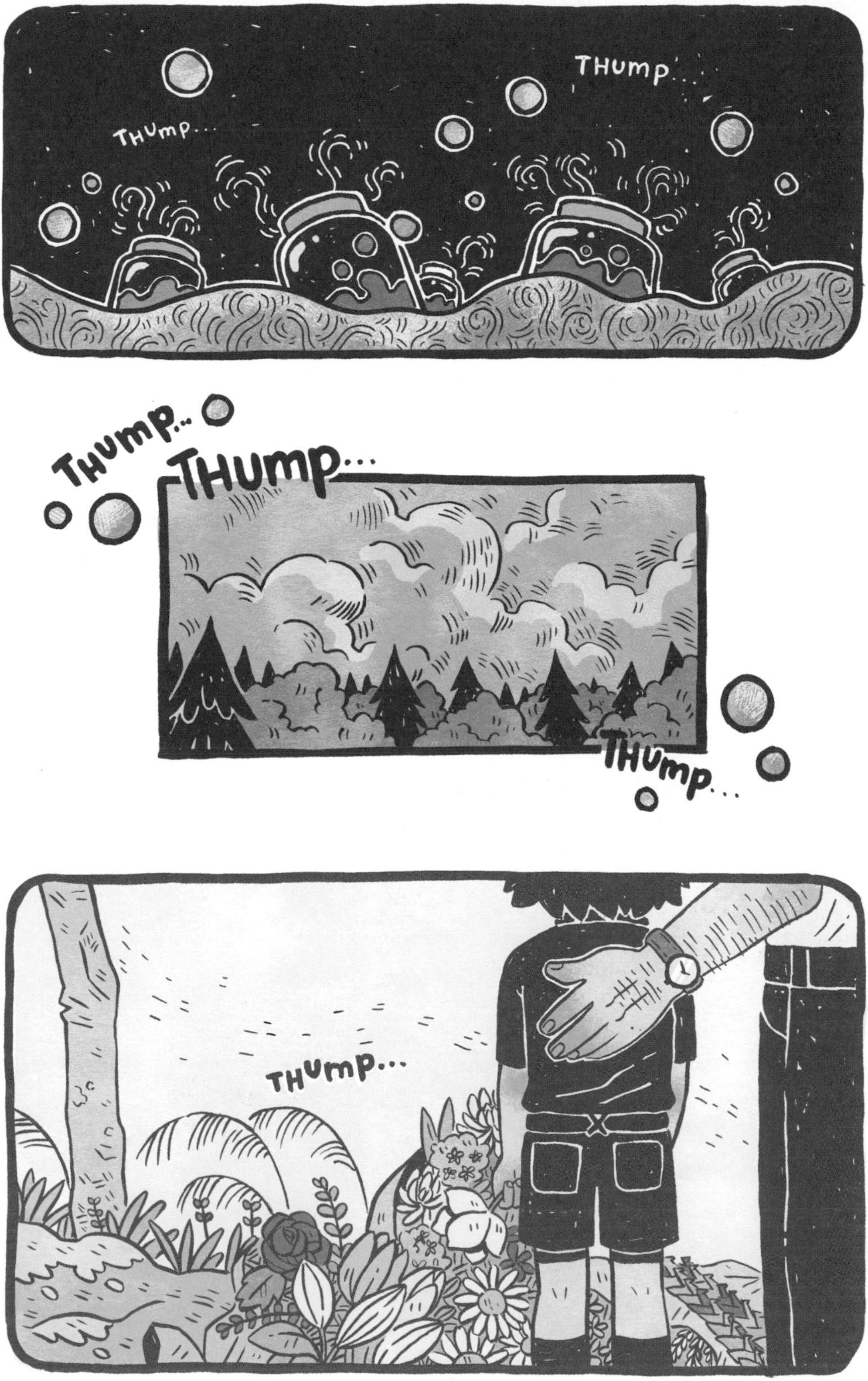
THUMP...
THUMP...
THUMP...
THUMP...
THUMP...
THUMP...

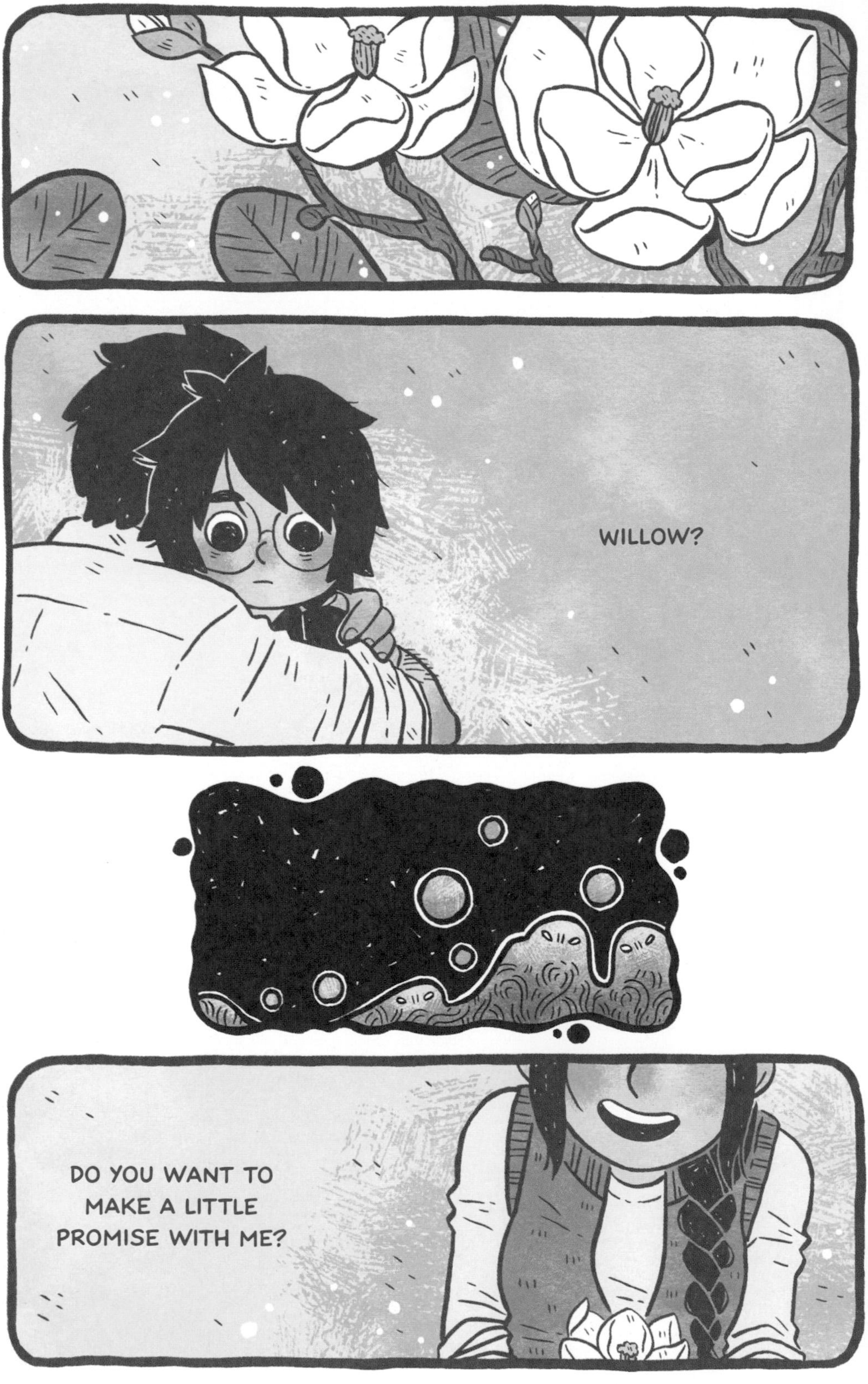
WILLOW?
DO YOU WANT TO MAKE A LITTLE PROMISE WITH ME?

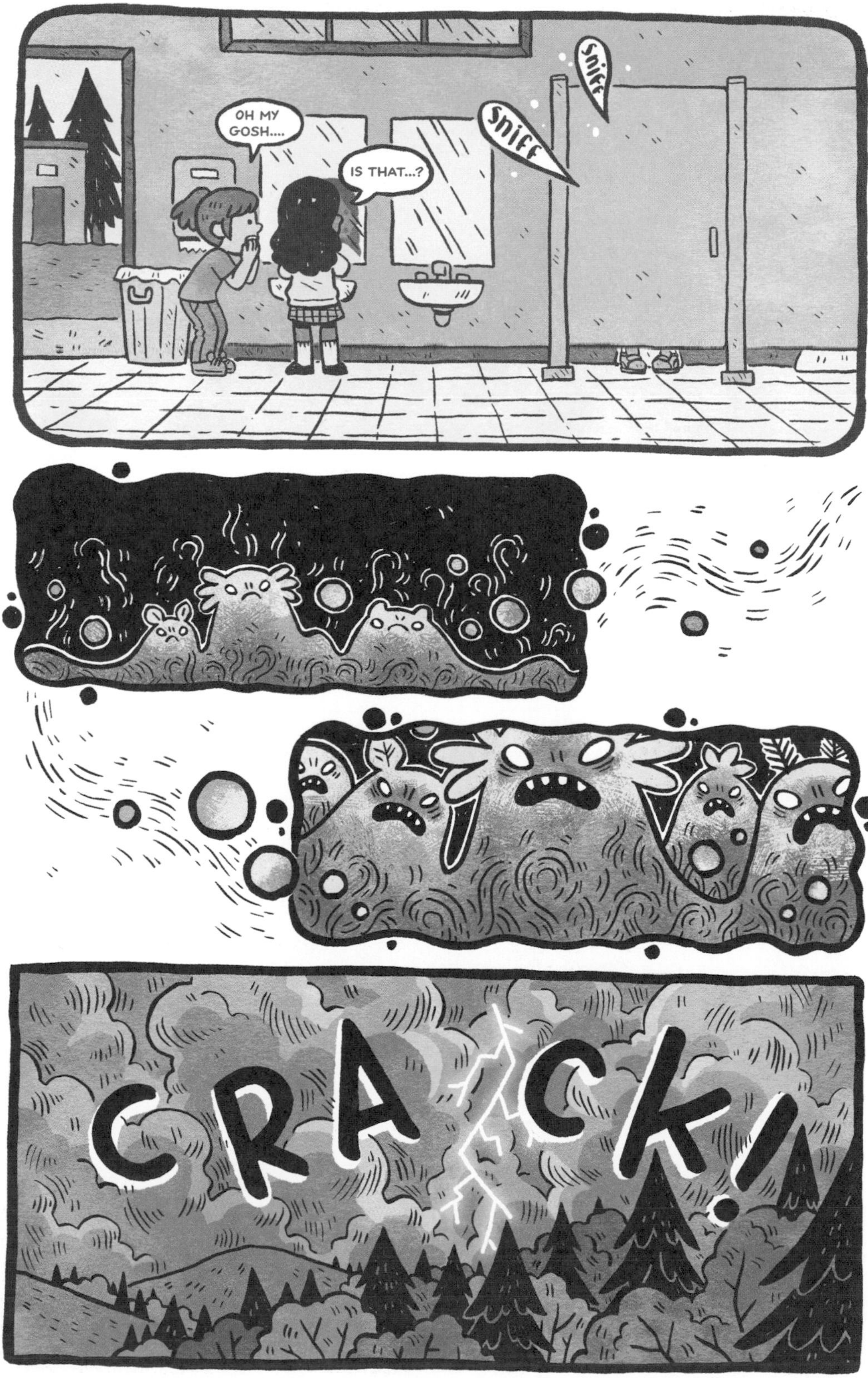
OH MY GOSH....
IS THAT...?
Sniff
Sniff
CRACK!

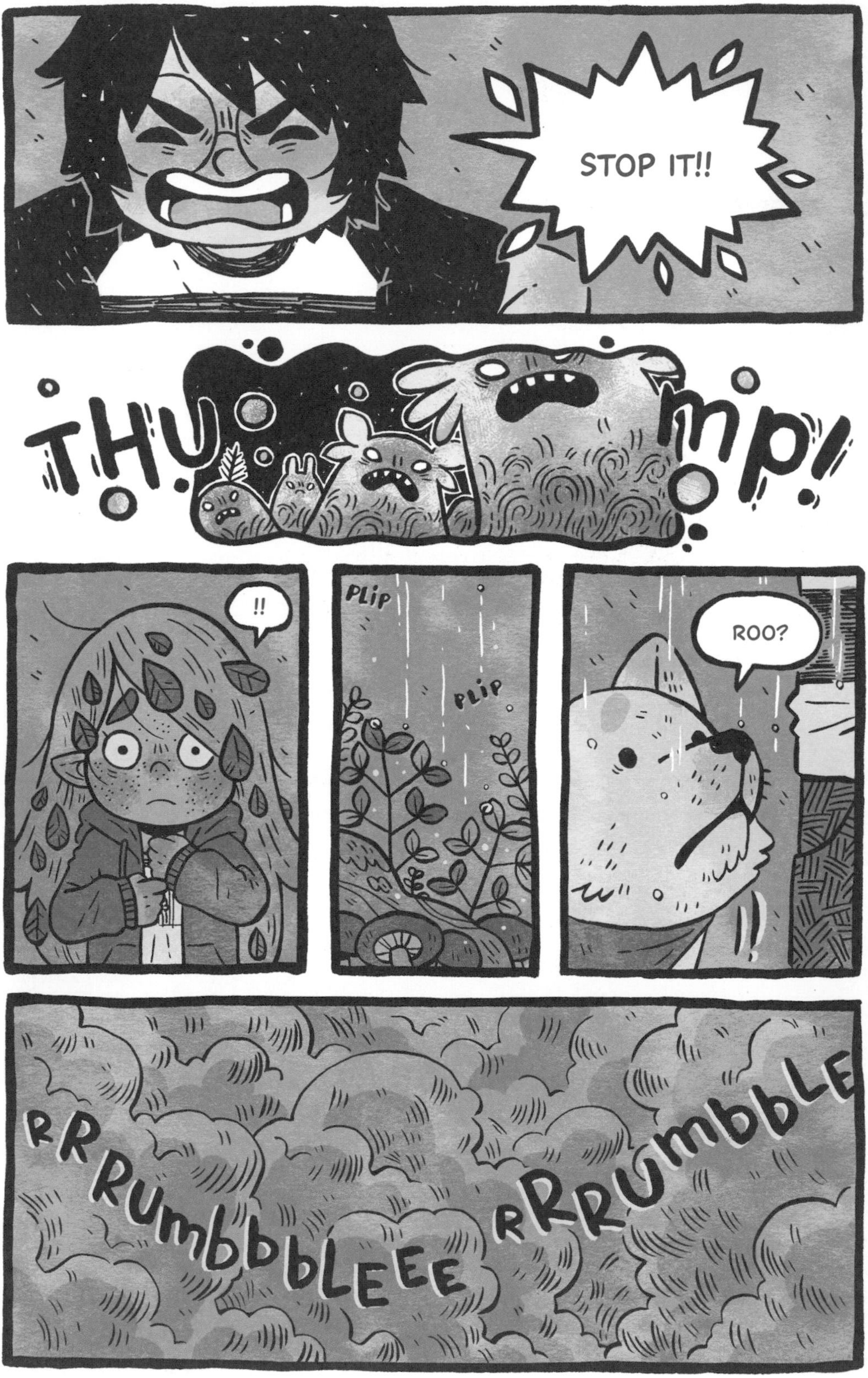
STOP IT!!
THUmp!
!!
PLIP
PLIP
ROO?
!!
rRRUmbbbLEEE
rRRUmbbLE

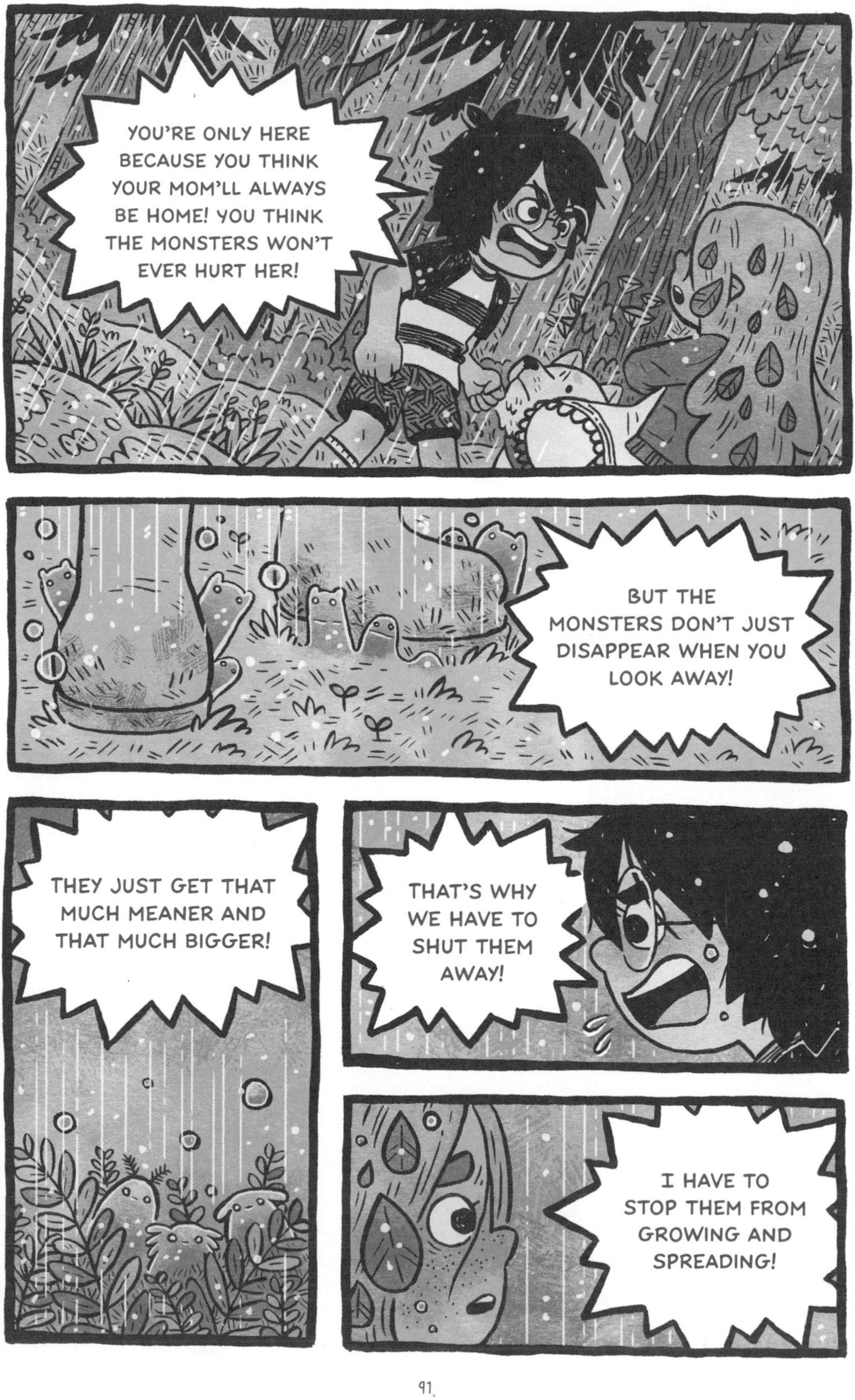
YOU'RE ONLY HERE BECAUSE YOU THINK YOUR MOM'LL ALWAYS BE HOME! YOU THINK THE MONSTERS WON'T EVER HURT HER!
BUT THE MONSTERS DON'T JUST DISAPPEAR WHEN YOU LOOK AWAY!
THEY JUST GET THAT MUCH MEANER AND THAT MUCH BIGGER!
THAT'S WHY WE HAVE TO SHUT THEM AWAY!
I HAVE TO STOP THEM FROM GROWING AND SPREADING!

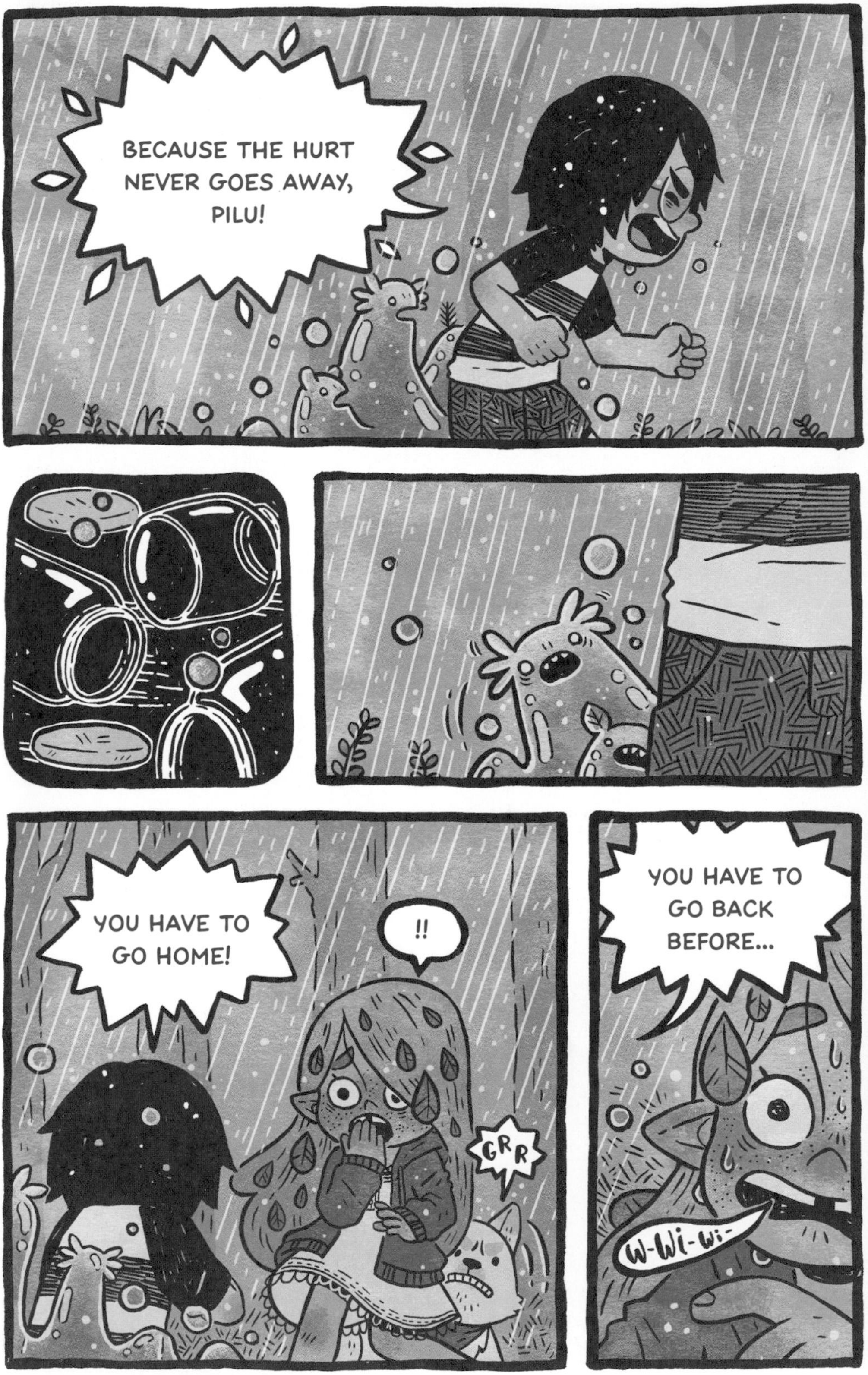
BECAUSE THE HURT NEVER GOES AWAY, PILU!
YOU HAVE TO GO HOME!
!!
GRR
YOU HAVE TO GO BACK BEFORE...
W-Wi-Wi-

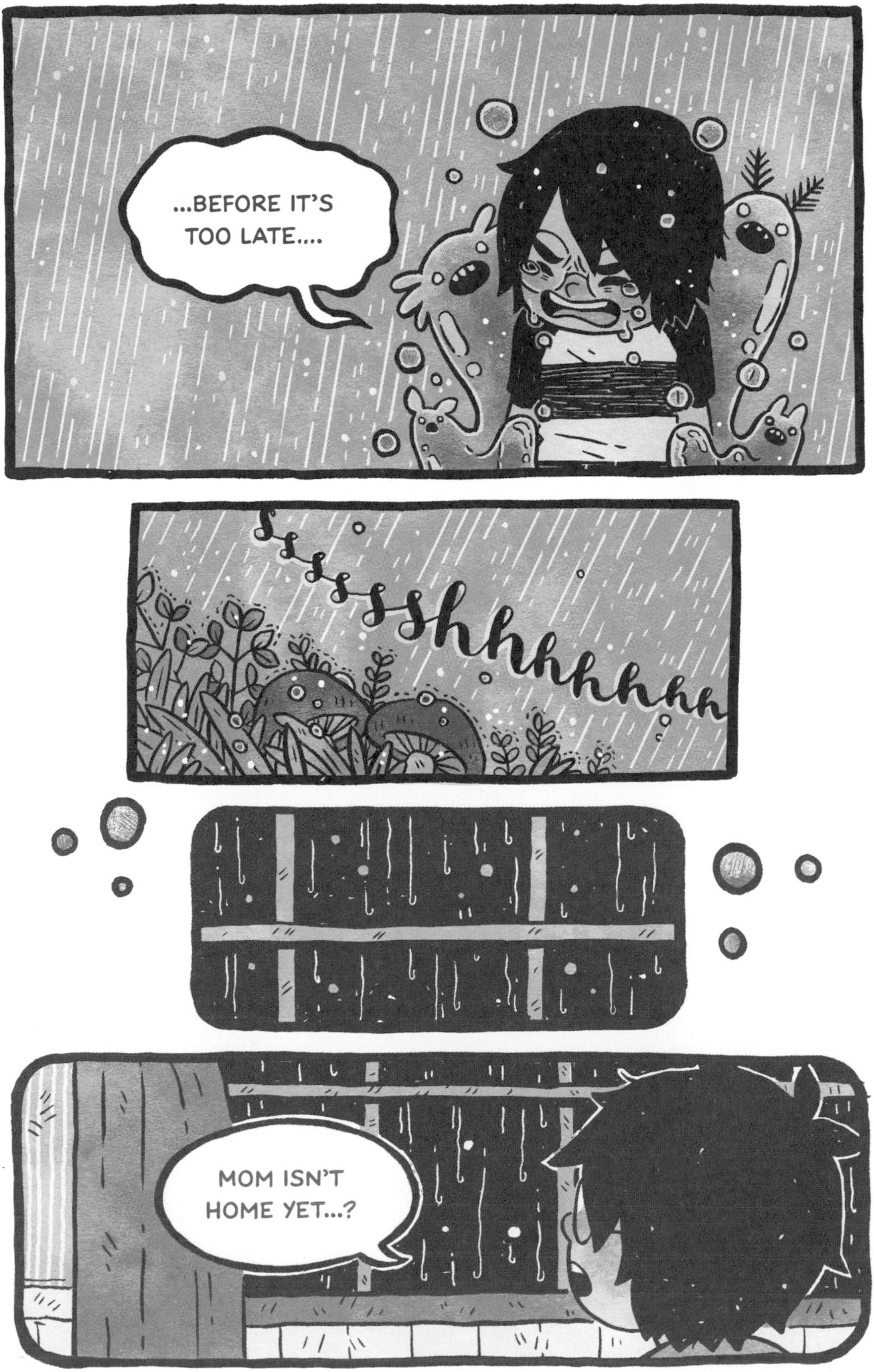
...BEFORE IT'S TOO LATE....
SSSSSSShhhhhhhh
MOM ISN'T HOME YET...?

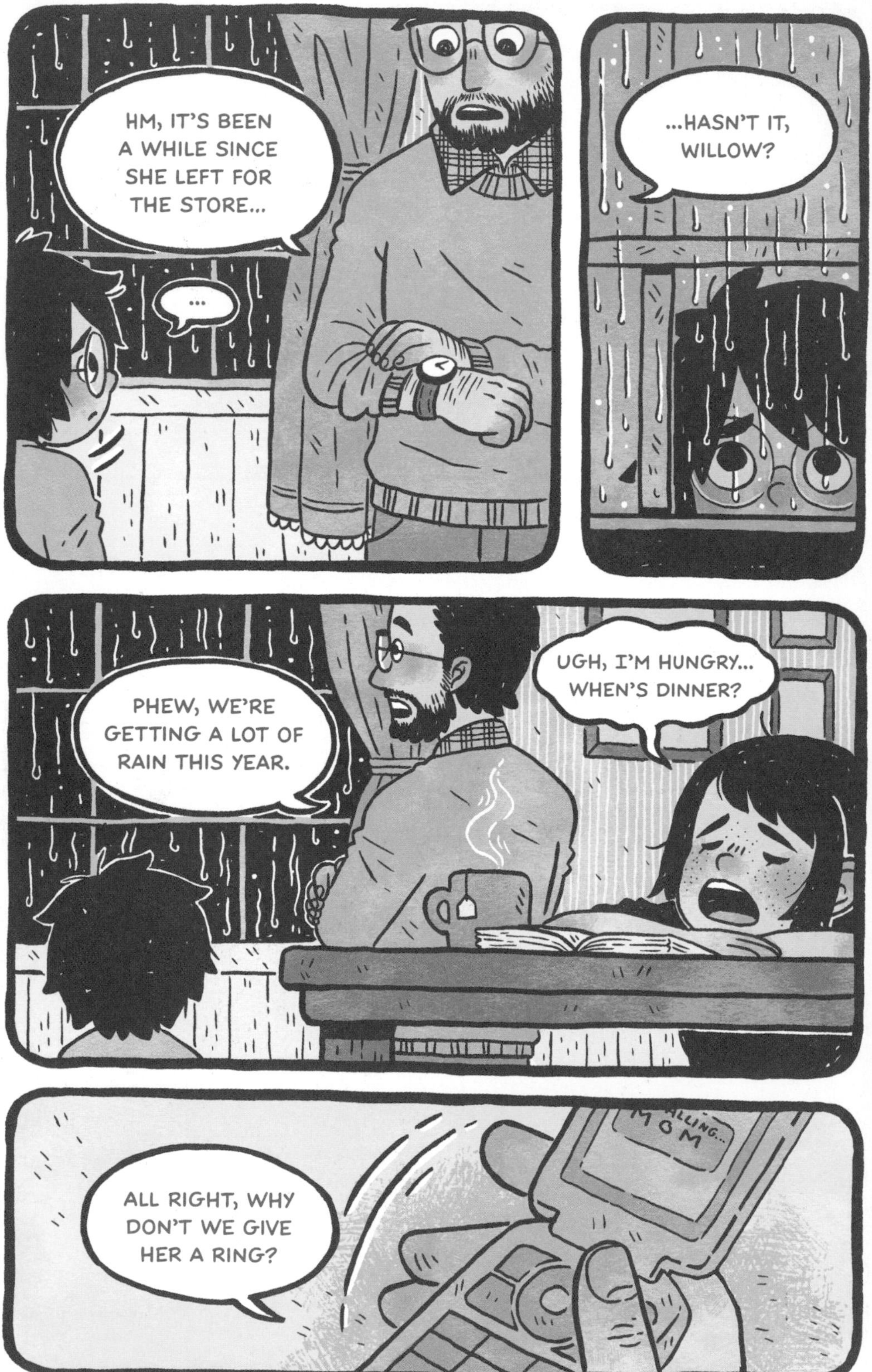
HM, IT'S BEEN A WHILE SINCE SHE LEFT FOR THE STORE...
...
...HASN'T IT, WILLOW?
PHEW, WE'RE GETTING A LOT OF RAIN THIS YEAR.
UGH, I'M HUNGRY... WHEN'S DINNER?
ALL RIGHT, WHY DON'T WE GIVE HER A RING?
CALLING... MOM

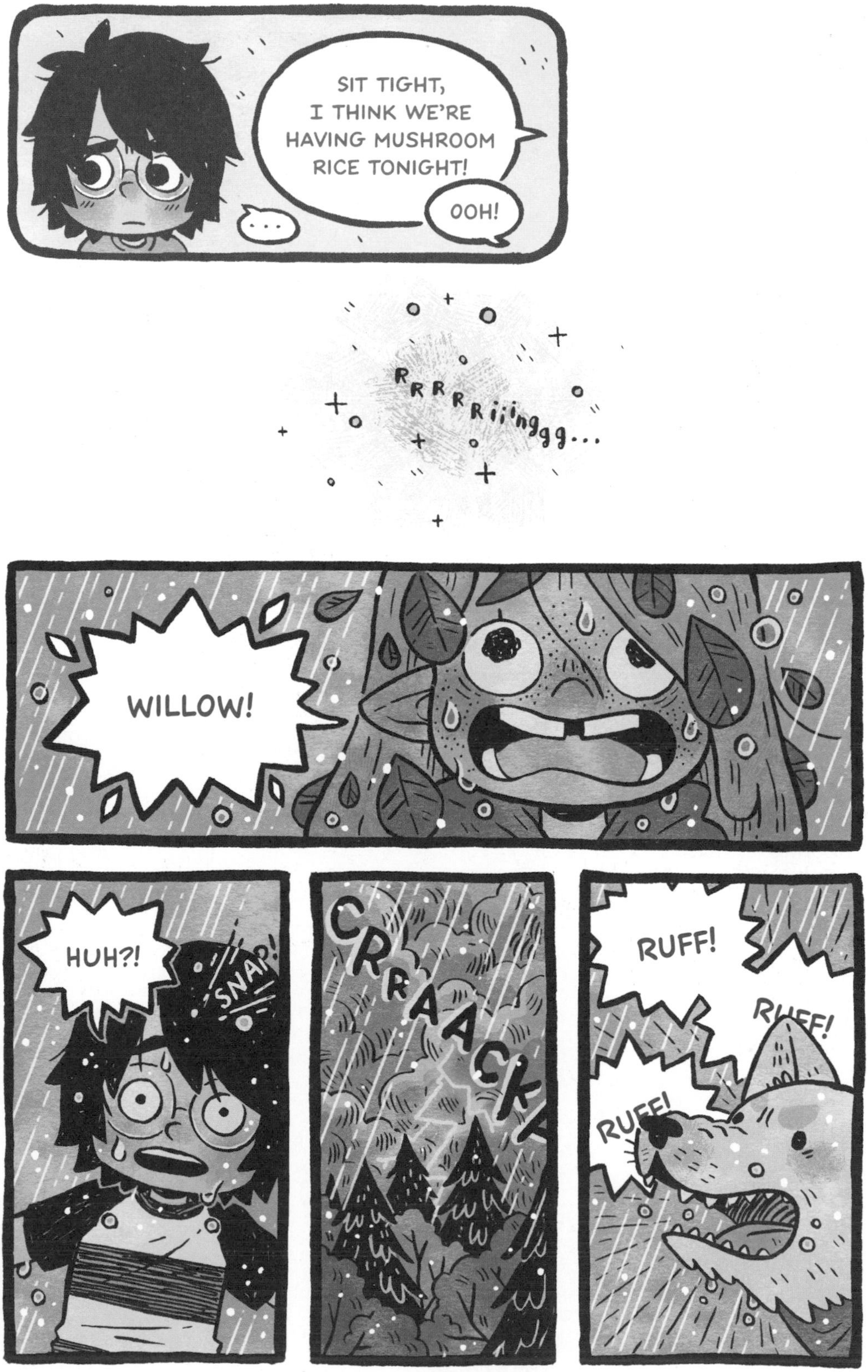

SIT TIGHT, I THINK WE'RE HAVING MUSHROOM RICE TONIGHT!
...
OOH!
RRRRRiiinggg...
WILLOW!
HUH?!
SNAP!
CRRAACK
RUFF!
RUFF!
RUFF!

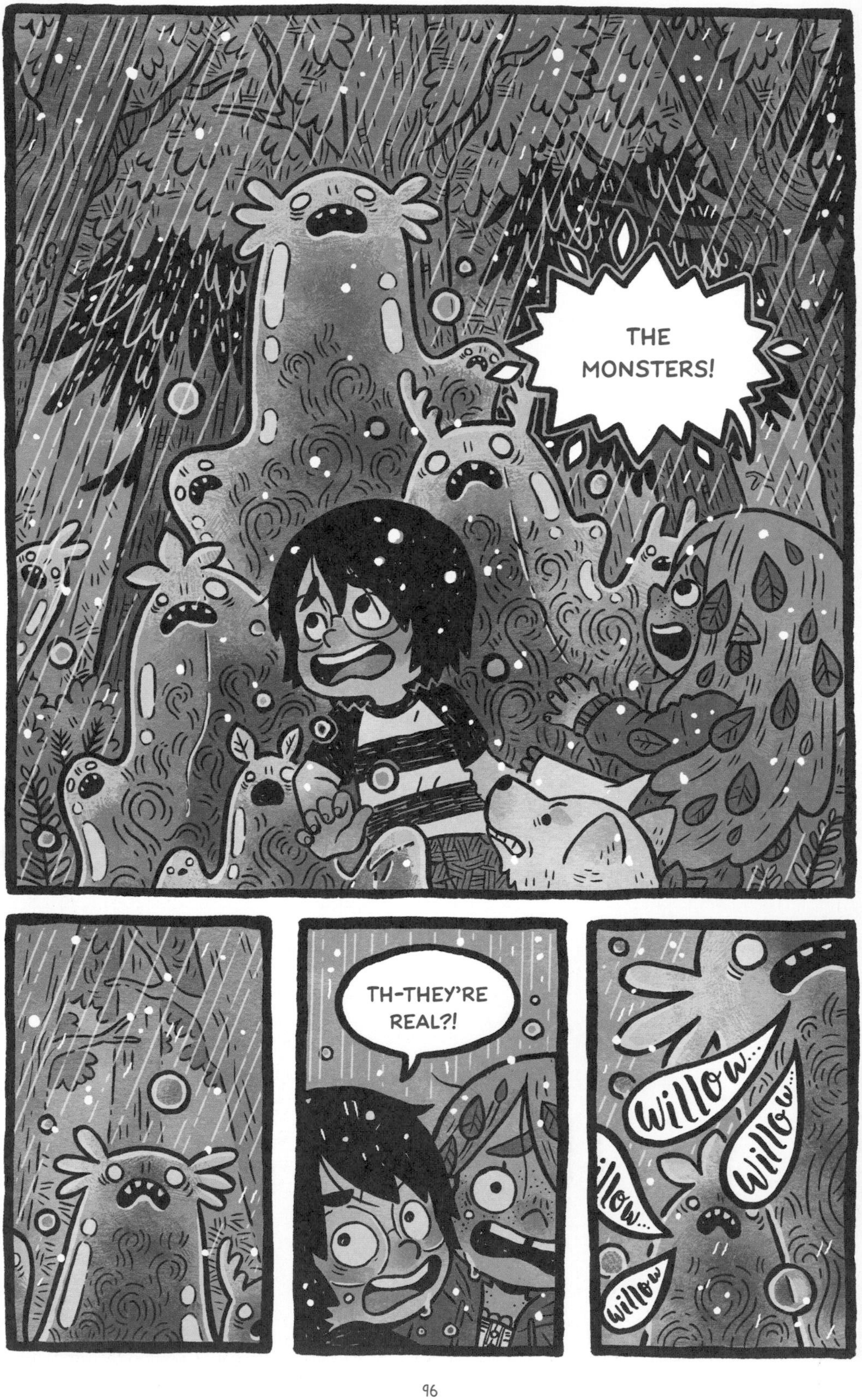
THE MONSTERS!
TH-THEY'RE REAL?!
willow...
willow...
willow...
illow...
willow

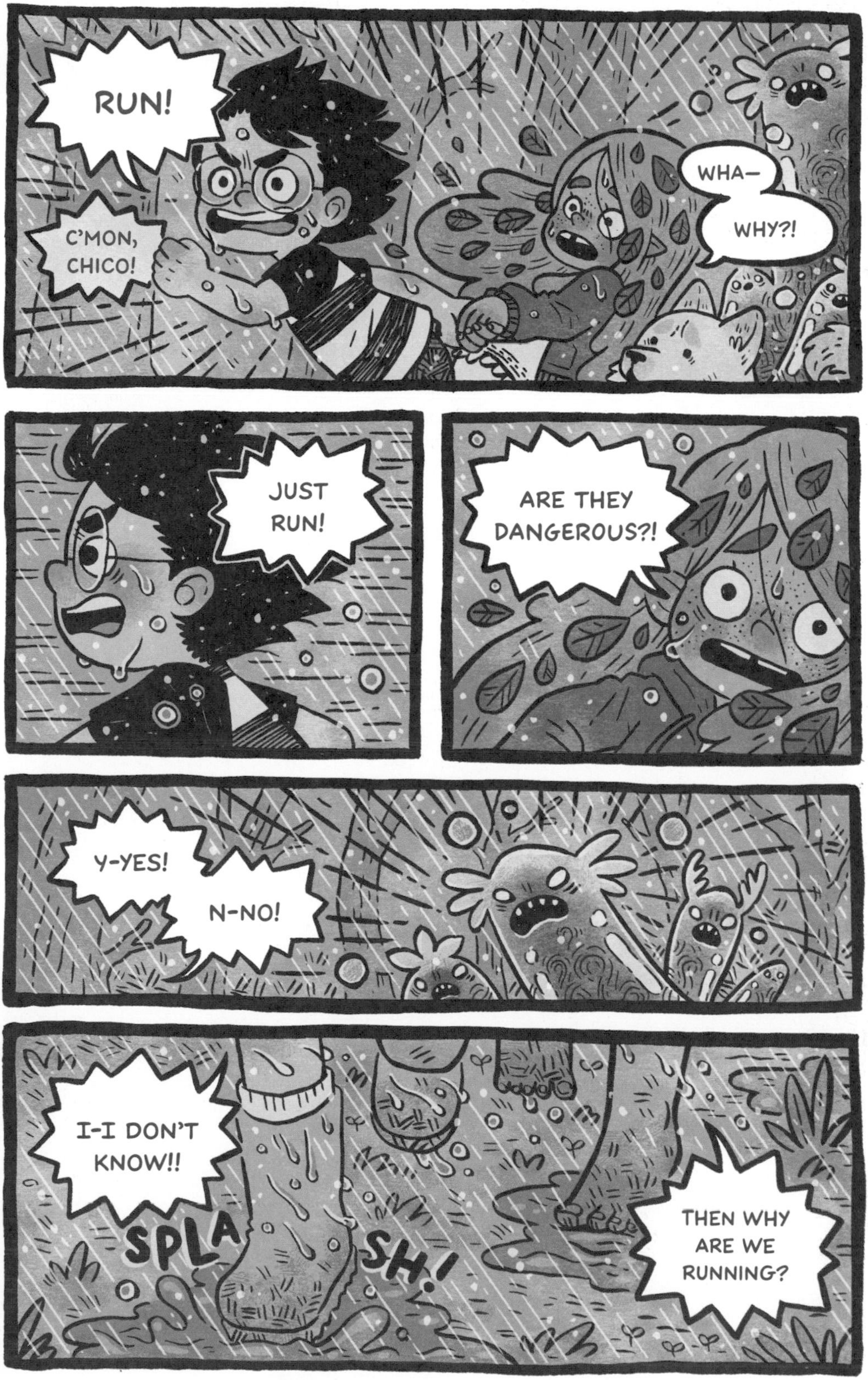
RUN!
C'MON, CHICO!
WHA—
WHY?!
JUST RUN!
ARE THEY DANGEROUS?!
Y-YES!
N-NO!
I-I DON'T KNOW!!
SPLASH!
THEN WHY ARE WE RUNNING?

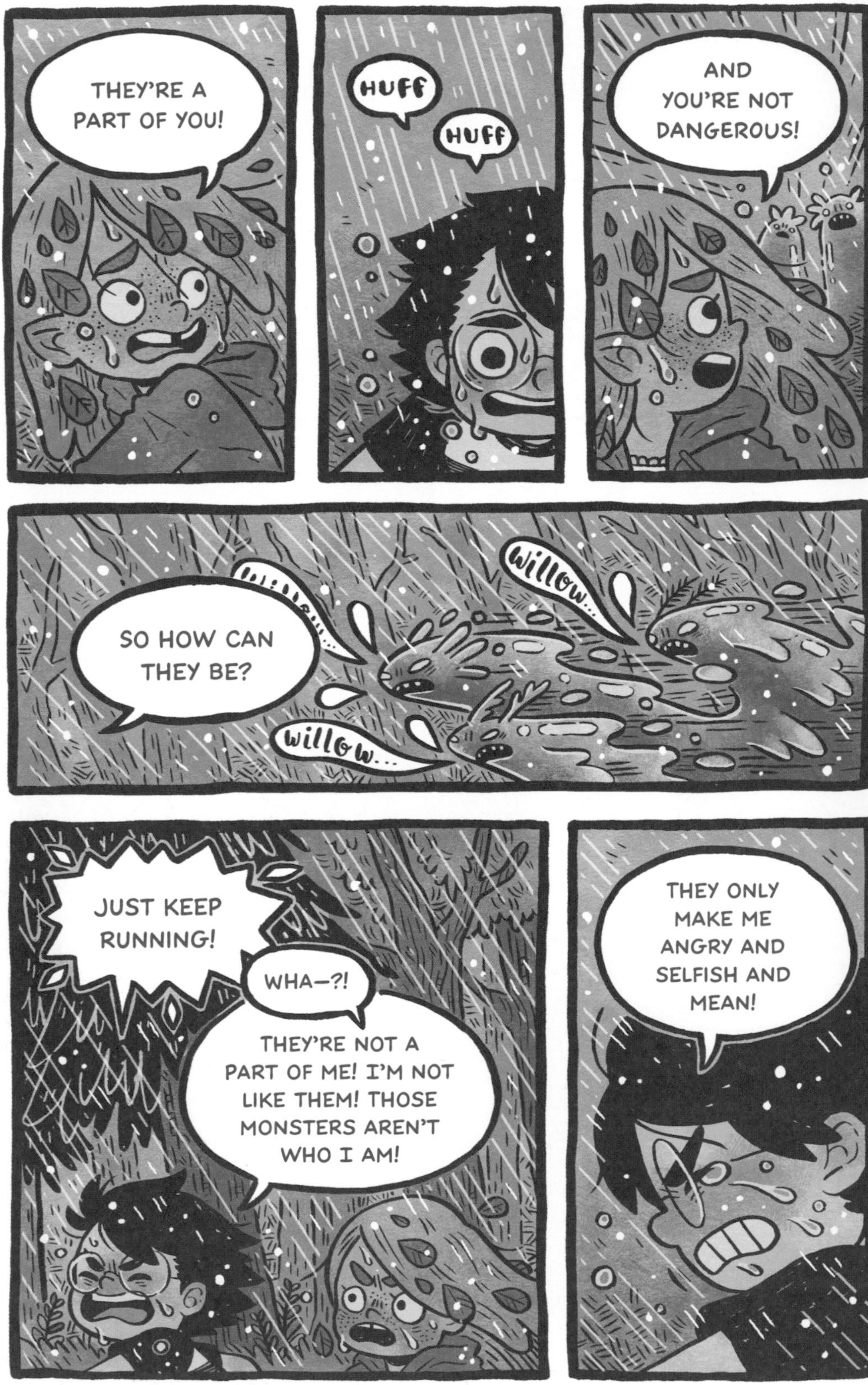
THEY'RE A PART OF YOU!
HUFF
HUFF
AND YOU'RE NOT DANGEROUS!
SO HOW CAN THEY BE?
willow...
willow...
JUST KEEP RUNNING!
WHA—?!
THEY'RE NOT A PART OF ME! I'M NOT LIKE THEM! THOSE MONSTERS AREN'T WHO I AM!
THEY ONLY MAKE ME ANGRY AND SELFISH AND MEAN!

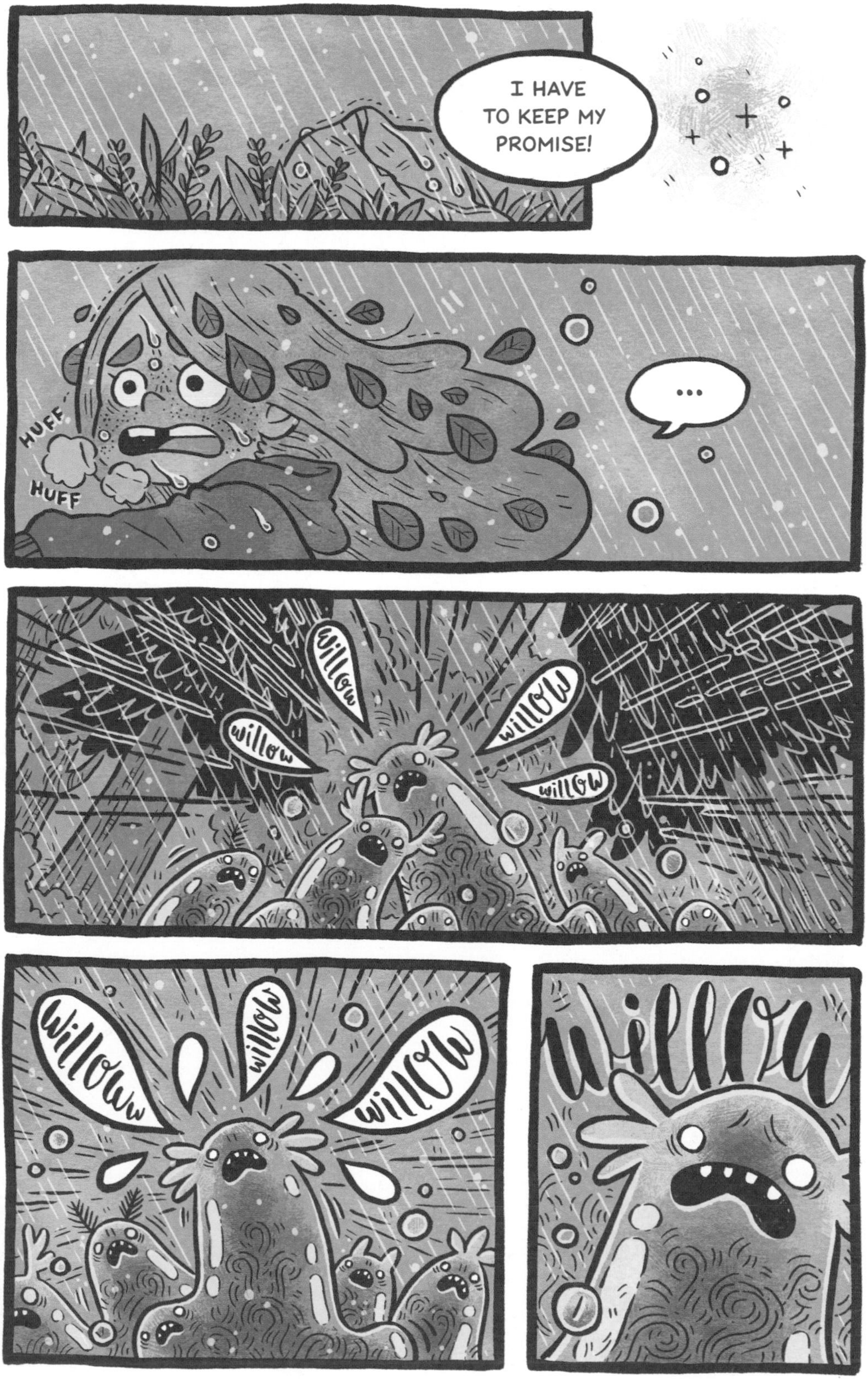
I HAVE TO KEEP MY PROMISE!
HUFF
HUFF
...
willow
willow
willow
willow
willow
willow
willow
willow

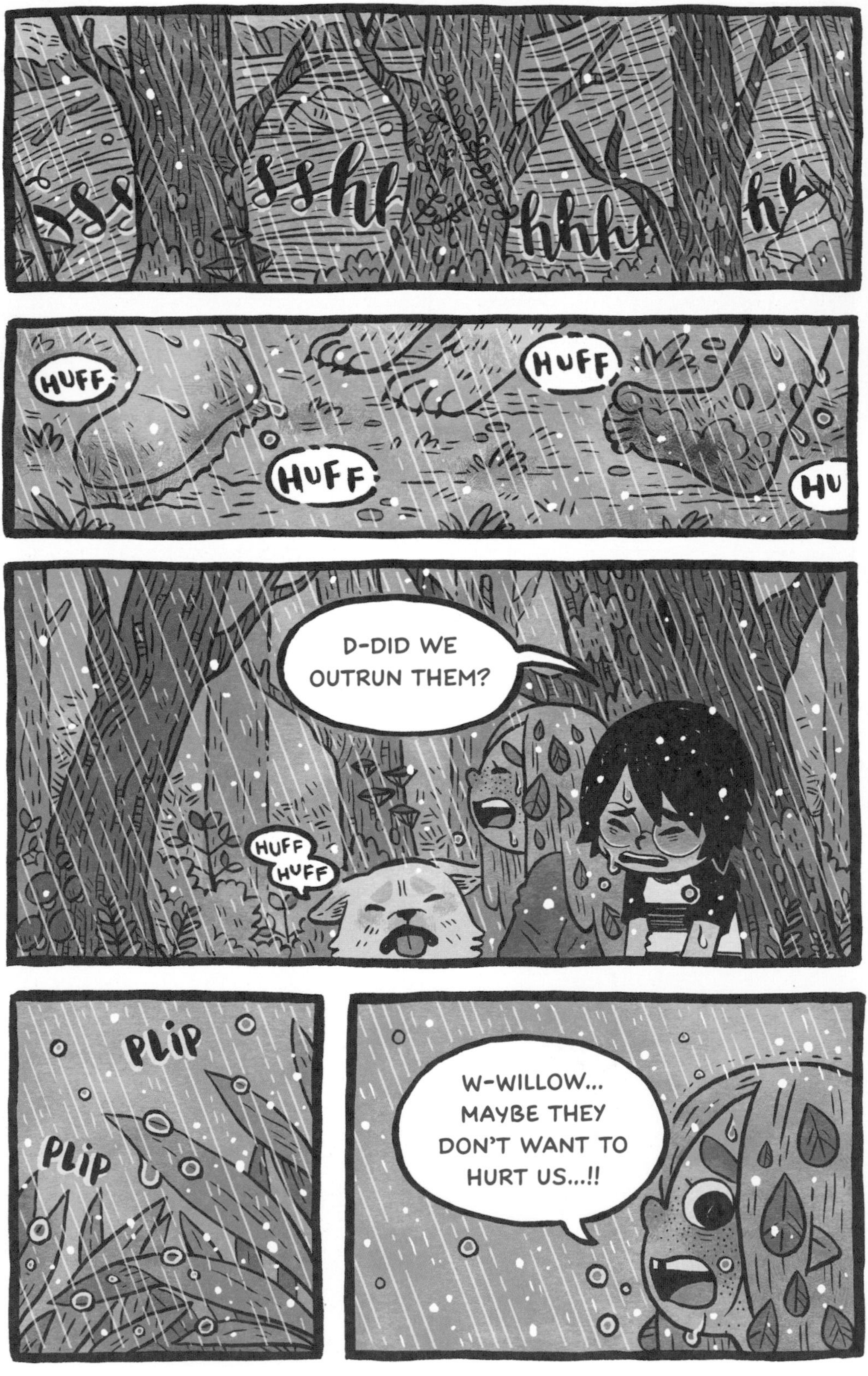
sshf
hhhh
HUFF
HUFF
HUFF
HU
D-DID WE OUTRUN THEM?
HUFF HUFF
PLIP
PLIP
W-WILLOW... MAYBE THEY DON'T WANT TO HURT US...!!

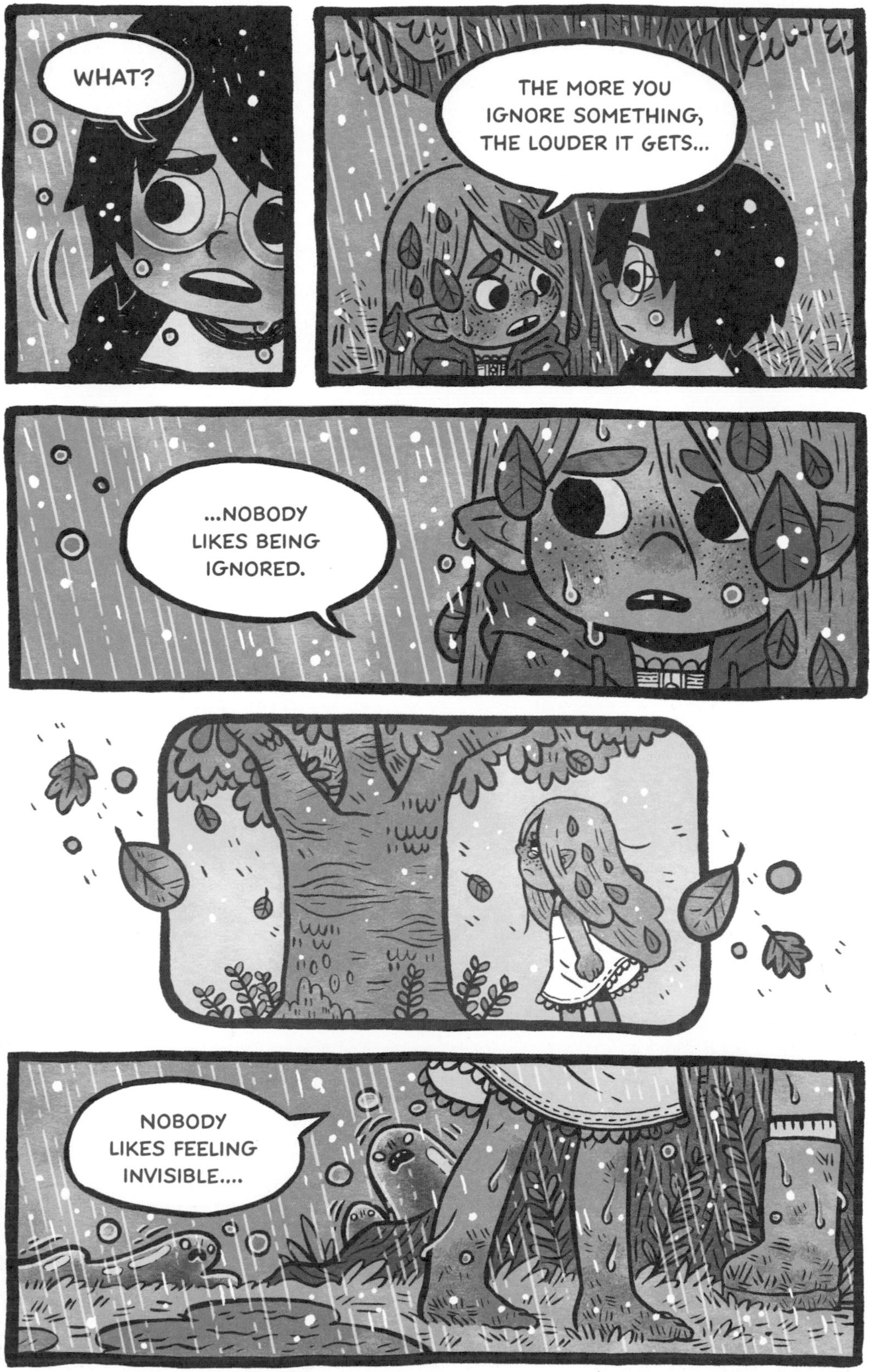
WHAT?
THE MORE YOU IGNORE SOMETHING, THE LOUDER IT GETS...
...NOBODY LIKES BEING IGNORED.
NOBODY LIKES FEELING INVISIBLE....

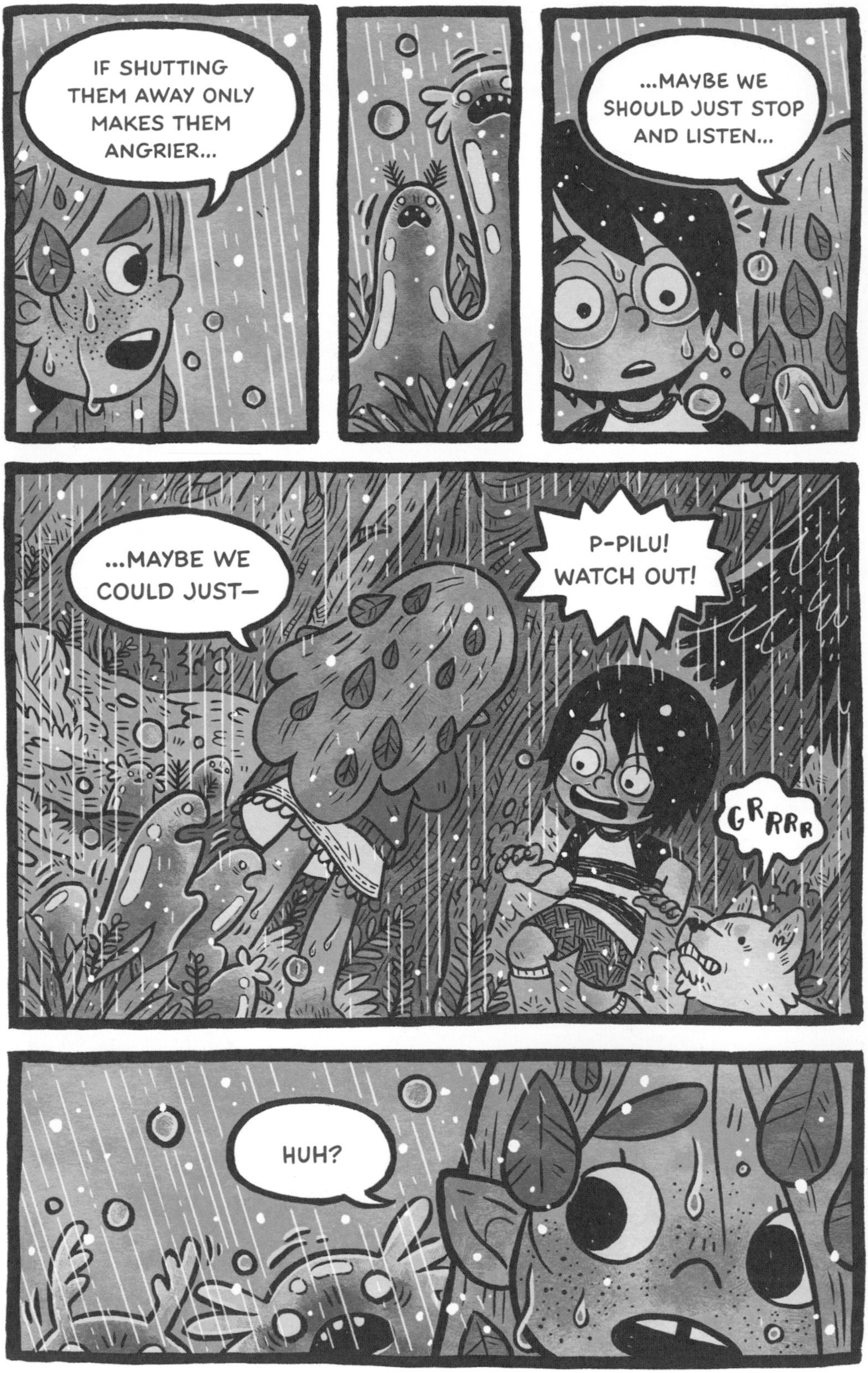
IF SHUTTING THEM AWAY ONLY MAKES THEM ANGRIER...
...MAYBE WE SHOULD JUST STOP AND LISTEN...
...MAYBE WE COULD JUST—
P-PILU! WATCH OUT!
GRRRR
HUH?

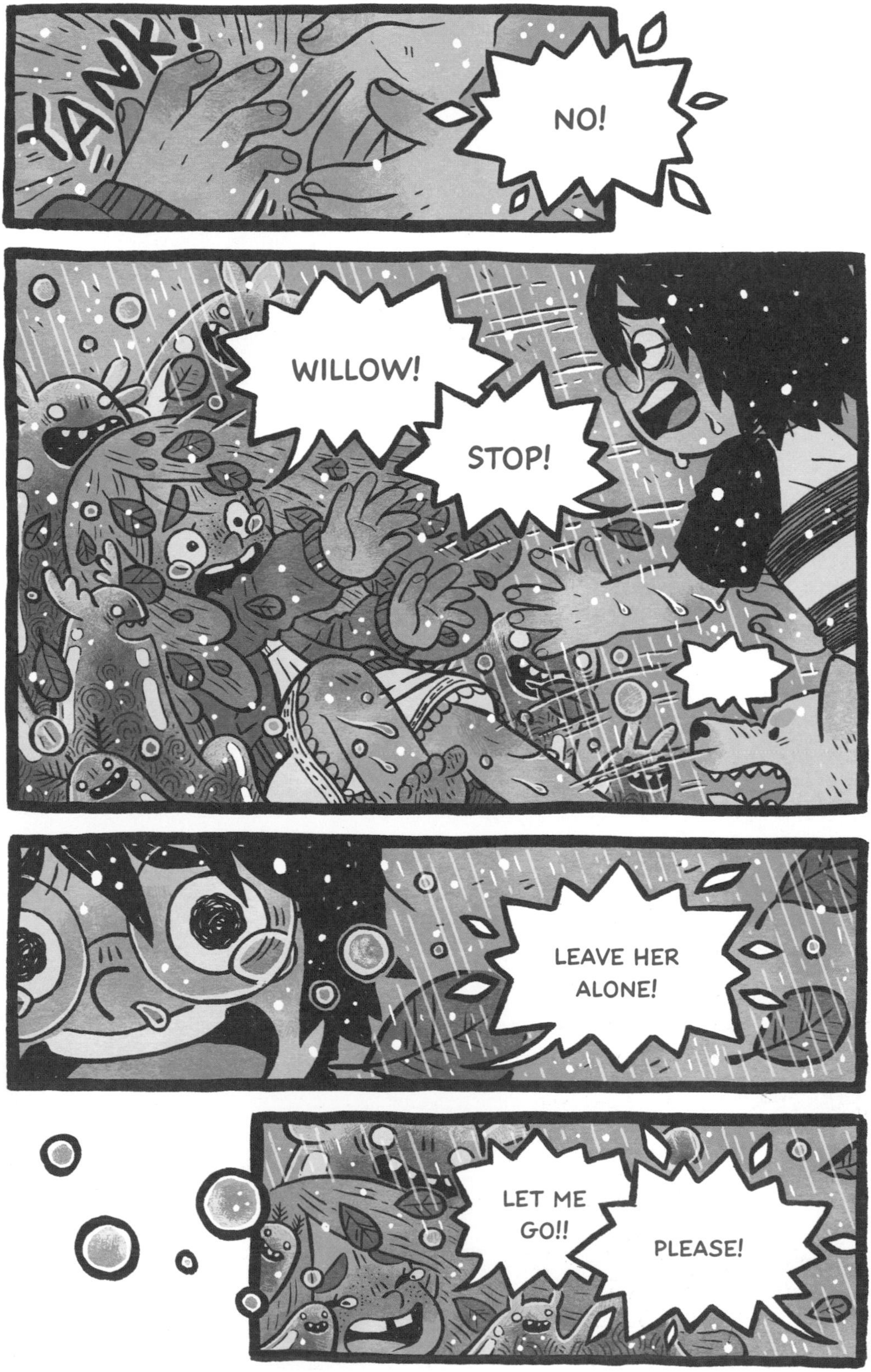
YANK!
NO!
WILLOW!
STOP!
LEAVE HER ALONE!
LET ME GO!!
PLEASE!

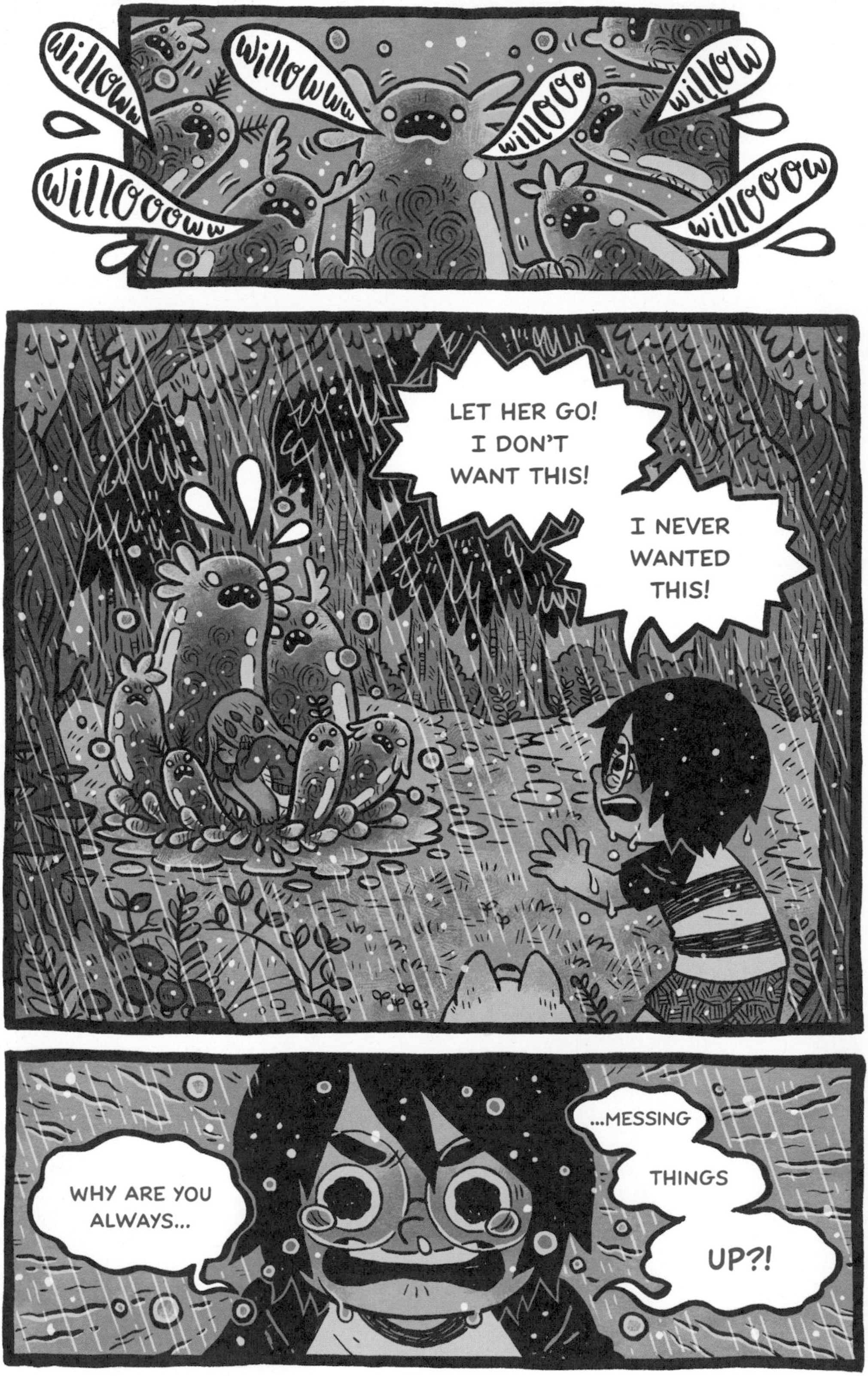
willowww
willowwww
willOOo
willOW
willOOOoww
willOOOw
LET HER GO! I DON'T WANT THIS!
I NEVER WANTED THIS!
WHY ARE YOU ALWAYS...
...MESSING
THINGS
UP?!

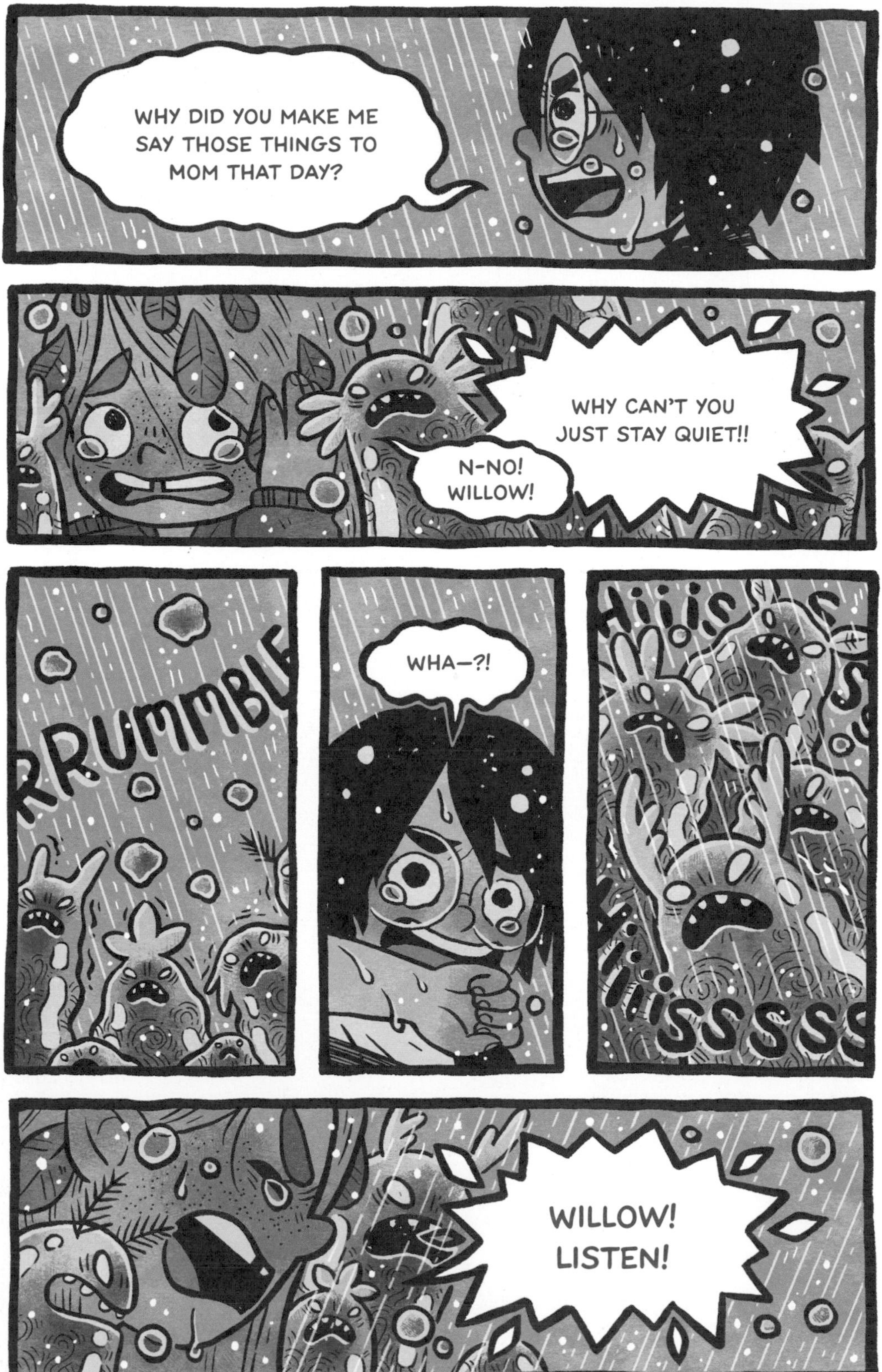
WHY DID YOU MAKE ME SAY THOSE THINGS TO MOM THAT DAY?
WHY CAN'T YOU JUST STAY QUIET!!
N-NO! WILLOW!
RRUMMBLE
WHA—?!
HIIISSSSS
WILLOW! LISTEN!

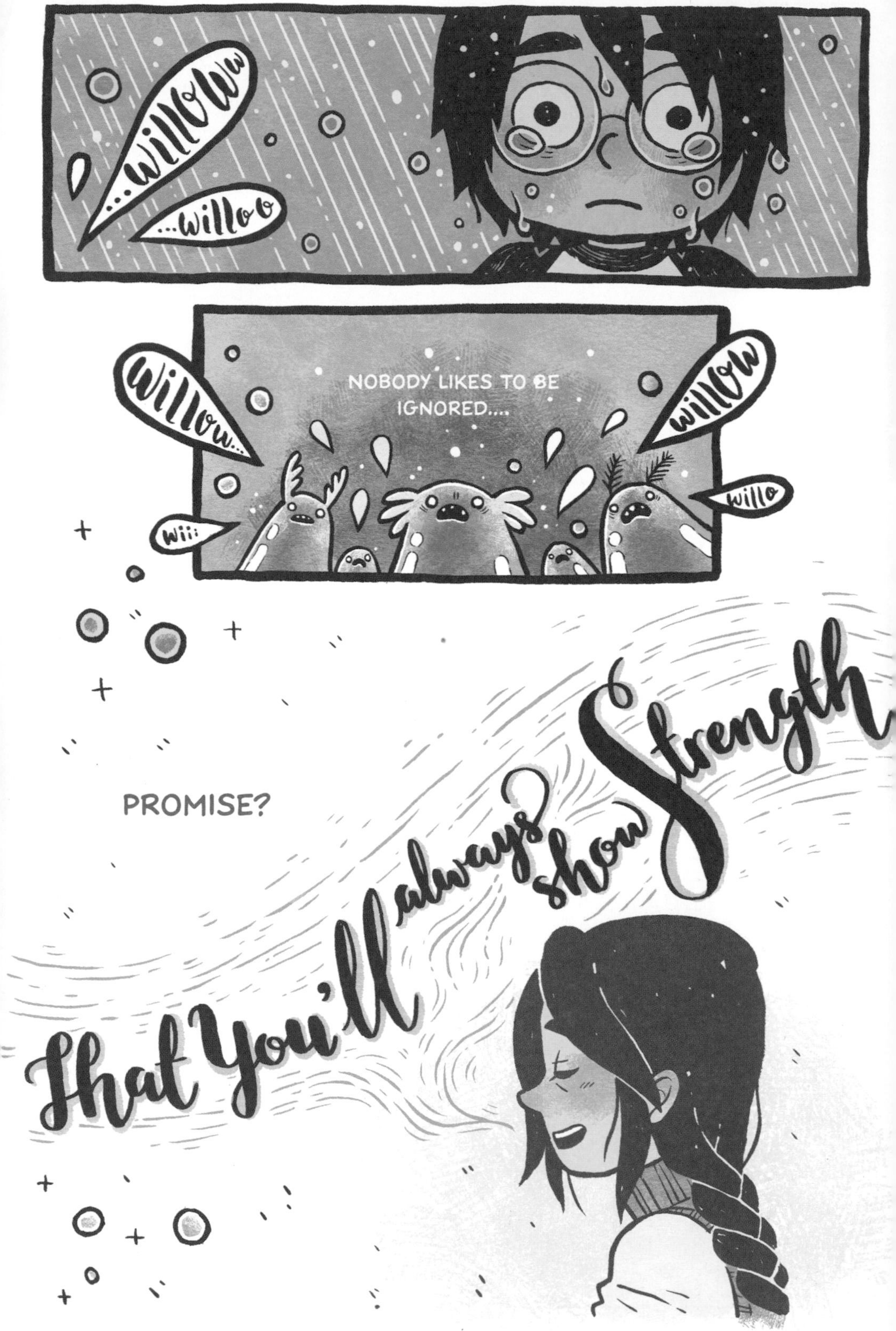
...willoww
...willoo
willow...
NOBODY LIKES TO BE IGNORED....
willow
willo
wiii
PROMISE?
That you'll always show strength

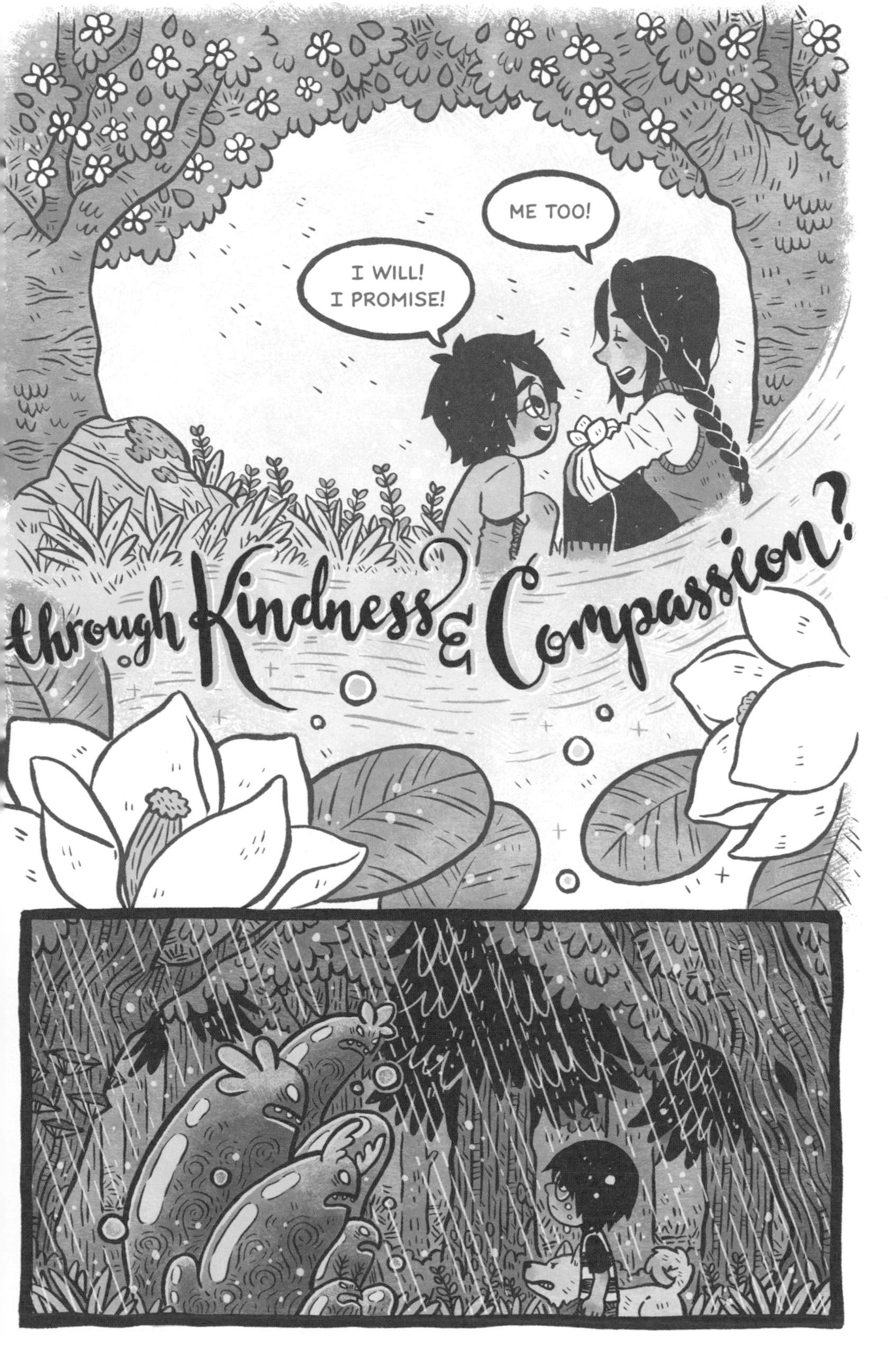

I WILL!
I PROMISE!
ME TOO!
through Kindness & Compassion?

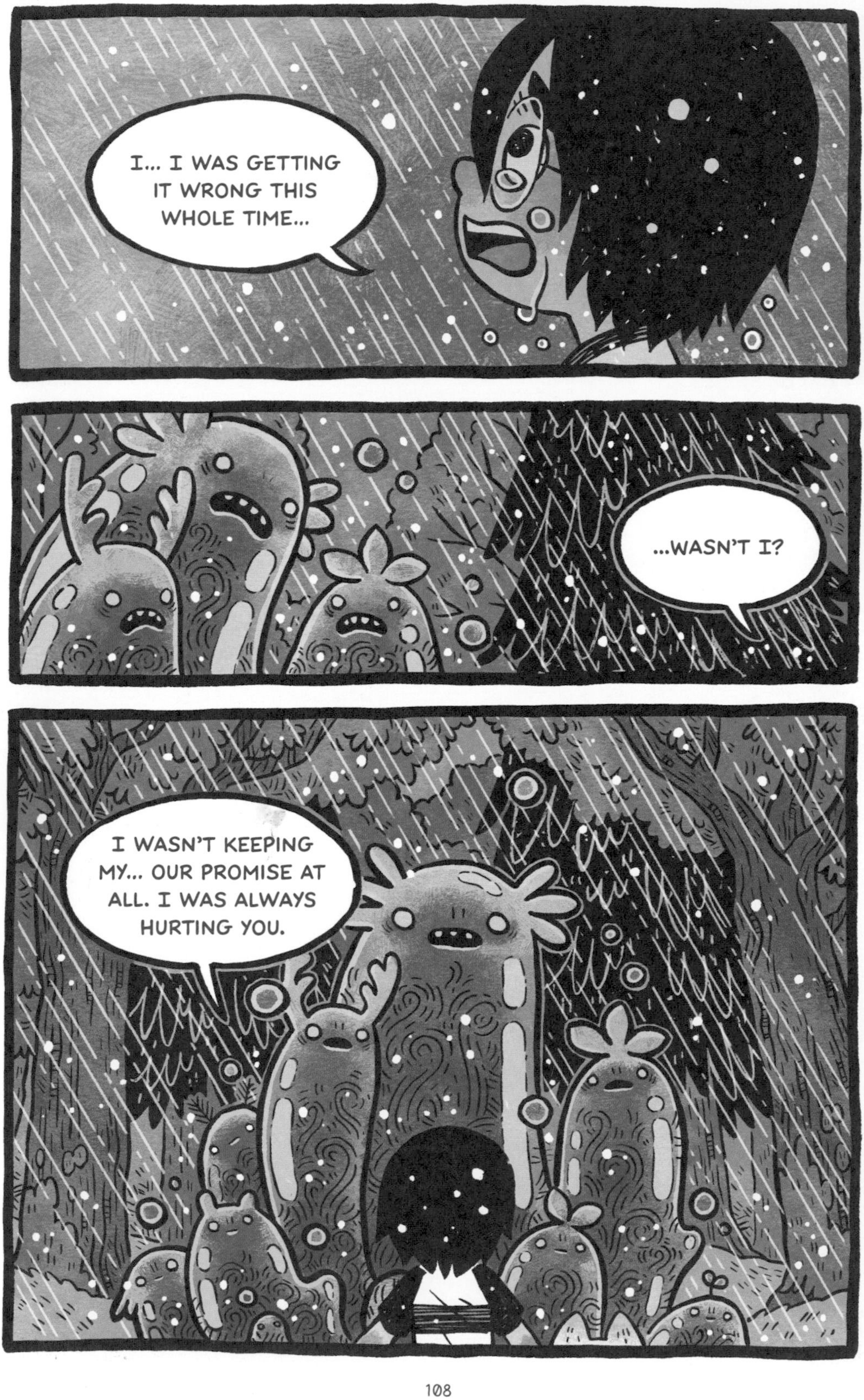
I... I WAS GETTING IT WRONG THIS WHOLE TIME...
...WASN'T I?
I WASN'T KEEPING MY... OUR PROMISE AT ALL. I WAS ALWAYS HURTING YOU.

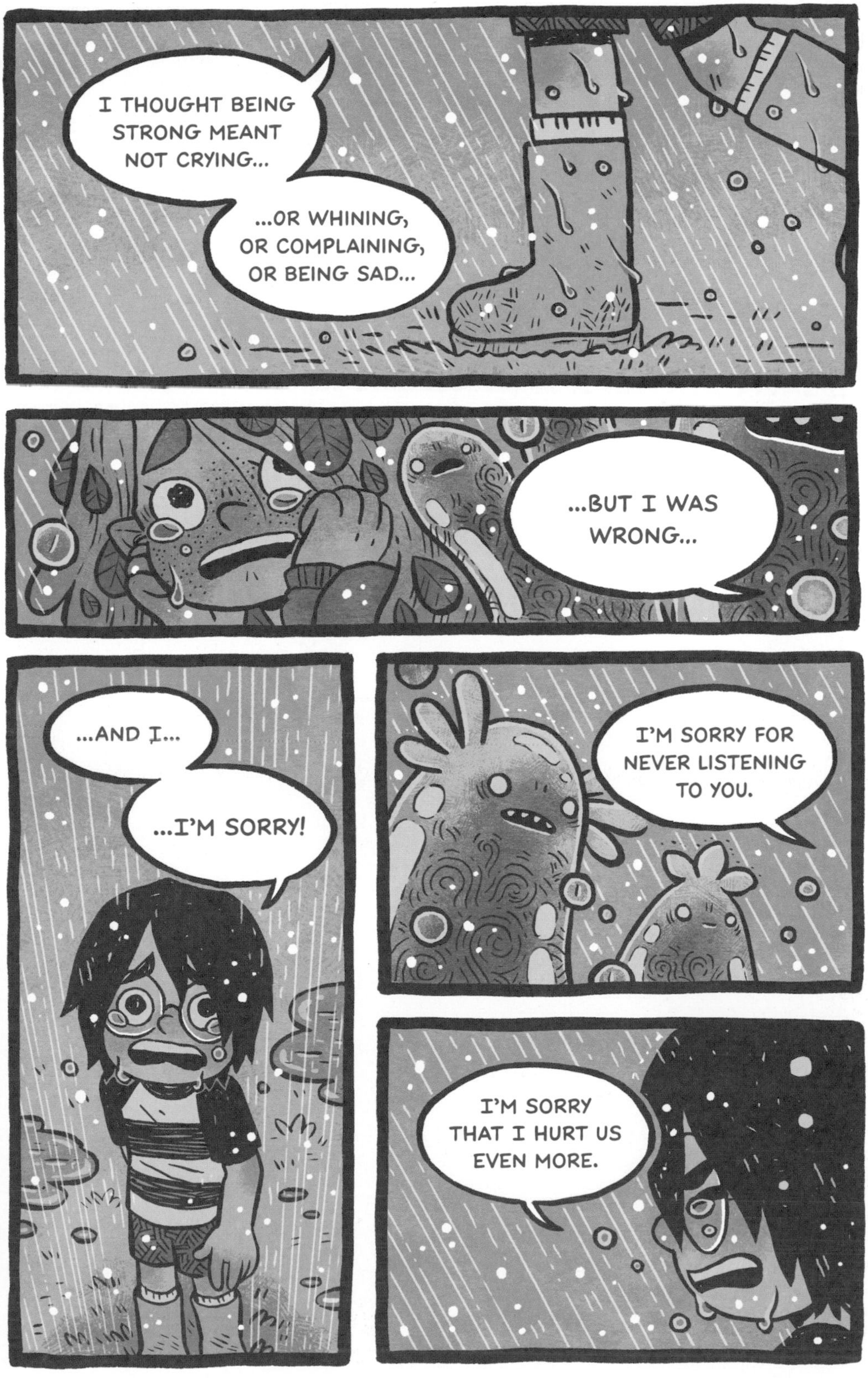
I THOUGHT BEING STRONG MEANT NOT CRYING...
...OR WHINING, OR COMPLAINING, OR BEING SAD...
...BUT I WAS WRONG...
...AND I...
...I'M SORRY!
I'M SORRY FOR NEVER LISTENING TO YOU.
I'M SORRY THAT I HURT US EVEN MORE.

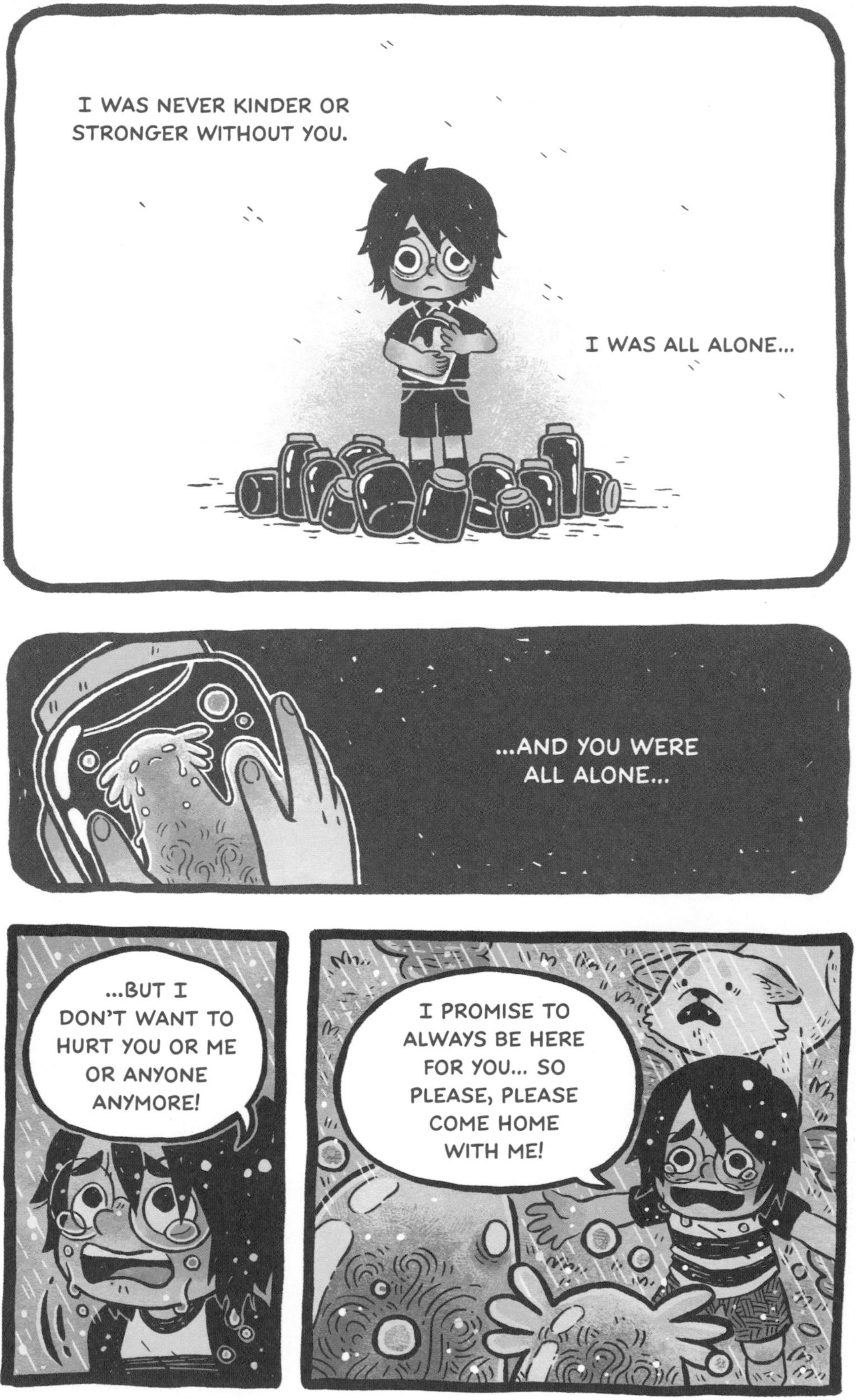
I WAS NEVER KINDER OR STRONGER WITHOUT YOU.
I WAS ALL ALONE...
...AND YOU WERE ALL ALONE...
...BUT I DON'T WANT TO HURT YOU OR ME OR ANYONE ANYMORE!
I PROMISE TO ALWAYS BE HERE FOR YOU... SO PLEASE, PLEASE COME HOME WITH ME!

PLEASE!

RRRRUUUMMBBL!

RRRUUUMm

BBBLLE

W-WILLOW!

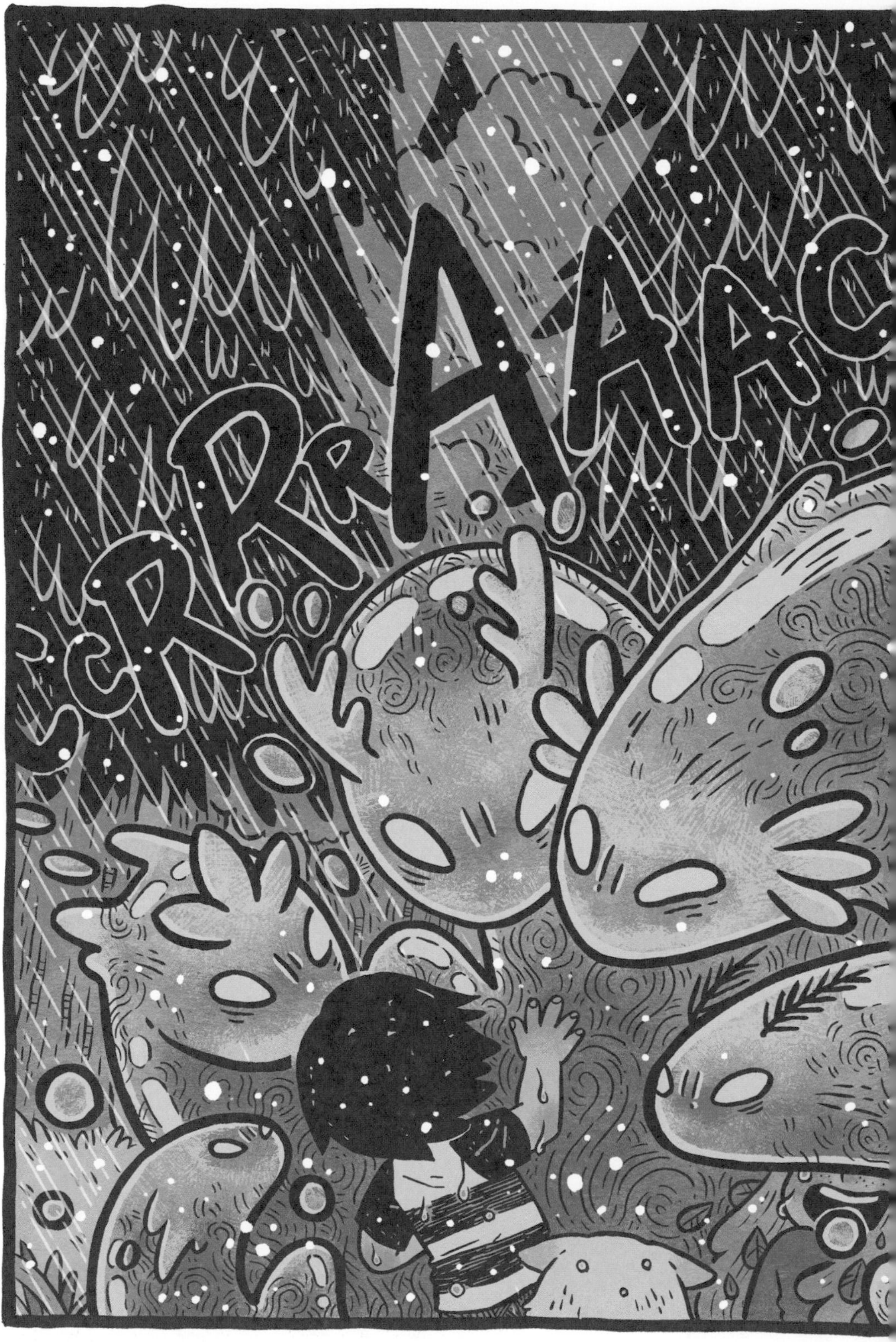
CRRRAAAC

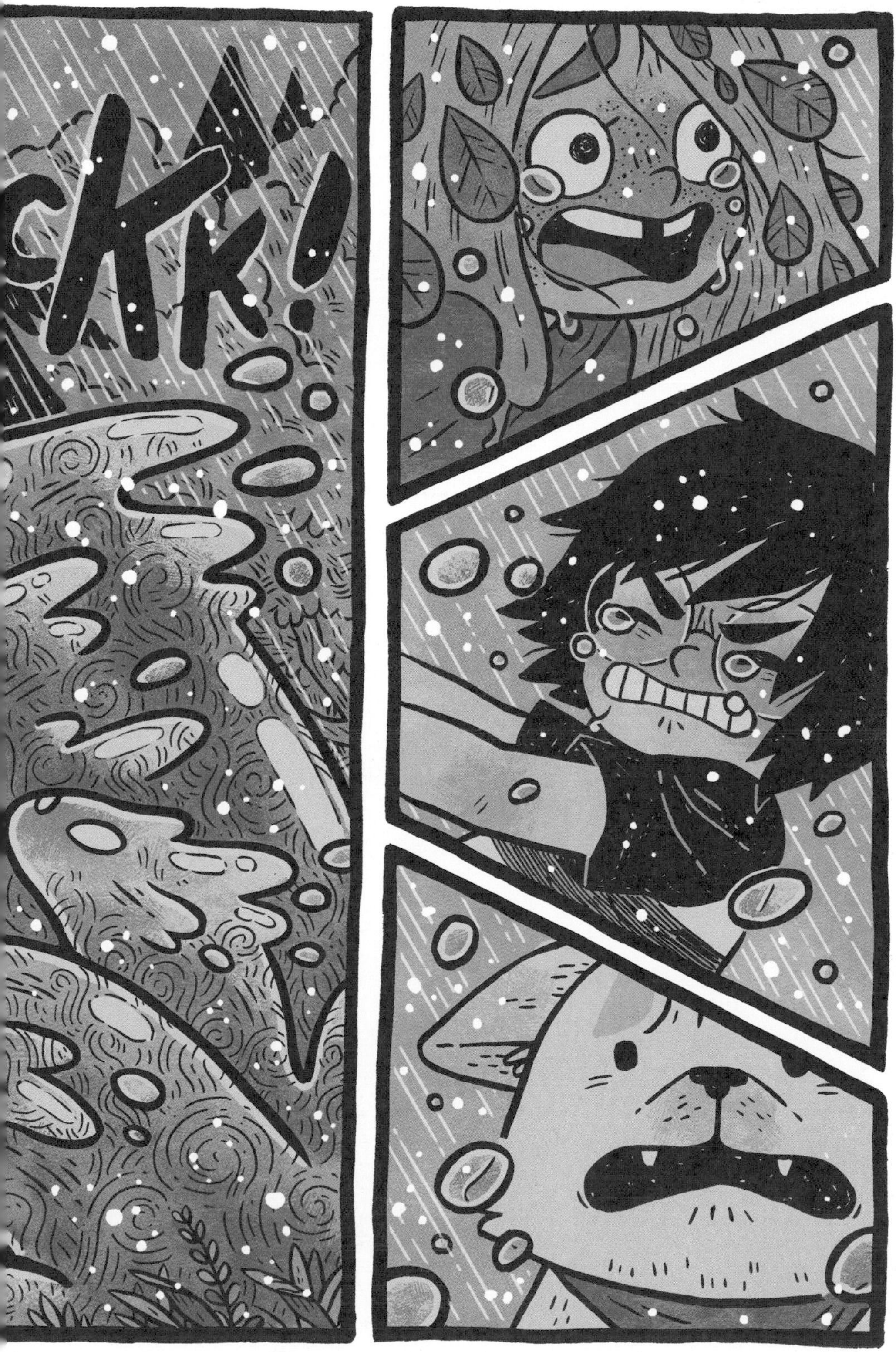
CKK!

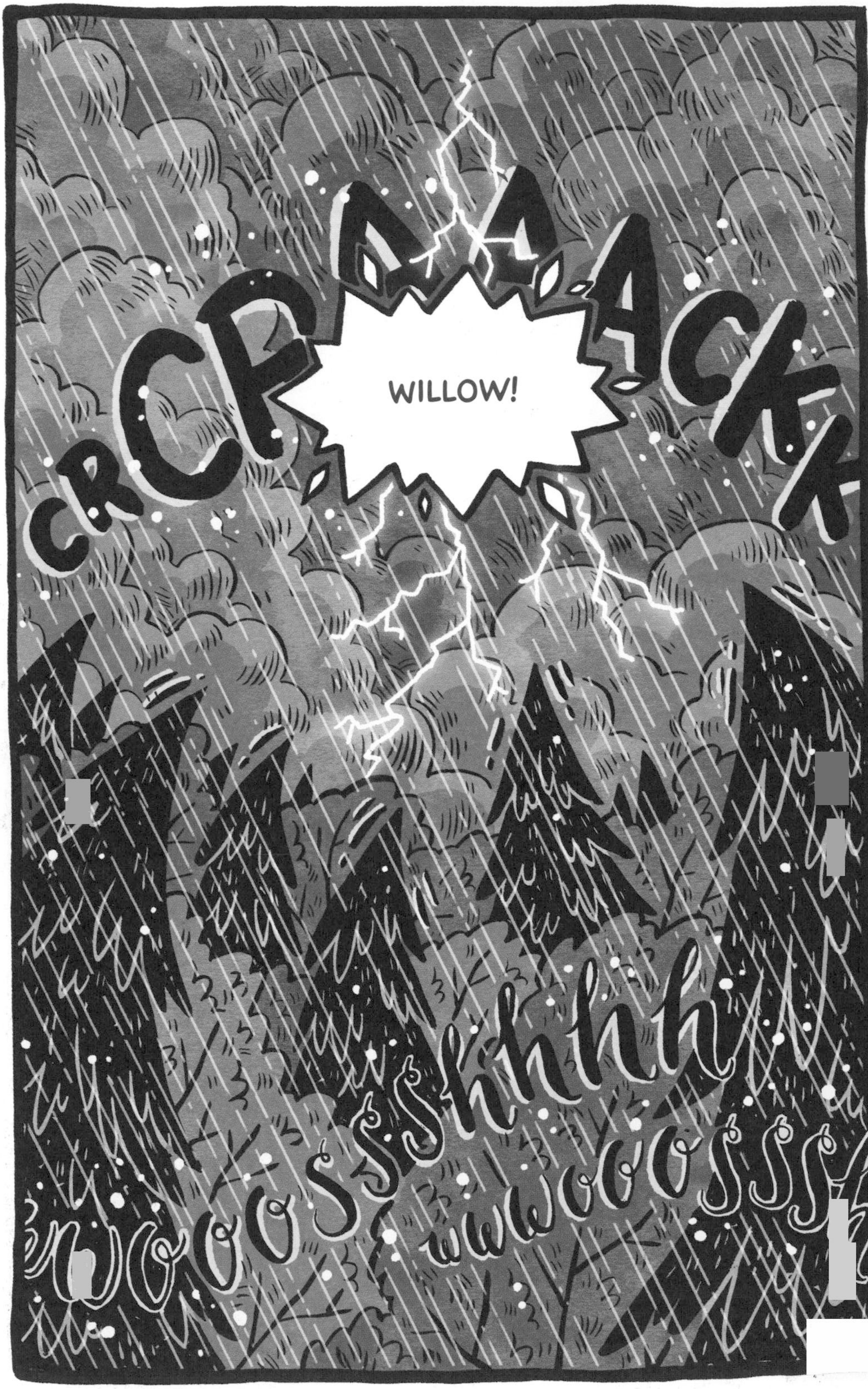
WILLOW!

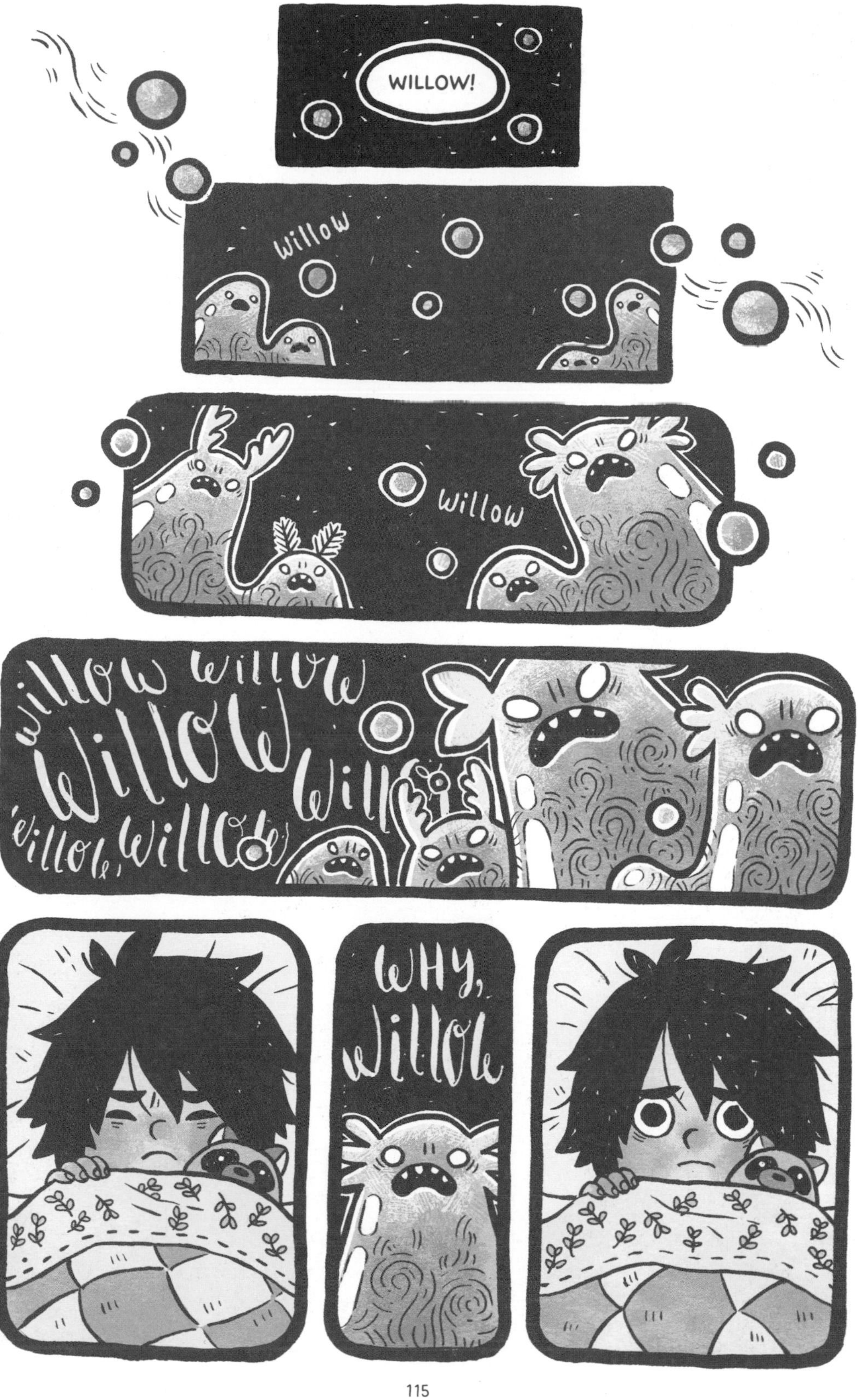
WILLOW!
willow
willow
willow willow
Willow
WHY, WILLOW

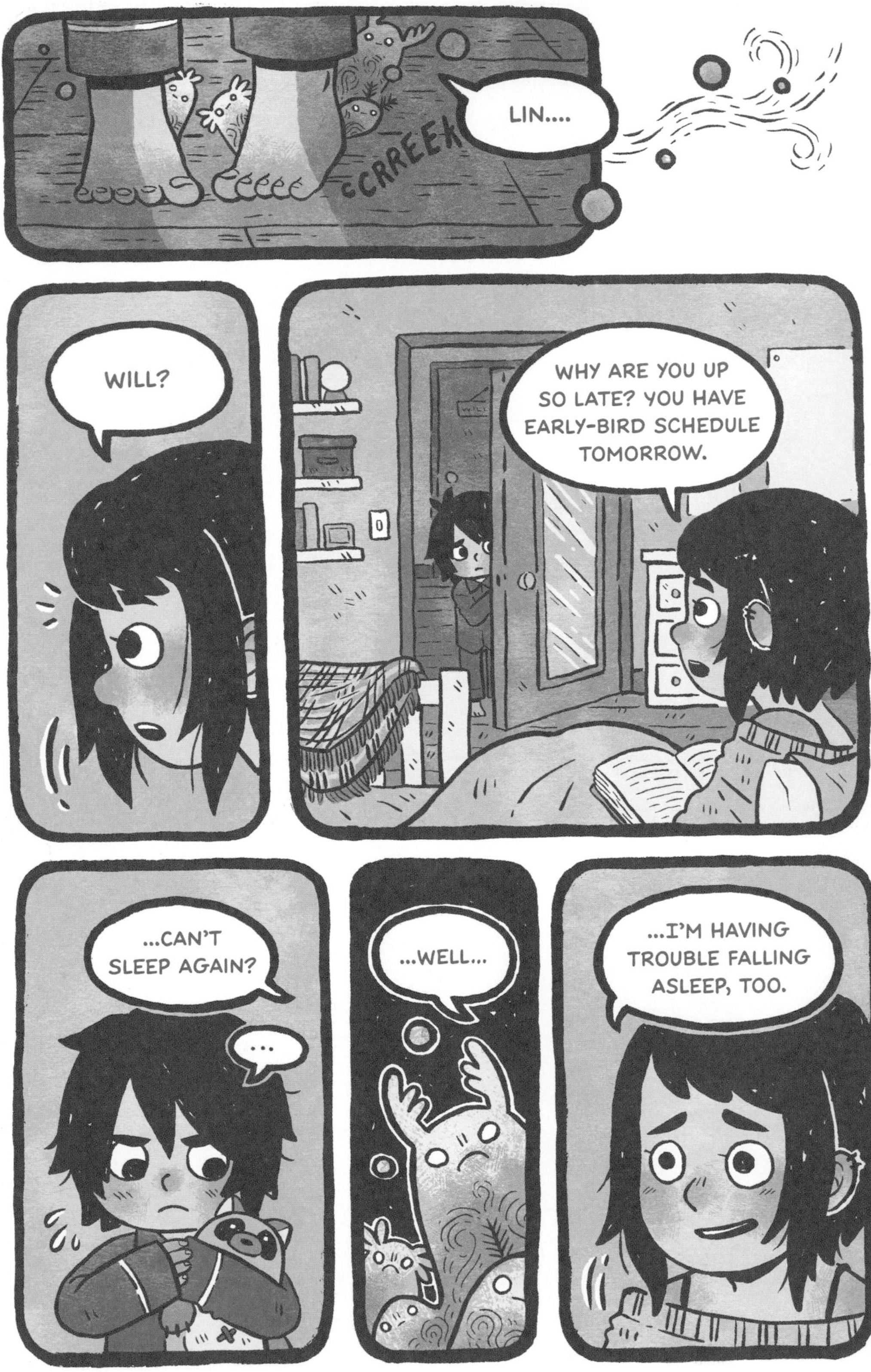
CRREEK
LIN....
WILL?
WHY ARE YOU UP SO LATE? YOU HAVE EARLY-BIRD SCHEDULE TOMORROW.
...CAN'T SLEEP AGAIN?
...
...WELL...
...I'M HAVING TROUBLE FALLING ASLEEP, TOO.

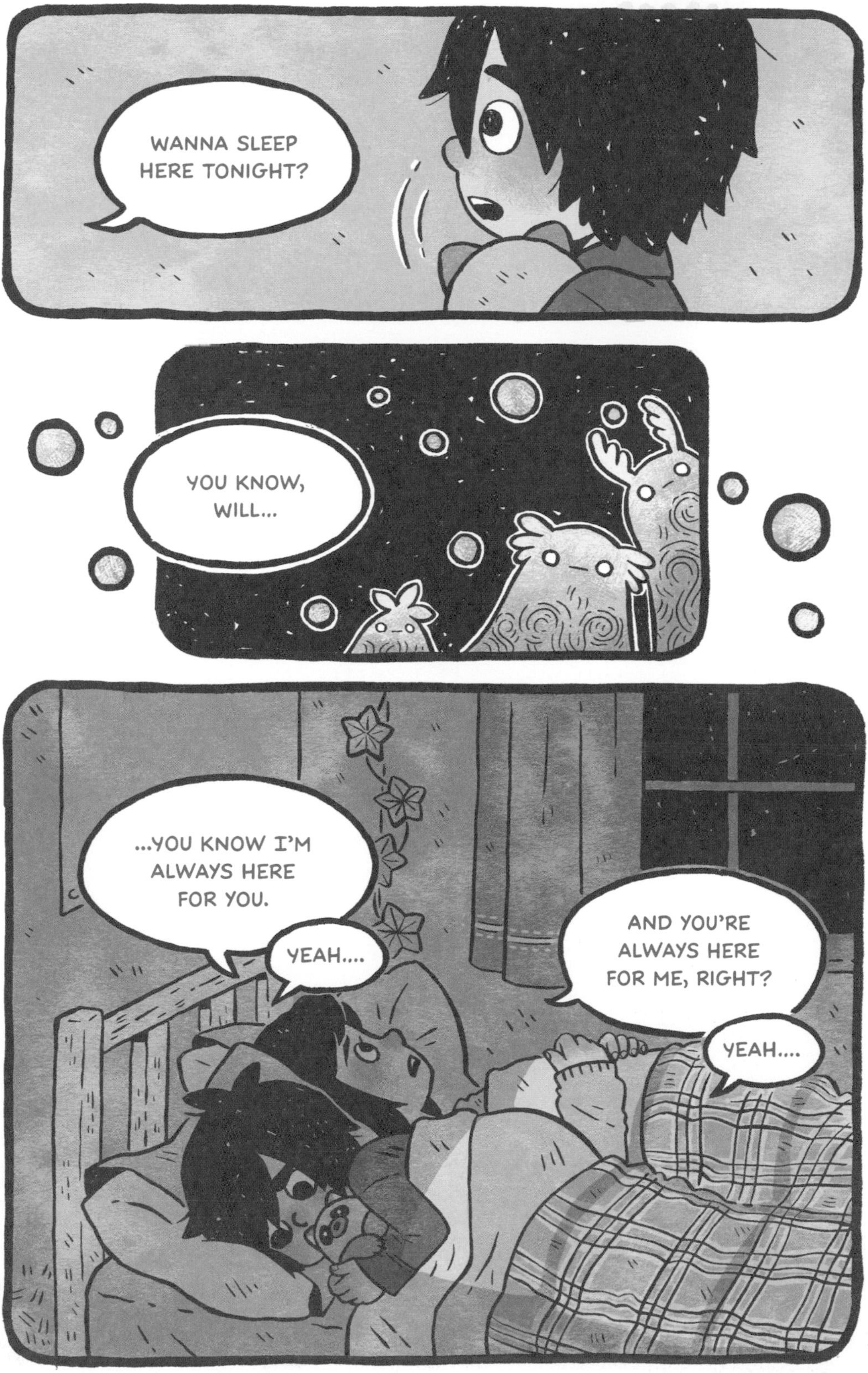
WANNA SLEEP HERE TONIGHT?
YOU KNOW, WILL...
...YOU KNOW I'M ALWAYS HERE FOR YOU.
YEAH....
AND YOU'RE ALWAYS HERE FOR ME, RIGHT?
YEAH....

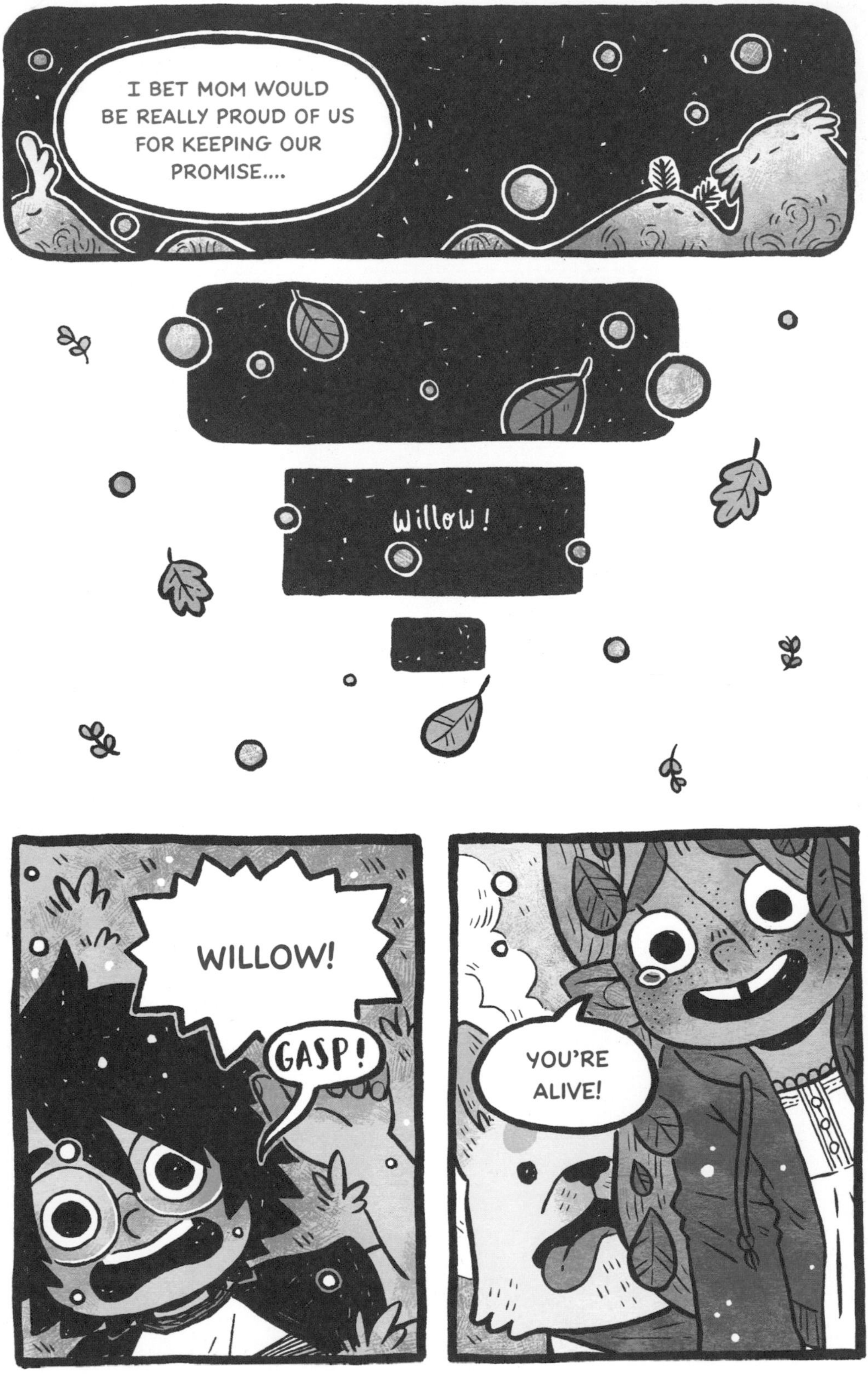
I BET MOM WOULD BE REALLY PROUD OF US FOR KEEPING OUR PROMISE....
Willow!
WILLOW!
GASP!
YOU'RE ALIVE!

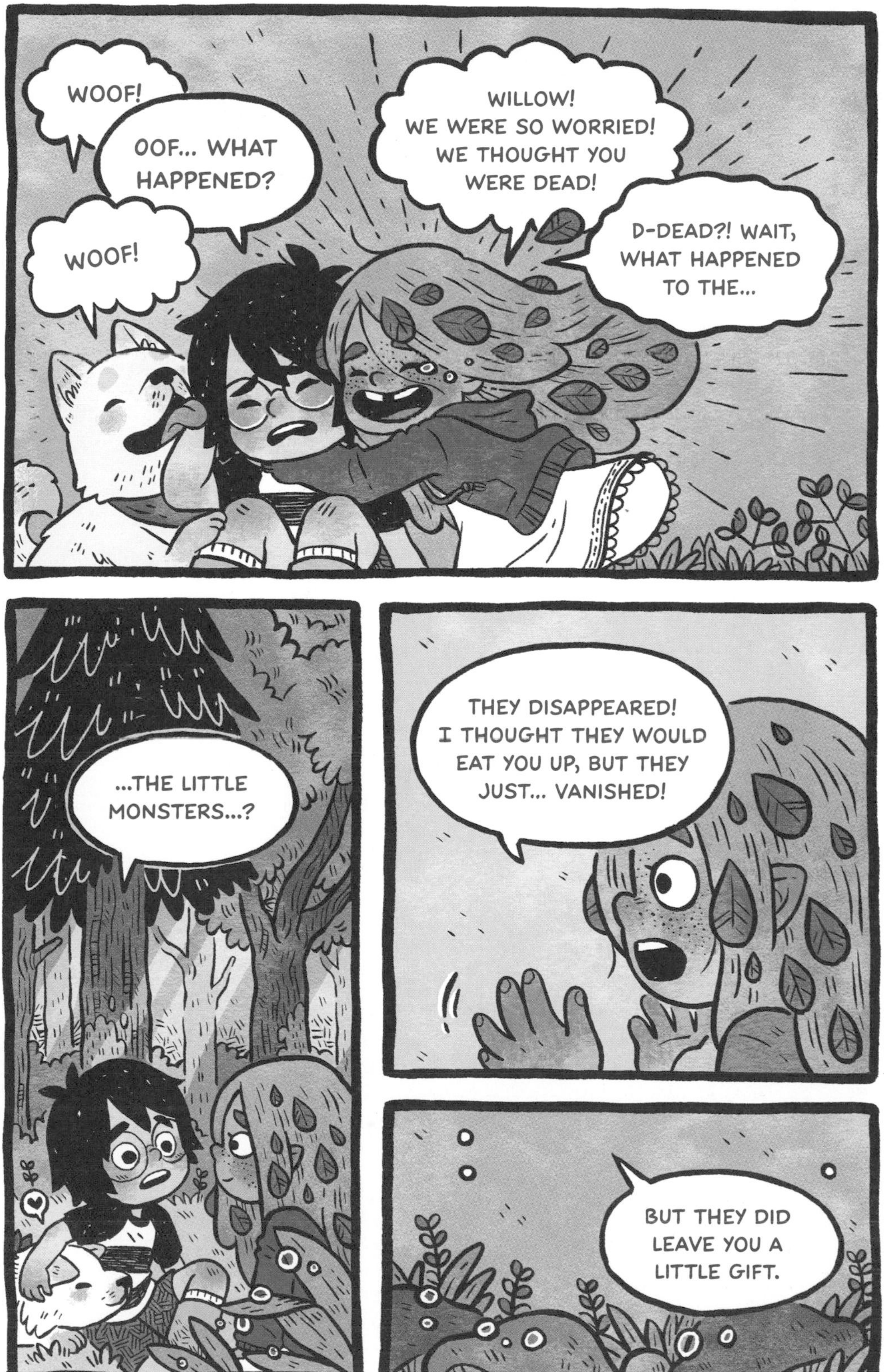
WOOF!
OOF... WHAT HAPPENED?
WOOF!
WILLOW! WE WERE SO WORRIED! WE THOUGHT YOU WERE DEAD!
D-DEAD?! WAIT, WHAT HAPPENED TO THE...
...THE LITTLE MONSTERS...?
THEY DISAPPEARED! I THOUGHT THEY WOULD EAT YOU UP, BUT THEY JUST... VANISHED!
BUT THEY DID LEAVE YOU A LITTLE GIFT.

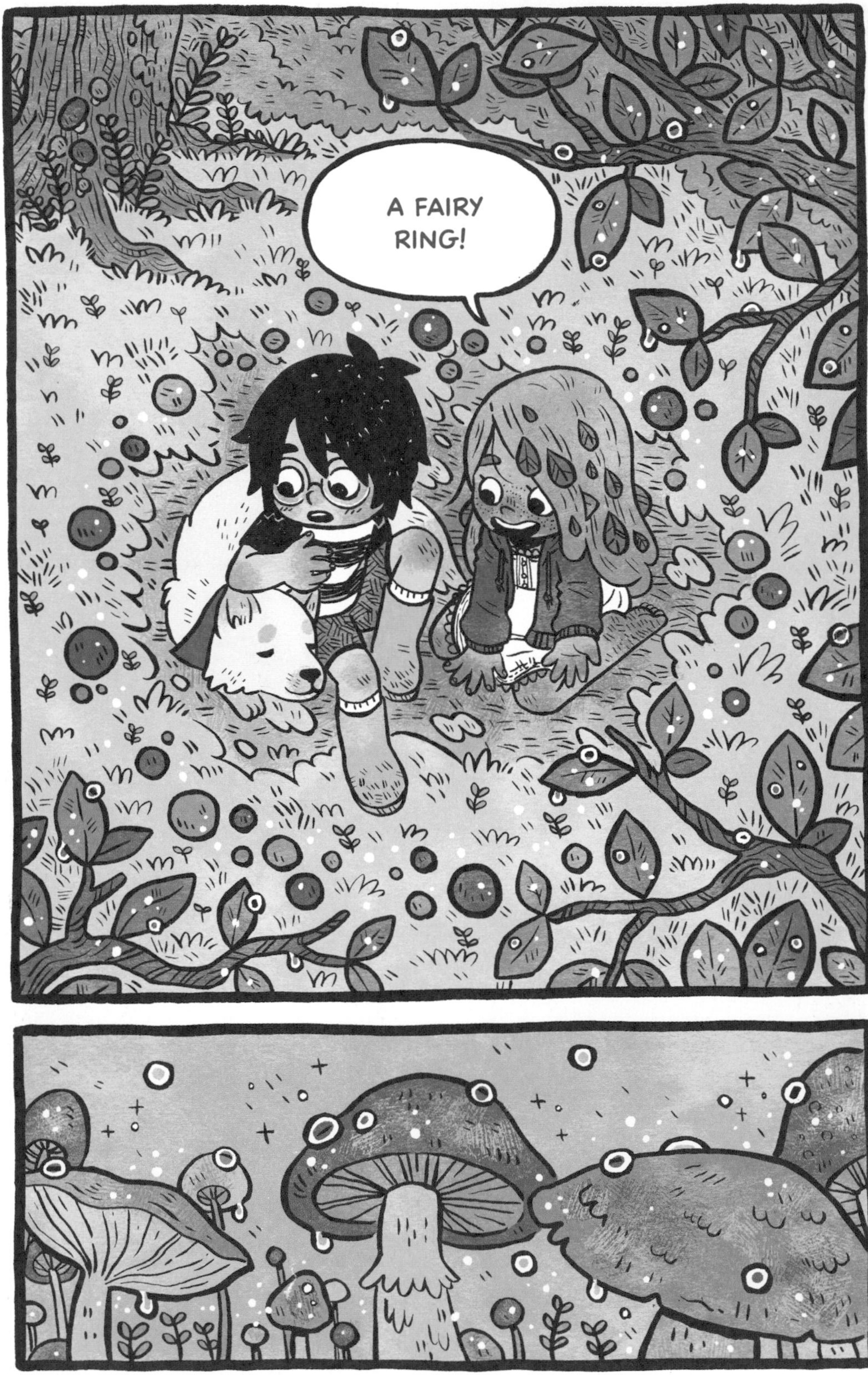
A FAIRY RING!

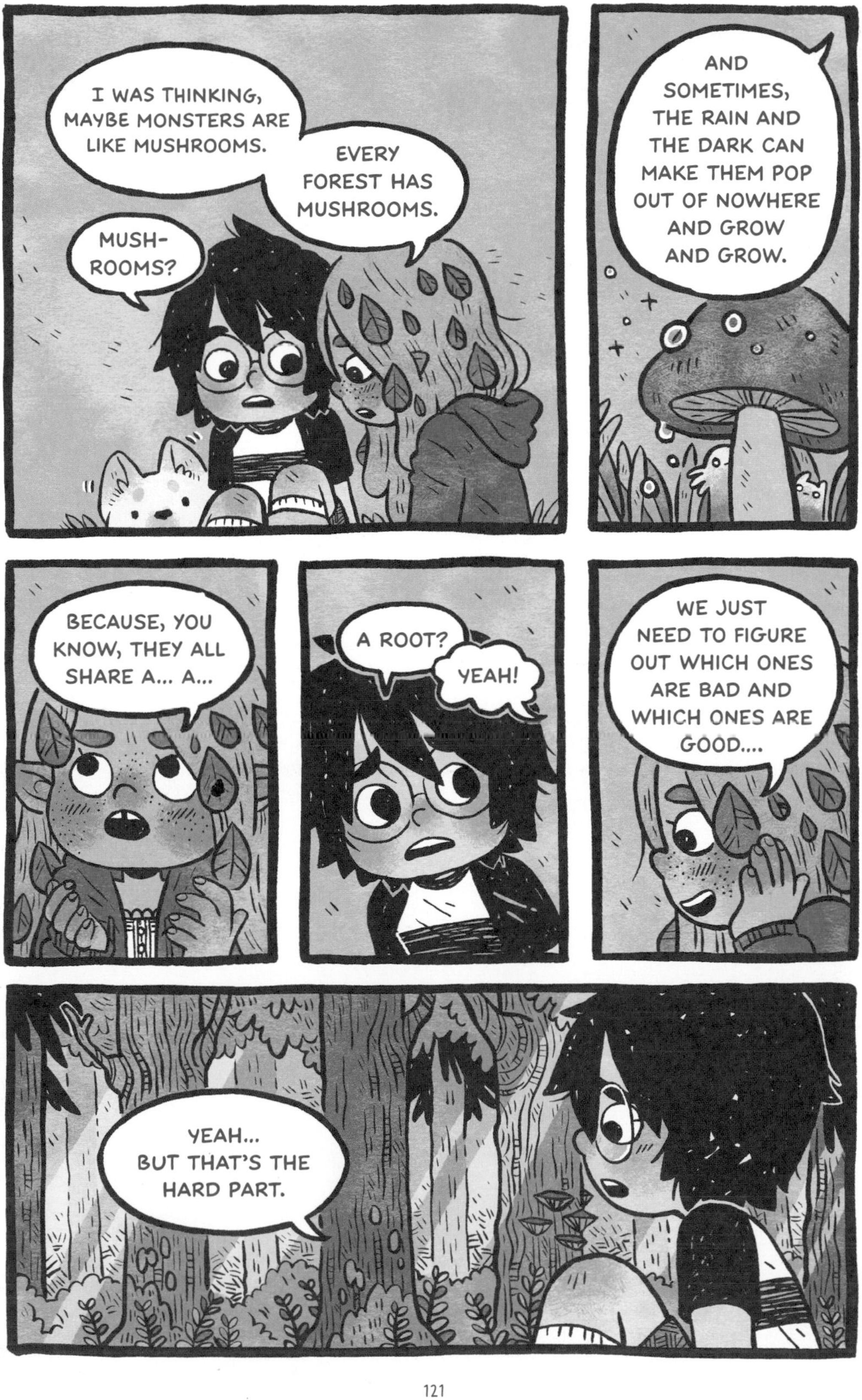
I WAS THINKING, MAYBE MONSTERS ARE LIKE MUSHROOMS.
MUSH-ROOMS?
EVERY FOREST HAS MUSHROOMS.
AND SOMETIMES, THE RAIN AND THE DARK CAN MAKE THEM POP OUT OF NOWHERE AND GROW AND GROW.
BECAUSE, YOU KNOW, THEY ALL SHARE A... A...
A ROOT?
YEAH!
WE JUST NEED TO FIGURE OUT WHICH ONES ARE BAD AND WHICH ONES ARE GOOD....
YEAH... BUT THAT'S THE HARD PART.

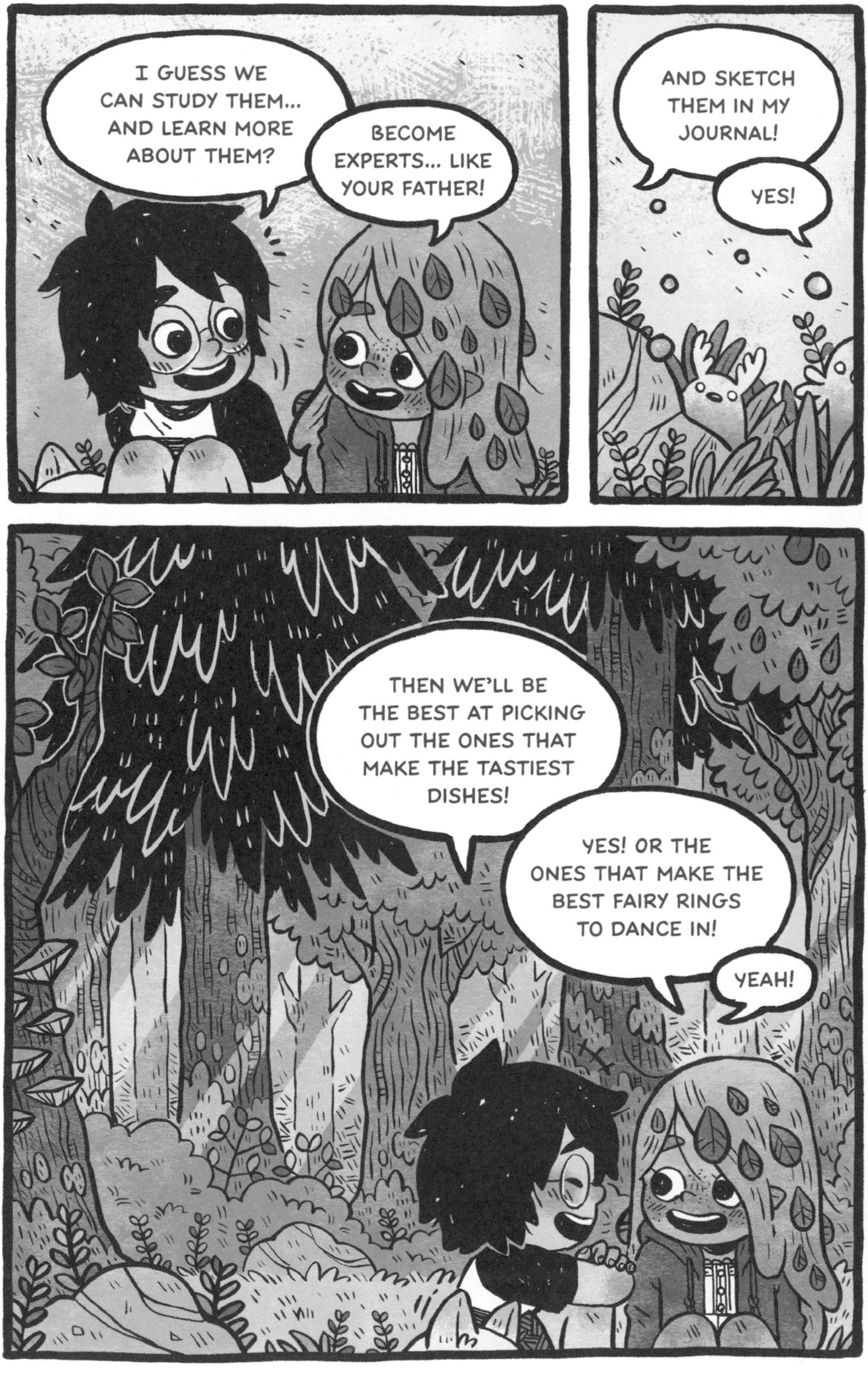
I GUESS WE CAN STUDY THEM... AND LEARN MORE ABOUT THEM?
BECOME EXPERTS... LIKE YOUR FATHER!
AND SKETCH THEM IN MY JOURNAL!
YES!
THEN WE'LL BE THE BEST AT PICKING OUT THE ONES THAT MAKE THE TASTIEST DISHES!
YES! OR THE ONES THAT MAKE THE BEST FAIRY RINGS TO DANCE IN!
YEAH!

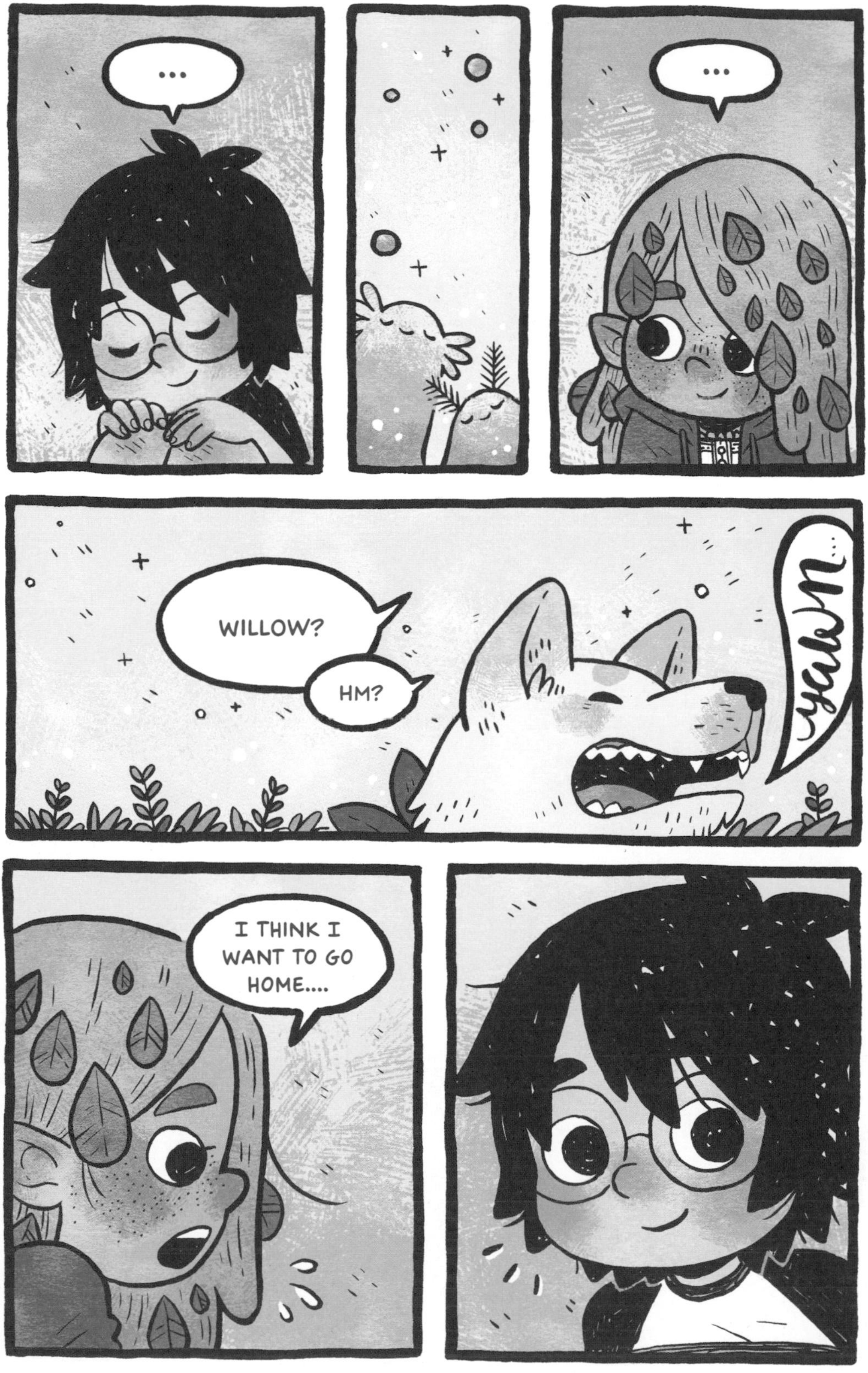
...
...
WILLOW?
HM?
yawn...
I THINK I WANT TO GO HOME....

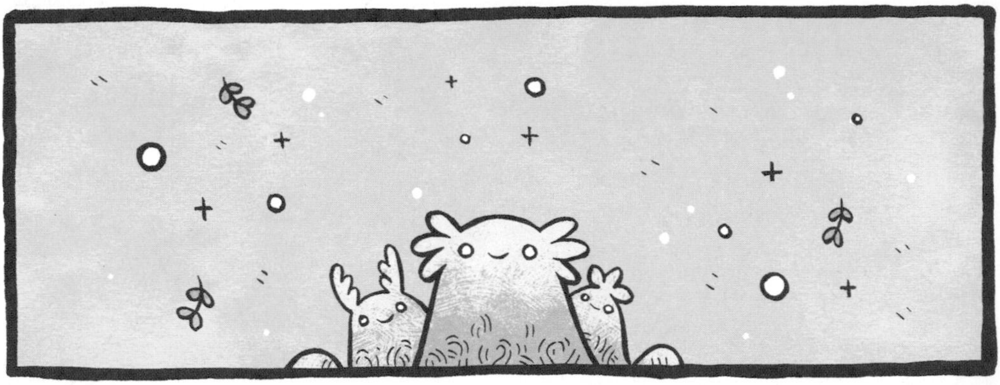

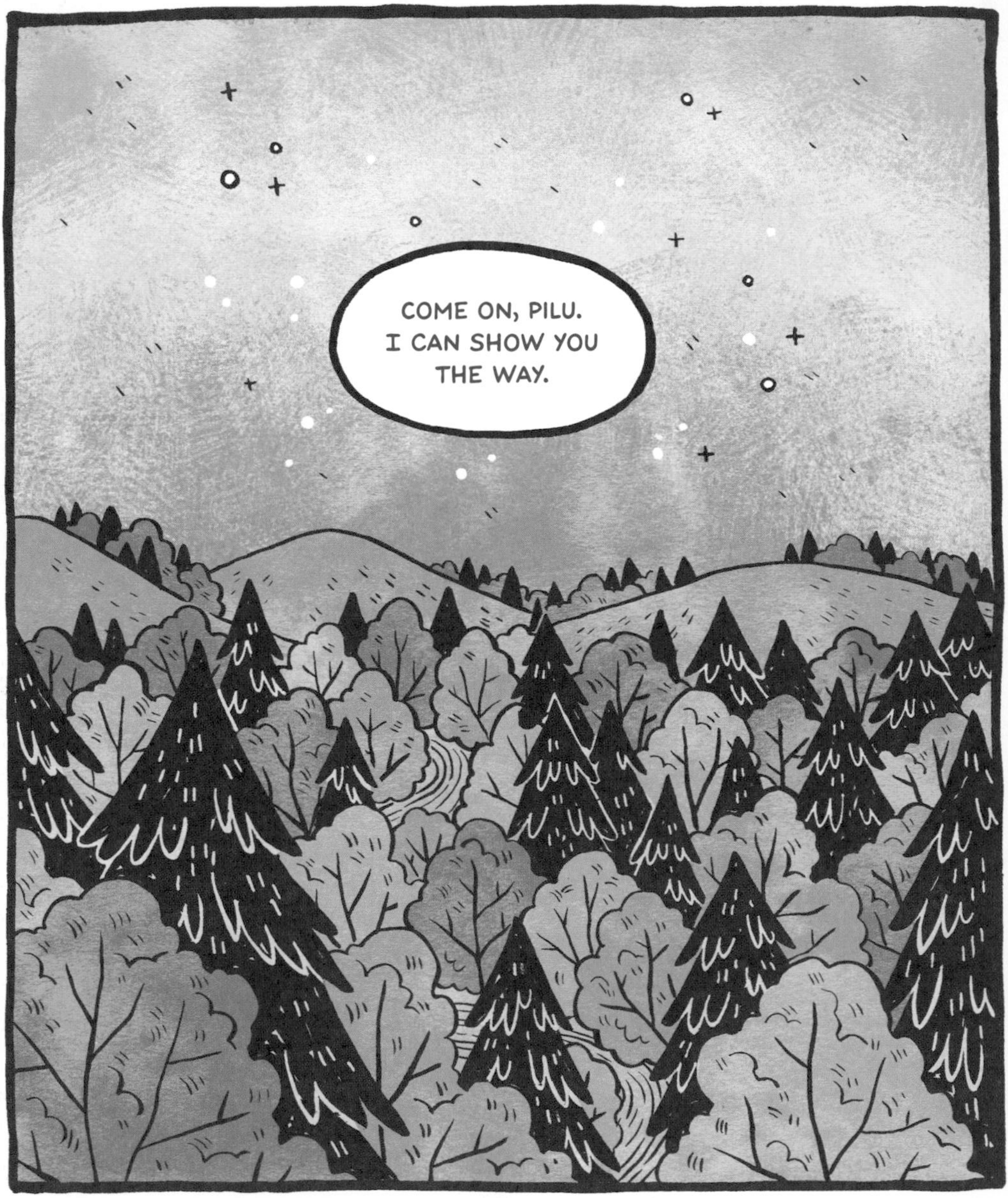
COME ON, PILU. I CAN SHOW YOU THE WAY.

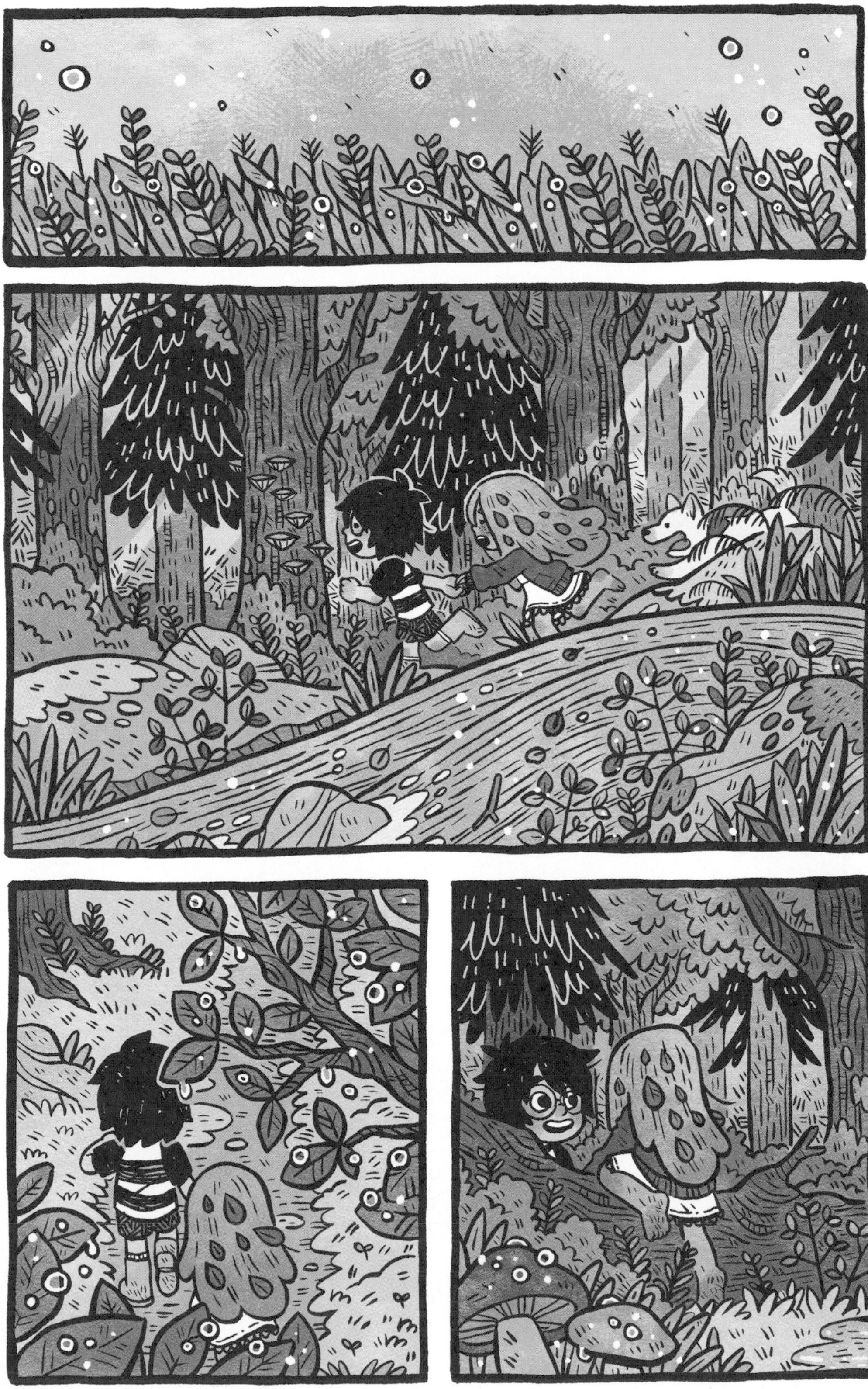

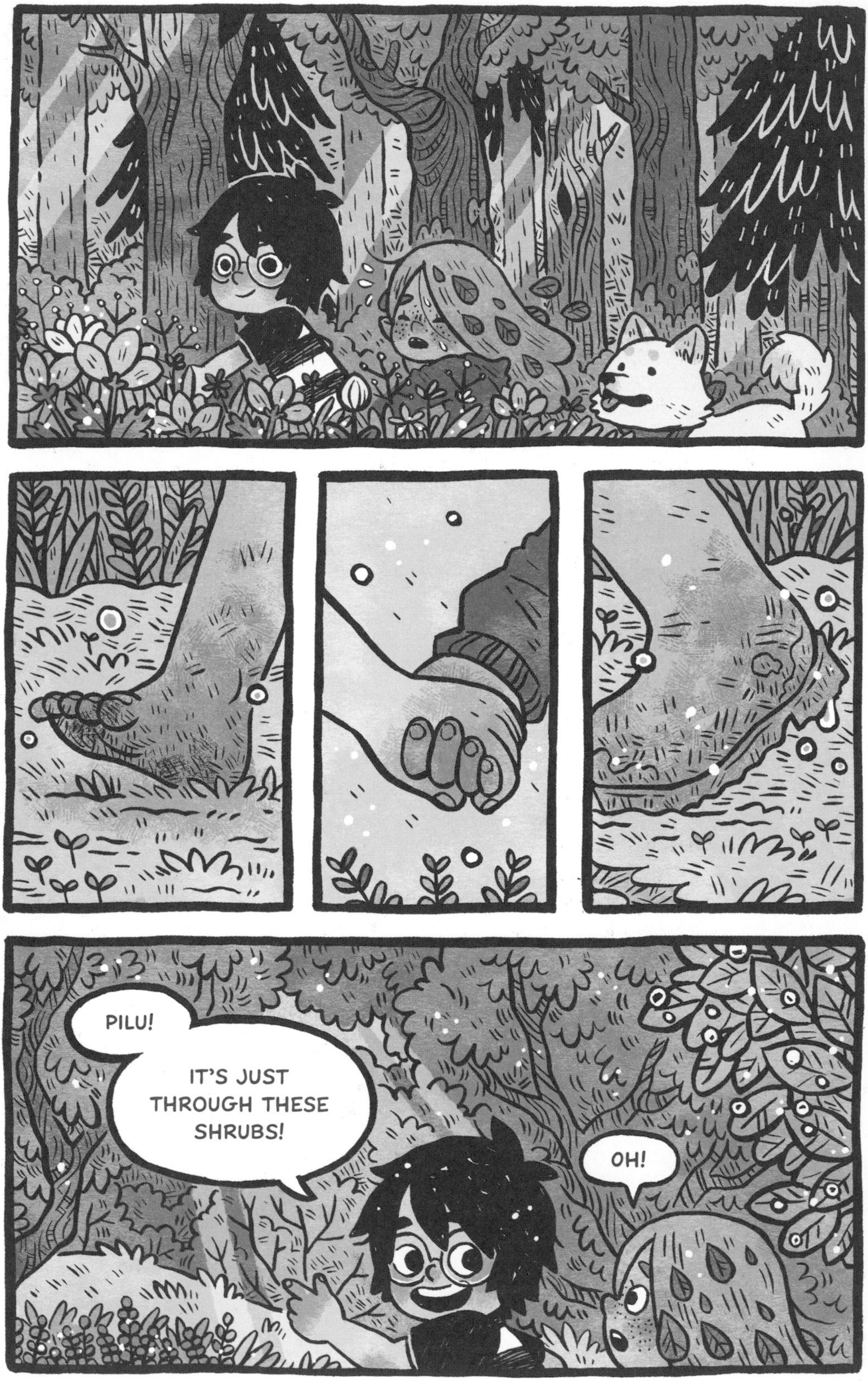
PILU!
IT'S JUST THROUGH THESE SHRUBS!
OH!

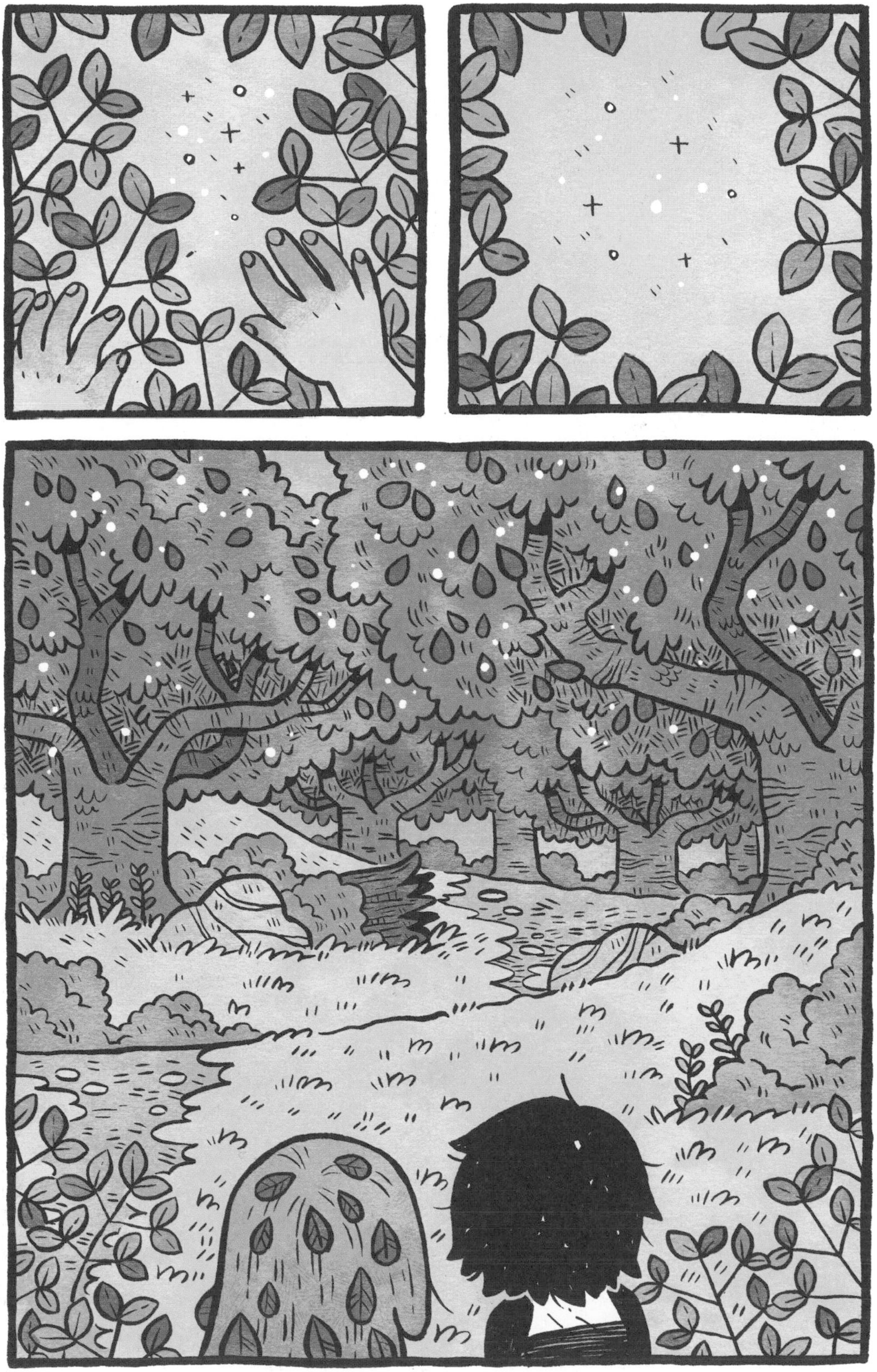

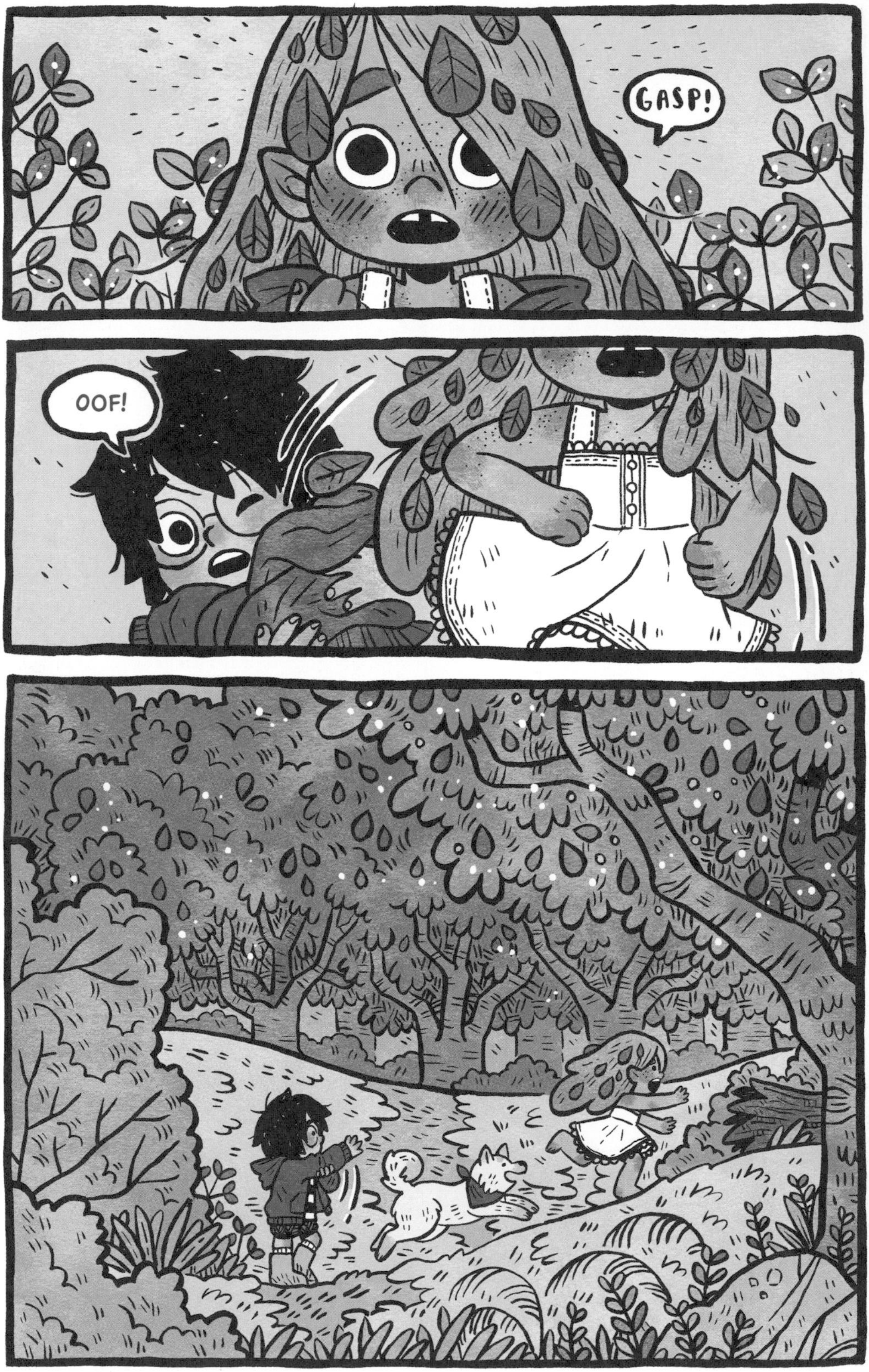
GASP!
OOF!

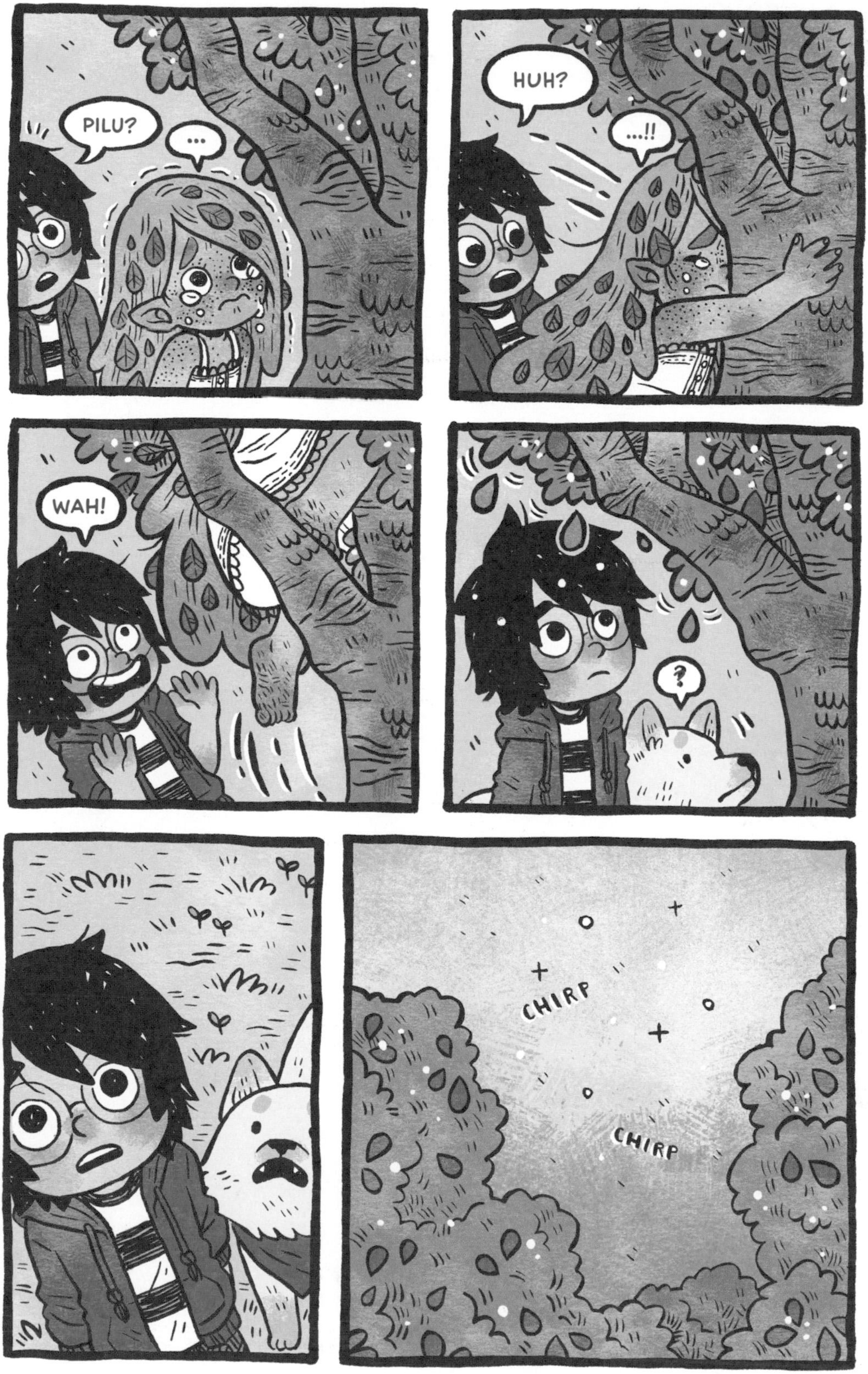
PILU?
...
HUH?
...!!
WAH!
?
CHIRP
CHIRP

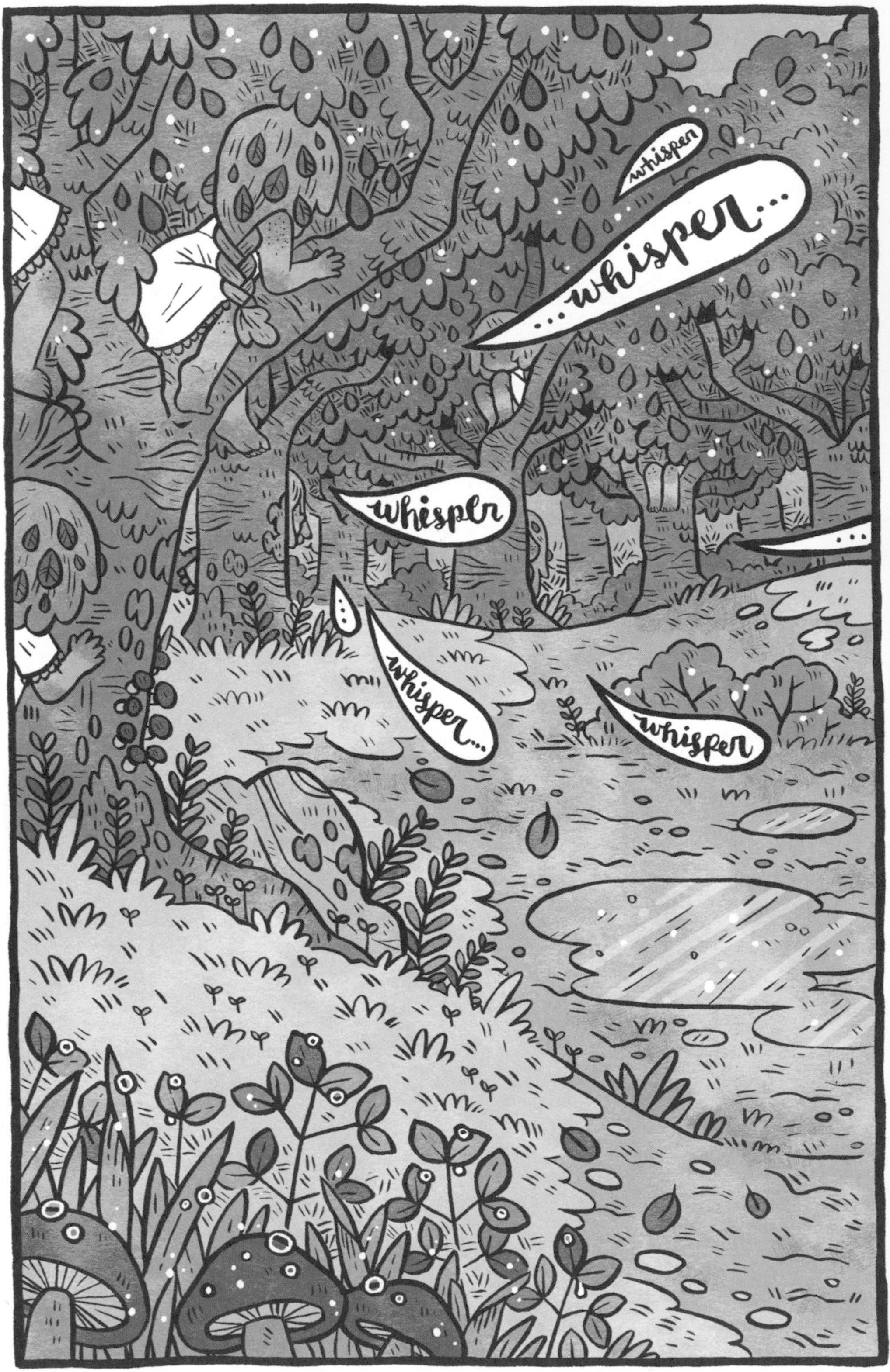
whisper
...whisper...
whisper
whisper...
whisper

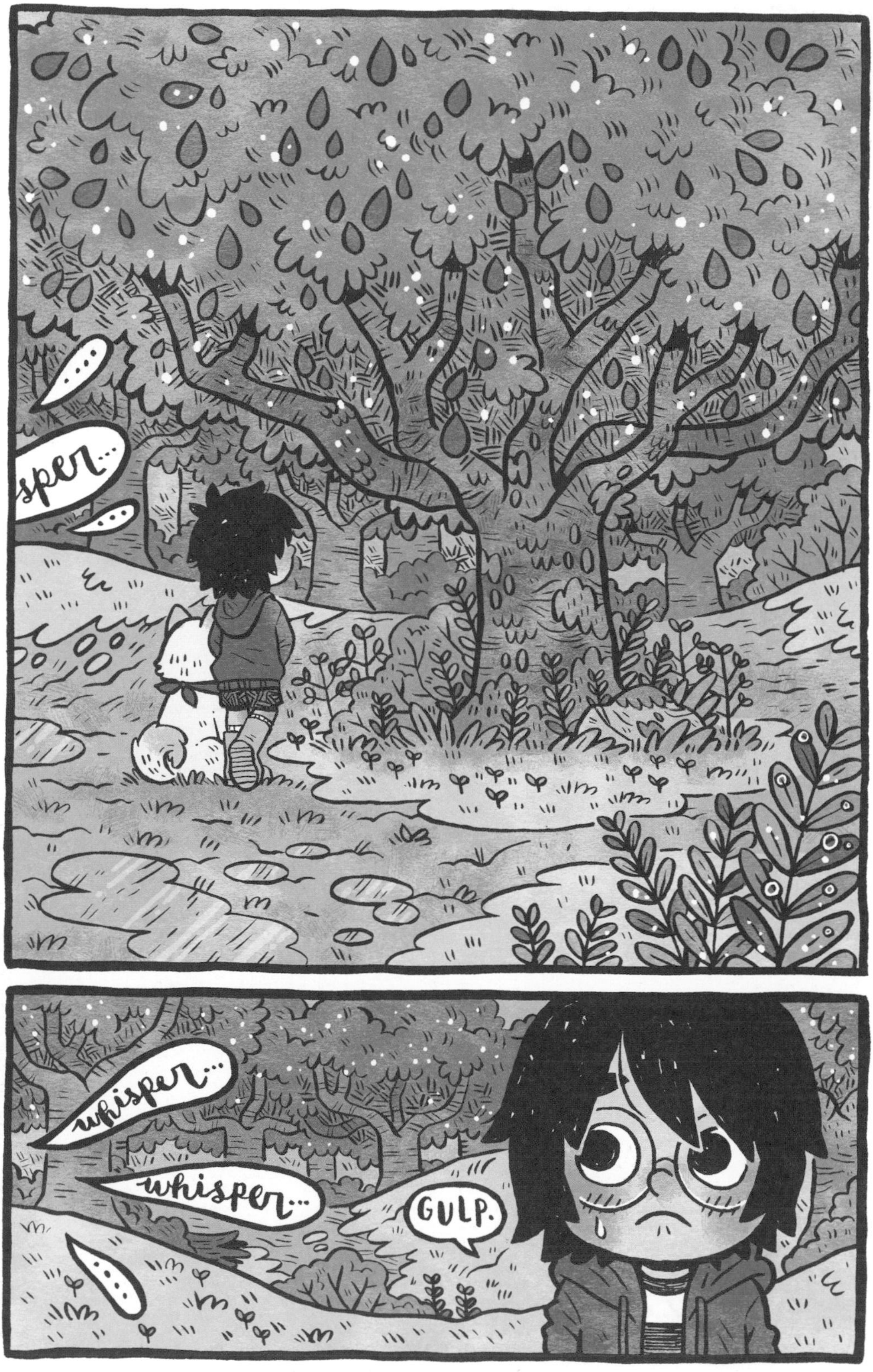
...
sper...
whisper...
whisper...
GULP.

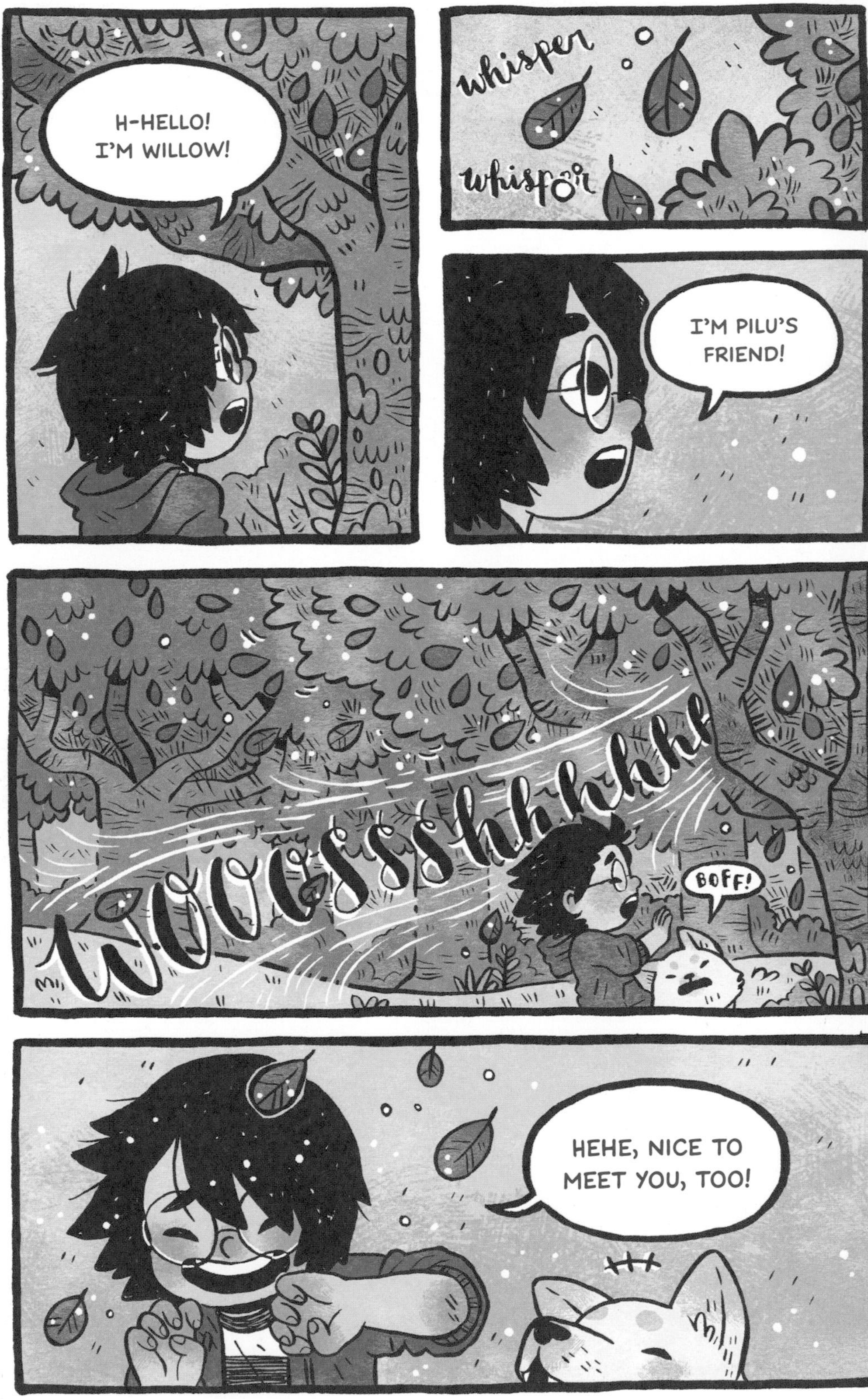

H-HELLO! I'M WILLOW!
whisper
whispoir
I'M PILU'S FRIEND!
WOOOSSSHHHHH
BOFF!
HEHE, NICE TO MEET YOU, TOO!

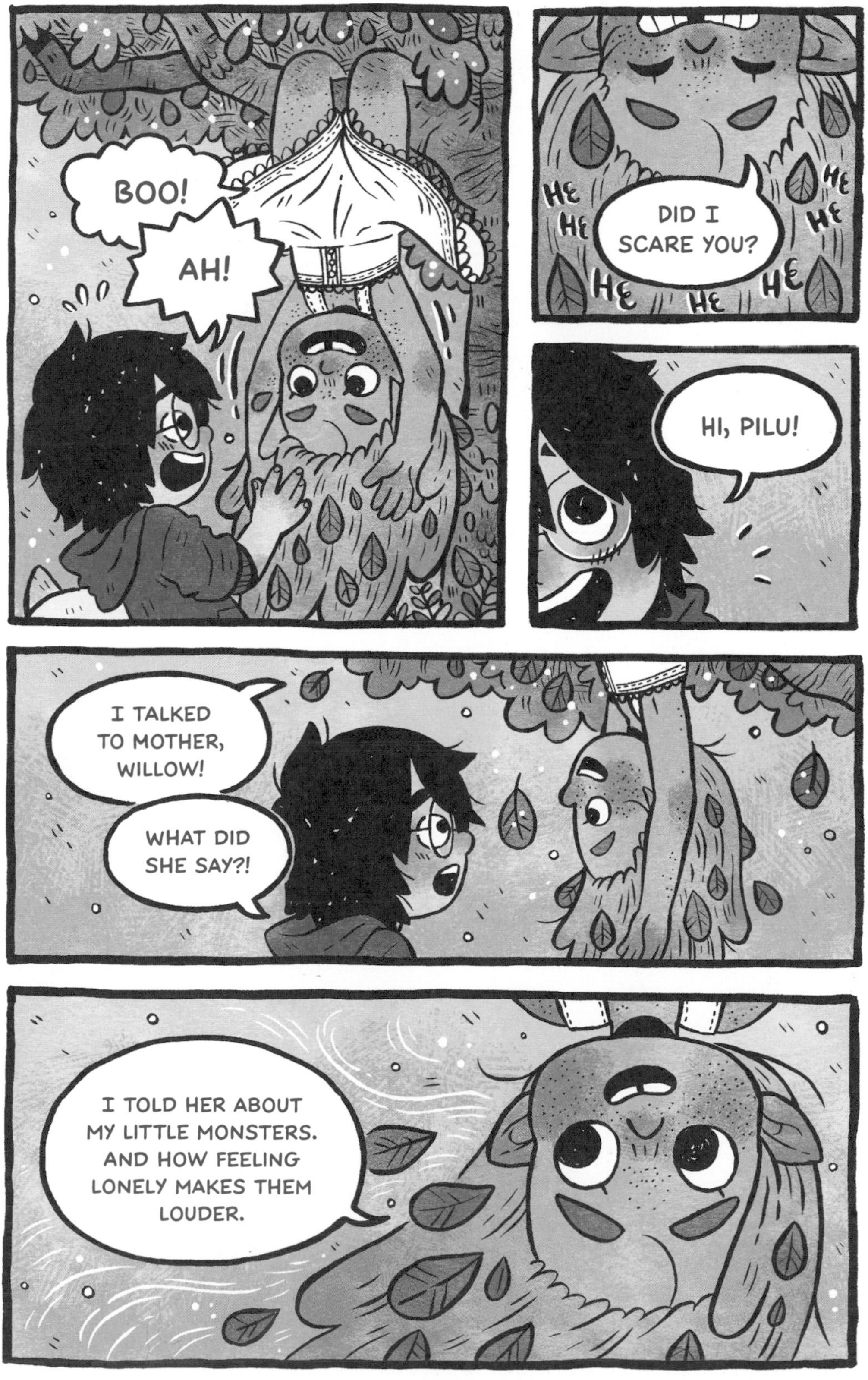
BOO!
AH!
DID I SCARE YOU?
HE HE HE HE HE HE HE HE
HI, PILU!
I TALKED TO MOTHER, WILLOW!
WHAT DID SHE SAY?!
I TOLD HER ABOUT MY LITTLE MONSTERS. AND HOW FEELING LONELY MAKES THEM LOUDER.

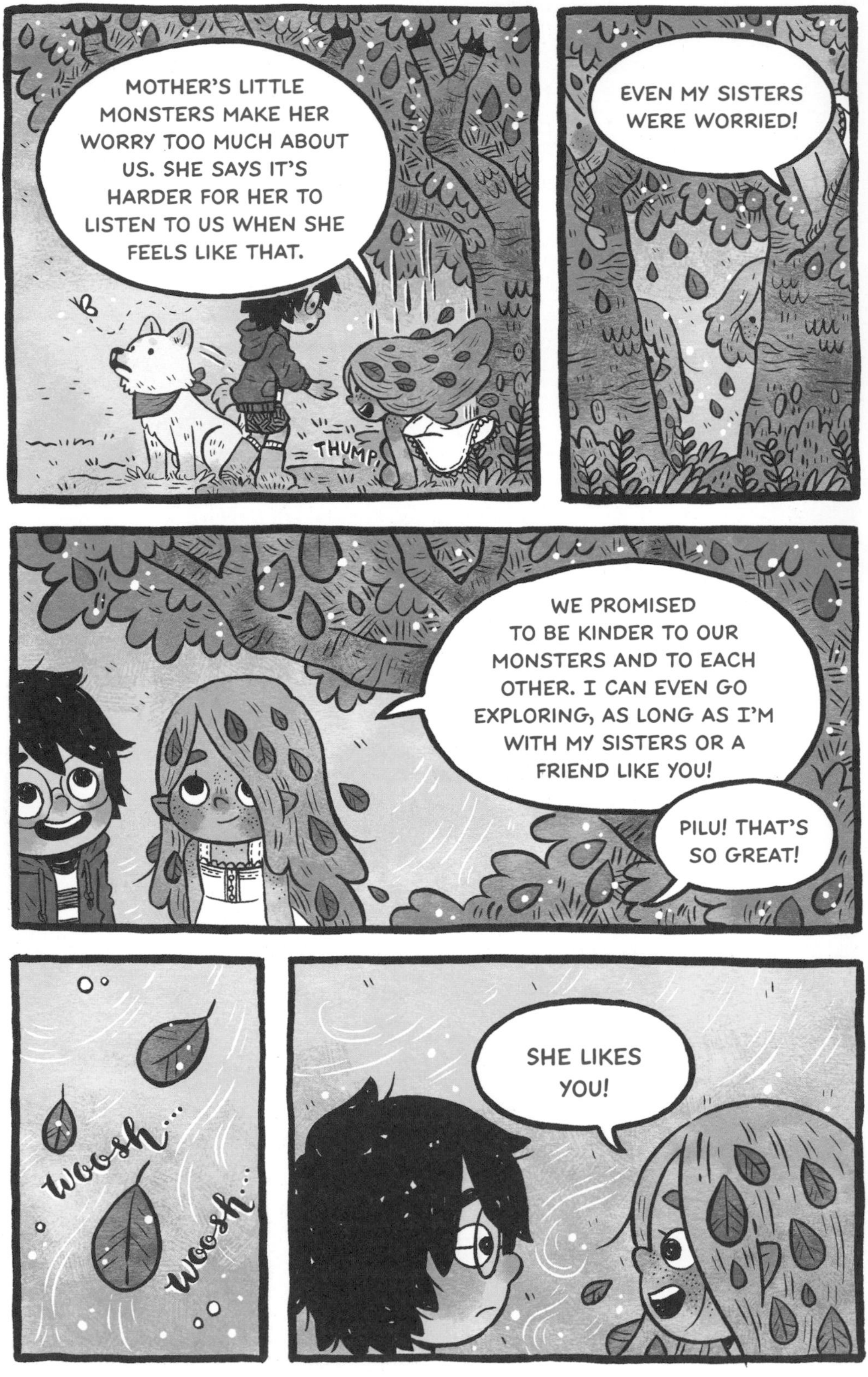
MOTHER'S LITTLE MONSTERS MAKE HER WORRY TOO MUCH ABOUT US. SHE SAYS IT'S HARDER FOR HER TO LISTEN TO US WHEN SHE FEELS LIKE THAT.
THUMP!
EVEN MY SISTERS WERE WORRIED!
WE PROMISED TO BE KINDER TO OUR MONSTERS AND TO EACH OTHER. I CAN EVEN GO EXPLORING, AS LONG AS I'M WITH MY SISTERS OR A FRIEND LIKE YOU!
PILU! THAT'S SO GREAT!
woosh...
woosh...
SHE LIKES YOU!

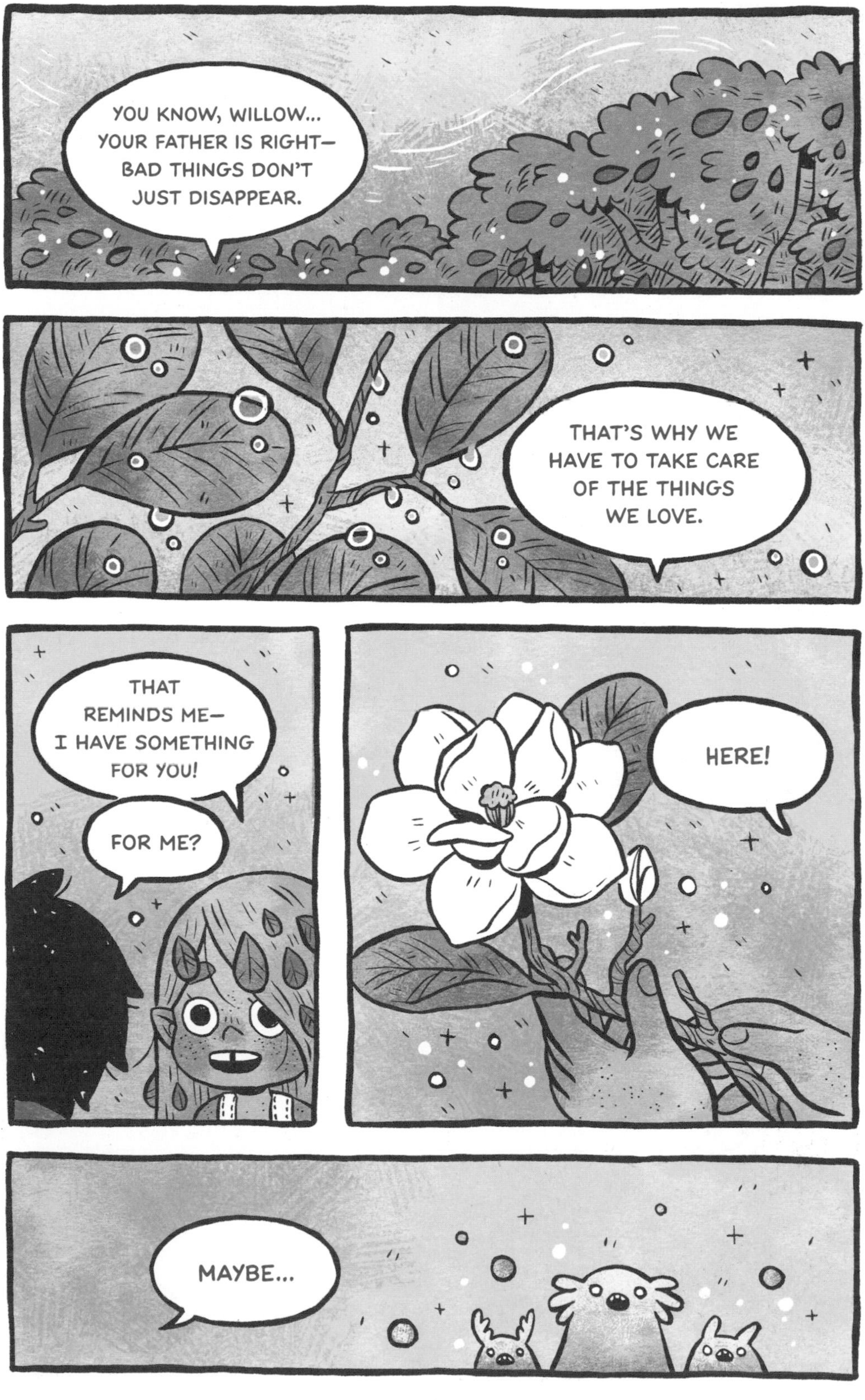
YOU KNOW, WILLOW... YOUR FATHER IS RIGHT— BAD THINGS DON'T JUST DISAPPEAR.
THAT'S WHY WE HAVE TO TAKE CARE OF THE THINGS WE LOVE.
THAT REMINDS ME— I HAVE SOMETHING FOR YOU!
FOR ME?
HERE!
MAYBE...

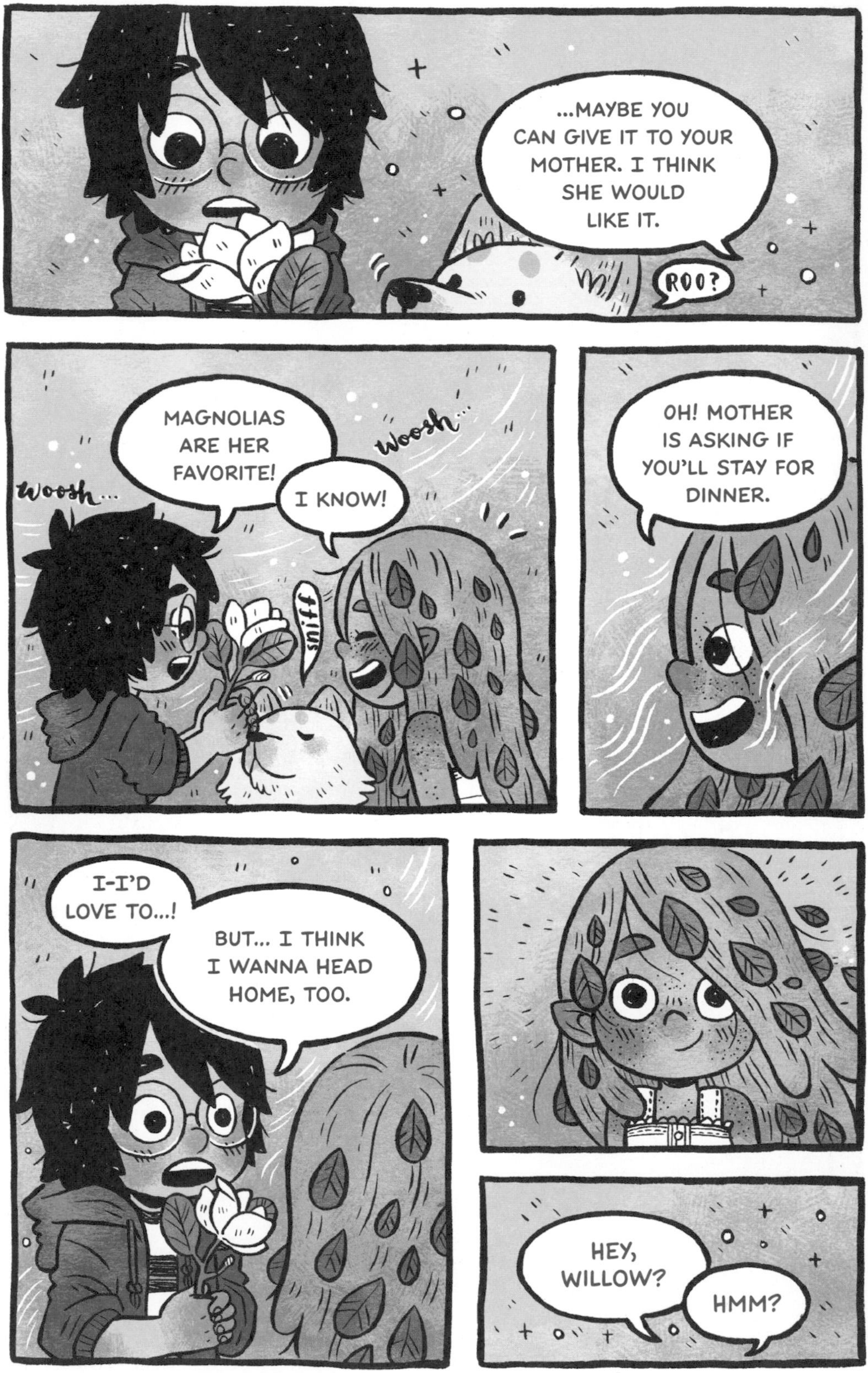
...MAYBE YOU CAN GIVE IT TO YOUR MOTHER. I THINK SHE WOULD LIKE IT.
ROO?
MAGNOLIAS ARE HER FAVORITE!
woosh...
woosh...
I KNOW!
OH! MOTHER IS ASKING IF YOU'LL STAY FOR DINNER.
I-I'D LOVE TO...!
BUT... I THINK I WANNA HEAD HOME, TOO.
HEY, WILLOW?
HMM?

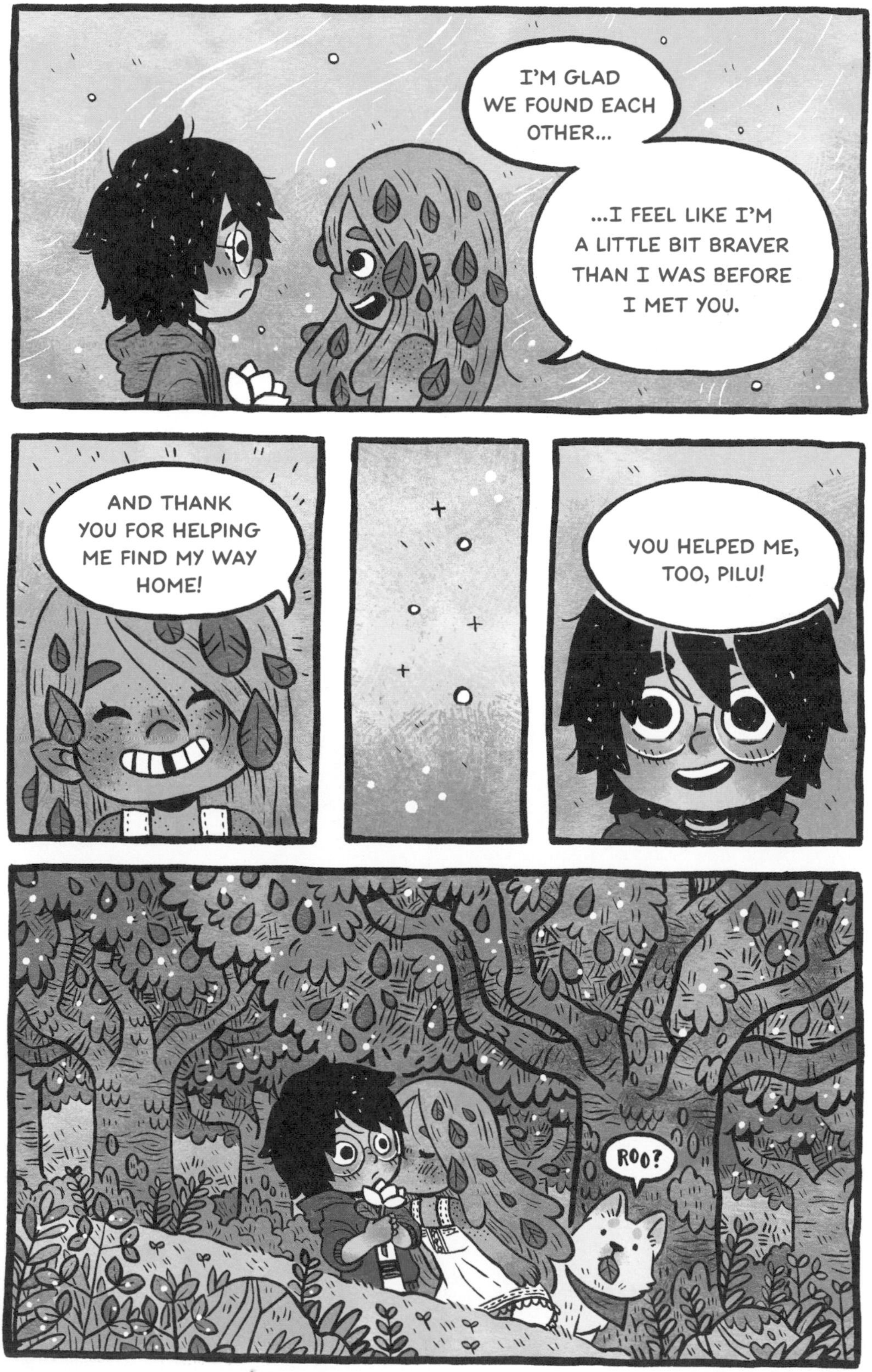
I'M GLAD WE FOUND EACH OTHER...
...I FEEL LIKE I'M A LITTLE BIT BRAVER THAN I WAS BEFORE I MET YOU.
AND THANK YOU FOR HELPING ME FIND MY WAY HOME!
YOU HELPED ME, TOO, PILU!
ROO?

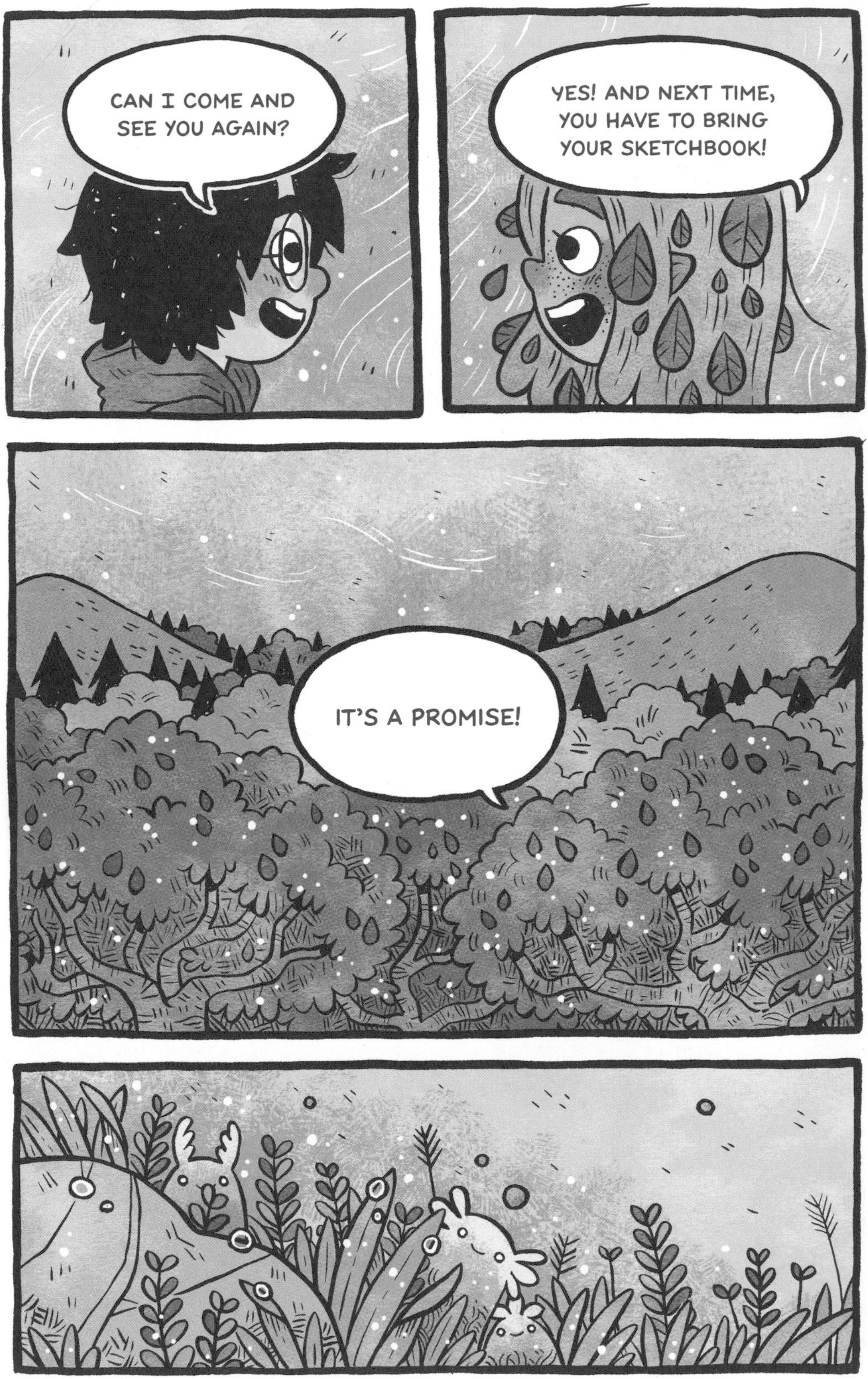
CAN I COME AND SEE YOU AGAIN?
YES! AND NEXT TIME, YOU HAVE TO BRING YOUR SKETCHBOOK!
IT'S A PROMISE!

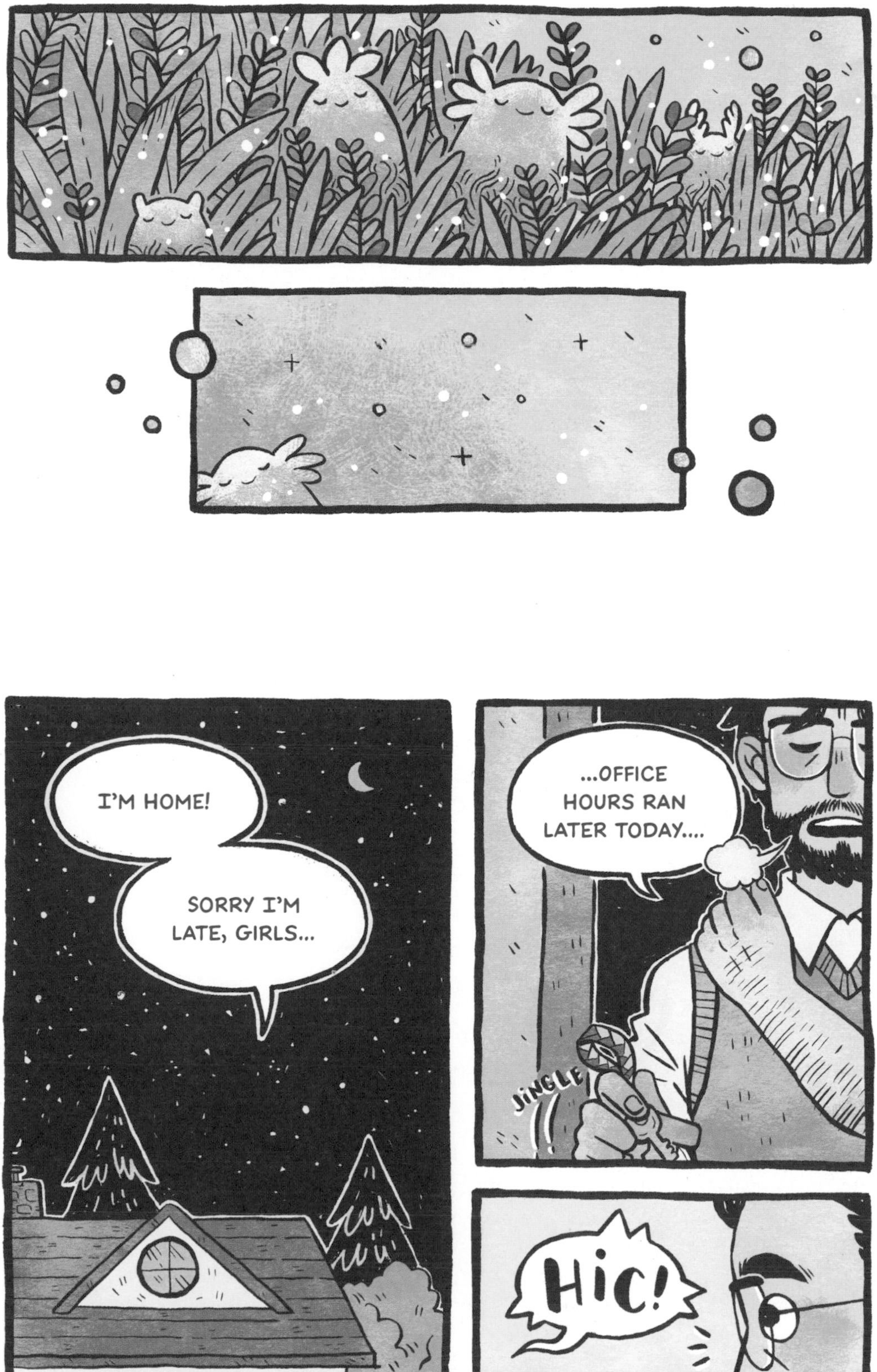

I'M HOME!
SORRY I'M LATE, GIRLS...
...OFFICE HOURS RAN LATER TODAY....
JINGLE
HIC!

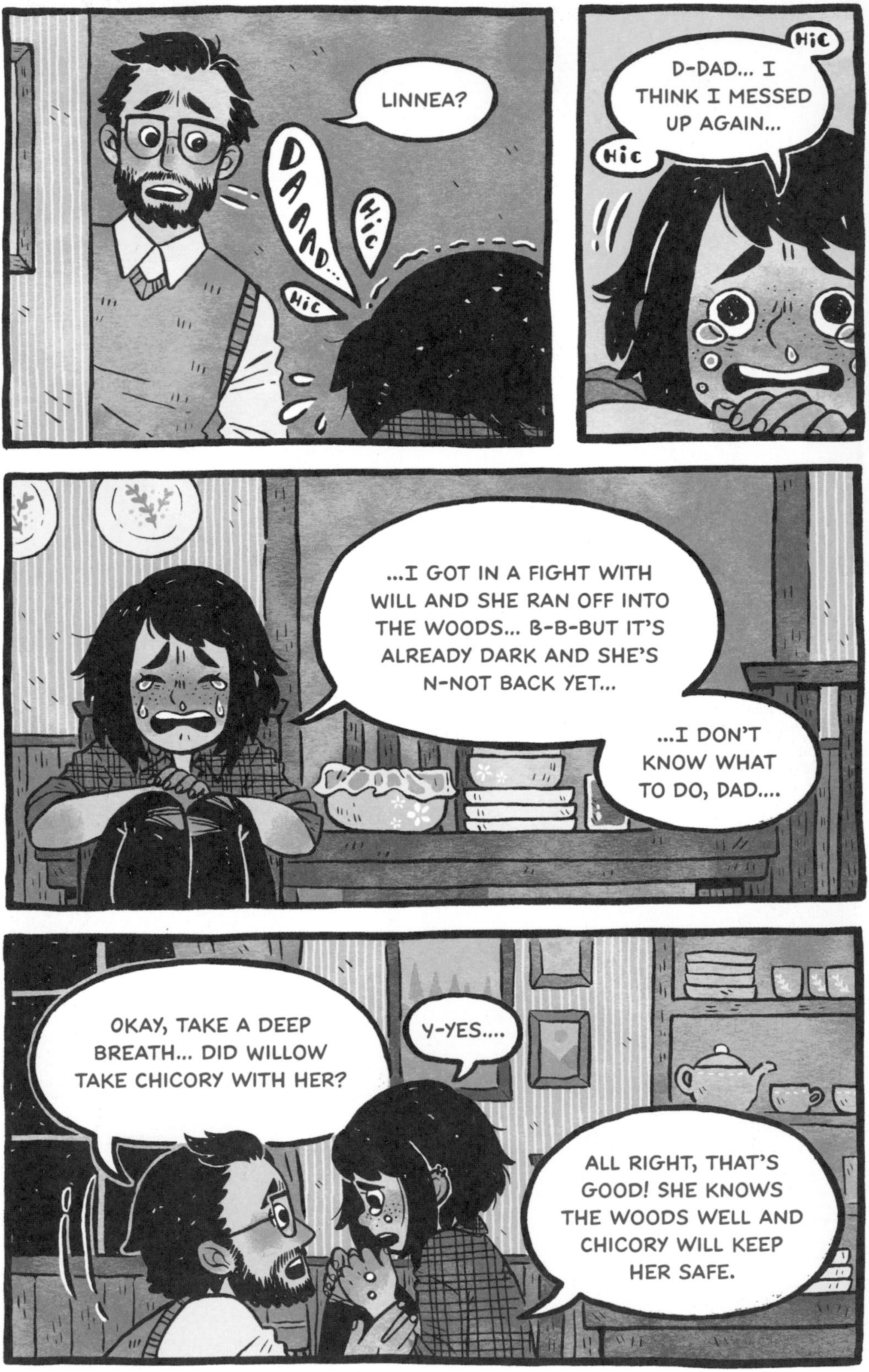
LINNEA?
DAAAAD...
HIC
HIC
HIC
D-DAD... I THINK I MESSED UP AGAIN...
HIC
...I GOT IN A FIGHT WITH WILL AND SHE RAN OFF INTO THE WOODS... B-B-BUT IT'S ALREADY DARK AND SHE'S N-NOT BACK YET...
...I DON'T KNOW WHAT TO DO, DAD....
OKAY, TAKE A DEEP BREATH... DID WILLOW TAKE CHICORY WITH HER?
Y-YES....
ALL RIGHT, THAT'S GOOD! SHE KNOWS THE WOODS WELL AND CHICORY WILL KEEP HER SAFE.

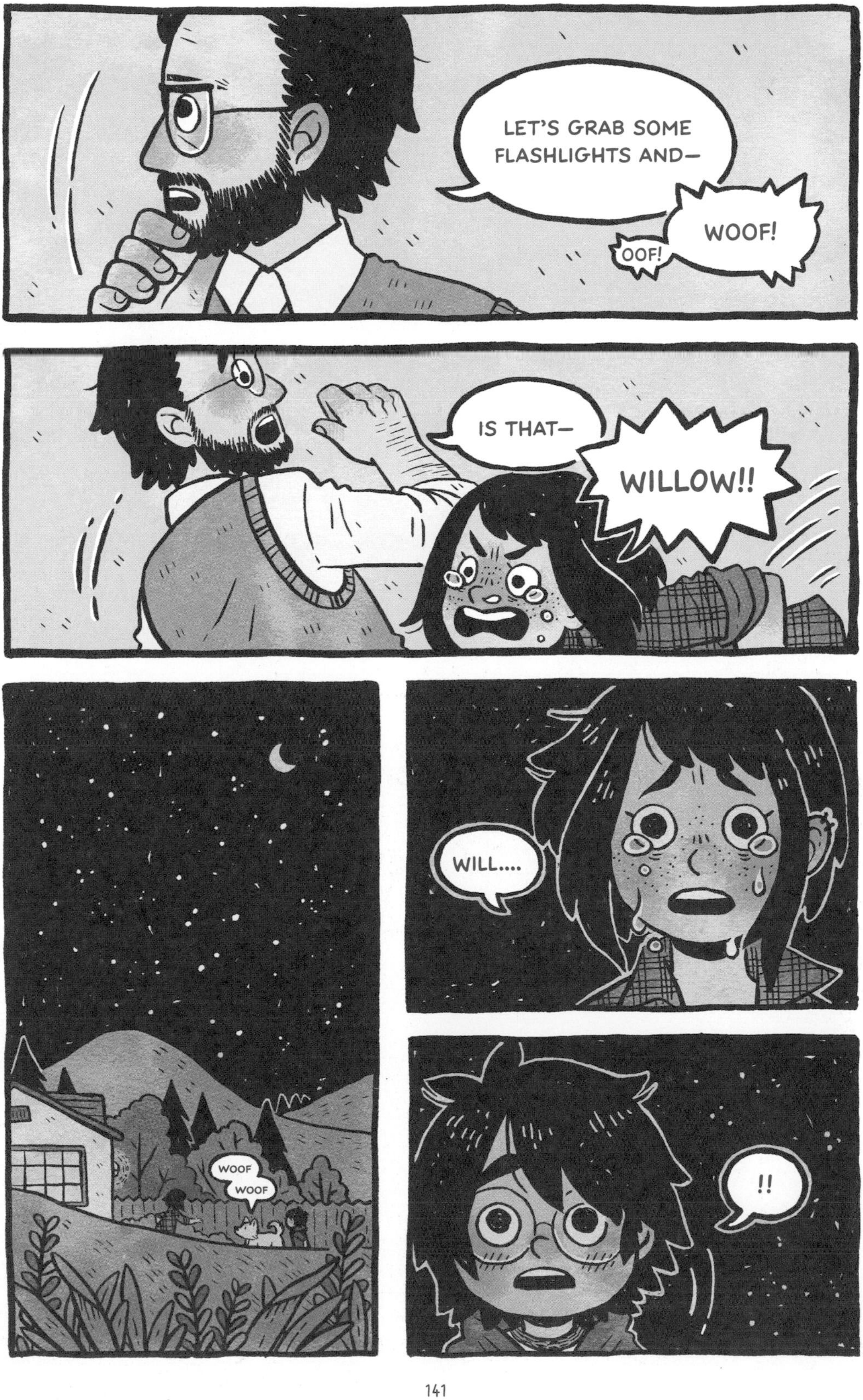
LET'S GRAB SOME FLASHLIGHTS AND—
OOF!
WOOF!
IS THAT—
WILLOW!!
WOOF
WOOF
WILL....
!!

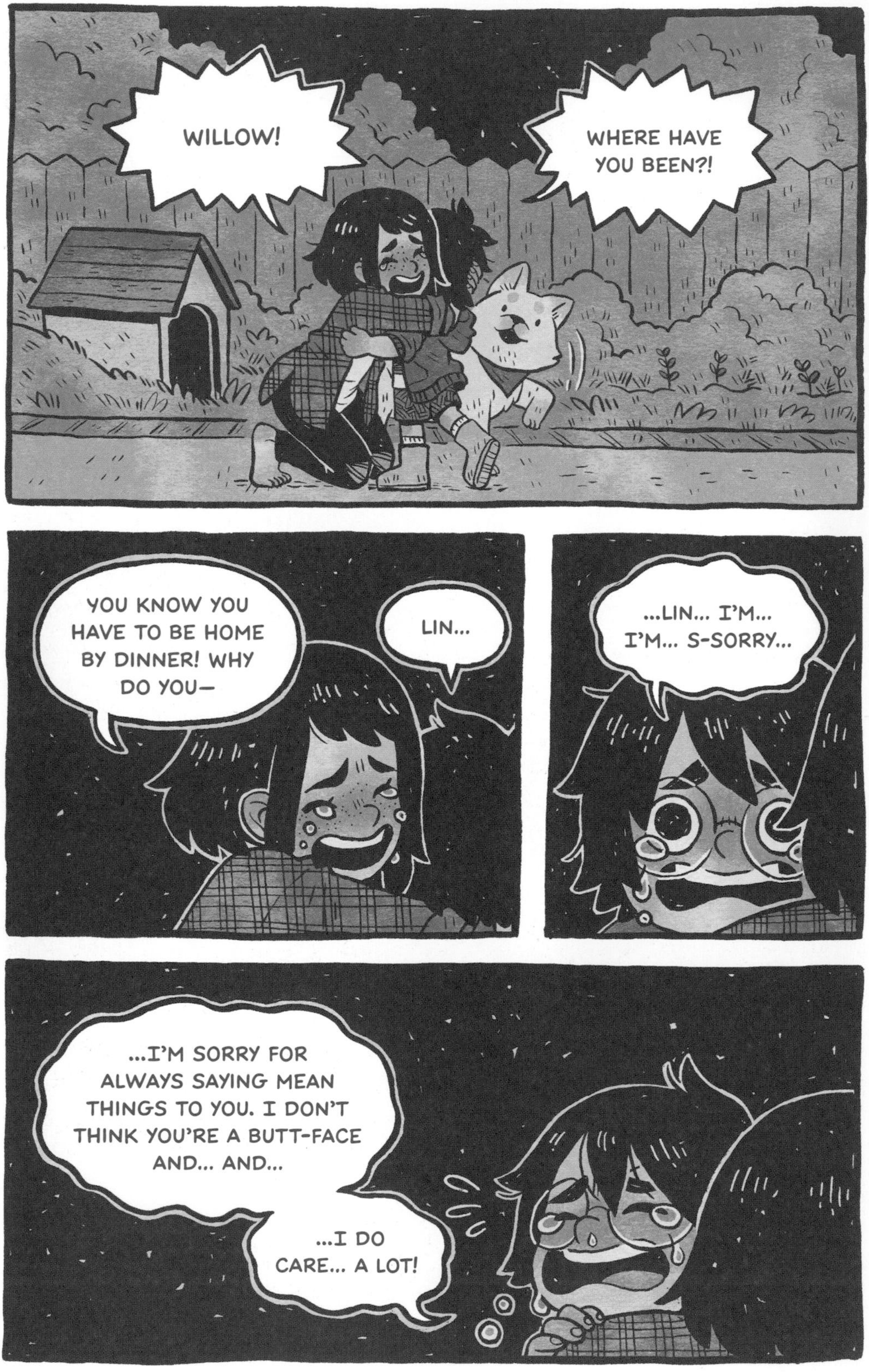
WILLOW!
WHERE HAVE YOU BEEN?!
YOU KNOW YOU HAVE TO BE HOME BY DINNER! WHY DO YOU—
LIN...
...LIN... I'M... I'M... S-SORRY...
...I'M SORRY FOR ALWAYS SAYING MEAN THINGS TO YOU. I DON'T THINK YOU'RE A BUTT-FACE AND... AND...
...I DO CARE... A LOT!

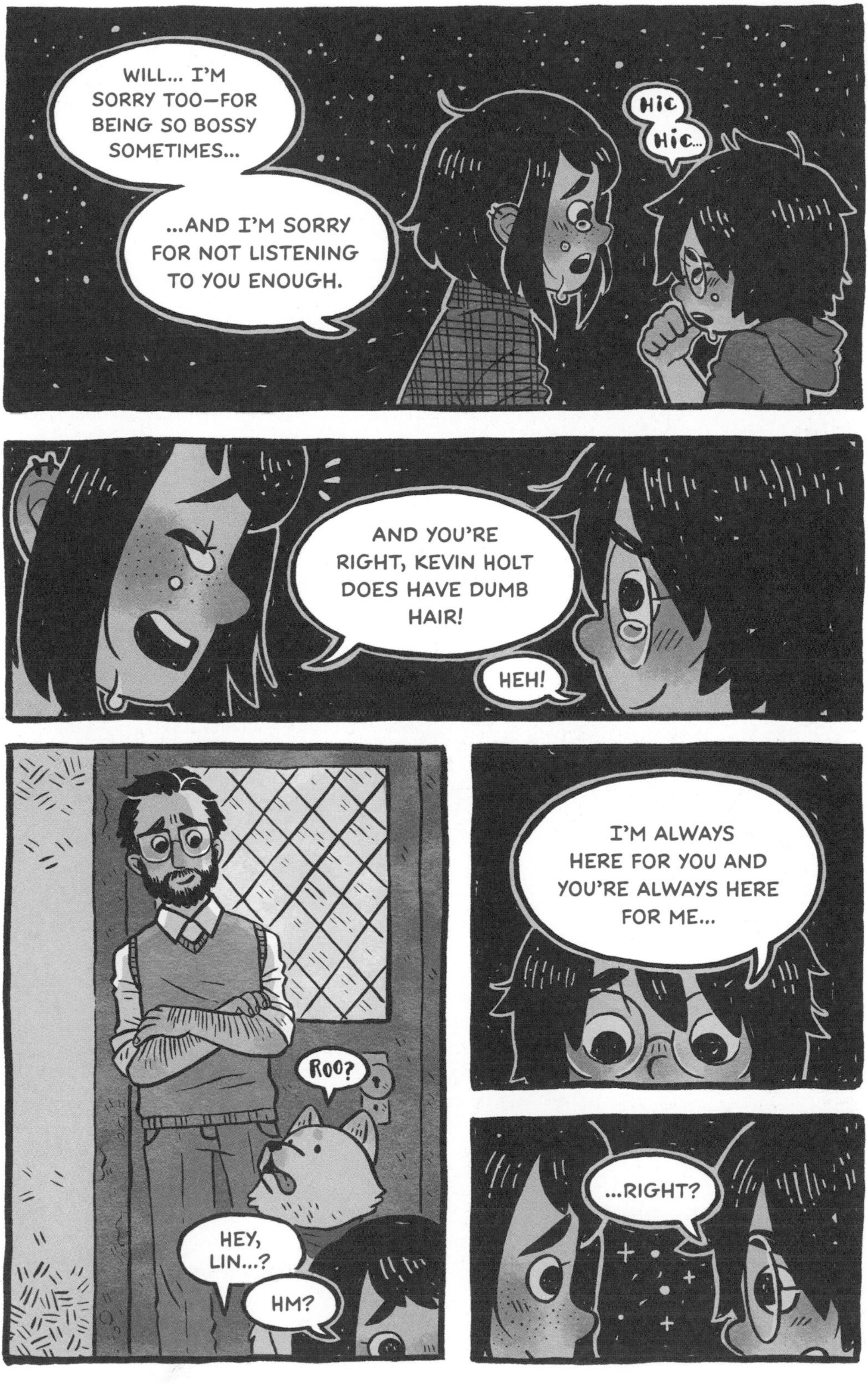
WILL... I'M SORRY TOO—FOR BEING SO BOSSY SOMETIMES...
...AND I'M SORRY FOR NOT LISTENING TO YOU ENOUGH.
HIC
HIC...
AND YOU'RE RIGHT, KEVIN HOLT DOES HAVE DUMB HAIR!
HEH!
ROO?
HEY, LIN...?
HM?
I'M ALWAYS HERE FOR YOU AND YOU'RE ALWAYS HERE FOR ME...
...RIGHT?

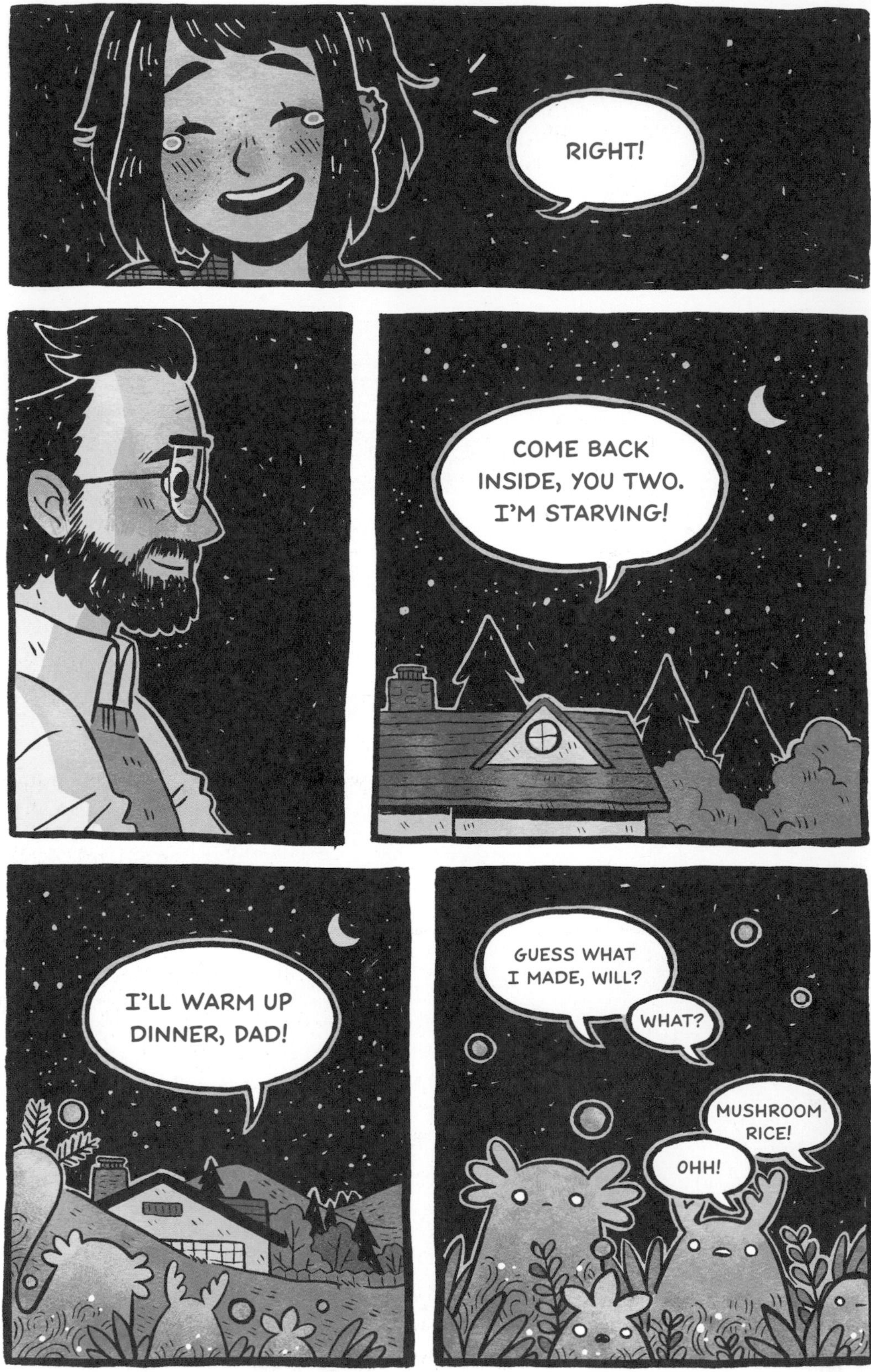
RIGHT!
COME BACK INSIDE, YOU TWO. I'M STARVING!
I'LL WARM UP DINNER, DAD!
GUESS WHAT I MADE, WILL?
WHAT?
MUSHROOM RICE!
OHH!

SSSS shh h hh hhhhh...

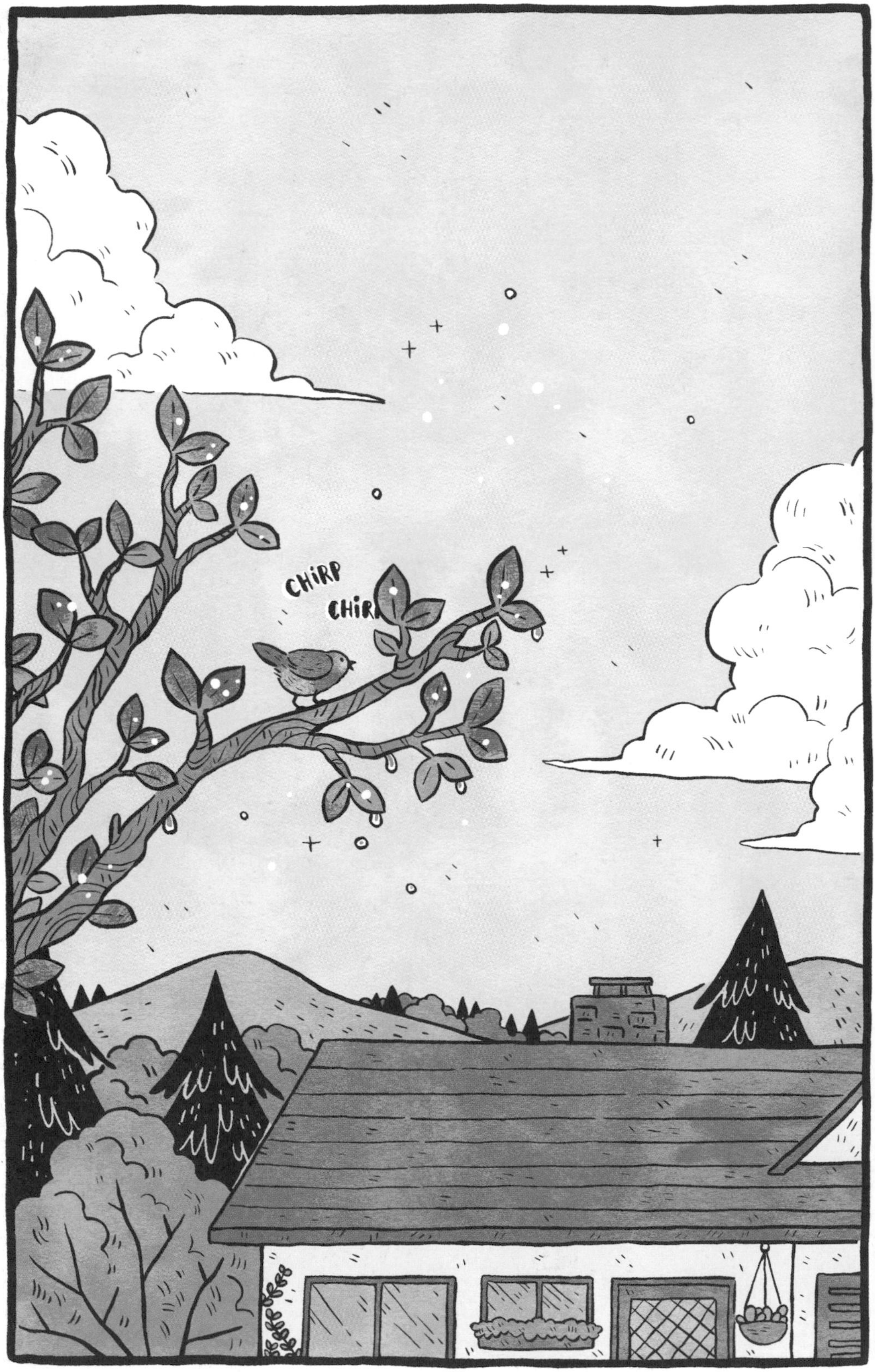
CHIRP
CHIR

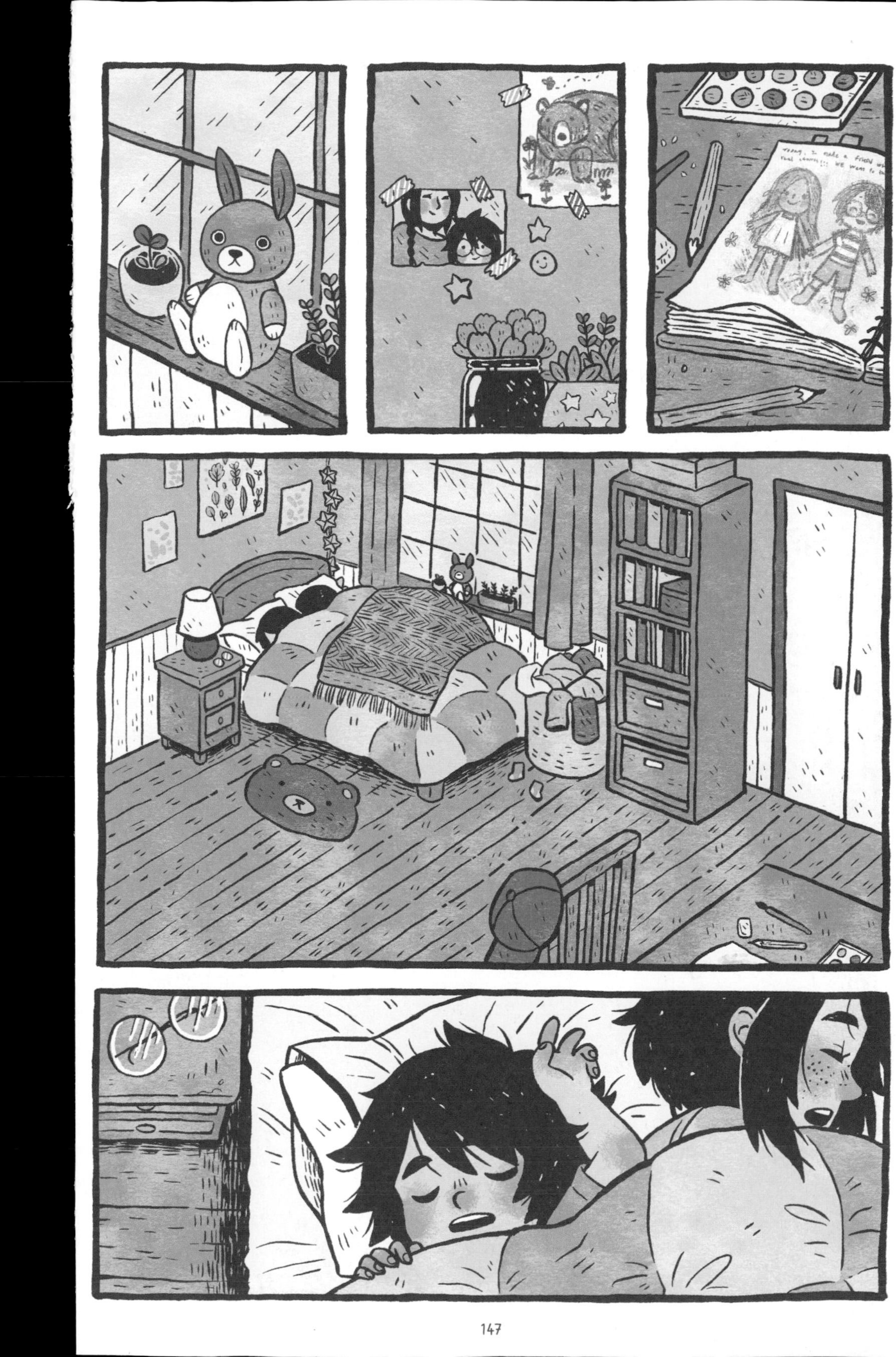

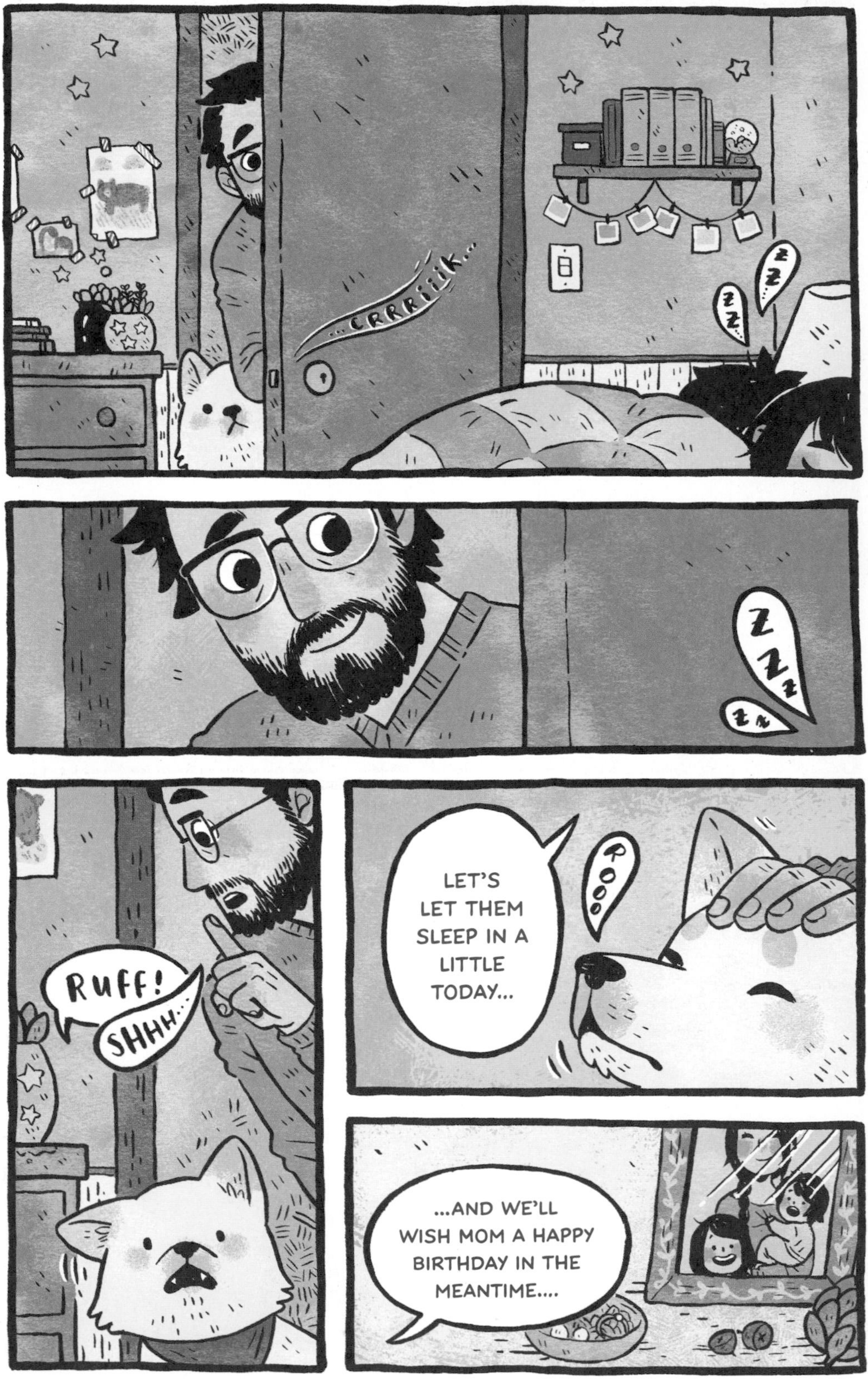
...CRRRiiiik...
Z Z Z
Z Z
Z Z Z
Z Z
RUFF!
SHHH...
LET'S LET THEM SLEEP IN A LITTLE TODAY...
ROOO
...AND WE'LL WISH MOM A HAPPY BIRTHDAY IN THE MEANTIME....

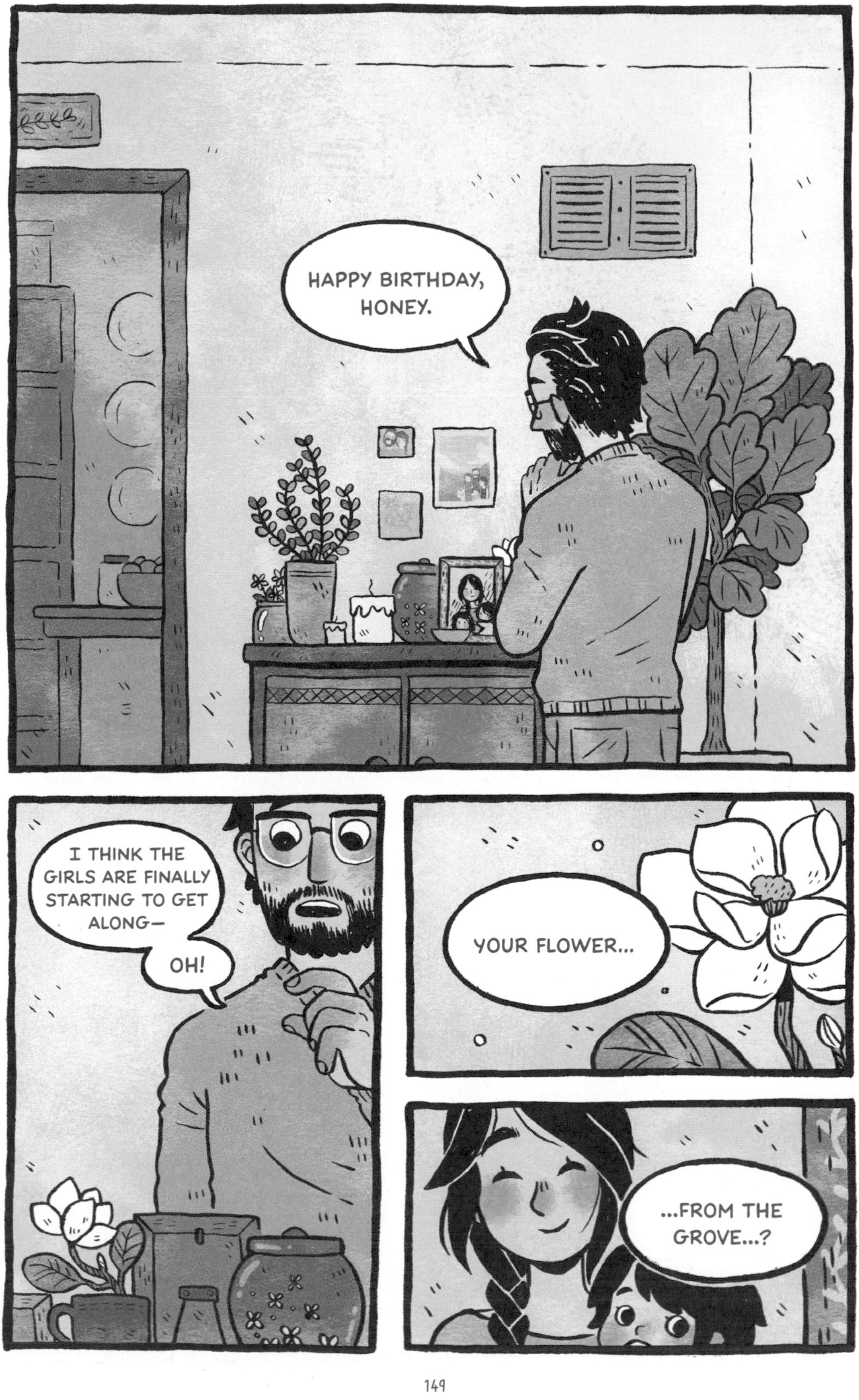
HAPPY BIRTHDAY, HONEY.
I THINK THE GIRLS ARE FINALLY STARTING TO GET ALONG—
OH!
YOUR FLOWER...
...FROM THE GROVE...?

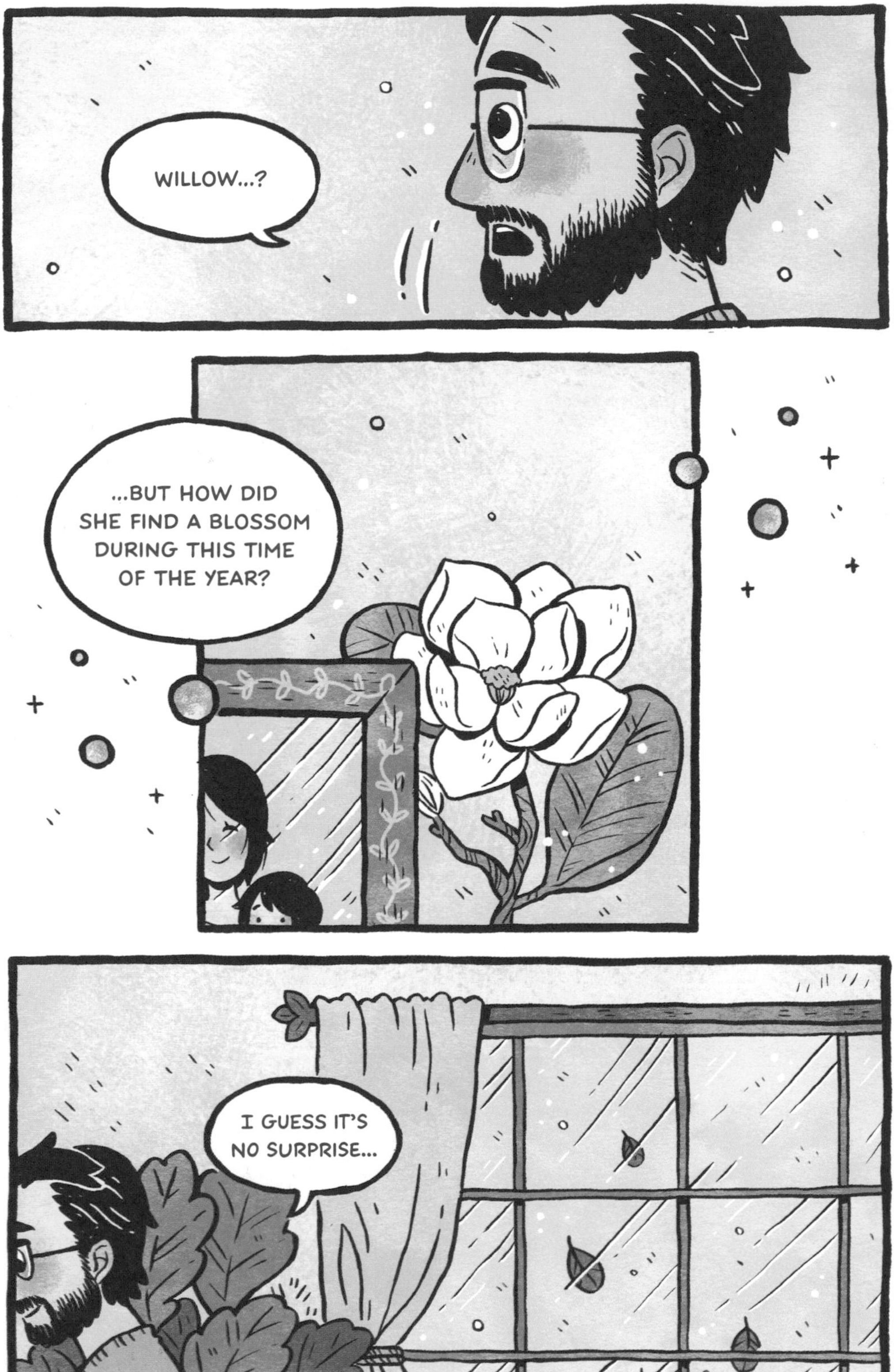
WILLOW...?
...BUT HOW DID SHE FIND A BLOSSOM DURING THIS TIME OF THE YEAR?
I GUESS IT'S NO SURPRISE...

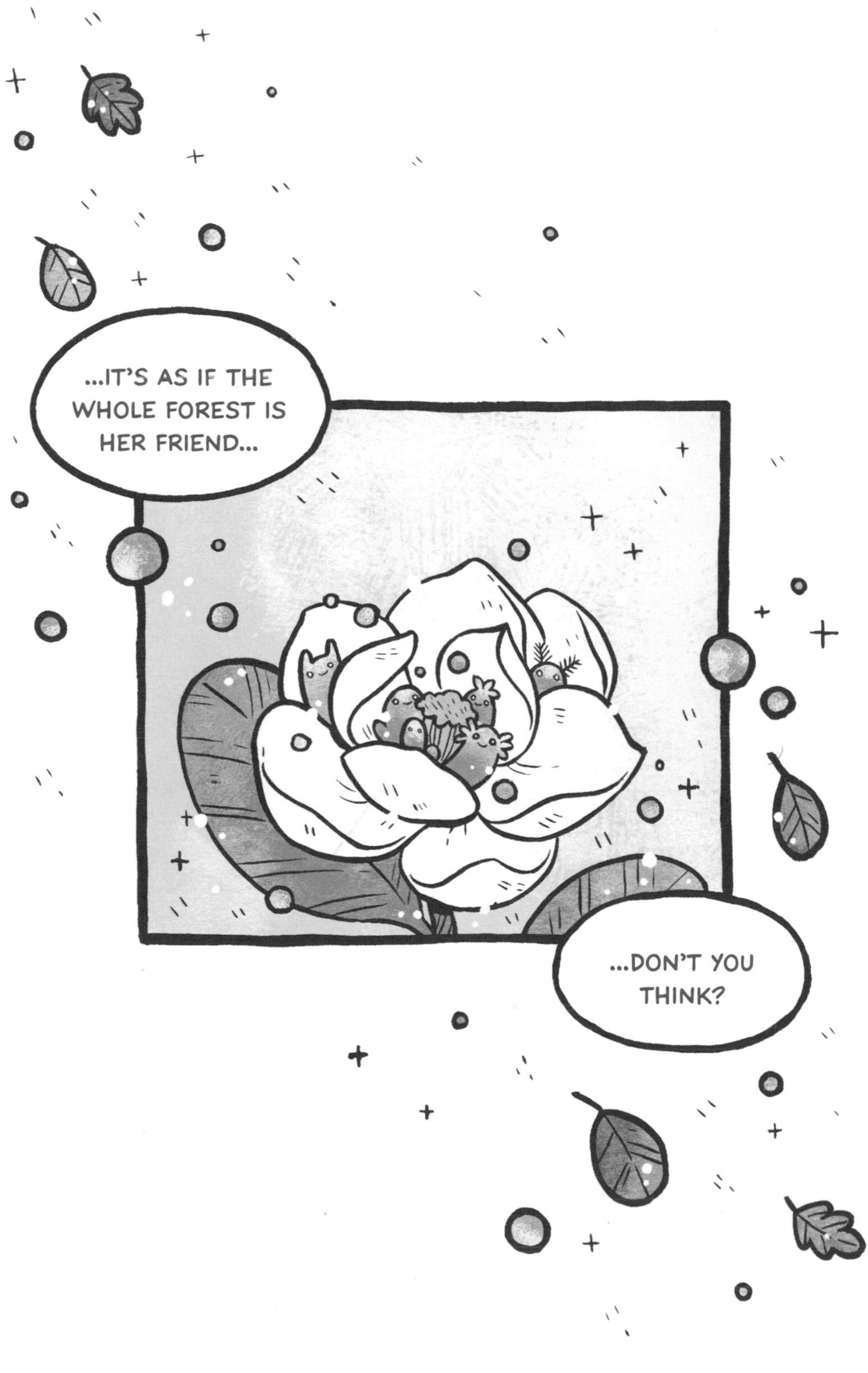
...IT'S AS IF THE WHOLE FOREST IS HER FRIEND...
...DON'T YOU THINK?

NATURE JOURNAL

HERE'S A CHANCE FOR YOU TO RECORD THE THINGS YOU SEE IN NATURE, just like Willow does! WIllow loves to draw her favorite plants, flowers, and trees, and there are many other ways to interact with nature in your own journal. Use these pages as a jumping-off point.

Is there a plant, flower, tree, or animal that you see often in your daily life? Try drawing it here.

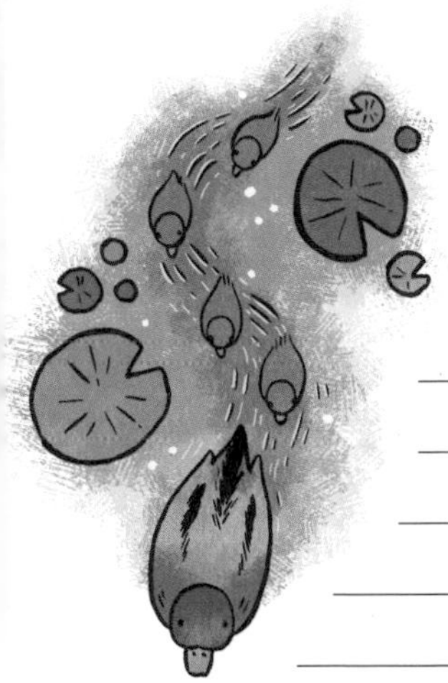

Try describing it here. What does it look like? If it's a plant, describe its smell. If it's an animal, describe the sounds it makes. What else can you describe about it?

Now, write about how it makes you feel. What memories do you associate with this plant or animal? What feelings does it give you? What other things does it remind you of?

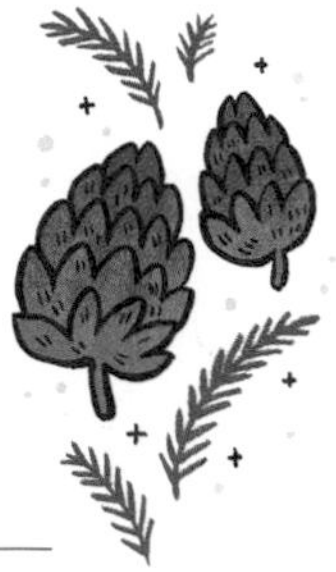

Go to your backyard, or a park, or another place where you can see a lot of nature. (The zoo counts!) List ten things you find in these places. You don't have to know the names of them, but you can make up descriptive names. (Like "Pretty Yellow Flower" or "Tall Tree Shaped like a Triangle.")

Look up at the sky. Clouds are a part of nature, too! What kind of clouds can you see? Again, you don't have to know the names.

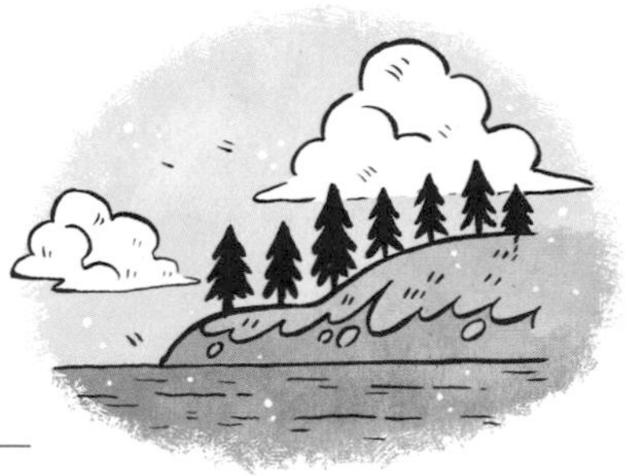

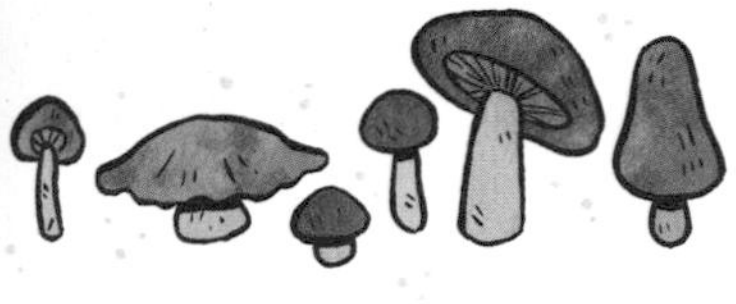

Are there plants and animals that don't exist where you live, but you want to know more about them anyway? What are they? Write them here. Find out where they can be found.

Draw one item from the list you came up with on the previous page. Draw while looking at it to try and get as accurate of a picture as possible.

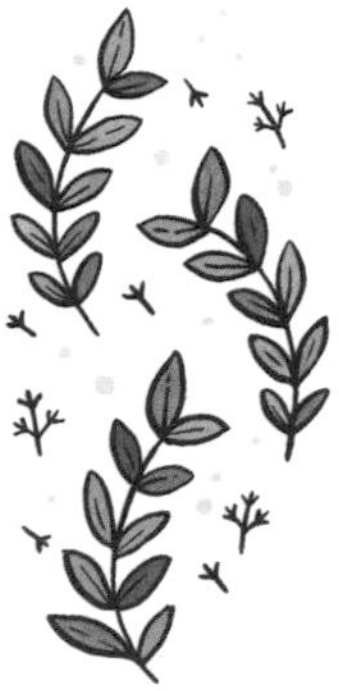

Pick one small part of what you drew—an ear? A leaf? A petal? —and draw it here, being as detailed as you can.

Draw one item from the list you came up with on the previous page from memory. This means you are remembering what it looks like instead of using your eyes to look at it. You can look at your written descriptions, though.

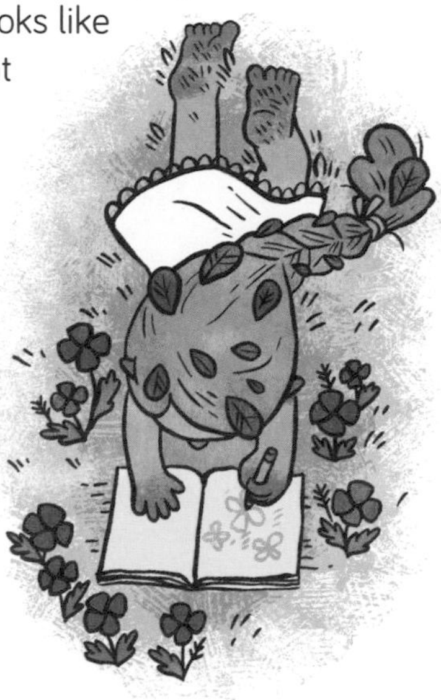

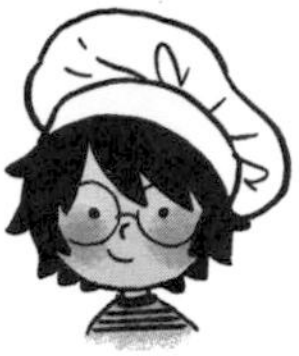

MOM'S MUSHROOM RICE
(KINOKO GOHAN)

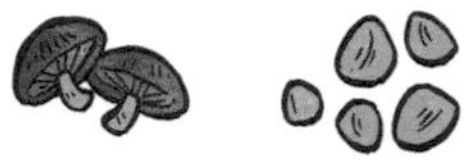

2 CUPS OF RICE

250 G OF ENOKI AND SHITAKE MUSHROOMS

150 G OF SKINLESS CHICKEN THIGHS, CUT INTO BITE-SIZED PIECES

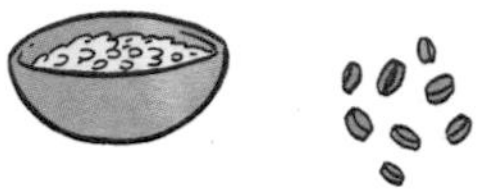

1/4 CARROT, SHREDDED OR DICED

1.5 CUPS OF BROTH, PLUS MORE

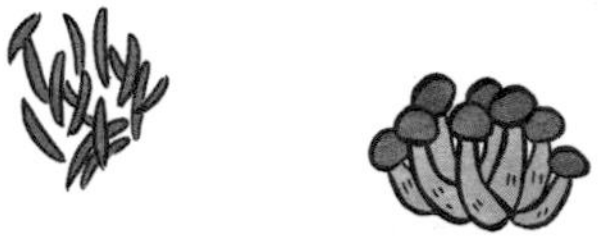

1 TBSP EACH OF SOY SAUCE AND COOKING SAKE

2 TBSP EACH OF SOY SAUCE, COOKING SAKE, AND MIRIN

½ TSP EACH OF SALT AND SUGAR

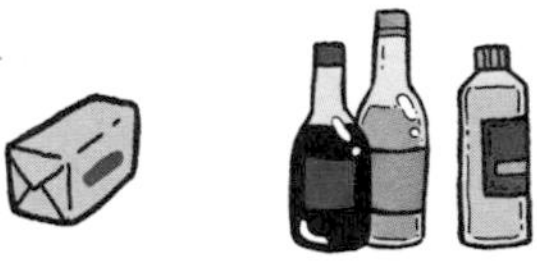

1 TBSP OF BUTTER

CHOPPED GREEN ONIONS

In a small bowl toss the chicken in 1 tbsp of soy sauce and 1 tbsp of cooking sake. Set aside.

Rinse 2 cups of rice until the water runs clear. Let it soak for 30 minutes (letting it soak will give you fluffier rice!). To ensure your rice is dry, put it in a sieve and let it drain for at least 15 minutes.

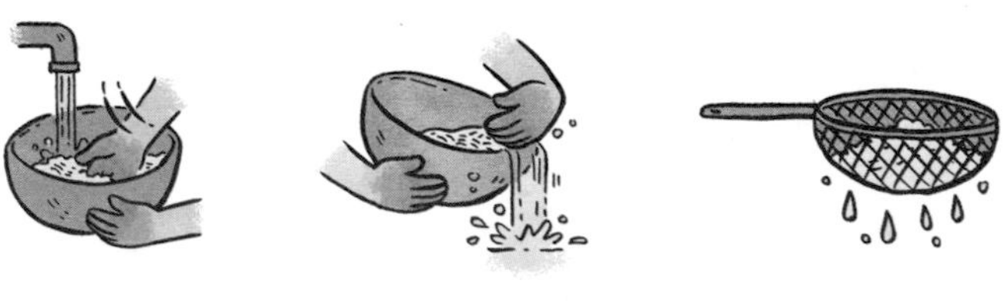

In a small pot, combine the chicken and carrots. Add 1.5 cups of broth (or enough to cover the chicken and carrots) and bring it to a boil. Lower the heat and let it simmer for about 10 minutes, skimming any foam.

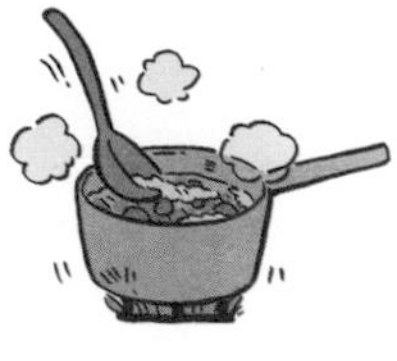

Use a sieve to separate the chicken and carrots from the broth. Don't throw out the broth—we'll use it to cook the rice in!

In a heavy bottomed pot, combine the rice and 2 cups of chicken broth—use the broth in step 3 and add regular chicken broth to make 2 cups.

Add 2 tbsp of cooking sake, 2 tbsp of mirin, 2 tbsp of soy sauce, 1/2 tsp of salt, and 1/2 tsp of sugar.

Add the mushrooms, chicken, carrots, and 1 tbsp of butter. Don't mix it! Let everything sit on the rice.

Cover the pot and bring to a boil over high heat. It's best to not lift the lid, so try and listen for the clattering of boiling water. Reduce the heat to low and let the rice cook for about 12-13 minutes, or until the water has been absorbed (it's okay to take quick peeks).

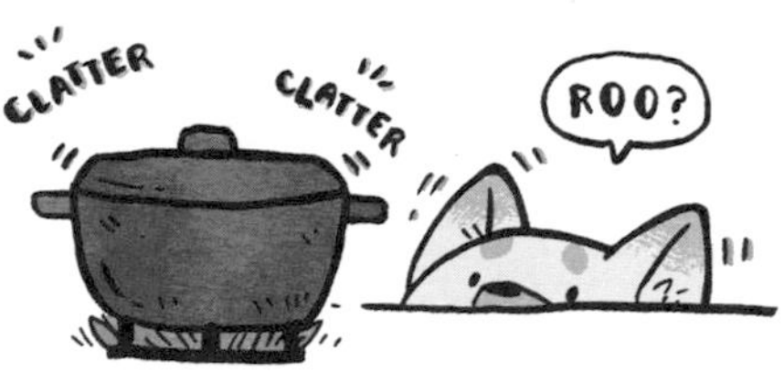
CLATTER
CLATTER
ROO?

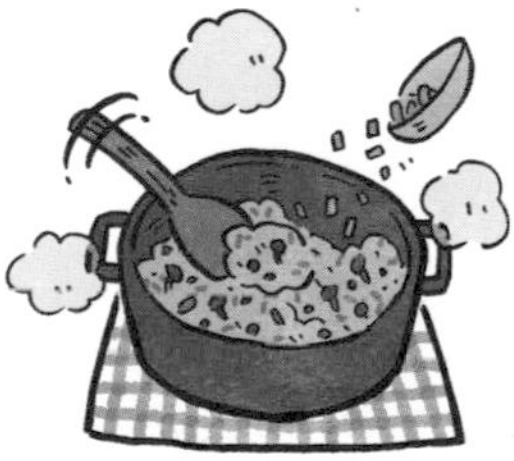

Remove the pot from the heat with the lid, and let it steam for about 10 more minutes. Lift the lid and fluff the rice, making sure everything is evenly mixed.

Finally, add some of the chopped green onions and enjoy your mushroom rice!

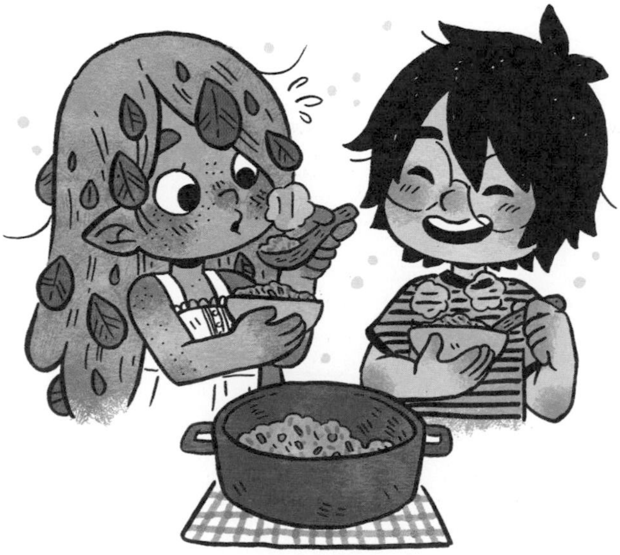

MAI K. NGUYEN is a comics maker, illustrator, and ice-cream enthusiast living in Northern California. She has previously self-published two short stories, *Coral and the King* and *Little Ghost*. When she's not doodling, she's hustling as a visual designer in San Francisco, watching too many true-crime documentaries, or dreaming about all the other comics she wants to make. Not unlike Willow, she loves feeling small amongst redwood trees and inhaling the salty-grassy smell of coastal bluffs.

THANK YOU

FOR HELPING WILLOW & PILU FIND THEIR WAY HOME

ILA, who has been my favorite artist ever since I was little. This book wouldn't exist, like really really wouldn't exist, if it weren't for you pushing me to share my work with a bigger audience and to take my passion more seriously. Thank you for always finding time to look over my pitch, my script, my thumbnails, my sketches, and everything in between countless times.

AKSHAYA, for two years of dragging me to coffee shops every Thursday night to work on our books. You've been my accountability buddy, my tomato buddy, my compassion buddy, my wisdom buddy, and every other type of buddy. Thank you for reminding me every day of the importance of pursuing what you love with all your heart.

IAN, for always, always cheering me on. This book is better because you gave me honest and actionable feedback, helped me letter pages during crunch time, and scooped me up whenever I wallowed in too much self-doubt. Thank you for being the absolute best.

SHIRO, who kept me company during late night drawing sessions for most of the creation of this book, and who looks suspiciously like Chicory (or Chicory like Shiro?). I miss swiveling around in my chair to find you snoozing away.

MOCHA, because I learned to love drawing comics in middle school based on your angsty Fictionpress stories. At age 13, I thought, "When I publish my first real comic book, I'm gonna put Mocha's name in it somewhere." So here it is.

And last but not least, my first ever editor, **ROBIN** and the wonderful folks at **ONI PRESS,** who helped bring to life a little idea I had in 2012.

MORE FANTASTIC TITLES FROM ONI PRESS!

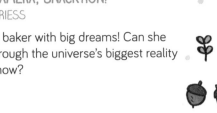

SPACE BATTLE LUNCHTIME VOLUME 1: LIGHTS, CAMERA, SNACKTION!
BY NATALIE RIESS

Peony is a baker with big dreams! Can she make it through the universe's biggest reality cooking show?

THE TEA DRAGON SOCIETY
BY KATIE O'NEILL

When Greta finds a lost creature in the market, she learns about the nearly-forgotten art of Tea Dragon caretaking.

AQUICORN COVE
BY KATIE O'NEILL

Unable to rely on the adults in her storm-ravaged town, a young girl must protect a colony of magical creatures she discovers in the coral reef.

GHOST HOG
BY JOEY WEISER

Truff, the ghost of a boar killed by a hunter, navigates her new afterlife as she seeks revenge.

SCI-FU BOOK 1: KICK IT OFF
BY YEHUDI MERCADO

Wax might be the greatest DJ in Brooklyn, but what happens when robot aliens expect him to save their planet, Discopia?

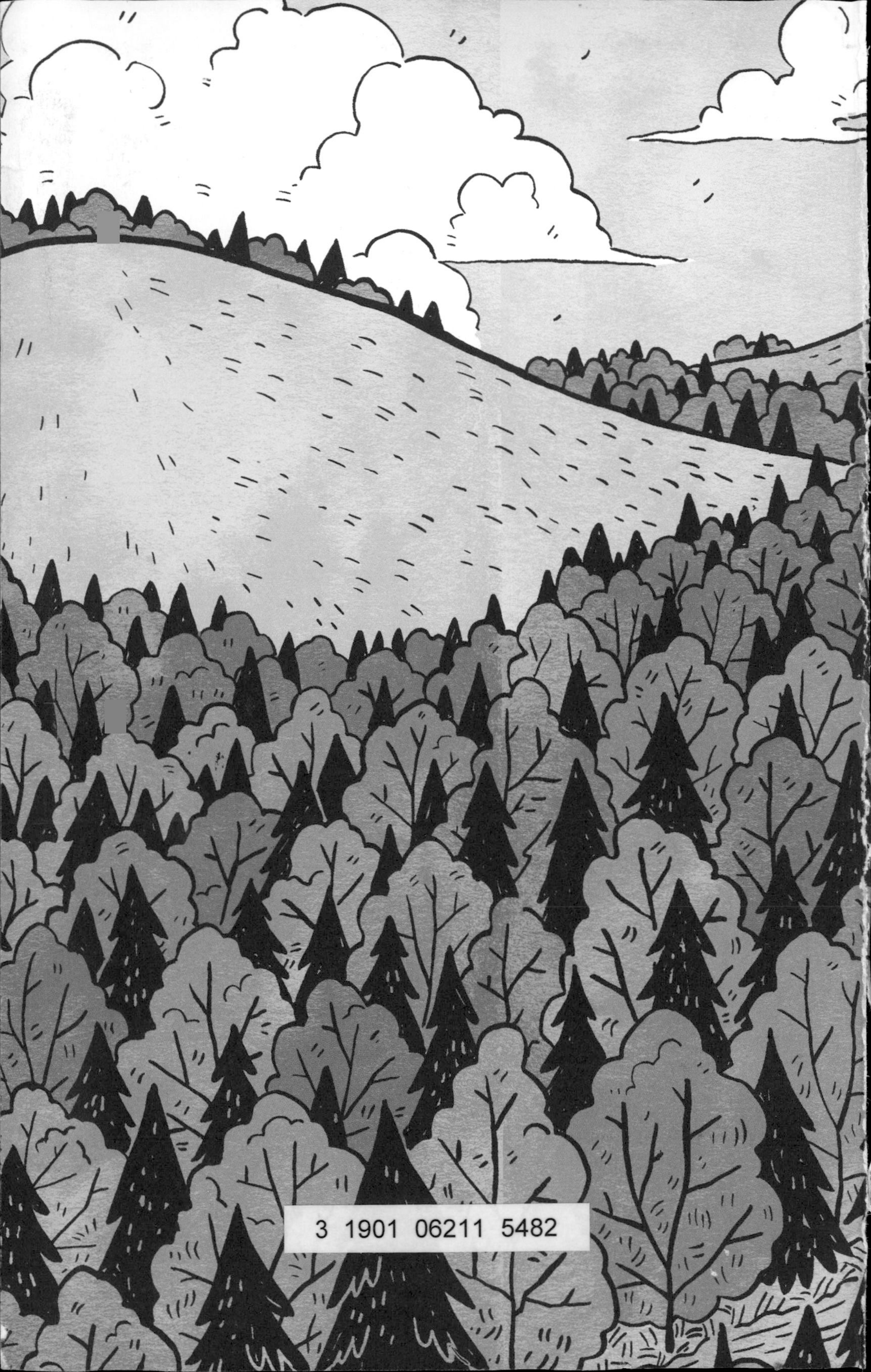